ST. MICK

a novel by
Jack Challenge

Ross–Erikson, Publishers
Santa Barbara

First Edition
©1981 by Jack Challenge

Challenge, Jack
St. Mick
  I. Title.
PS3553.H248S7   813'.54   81-5867
ISBN 0-915520-38-9   AACR2
ISBN 0-915520-41-9 (pbk.)

ST. MICK

To C.I., seer and believer

—*for the cruel priapic god is mad, bad and dangerous*
Gore Vidal

Part One

1.

Naked to the world I felt the fever rise, heating up my belly, humming in my ears. *NOW what?*—I mumbled to my pillow. *Only sirens in the night. Go back to sleep.* I awoke. I didn't always listen to that kind of inner voice.

I didn't always listen to the sirens. Sirens were the background music of the city, Muzak of Greater Los Angeles, song of civic servants in rescue and arrest. But when sirens wail in packs and keep on wailing, a listener begins to sense there's something wrong.

The ivory ceiling had turned Sunkist orange. Why was that—a UFO? A missile launch? The sun coming up in the west? That ceiling wasn't kidding. I wasn't dreaming, either, or full of drugs or drink—for the bed trembled and the walls shook to the roar of full-bore engines as they thundered by the house. *Four o'clock.* As good an hour as any to get up.

The ocean glittered orange and crimson, too. Flames—huge ones—danced across the foothills, as in scientific photos of the sun's eclipse: a field day for photographers. I grabbed my clothes and cameras and joined a parade of engines charging west on the Pacific Coast Highway, State Route 1.

Malibu was burning, the film colony *perhaps.* Scores of cars were streaming down the canyons, racing fires that raged through the brush. The sheriff's men had set out warning flares and roadblocks. My car darted through, like the animals that fled with smoking pelts across the highway. I longed to run from the fire—then toward it.

The real sun had risen in its normal place. I stood by a new hilltop ranch house exposing Kodachrome while an engine crew filled tanks from garden hoses. It was taking a long time. The residents served coffee from a patio cart, for it was otherwise a sunny Southern California morning, of the kind seen in *Sunset* magazine.

"Sugar and cream?" asked the hostess, who wore a silk bandanna over curlers and a pink pair of toreadors from Jax. "Just straight, please," said the fireman, a black. His sleek rubber boots and quilted jacket were tailor-made for that day's event.

Just then a dazzling screen of flame rose up before us, like a wave surprising bathers at the beach, and we all rolled and scrambled down the newly-landscaped bank. The children screamed for their parents; a fireman crawled back up to look. The colonial white and mustard-color ranch house went up in a wild sort of crackle, a balloon of black smoke. Borne on the wings of a Santa Ana wind, another California fire was clearly out of control.

The flames swept through dry grass like infantry, wasting houses, torching trees. Like armies in red enamel, equipment had been sent from other counties; then Seabees from Port Hueneme, sailors from Point Mugu. The sailors were defending a stand of eucalyptus trees.

Through a telephoto lens I caught a boy in dungarees, his hair a blaze of red, his back burned bright with sun. He sprinkled the earth as though wetting a lawn, or writing his name in pee. He turned to see who noticed, and grinned into the lens.

"Hey *Mickey!*" yelled another sailor. "Haul that fucking hose down here!" The fire was moving up the hill, the water pressure falling.

"You mean my fucking *hose?*" the redhead shouted, sticking it between his legs, spurting jets of water at his crewmate.

"Motherfucker," the wet mate said. *"MOVE it."*

As the boy began to drag his hose-line down the slope, the treetops burst into crowns of yellow flame. Like a routed band of fiends, the sailors turned and vanished in a swarm of flying cinders, clouds of whirling smoke.

Maybe it seemed heartless to be taking color photos while others fought for property and lives. I helped wet down roofs and dig firebreaks, but it wasn't much use. The flames flew one way then another, through valleys, up ravines. It grew monotonous, almost boring, to see yet another homestead snatched up in fists of fire. Trucks full of furniture bounced down rutted trails, horsemen behind them, collie dogs barking in the dust.

The hills took on the look of a battle-leveled plain scorched by a hostile sun. I sat on a hot rock to rest, all adrenaline drained, sweating ashes and dirt. Browbeat, bone-weary, I found myself strangely aroused. But no secret thrill like an arsonist's deed inflamed that unutilized limb. The bare-bouldered land, the sun's staring eye, the barebacked boy on film were potent recollections of another place and time. The vision hovered on the super-heated air, a quivering illusion, a mirage.

A few miles farther west an immaculate Pacific displayed a calm burnished surface of deep blue, the pure white surf-line sculptured by the offshore breezes. Out there gleamed the station wagons of the beach-front homeless, with their unplugged TV sets and unfed kids.

I wanted to go for a swim.

2.

Southern California had always seemed a land of more than natural disaster. The drenching rains of the early months, the flames of parched late summer, the temperamental rumblings of the restless earth—these were more like extensions of the movie lots, expensive magical effects exceeding budgets and expectations of their masters. Los Angeles had the look, indeed the purpose, of a place made for ready use and quick recycling—a kind of throwaway city. Sluicing knee-deep through flooded streets or chasing midnight blazes gave sensations of taking part in an ongoing production of colossal scale, while God's hidden cameras turned silently. In dramas of converging sirens and scarlet footlight flares even crashes on the freeway seemed events of special staging. Unless, of course, the leading role of victim was taken by oneself.

I was a working part of such an order. *JEREMY CARR, VISUALS*, my business card read, with an all-seeing eye like the iris of a lens for a logo, and below it: *Photography, Planning, Design*. Then a call service number and my address. A jack- or sometimes jerk-of-all-trades was a title I had won for these chameleon callings. The fact is, I performed them rather well. From my apartment on the bay I worked on demand and swam at leisure.

In the wake of that year's fire I took photos of burned properties, made sketches of possible houses, and offered myself as planner-builder, ready to put owners under roof. Helped by low-rate disaster loans I got several jobs, the best of these a site on a bluff where the fire had burned to the sea. The owner liked a plan of many levels, and early in the spring gave orders to begin foundation work.

The house on the next lot had merely been singed. Expecting its destruction, the occupants had gone wading in the surf. The lady of the house, a mother of three, granted phone and bathroom privileges in exchange for small repairs. The home of Linda Lee Fedderman, then, became a restroom for the workmen, a snack bar and office for myself.

When we arrived on weekday mornings the children were long gone down the highway on the schoolbus. Linda, cleaning up, would have our coffee ready. She served it on the red brick terrace that looked across the Pacific from southeast, and the land of Mexico, to the misty blue humps of the west Channel Islands. We could still be in cool shade as the sun climbed up behind the mountains, gradually changing the color of the sea, and sometimes catching the sails of passing boats like exclamation marks. On some days a rusty kelp-cutter churned through beds of purple seaweed in the gilded daybreak colors of a royal barge. It was a nice way to start a piece of work.

The workmen gulped their coffee and set about their jobs. They were married and hadn't much to say, instead putting in paid hours. But Linda and I would linger over several cups. We found lots to say to one another, mundane thoughts at first, such as our stations in life and attitudes upon this planet. Then regrets for the past and hopes for the future, good times and bad times, and at last, our approximate ages and true worth in dollars. She held the lead in years and was also ahead in real value—she owned the unburnt house. Our morning conversations might run along like this:

"That was fascinating, Jerry, really. Here, let me fill your cup."

"Okay, Linda. Look. Do you see the whales?" The gentle monsters would be cruising just a few miles out, a fleet of spouting submersibles.

"Yes, I see the big ones up front. And lots of little ones."

"Those are the calves. From last year, I suppose."

"I know. I always watch them. It's their mating season."

"How do they ever—*Ouch!* You spilt it all over my *lap.*"

"I'm sorry, Jerry. Here. Let me wipe it." Long, lingering wipe with red-checked apron as camera irises out. Or the phone rings.

About mid-afternoon the bus returned the kids from school. On fine days they ran to the beach like uncaged beasts, and on foul ones they played in the unfinished house. The children were living in that careless West Coast fashion that made them good companions and fun to have around. Like their mother they were fair-haired, even-featured, and in abundant outdoor health. Brenda was thirteen, Steven eleven, and Starkey was a boy of eight—the brightest of the family so far as I could tell. The names recalled popular television series of their natal years.

Of her departed husband Linda spoke without illusion or regret. It was a subject I rarely pressed. He ran a firm called BUG-A-BYE INC. and drove a yellow pickup truck. Harry Fedderman had done and said terrible things to Linda, and had punished the children and pets. The divorce had only recently been final. Linda lived on child support, her alimony, and the love and affection of those near and dear—plus a trust fund established by her rich Uncle Stanley on behalf of his favorite niece.

Sole child of an absent father and busy mother, I too had grown California style, running loose in the hills above Eagle Rock before capture by the public school system and later on, the military service. A year at art school on the G.I. Bill had got me into motion picture companies, where I learned the variety of trades that kept me from immediate want. My social life was also of this nature. The concept of marriage in a permanent legal form had not stayed in mind over any long period of time.

"Jerry?"

"Hmmm? *Yes,* Linda."

As soon as the hammering and power saws had ceased, Linda would appear in any kind of weather for an inspection of the work. On that afternoon I was stowing away the tools against the salt air corrosion of a springtime mist. The workmen had left and the kids had gone off without telling us.

"Is it a surprise then?"

"You might call it that." She flourished two bottle-green bottles of Heineken beer, dripping foam and dewy moisture exactly like the ads. Putting one to her lips Linda slid the other down my jeans behind the belt. Our reactions were instinctive—she was blushing.

"Then I've got one for you," I said with a quick swig, and throwing sawdust-crusted arms around her neck I hugged her to me. As the Dutch beer mingled in our mouths, the bottles dangled coldly down each other's spine. She wore a monk's cloth tunic. Her fabric-armored nipples plunged toward either armpit. My back was straight, our hips aligned, and her bare toes curled across my boot-tops. I tugged the back length zipper to its nether end; it rasped in the thickening fog. The dress dropped away from bra-less, bobbing breasts that now faced impudently forward.

Linda put aside her beer to spring the clasp of my carpenter's belt. She opened the fly and let gravity tug the pants earthward. There was nothing beneath these, either, except of course, myself. Like two intoxicated, uninvited guests, we struggled grotesquely with our failing clothes down the flagstone steps to the game room, led by my waggish wing-wang. We fell on a tarpaulin where the wet bar would be, in a rolling, wrestling embrace. She wanted to play games, did she? We twisted, turned, until our tongues met. Linda's body yielded as though the bones turned soft—I suddenly slipped inside her. Two teammates, we worked swiftly to complete ourselves, raw trunks arching at the same breath-catching moment. I swallowed and lay still. In the silence of the uncompleted room I felt I'd come home at last.

The tarp gave off a pungent scent of resin; I could smell my own sweat. The fog had turned blue with early evening and began to blur the outlines of the room. A chill fell on my naked buttocks but my feet were still warm in their socks. Linda lay in a kind of warming revery, a forearm clinging to my rib cage.

"Oh, lover," she murmured. "That was *so* good. It's been so *long*." She gave a long sigh. "I do think I love you, Harry." My thigh twitched. "*Jerry*, of course. I wanted to know if you were listening."

I didn't know what to say at this first mention of her husband's name in its new and intimate context. I reached for the bottles of imported beer. We guzzled as darkness fell around us.

"Hey, MOM! Where's the *milk?*" That would be Starkey out there somewhere. I wasn't sure where I was. We had probably gone to sleep, curled like other mammals in some primitive cave. Linda snuggled even closer before sitting up to shout, "Behind the *orange juice*, dear! If there *is* any." An affectionate pause. "Tell the others Jerry will be staying on for dinner."

It seemed entirely possible that the others already knew.

3.

Over outsize Old Fashioneds Linda Lee and I expanded our rapport, bumping elbows, rubbing behinds in the cluttered kitchen hung with garlic chains. As the kids ran in and out I carved a roast of lamb. And while they bolted food before the flickering tube I dined with their mother by candlelight—silverware and crystal sparkling in the big plate glass window and its everlasting picture of the sea.

The sky had cleared and stars began to multiply above the flat black rim of the Pacific—one third of the surface of the earth, I told Linda between bites. Already she seemed impressed by my command of random facts. Against that dark immensity I saw something soft and birdlike, something eager to be sheltered in its nest.

I built a fire in the tall brick stack. Two calico cats and the Irish setter, Randy, gathered on the hearth, then Brenda in a nighty, the boys in flannel p.j.'s—pictures of a childhood innocence I could not remember in myself. Even their laundered scalps smelled pure as they bid us goodnight.

As soon as they had gone Linda put out the pets. We lay writhing and whispering before the dying coals. When their glow faded a shaft of brilliant moonshine began to pierce the room.

That was the first of our cozy dinners in the house above the sea. I began to spend the evenings, then the nights as well, on the queen-size living room couch. We played delicious games beneath the blankets; I wondered if the children ever heard.

One Sunday morning they surprised us lying naked in the sheets.

"Hi, there!" called Brenda, "I hope you all enjoyed yourselves. Whatever."

"Here's the paper," said Starkey, stretching out with the comics, obliging Linda and me to move aside.

"How do you like Prince Valiant?" I asked for openers. I compared my golden-haired Linda to his Aleta, Queen of the Misty Isles.

"Ah, he doesn't do anything but have adventures. When is he gonna grow up?"

I glanced across the young critic's shoulder at a four-color Frito ad, and below it a tale from the Bible, the one about the replicating loaves and fishes.

"Do you follow those stories, too?"

"Naw. They're too crazy."

"How about Dick Tracy?"

"His head's as full of holes as his hat is. He's always busting people's doors down, like our dad." Starkey turned the page. "Hey, *Jerry*. Look at this. It's Fearless Fosdick!" the boy cried with glee.

I shared his crinkled view of the needle-jawed detective in his derby, eyes-a-bulge, slobbering over the platter-size tenderloin served up by Prudence Pimpleton, his lifelong sweetheart. Starkey's restless squirming shook the couch. When Linda took a sheet and strolled off to the bathroom, I wished I had thought to go first.

"A steak a night for life," the boy soliloquized. "I'll bet he doesn't even have to sleep with her."

"You wouldn't, either," I remarked man-to-man, "if she looked anything like that." Linda didn't look so great herself that morning, it occurred to me. Starkey had begun to frown at Mary Worth. Too many words floated in the speech balloons. He turned another page.

"When are you and Mom getting married?"

"Oh, I don't know. We haven't really talked a lot about it. Yet. How did you happen to ask?" I was growing uncomfortable under the cover, littered with the week's crimes and news. What was Linda doing in the bath so long? She didn't look all *that* bad. It was a test of both my patience and my bladder, whose fullness had already raised a useless lump.

"I think it's a good idea," said Starkey, "before she finds somebody else. Someone we might not like as much as you." He went on reading. Flattery sparred with annoyance in the practice ring of my emotions.

"I'll take it under advisement," I replied.

In September and early October the California coastline shows its true summer season, climax of the year. Hot winds from the desert sweep clear the overcast that lingers on the shore throughout vacation time, and cleanse the near-deserted beaches, leaving patterns of their passing scribbled on the dunes. The surf rolls majestically in shapes of liquid glass.

Then the deep-water blues of the Pacific turn red as old blood with tides of plankton flashing on the waves at night in streaks of pale sea fire. A skinny-dipper's body looks green as any ghost's; his stride leaves footprints glowing in the sand. Behind him crowd the jaws of jagged ridges, hell-black and death-close in the totally clarified darkness. The air itself is charged with nameless currents.

"The wine dark sea," mused Linda Lee, who had done her share of reading. "Homer's red ocean."

"Appropriate!" was my comment. "But what Homer really meant was the *darkness* of the sea. Not its *color*. It's a flaw in the translation. They don't have the Red Tide in Greece, you know. At least not under their new government."

Linda, absorbed in the sunset, did not respond to this political aside. We lounged in torn campaign chairs on the terrace as the sun sank through veils of vapor to drop like a hot coin in its ocean slot. Seconds later the sky lit like a cosmic jukebox, or a nuclear bomb going off—the illustrious Green Flash, the setting sun's refraction, and a sure sign of favor from the gods.

"That was nice," said Linda. "Like wishing on a falling star. I'm going in to see about the dinner. Can I fix you another drink?"

"Not right now, thanks. I'd like to think for a minute." I was pondering our future, with or without its new good-luck sign in the skies. I wondered what Linda had wished for. In a while she was back with fresh drinks.

"I don't think I want one, oddly enough."

"Then what are you thinking that's so serious, dear?"

"About the nature of physical reality. Life and its permutations. The expanding universe. About us, I suppose."

"You mean about our getting married, don't you?" Linda laid an arm on my campaign chair.

"I guess that's the problem. When you come right down to it."

"Is it a big one, Jerry?"

I took her hand in my lap. "Not really. It's just something I've never done before. You know? I wonder if I'd be any good at it."

"You've done all right so far," she reassured me. The children were teasing Randy; and his excited bark, mixed with their laughter, came from the amber windows of the house, a lantern in the dusk.

What I *had* been thinking of was previous affairs, most of them delightful in their fashion, and how each began and how it ended— the painful part. I was also seriously thoughtful about taking on an instant family, adorable though its members might be. In some slippery convolution of the brain, freedom tangled with security—like a thief in a condominium hallway.

"Well, you know how I feel about you, Jerry. And the children like you too. They really do. They *need* some kind of father."

This last point struck home: I'd hardly known a father of my own.

"I don't know, Linda. There're things in my past the kids might not think so much of. If they ever found out, that is." I thought of a number of occasions that would not be approved by any child that I could think of. But why did I *need* their approval anyway—a full-grown, resourceful, self-employed male adult?

"It's all right, Jerry, I understand. Don't forget. They're going to grow up too, some day."

It was a truth with the light of revelation. I'd failed to visualize the children beyond their present tender years. I hadn't been around to see them *grow*. I saw an even more complicated future.

"So it wouldn't hurt too much to try. You're practically living here already." Our hands relaxed their clasp.

Strike two! This was truer than I'd wanted to admit. I was spending days and hours—no, damn near my entire *time* there—playing House. Where would we get the money? I began to feel depressed. "Well, it's nothing to rush right into. Shouldn't we figure it out?"

Linda brought a legal pad and began to compare our incomes by the light of the hurricane lamp. Hers was easily the larger, I saw. But combined, she reasoned, we'd have enough for normal purposes. "We'll keep a budget," she said brightly.

My heart sank even lower, to the bottom of my ribs. Keeping budgets. Making payments. Saving dollars. She sounded like a car-lot salesman closing a dubious contract. Why buy this used mother—and her three minor accessories? Why marry at all? Why her? *Why them? WHY ME!*

"I do think I love you, Linda, but I don't know about our marriage."

Her turn to experience depression! She was silent, save for the clinking of her drink.

"I have a problem, too," she said finally, in a low flat voice.

"What's that? Is it a *big* one?"

"I think I'm going to have another child."

Four extra features included in the deal! I did not think at all before answering, "I think I'll have that other drink now, after all."

4.

"That *hurt*," I complained to the girl in black who had just finished pinching my ass. "Margo!"

"I'd know you anywhere, Jerry, even without your makeup. Kiss me, but don't let it smear."

"*Mmmmmmmmm-ff.* Do you miss me?"

"Sweet, foolish man, of course I do. There's no one quite like you. Here's Fred. He talks to computers."

He was a defrocked priest with a beard, she a spirit from the past. Her thick black hair crackled electrically as always, as Linda's never did. It grew thick on her body, too, and had left deep impressions in my memory book on the order of well-pressed ferns. The two went out of doors.

Inside the house were Linda's friends and neighbors, couples in their thirties like ourselves, with new cars and nice homes, a problem child or a psychiatrist. Tonight they were all someone else—space freaks and mutants of the Sixties, flappers from the Twenties, western types. Or an imitation whore, a devil in tights, Dracula, Bette Davis— like lunchtime on the old backlot. I'd asked a few workers from studio days who knew how to dress and act. No one had invited the surfers and their girls, freeloading booze and groceries. They would be themselves anywhere, the normals. Every now and then a small but human face peered around a corner—Starkey out of "Gunsmoke." The kids were keeping score.

Lights revolved, records plopped, people danced. It was a good noisy Halloween party. Only one thing was wrong. I wasn't having any fun, even after six or seven drinks. So I stood by the door in my breechcloth and beads, a silent redskin, embarrassed beneath my red paint—last of a race of doomed romantics, follower of buffalo and eagle down the sunset trail, without an Indian nickel's worth of dust to lay my braids in. What was I doing getting hitched? I was no more a natural husband than a son of native tribes.

Where the hell was Linda? In the kitchen of course, fixing something to eat—in a Mother Hubbard dress and coal-scuttle bonnet, a migrant widow on a wagon train, a true pioneer! She would have flung back flaming arrows, staked a homestead on rich bottom land and reared a dozen offspring, still darning socks with cats in her lap at the age of a hundred-and-four—a matriarch. And here she was in Malibu, as far west as she could get. Did that make her stronger that I was? *Suppose it did!*

"Why the long face, Jerry? Is something wrong?"

I hung my braids. "I think I lost my I.D. That's all."

"Let's see if we can find it." She led me to the bluff, down a trail of wet iceplant to a secret cove at the base. Frenzied screams reached us from the ocean, where shining bodies reveled in the surf. Linda stripped off the breechcloth, then her dress. For a long time I wriggled and panted, till her hands told the effort to stop.

"That's all right," she murmured. "It doesn't have to happen every time."

"I *want it* to happen every time. Why would we want to get married?"

We lay back and stared at the stars, now grouped in unfamiliar patterns that seemed nearer than necessity might dictate. I thought of flying saucers seeking specimens from Earth. Linda started, then aborted a yawn.

"What do you think they're doing on other planets, Linda?"

"Probably the same things we are." She rubbed my painted chest.

"Do you think they do stuff like this?" I flexed my limbs like groping tentacles joined in strange organic congress.

"I *do* love you, Jerry," said Linda with extra sincerity.

A bright light shot across the sky—a star had decided to fall. She watched it head for Mexico.

"What did you wish for this time?"

"The same thing as last, I think. A boy."

"Me, too," I said and kissed her, tongue to navel. That night we slept in her bed.

As dawn's rosy fingers came stealing through the room I got up for a handful of aspirin. The bathroom was a bin of used disguises. No Indian brave in war-stripes but a clown in smeared grease paint surprised me in the mirror. *You're the one who's been savaged,* it might as well have said. I made terrible faces, then scrubbed myself clean.

In the living room was Margo, arms around her lover, face in his beard—a hairy pair of couch-mates. Her furry armpits still held strong attractions for me, like pubic zones kept in reserve. But those were usually found on *guys*, weren't they? I moved on to the terrace.

Turning slowly on the bearings of its frozen poles that ultimate party light, the planet earth, revealed the luscious colors of the sunrise—purple grape to cherry, peach to yellow-orange. The kelp-cutter, grazing seaweed pasture for its iodine crop, moved at the pace of a private yacht, flashing back the wet metallic shimmer of a gold November morn.

Then I saw in mind, like the disc of rising sun behind me, the calm reformed profiles of Linda and myself, stamped upon the bright, new-minted surface of a noble coin.

5.

"What a mess!" wailed Brenda's voice. The refrigerator door slammed. "I thought they'd never leave. Let me have one of those, Stevie."

"It's not your brand."

Her brand of what, I wondered. Linda and I had just done it in bed—successfully, and she got up to close the door. I stopped her. It was our chance to spy on the kids.

"What happened then?" That was Starkey.

"Oh, they all fooled around and ran naked on the beach and smoked some marijuana. Mom and J.C. played man and wife." She took my name in vain, I said to Linda.

"Just make believe?" continued Starkey.

"Well, it *was* Halloween, wasn't it? I didn't get any sleep. Some people in the next room were doing things, right against my wall."

"Oh, yeah?" said Steve. "You mean the robot and his chick? She's neat. I'll bet he balled her all night. I wish I could."

"Shut up, Steve. Starkey isn't old enough for all that."

"Sure I am. I saw Mom and Jerry doing it, over in the new house and right here on the couch. It looked funny." I saw them staring at the violated couch, maybe changing seats.

"Well, now you know how they make babies." Brenda made a noise of stacking plates.

"How about the guys in the bathroom?" said Steve. "The fag in drag and the sailor. They forgot to lock the door." The clatter ceased.

"You shouldn't even mention such things. They're too perverted."

"I know what that means, too," said Starkey. "A Hollywood fruit cocktail. What'll we call the baby?"

"Mom wants to call it Casey, after Doctor Ben Casey on TV." Linda shook her head. We heard scores of preposterous namesakes. The childish puns, the needless jokes were revving up my head pains.

"Let's say it's a girl," Brenda finished. "Even though it's a bastard."

"How can a girl be a bastard?"

"Look at your sis."

"What makes you think it's a girl then?"

"Because there's *pricks* enough around here already."

"Don't knock 'em till you've tried 'em," Stevie laughed.

Now what in hell had Brenda meant by that? Was it a general remark? Or personal? Maybe she only wanted a one-to-one ratio on the good old family team. We got up to see what they were doing.

The three were lounging in the living room, cleaning the glasses by draining the drinks, and puffing away on Kools. The setter lapped a bowl of beer suds.

"You children shouldn't be doing that," said their mother.

"Put those damn things out!" I commanded, first order as nominal parent. I was glad to see it obeyed.

"We were having our own little party," said sensible Brenda. "We'll go down to the beach. You guys can clean if you want to. I'm not making up the beds." Hers was as clear as any head that morning.

"I didn't know they smoked and drank, for Christ's sake," I said to Linda, scouring pans. "What are some other vices?"

"They usually don't behave like that. They're good children, really."

"I suppose they really are." I thought of Starkey in his cowboy suit. "But don't you tell them anything? Aren't there any house rules?"

"Harry took care of all that. He used to whip them and lock them in their rooms. Once he used his roach-spray on Starkey, and cut off most of Stevie's hair." As she bent at the sink Linda's eyes were glistening. "He did some rotten things to Brenda, too ugly to describe. He put laxatives in the food for the cats."

I wrapped an arm around her. I didn't want to be a dad like that at any cost, especially now that I would soon be an authentic father.

"They called him the Great Exterminator." Her list of crimes ran on. "They ran and hid when his truck came down the driveway. I did, too. That's why we're divorced. That and a few other reasons, too painful to go into now."

I didn't want to know the other reasons. She was lucky to be rid of that Nazi! There'd be no child abuse in our house, I resolved, or juvenile debauchery, either. What we adults were doing was probably bad enough. To set new sights in home morality, Linda and I took our blood tests and were duly attached by a justice of the peace.

A few weeks later I gave up the apartment-office by the harbor and brought my clothes, drawing board and records to the house. If it was more than a game we were playing, I was going to play for keeps.

6.

Periods of real content escape description. Time flows too smoothly, a pure stream of being, reflecting only pleasure in its surface calm. The weeks went by in the way of those unscripted days that fly from the calendars of early movies, leaves of time's passing that can never be recalled.

Sprawled on the terrace we watched the world glide by: racing boats and trawlers, whales going back to where they came from, and, at night, patterned lights like glowing rivets of great steel ships along the sea lanes. What lay deep beneath their buoyant hulls, I wondered, on the dark drowned ledge of the continental shelf? I thought of Huck Finn and black Jim, euphorically afloat on the miles-wide Mississippi, oblivious to snags and gars and hidden sand bars, drifting toward fates the river made for them. Obstacles yet to be sounded might lurk in our future also. I didn't want to think of them. They were too far around the next unwinding bend.

Like that free pair, we were sometimes naked, too. The boys thought it odd, but Brenda took offense. Overweight and physically mature, she wasn't yet ready for nature's manifest duality. She slammed the door on Starkey each time he made a fountain in the toilet bowl—his proof of being male. Steve had grown a coat of fleece, white against his surfer's tan.

So the children were growing, just as Linda said they would, though not so fast as the small prisoner of her womb. In the springtime he would make his escape.

I loved the womb-like warmth of our common security blanket. I often woke in the late cool hours when body heat ebbs lowest, an arm or a leg around Linda, to monitor her light untroubled breathing, the beating of her healthy mother's heart, a living metronome. I would snuggle even closer. Like cooling oil to a crankcase my blood drained from idle brain to pelvis, raising there a little club of flesh. Sometimes Linda would awaken too. My God—I would be startled to realize—this extraordinary woman is my wife!

In that profound early silence the others could be heard as well, astir in tiny spasms of their growth, or twitching like Randy in uncomplicated dreams. Their lungs shared the same night air, were open to the same night spirits. I would lie then as in a spell of mindless, timeless ambience; father and protector, keeper and defender of the family flame. *Like the pilot light on the water-heater,* as Linda had once paraphrased the concept for me. Woman the realist. Man, the Idealist. Some things never changed.

From a hundred yards at sea against an epic mountain backdrop the terrace of our home became a puppet stage. Linda entered from the glass doors, right center, shed water from a sprinkling can, and rubbed her belly. Next door at the just-finished house appeared my client and our neighbor, Lieutenant Colonel Everett Vandenberg, United States Army Corps of Engineers, retired, to direct short hose-bursts at each of his seedling plants. Exchanging greetings, these tillers of the soil began to talk. Why wasn't she inside to baste the turkey?

I was treading water in my swim fins, waiting for the ultimate wave; waiting to twist into the crest, slice through the face like a dagger, arms back, chest out, the foam gurgling under my exalted loins—a kind of *sea rape.* The sea was warm on top, slick as a motel bedspread; below, cold as bedsprings.

Waiting for the sun to melt fat from her bones, Brenda lay becalmed on an airmat. Steve took rides on his short-tailed board, his towhead sliding out of sight behind the surf-line. And there was Starkey's cry as he threw sticks for Randy—*It's a bird, it's a plane, it's SU-PER-mannn...* The schizoid from Krypton was still a kind of hero, despite the knocking off of national leaders in Big Town, U.S.A.

Who among our number was the happiest? Not me. My teeth chattered and my groin ached. I was freezing my buns off. Where was that overdue set of waves? And what the hell were those two talking about? Me? I projected my will across the waters, only to see the pair take seats in the campaign chairs. My powers of psychokinesis had been drained by the covetous ocean. I began the long swim to shore.

"Hi," I said to the Colonel, lips blue and trembling, dripping water on the bricks. "Welcome aboard, sir." The building of his house had its differences: designer versus engineer, art against authority. But today he was affably relaxed, sipping sherry in the sunshine with my wife.

"You can call me Everett, Jerry, now that the job is done. I've just been asked to dinner. Here's to you, friend to friend."

In the shower, while gallons of hot water ran, I considered our two careers. His had been a true profession: military school, West Point, a command in Allied defenses during World War II, administrative posts and now retirement, still fit in his late forties with options for a whole new career.

Where-*as*, my life in the Air Force had been much like the one outside it: a fumbling start, opportune transfers, and then flight school, where I'd torn up a trainer in a ground loop. I had put in my time on the ground and got out, permanently outranked by my neighbor. If he'd done his job so frigging well, why wasn't he a goddamn general?

My flesh began to thaw like the tom turkey's—soft at the surface, frozen at the core. A profile—Linda's—fell across the etched glass door. She swung it and crowded in beside me.

"*Oouuow*. It's *hot*, honey. Are you really that cold?"

"A human popsicle, Linda. Feel." She soaped my back, then my trunk. As the shower poured and steam filled the chamber, we fondled, kissed, and joined—a fantastic kind of heart-throbbing hip-throwing mind-blowing holiday *fuck*. Another shadow crossed the streaming glass.

"Shall I turn the turkey *now*, Mom?" *Jesus*. What timing! We were hanging on the crest.

"Do anything you *want* with it, Brenda. Your mother's busy."

"I can see that she's otherwise occupied. Dinner's nearly ready." What a daughter—a *step*-daughter of course. We resumed but it wasn't the same. The showerhead ran lukewarm, then cold. Still sudsed I turned the dials to OFF. Linda brought a towel.

"How come you had to ask the Colonel?"

"Because he's up here all alone, poor man. His wife's at Fort Myers in Florida, with the children. I think she's having an affair."

"What's that got to do with us?"

"He's your client, Jerry. Don't you want him to have Thanksgiving dinner? Try to be a little generous. He's been pretty good to you, you know." And so have you, sweetheart, I sighed to myself.

"You can do the carving," Linda said. Our first big family dinner was a set piece: the sun-splashed linen, the flashing crystal glasses, the steaming platters, the Colonel on Linda's right—erect in trim grey hairs and mustache. A viewer would take *him* to be master of the table. Until the children began to speak.

"You forgot my stuffing, Jerry dear," said Brenda.

"She don't need it," Stevie said. "Lemme have the other leg."

"That's my leg," said Starkey. "There's only two, you know."

"No I didn't. Did you count 'em?"

"Screw you." Starkey grabbed it.

"Don't you wish!"

"Children, please," said their mother. "Don't forget what day it is. Just be still and eat your dinner."

"Just what we're trying to do. If we're permitted," Brenda added.

"Here's your stuffing, girl. Now stuff it."

"We don't eat this well in the service," said the Colonel. Nor as badly, either. Not exactly an Officers' Mess.

"You were abroad, weren't you, Everett?" asked my wife. Over-*seas* is what you mean, dear. It wasn't everybody's pleasure trip. I already knew what we were in for—a big serving, a super-helping, a generous shovelful of all that military crap. I'd had enough to last a lifetime.

"I was in England before D-Day. We built the floating harbors for our invasion forces, and then the mobile bridges for our tanks. We really took Jerry by surprise." Linda looked perplexed. The Colonel smiled.

"By Jerry I mean the krauts, of course. That was the English nickname for the Germans." The kids were silent, their tummies full, as the Colonel rambled on about the Nazis and their buried forts of concrete, the flak towers built like castles, the factories run by starving slaves, the globe-threatening Fascist order designed for a millennium.

"Even V-1's, the V-2's, all the weapons of terror could not save the doomed Third Reich. They even planned a plane to bomb New York." That caught the kids' drifting attention. L.A. next time! "It takes more than blood and brains to win world conflicts." The Colonel dabbed his mustache.

"What then?" I felt compelled to ask.

"A sense of purpose, hence of being. The enlightened will to victory." It was Linda who listened now. The words had been those of the Master Race.

"Did you get wounded?" Starkey asked.

"I did, but I can't tell you where. It's a military secret."

7.

"What are you going to do today, Jerry?"

That was another from Starkey's large reserve of touchy questions. Ten o'clock Monday at the end of a three-night weekend and I was still in bed waiting, in fact, for my breakfast. This boy's vacation was legitimate. It was enough to make anyone feel guilt.

"What is your need to know?" I asked him.

"Mom wants you to take us all downtown to do our Christmas shopping. She gave us each ten bucks."

I yawned and scratched myself beneath the covers. It was snug there. I knew what the assignment meant: a trip from parking lot to overloaded parking lot in a driving winter rain, the wipers clicking and the windows sweating over, so the kids could spend themselves delirious in expensive Beverly Hills.

"What do you want for Christmas, Starkey?"

"A three-stage rocket and a gun."

"Your mother said no war toys."

"Those aren't toys, dumbo. The rocket really works. It's got a hundred-foot ceiling with a payload. The gun's a twenty-two repeating rifle, with telescope sights." The boy was practical for nine. I would have asked for the same at his age, if I'd thought there was any chance of getting them.

It was dark when we returned—tired, broke and irritable. The children went immediately to watch TV. As in earlier times, Linda had set our table by the fire and brought me a hot drink. She touched my hand to her abdomen. "Can you feel it? He does that a lot of the time now."

At the sense of this new individual, our first contact, a curious apprehension seized me. What was happening here? Instead of the pride of parenthood, I felt fear of a strange symbiosis, like a roving creature trapped in jungle vines.

"Poor man," she said later, with brandy.

"Who. Me?"

"Not you, Jerry." I couldn't always be first, she was telling me. "Who then?"

For her audience of one Linda sighed. "Everett, of course." My new rival. "He's gone to Florida to see his wife. They've been married twenty years, you know. A Southern girl." I knew the type— so marvelously entertaining in small talk on the post, free of troublesome ideas in politics. "She's going with his former aide. A major! Can you imagine?" I could imagine. "He's such a fine man, too."

"Well, we have each other. Don't we, hon?"

"I think I know where he's been wounded. In the place where it never quite heals."

I frowned, waiting to show sympathy.

"In the heart, of course, dear Jerry. Please do try to understand."

For once, I thought I could. I was glad my wife was pregnant.

> Good King Wenceslas went out,
>   on the Feast of Stephen
> When the snow lay round about,
>   deep and crisp and ee-ven.

The children in tumble-dry p.j.'s were pillow-fighting on the couch. The old carol played on the radio:

> ...underneath the mountain
> Right against the forest fence,
>   by Saint Agnes' fou-ountain.

I loved the image of the good man, staff in hand, crunching through the night in tails of ermine, his shivering page matching footprints on tingling, bell-tipped toes—me and Starkey—and the mountain cloaked in hoary woods beyond the glittering plain. A carved stone basin hid there, hung with chimes of ice. Wolves howled from the timber line. It was a sharper picture than any that those other three kings—the Wise Men, slogging through the sands on over-burdened camels—had ever brought to mind.

"Who was he, anyway?" asked Starkey.

"The King of Bohemia. In the fifteenth century." I went on about the Yule log and mistletoe, the Roman Saturnalia, the birth of Christ, the climes and times of Christmas. The children heard me out with bored distraction, bright eyes locked on heaps of treasure stacked beneath the gem-colored tree lights. Three wise moppets, for sure. If Linda and I could help it, and I thought we could, they weren't getting into any of that stuff until morning.

"...but the Saint was a real life person, beloved by young and old because he was so generous. He chucked a bag of gold through the window every time the daughter of a certain house got married. There were three daughters. And that's why you see three gold balls on pawn shops today. They give out money."

"And rob you blind," said Brenda.

"I always thought one ball was a spare."

"*Steve!* On Christmas Eve. You won't get anything in *your* stocking."

"I can stuff it myself, with my own candy cane."

"...and that's the story of Saint Nicholas. Or Saint Nick, the Giver," I concluded. "We sometimes call him Santa Claus."

"It's a lovely story," said Linda, lover of myths and legends. "I wish we could have lived in those times."

"Who's Old Nick then?" asked my other loyal listener—Starkey.

"Old Nick is a nick-name for the Devil."

"Oh, I love it, I *love* it," laughed Brenda, showering herself from a flask of Chanel Number 5. "Thank you, baby brother."

"Don't thank me."

"Thanks for the diver's watch, Starkey," said Steve.

"Forget it." He was setting up the rocket for an early launch. As the others sorted out their loot I trod to the kitchen for our breakfast juice, a quart of California bubbly.

"Why don't you open your presents, Mom and Jerry?" And we did. A string of cultured pearls for their mother, a blue nylon flight bag for me. The bag contained a gift-boxed fifth of Jack Daniels Old Number Seven.

"I don't know what to say, kids. Thanks a million." Where had they scored that kind of merchandise for under thirty bucks, plus tax?

And where did they buy the booze? They either had private cash reserves or were smart junior spenders without equal.

"This is yours, dear husband," Linda said. *Your time is my time,* read the tag on the box. Another watch, this one a self-winding sports chronometer whose case matched my Navajo ring. Then I helped rip the tissues from Linda's gift, a king-size alpaca bedspread. The tender skins, cream and tan and umber, were stitched together like an intricate puzzle of the Incas. The hairs raised at our touch. There were magic nights ahead beneath that fuzzy crazy-quilt.

Champagne in hand we went outdoors to watch the rocket launching. As Starkey mixed the chemicals we all stood back. The mixture hissed, the plastic tube trembled—a pulsing white phallus stenciled U.S.A.F. The rocket lurched aloft, dropped the dummy booster, and arced above the trees. I felt a sting of pride in its performance—my years in the Air Force had a meaning after all. At the apogee of flight the cone expelled a parachuted astronaut who fell into the topmost branch of a eucalyptus. Randy barked and clawed the trunk.

"Scratch one moon shot," said Stevie.

"Balls," said the frustrated crew-chief. Starkey went inside and got the rifle, slipped in some shells, and in two shots dropped the spaceman from his perch.

"*Bull-zai!*" yelled Steve. "Let's go shoot some bottles in the gully."

"Wait a minute, guys. I'll go with you." So I thought. But Linda held my sleeve. What did she want, more champagne? A greater gift? A trial run with the alpaca?

"Let them go, Jerry. Starkey's worried. He's afraid you'll find out about the presents."

"Find out what about the presents? They're not all opened yet."

"They weren't exactly purchases, you know."

"How do you know? Are you psychic?"

"Brenda told me. She's crying in her room right now."

"You mean they're *stolen?*"

Linda nodded. What a scene—Brenda's teenage tears of larceny mingling with the purloined #5 Chanel! We went into our room.

I fell into the warm alpaca spread as Linda began her Christmas story. The three precocious raiders had hit three stores within the hour: Bullock's Westwood, the Fancy Pantry, Gifts To Go. While Steve and Brenda had made selections, Starkey, with their first choice, my—*my?*—flight bag, had served as bag man—or boy—until it filled.

Shopping done, they had stopped for club sandwiches and sodas to celebrate by spending hard cash. In their well-bred looks and charge card clothing they had gone without detection—a clean, efficient, first-class holiday heist. "So many others were doing it," Brenda had explained between sobs. "We saw a woman snatch a purse, and a man take a carved ivory chess set. Board and all."

I lay back and stared at the ceiling, where a spider had started a web. What in hell could be done about such things? Their responsible legal guardian, I probably should have stayed with the kids, instead of disappearing at the Fame & Fashion Faire to compare imported shirts. I'd had the dim half-thought of maybe *lifting* one, just to see what it was like. But the mad idea had scared me, and sent me to the basement john with loosened bowels. *MY PLACE FOR B.J.*, I read idly on the paper-holder, tensing. *BLOND STUDENTS ONLY PLEASE 18-24.* And a telephone number. No doubt a clever vice squad trap for wayward college students. Then I had gone to find the children, pushing through the line at Santa's Throne.

What were we going to do now? That was the Number One question. Take it all back again on Monday? Or wait to see if anyone got caught? For these first offenders, I saw the hard truth and its train of bitter consequence—Lincoln Heights, a night among hardened hard-up criminals, Juvenile Hall, probation. And for us? Canceled credit cards at important retail outlets, a damaged image, the talk of upper Malibu. What, for example, would the Colonel think? Eventually the blame fell on our heads. And how would we punish them now, on Christmas Day, as we helped destroy state's evidence? I had just drunk an Old Jack Daniels drink.

Linda was apparently reading my thoughts or had already thought them, for she drew even closer as our troubled eyes met.

"After all, it's just the first time." How could she know that? "And they were shopping mostly for us." Okay, okay. But the operative verb is shop-*lifting*, sweetheart. She was stoked on that new string of pearls! "You'll have to talk to them, Jerry."

Jesus. *My* job to clean up the dirty work. I felt like a fallen prince consort making deals in the shadow of the throne, while my Queen smiled on her stolen necklace, and our commemorative medal tarnished in its mildewed case. We got out of our clothes and wrapped ourselves entirely in the patchwork of skins from the Andes.

As we were thus engaged, a car or loose-framed vehicle of sorts rattled down the driveway and stopped. While the motor ran, three heavy knocks, hard as fate, sounded on the plank front door. We could almost hear the knocker's breathing. Would it be the Sheriff, on this Day of days, armed with a fistful of warrants? We lay still, rolled in darkness.

After four long minutes by the radiant sweep-second hand of my legitimately purchased sports watch, the car door slammed and the driver drove away. I peeked from our cocoon to spot the caller. Waiting to join traffic at the crest of the drive was a yellow Chevy pickup, on its tailgate the faded letters, BUG-A-BYE INC. When he had gone we opened the door and found there wrapped in ribbons a big tin of pretzels, six-packs of beer and Coke, and at least a year's supply of DEE-DAY Pest & Insect Killer.

"Good old Harry," murmured Linda, the former Mrs. Fedderman, at my side. The Great Exterminator, she had called him more than once. From those toxined loins had sprung these same misguided offspring, the budding young kleptos of our joint address. I was open to the holiday opinion that perhaps he hadn't punished them enough.

8.

Like the honey-color crown of the queen bee, regnant, Linda Lee's corona of lamplit golden hair flared out above the vast terrain of furry comforter. In her soft lotioned hands lay a beautifully illustrated copy of *Perrault's Fairy Tales*.

"Are you sure you won't come with me?"

"I really don't want to go, dear. You go if you want. You've always done it before—what you wanted."

"It's New Year's Eve, for Christ's sake. It's going to be a party like you've never seen before."

"I don't especially want to see it, Jerry, believe it or not. Besides, the baby's acting up tonight, just like the infant year. We're happy right here in our bed."

Already showered and dressed, I sat down on the edge of the mattress and rattled my preparatory drink, my free hand taking in it one of hers.

"What are you reading, *Sleeping Beauty?*"

"No, the story of Patient Griselda."

"Griselda? Who was she?" I glanced at the digital alarm, the digits at 9:0:6. Linda turned back the pages and began to read in a girlish singsong voice:

> *"At the foot of the mountains...there once lived a youthful and gallant prince, the favorite of the whole countryside."*

Despite the hour, she had caught my attention immediately.

> *"...Combining in himself all the gifts of body and spirit, he was strong, clever, skillful in war, and displayed great enthusiasm for the arts."*

Right up my alley! "Go on, Linda," I encouraged her.

> *"He loved fighting and victory, too, along with all mighty endeavors and deeds of glory—everything which makes one's name live in history. But more than all these, his greatest pleasure lay in the happiness of his people."*

"What else does it say?" *Those* words sounded more like the Colonel. She gave me a long look before continuing:

> *"This splendid disposition was obscured, however, by a somber cloud, a melancholy mood which caused the Prince to feel, in the depths of his heart, that all women were faithless and deceivers. Even in a woman of the highest distinction"*—meaning herself!— *"he saw only the heart of a hypocrite, elated with pride. To him she was a cruel enemy whose unbroken ambition was to gain mastery over whatever unhappy men might surrender to her..."*

That was the writing on the wall, all right. No need to go any further. Besides, it was already 9:2:3. But she went on:

> *"...Each day the Prince gave his morning to his royal business. He ruled wisely, doing everything he felt best for his people—the frail orphan, the oppressed widow, protecting the rights of all. The remainder of the day he devoted to the chase, either the stag or the*

bear. These, in spite of their ferocity, frightened him less than the charming women he shunned daily."

"You'd rather read that than go with me?"

Linda closed the book. "It's just the way I'm feeling, hon."

All right, then. I could have a good time by myself. There I'd have a hundred other people. I'd known all along I was right. I was also right to make the gesture. 9:3:2! I stood up, jingling the car keys in one hand, the glass of melting ice cubes in the other. "Let me know how it all turns out."

"Please watch your driving. And your drinking, too. You won't be the only one out there tonight, you know. We need you for a father."

I was gratified—not a word about the absent Everett. We were going to start the new year right, after all.

"I'll be among friends," I promised. "Happy New Year." Planting a wet kiss on either cheek, I checked the hour once more by her present, the Christmas chronometer, and left the silent house. The children had gone to a party down by the beach and were probably even at the moment sunk deep in some iniquitous teenage folly.

Like a luminous gas balloon, a full moon was rising after showers. The moist air made the car run like a winner. The old year's new word, *groovy*, described the way the wheels took to the Pacific Coast Highway. The scenery slid by with the slickness of a process shot. My face lit by dials, I might have been the driver at the wheel of a sound stage mock-up on the road to the next reel's successes.

The party had begun above the Merry-Go-Round at the ramp of Santa Monica Pier. That pier, a fingery projection of the city, probed the broad and murky bottom of the bay. The trestle was a relic of prewar days. The ballroom, the fun rides, the roller coaster had long ago burned down or been demolished. What remained were snack shacks, seafood restaurants and porcupine rows of fishing poles along the rails. The forest of pilings down below, cold and forbidding at all hours, was a gallery for the commission of lewd deeds, or crimes of an unspeakable violence. The rolling waves, trisected by the piles, beat heavily at their sockets wrapped in barnacles and starfish. The vibrations could be felt throughout the pier.

The last of the good-time buildings housed a carousel, whose wheel still turned with plunging horses to the clang of iron chords. It lived in a well of wood beneath a tent-like silver roof anchored to four corner turrets. In the tallest of these towers were the quarters of Leonard Faircycle, my host.

"Oh, hello. *Jerry?*"

"It's still me, Leonard."

"And you're *married,* clever boy. Where's the lucky lady?"

"She's busy having a baby."

"Yours? Not *this minute,* New Year's *Eve?*"

"It's a nine-month process, it turns out."

"I know just what you mean," said Sheila Eggers. "I've been through it all four times. Thirty-six months of unpaid labor."

"And that's why you're divorced?"

"That and one other reason."

"And she's not *here* tonight."

"Lenny, you're a bitch. But you know that."

Oh, Lordy, I thought, it was going to be one of *those* affairs—two mommas and no pop. Pity the poor kids!

"They're all in private schools, if that's what you're thinking, Jerry."

"I was thinking of getting a drink."

"I'll join you." And she did.

I knew them both from the studios. Since a change of name from Fleischaker to Faircycle, Leonard had done rather well. He ruled a section in Wardrobe. A few of his employees—young men he was said to favor—were here and there about the room, showing charm to lady guests. They would call him Leonard Farcical when the favors or the jobs had ceased.

The room was an octagon with tall rounded windows. The enameled white wainscot, the ceiling fan, the wicker chairs and potted palms were reminiscent of a Mississippi River steamboat. An intermittent striking of the harbor bell supported this idea. Mingling guests of assorted age and talent were much like those of Halloween.

"*Hi,* Sheila," said Beverly Bristol, an actress with a job.

"Bev! You got the part. I knew you would."

"We *both* know whom to thank."

At her side stood a near-human monster, a hundred pounds heavier than me, at least, a good ten inches taller, and all of it solid meat and bone. The giant's head had unobstructed views of every other.

"I want you to meet my friend here, Sheila. Buster Mirador. He plays fullback with the Rams." It figured. That skull of tough-skinned concrete was the perfect rack to hang a helmet on, the mountain goat logo curling round the ears. A big contrast to my symbol—the all-seeing mechanical eye.

"And this is Jeremy Carr. He does visuals."

"Hey, man," said Buster, mashing hands. "Is that something you eat?"

"That's pretty funny, Buster. How do you like the party, so far?"

"It's Fruit City here tonight. Like I expected."

"Buster! Can't you just have a good time?"

"I will if they let me." He crunched his calloused joints.

"Buster's only mad because a boy made a pass at him. Off the field, you understand," said Beverly.

"He asked for my number. My goddamn *telephone* number. The flit."

"And you didn't give it," said Sheila.

"Be glad you're not a man," warned Buster. While he sulked his manly sulk, the women went off by themselves. For a change of body fluids I made the kitchen/bathroom tour. A line locked the door to the red velvet bath. "What's happening in there?" I asked, legs crossed.

"A little home surgery," said another waiting guest.

"Keep your *hair* combed down. No one will notice," Leonard was counseling a friend when the door swung. "And stay out of his *way*, like I *told* you." The friend's face flushed.

"That's not a fullback, it's a *throw*back," he complained, a swollen eyelid blinking.

"Be glad you have a *family*," said Leonard as he passed. I wished I had Linda there with me. There was Jason Chisholm and his new girl—"Hi, Jase." *"Jerry."* And Margo, of course, whom I'd talk to when *she* was not the center of attention, and many many others, well or lesser known. But I found no companion, cute, kind, or sexy, to help usher in the year. A breeze was disturbing my hair. I turned to climb steps to a room overhead, above the blades of the slow-turning fan.

The top tower room was like the one below, but with oddly-pointed windows like a church. It had deep shag carpet and a huge platform bed bathed in pink and amber spotlights, a showcase for Leonard's love-life. On the bed lay piles of coats. On the coats lay Melody Landau in a spangled turquoise gown. Four or five others sat around the bed like kids playing games in the attic, an attic like the salon of a ship.

"Oh, hel-lo. I'm Captain Nemo. And this is Melody...Mermaid. We were...snorkeling." Here they snorted. "Do you know how to snorkel? Sir?"

"I know how to scuba dive."

"Ter-rif-fic! The man's a *scuba* diver. Scuby-do! What else can you do, mate?"

"I can skinny-dip and body-surf. On dry land."

"That's more *like* it. Would you care to body-surf, Miss Landau?"

She grew wide-eyed, holding her breath. "I might get rapture of the *depths*." Flaring her skirt like a mermaid's tail, she shook out her silvery hair.

"And of the *heights*," said a man on the bed. The two laughed alone.

"Come on, Jerry," said a woman I knew. "Let's find ourselves a drink."

"I just finished one."

"You might as well come down. They're higher than you'll get already."

As we descended, Buster shoved his way up the stair, shouldering the woodwork.

"Miss Landau has a full house up there," I said. "Standing room only."

"I don't care. I'm sick of dykes and fags. I wanta ball her."

"Lotsa luck then, Buster."

Bells rang and horns blew on the palisades, and from the public walk below came shouts of joy and anger. A handful of joints was passed around the room. I awoke in the corner by a potted palm; 3:15 by my chronometer. I finished someone's drink and crept back up the staircase. The tinted spots were out, but the room shared the light of the street lamps. I laid my eyeballs level with the lip of the stair.

The great bed quivered like the hide of some furiously agitated beast. Grunts and growls came from it. Suddenly the spread flew back. I had a privileged, unprecedented view of Buster Mirador in action—furry back, massive thighs and the Bull Durham sack that swung between them. Round his tree-thick trunk clung the slender legs of his currently favorite starlet.

"I think we got company," snarled the fullback.

"I *love* an audience," moaned Miss Landau, her sequined gown on the carpet. I crept back down the staircase hung with savage masks.

"Any fun?" asked Leonard in an apron.

"Sure. The Ram and the fish are making it."

"*Enchanting.* I have to *sleep* in that bed."

"A lovely party, Lenny." I gurgled another drink.

"Good. Now it's *over.*" He took the glass and dropped it in the sink.

Fog had drifted in across the harbor, swallowing the masts and hulls of fishing boats. From pier's end the foghorn bleated deeply, the only sound in the world. But far off in the distance...there it was... a siren.

The car to my surprise was where I'd left it, aglitter with sequins of dew.

9.

White lines wove a web inside the fog bank. Was I driving in only one lane? Stoplights glared as I ran an intersection. A uniformed figure flagged me over. A wheel struck a curb and stopped, the hubcap spinning into darkness. *Busted.* A white cap hove in the window.

"Some touchdown," said a sailor. "You shouldn't even be flying."

"Am I grounded?"

A patrol car had stopped for a signal change. The two officers watched, then took off after a sports car with whirling red light and siren.

"Shove over," the sailor said. "Let me drive." That was better than *shove off.* He flipped out two Lucky Strikes and lit them. The lighter's flare showed a swatch of red hair, a snub nose, an Irish grin, and dimples. I'd seen that face before...through my own eyes...or a camera's. The boy on the burning hilltop—the boy with the white canvas hose!

"Your name's...*Mickey.*"

"Right." He blew three perfect smoke rings.

"And you put out a Malibu fire?"

"Me and some others. Ship's Fireman McCoy here."

"The *real* McCoy?"

"You said it. Not me, bub. Where am I supposed to be taking you?"

I gave our five-digit number on the highway and watched the sailor drive, a sailor Leonard would describe as *cute*, or perhaps *a living doll*. I despised those kinds of phrases, improperly applied to human males. But some special, vitalizing essence held my eyes to a focus on his face. He grinned as he smoked without speaking, as though any further words would be mine. The words did not pronounce themselves. He stopped at the mailbox, got out, flagged the first car—a gold Eldorado—and was gone up the road to Point Mugu.

I drove at a burglar's creep along the gravel, eased the squeaking door of the house—the blood meanwhile pounding in my ears—and with exquisite courtesy and kindness shed all of my complicated clothes. I sneaked beneath the spreading tent of fur. The ceiling heaved and fluttered, like my stomach.

"Was it a good party?" Linda murmured. I tried to remember that far back in time.

"*Ter-rif-fic,*" I pronounced at last, the syllables about to make me puke. "What happened to...Patient...*Griselda?*"

"She waited till her prince got straightened out."

"And how long did that take?"

"Twenty years, in the book."

My vitals groaned at the sentence. No need to answer—she was probably correct. If I said one word more I'd throw up on the alpaca. It was best lying perfectly still like an accident case, keeping everything under control. The trouble was, my eyes refused to close and let me sleep. Linda's could and had. 4:5:3. Five early hours of another year.

I thought about the sailor who had possibly saved my life. Or my car. My driving record at the very least. Some other and similar person lingered on a memory trail that led all the way back to Eagle Rock High...in tenth-grade Physical Science class!

Jimmy Corey and I had made a scientific field trip on our bikes, far out to Big Tujunga Canyon. There we had clambered up the rocks to look down on a nudist camp. The rustic camp had tents, a cooking shelter, a leaky shower made from oil drums. The older campers played volleyball. The children painted clothes on one another with poster paints, then washed off the clothing in a stream.

We watched the ball game. Neither I, for certain, nor Jimmy Corey so far as I knew, had ever seen human parts so flagrantly exposed to view. Large, full-nippled breasts bounced up and down with every volley, their owners' legs wide-spread. And the guys—their ding-dongs flailed the canyon air.

"*Wow!*" said Jimmy, breathless. "Did you ever see anything to *beat* it?"

"I can't believe my eyes!" And I couldn't. I'd only been permitted anxious feels at drive-in movies, with limited visibility or none at all. The game ended with a great shout when the ball went out of bounds. The nudists went into their shelter and sucked on bottled drinks.

"What do you think we ought to do now, Jim? Do you think it's all right to go down there? Can't we just take our clothes off?" It was like getting tapped for the Big Game. Or going into battle—the first time under fire.

"I'd sure *like* to. I'm horny as a bitch in heat."

I caught my breath. "Why don't we?"

Jimmy shook his bright red head of hair.

"We can't," he said sadly, with regret. "It's a colony for lungers only. They're all supposed to have T.B." I was shocked. The well-tanned nudists were pictures of outdoor health.

We had skirted the forbidden camp and hiked up the stream bed of the canyon. Blueflies buzzed among the sun-warmed rocks. I wondered if they too might be infected. We came to a pool deep enough to dive into, laid our T-shirts and jeans across the boulders and sat down bare on a rock, our toes dangling in the cold mountain stream.

I had never seen a naked red-haired boy before. Jimmy Corey had a sprinkle of freckles on the shoulders, thin tufts of orange in the armpits, and copper-colored hairs in the crotch. He also had a perfectly normal red-tipped adolescent six-inch hard-on. He pulled up his legs, swiveled on his butt, and opened himself to inspection.

"You do it, too," he said. Jimmy Corey and I had masturbated one another there in Big Tujunga Canyon, face to freckled face.

We had rinsed our hands in the pool and gone swimming. Jimmy never spoke of it again, and in a few weeks he had made out with a popular girl who had grapefruit breasts. He was a tit man, Jimmy told me. As for myself, that was the first full experience of orgasm with a partner of either sex. Later in the school year I had scored with Marsha Brentlinger, although she had hardly any breasts at all.

My head felt straighter just thinking on these things, as though the brain itself achieved erection. I had a real one, too, in the usual place. I couldn't bring myself to rouse my Linda, my patient Sleeping Beauty, to foul her waking moments with my drinker's breath. I slunk off to the shower and did alone what Jimmy Corey and I had done together, my sex-strained heart and hand beating to the rhythmic litany—*what a-way to-start the-new year.* Then I turned the shower dial to COLD.

And then, and *then* it hit me. The model for my fantasized orgasm had not been the fabulous Miss Landau of the tower, all curves and moans and sequins, nor my wedded wife in our sanctioned marriage bed, nor even the long ago flat-chested Marsha, but a teenage boy and his counterpart—the red-haired Mickey of the road. My body blushed all over, and sank down on the toilet seat, sick with new-found guilt. If only Mother could be there to beat me *now,* I thought insanely. My headache returned with a vengeance.

When I felt well enough, I pulled on my pants and walked barefoot on the gravel to inspect the car: no unfamiliar dents, dings or gouges. Except for psychic damage and the headache, I had some-how got safely through the night. Cigarette butts and ashes soiled the floormat and a crushed wad was jammed into the ashtray—Mickey's pack of Lucky's, I recalled, with the poignant red circle of its brand. As a keepsake of that night's salvation, I flattened out and kept the souvenir.

10.

Like a long hangover after holidays, the rains came to Southern California, day after soggy day, until the roofs leaked and the floors ran, the streets were rivers and the valleys flood-plains. The robot snick-snack of windshield wipers became signals of insistent warning

—until slabs of mud slid off the shoulders of the weary hills, trees and houses with them.

The children had been kept in since the Christmas shopping caper. Now they were prisoners of the weather, without a workable TV.

"What'll we do tonight?" Brenda wanted to know. I was clipping *House Beautiful* and *Sunset* magazines for clever ideas in home storage. That was an example for the kids.

"You could all play Hearts," suggested Linda, knitting up a sock of baby blue.

"How *boring.*"

"Well, why don't you read some books for a change?"

"We've looked at all those pictures. A dozen times."

"Then why don't you play Monopoly? That's a fun game."

"Monotony, you mean."

"Come on," said Starkey. "At least we can play with money."

For a while we were like a model family. The wood hissed in the fire and the pieces toured the board, the players absorbed in their game.

"There!" said Brenda, "I landed on Ventnor Avenue. I've got all the yellow lots. I want houses on every one."

"Show us the color of your money." Steve was banker.

"One-fifty, three hundred, four-fifty...there. Gimme!" She arranged them with smug precision. Starkey landed twice. He was bankrupt.

"What'll you give me for Park Place?"

"One hundred dollars cash, please."

"That's not quite fair," said Linda. While *she* might know about real estate, I knew that Starkey was not a good loser. As I filed away plans for a wallful of cookie tins I decided to hold my tongue.

"Take it or leave it, little brother."

"What'll you give me, Steve?"

"I'll give you the sweat off my balls."

Starkey kicked the board into the air. The houses flew into the fire and flags of burning currency fluttered up the flue.

"*Fuck* you," Starkey said. Steve struck his mouth—his kid brother kneed him. When I pulled the two apart Stevie's eyes were bright, Starkey's lip was bleeding.

Linda picked up her knitting. "I think we should all go to bed now, children." The cats were unraveling the yarn.

"Why can't I stay up?" wailed Brenda. "I was *winning.*"

"Because I've had enough!"

"Leave her alone," said Steve. "She's off her Geritol."

"Get out. *All* of you! I'm *sick* of being your mother."

Though I had never seen her like this before I knew she meant it. The winter storm had moved inside the house. I ducked into the kitchen for a large Old Fashioned drink. On second thought I'd make one for Linda, an eggnog to soothe her savage breast. But first I'd let her cool out awhile. I didn't need both the tempest and her temper.

She was propped on her pillows with a storybook.

"Why, thank you, Jerry. You can be thoughtful when you want."

"Aren't I usually?"

"You are when you take time to think. It's not that you're really thoughtless."

"What am I then?"

"Well, you do tend to think of your needs first, don't you, hon? I suppose that could be considered selfish."

"What else can I get you?"

"It's not right now. It's all the time, you know. We all have our special needs, but yours seem more special than others, more than I can ever hope to satisfy." We listened to the rain beat on the roof and gurgle down the downspouts.

"What are you trying to tell me, Linda Lee?" About red-haired schoolboys from Eagle Rock, Irish chauffeurs from the Navy? She didn't even know such folk, unless I'd started talking in my dreams.

"Your sexual demands, for one thing. I'm not always up to it right now. It's different when you've got another child inside you."

"What do you mean, *another* child?"

"I didn't mean it that way, silly. You can't take everything personally. I've had three other children, you may recall."

"Tonight was a good recollection."

Linda sat up straighter. "Now don't take it out on *them*, Jerry Carr. You're the one we've been talking about. You might learn to be as patient with us as we've tried to be with you."

"Is that what you're trying to teach me?" I was beginning to get angry—she was right. And the *sex!* Now that it wasn't ready on demand, that standard home commodity had turned into a towering obsession. My crotch hurt at the very thought of it. "I wouldn't be

36

patiently sitting here, if it hadn't been your idea to have the baby."
At this she was briefly silent.

"I think you were right," agreed Linda at length. "You aren't prepared to be a father yet. That would require a grownup."
I gritted my teeth; we were back on home ground. The words had grown as common to my sense as a commuter's everyday bus ride, as a bathroom's week-old towel. The ritual went relentlessly forward.
"Like good old Everett?" I laughed. The laugh was not infectious.
"You're not far wrong, you know."
"Then why don't we call him right now, rain or shine? What's his Florida number?"
In a surprising show of strength Linda Lee leaned down, picked up a telephone directory, and threw the book at me. It knocked a third Old Fashioned from my hands.
"You swallowed your Geritol after all!"
"I'm sick of you, Jerry. I've indulged you far too long, I wish that Everett *was* here. He's twice the man you ever thought to be."
I was tempted to grab the alpaca and run out into the rain. Instead I went back to the living room and slept among the animals, on the couch of our initial affair. In the morning I was pleased to find an irritation of the throat and nasal membranes, sure signs of an oncoming cold. I'd wait for Linda to get up, then go on Sick Call. We would see who could feel the worse.

Two days later while I lay in bed the long-absent Colonel did return, again without his wedded wife Martha. Their son and daughter would join him in the summer, he said. The mustache looked less trim and the hair a little greyer. For once I was able to feel sorry.

11.

They came streaming from the showers in a cloud of steam, muscles sleekly gleaming—all the other members of the team.
"Let's get him."
Hands seized me in the locker aisle, stripped away the yellow jersey with the shameful **69** stenciled on it, the useless shoulder pads,

the mud-stained cross-laced pants—and laid me on my back, legs astride the hard slat bench.

"We said *throw* the ball. Not *hold* it!"

Why had I been out there in the first place—an underweight, second-team sub? I was perfectly happy sitting on the sidelines, watching others tackle and get hurt.

"It would have got there anyway."

They roared with lusty laughter. A dozen potent organs ringed my head. Fingers snapped the Bike supporter at my belly—then jerked the white elastic to my knees. My member quivered bare for all to see. It longed to hide itself in hairy sparseness.

"He's got *balls,* too! Would you believe it?"

Someone squeezed them.

"EAGLE ROCK. GRAB HIS COCK. GET HIM! GET HIM! GET HIM!"

"Let's blow him."

Red-haired Jimmy Corey drew a deepdown breath, knelt, and blew a hot blast of air across its head. Sensation was instantaneous. Liquid shot up the hollow column, traversed space, and spilled into a pool at the navel. It felt like heated mercury rolling there.

"It's a *touchdown!* Hooray for Jerry!" they all shouted, naked torsos flexed in a virile mirth. A whistle blast made them silent.

"YOU FUCKING FAGGOT!" their captain yelled into my burning ear.

I twisted sweating in the binding sheets and threw off the bulk of the alpaca. What a nightmare! The first wet dream since I couldn't remember when...high school days—or nights, probably. I ran my fingers slipperily down my adomen. No doubt about it—a redolent seminal odor stained their tips. Linda gave a snort and awoke.

"What's the matter, hon?" She touched me. "Why, you're all sticky there. Is something wrong?"

"They call it a nocturnal emission. I couldn't help it. It's when you don't get sufficient marital release."

"I'm sorry, Jerry. It's only going to be a few more weeks now. Did you dream about me?"

"Not exactly."

"Who was it? Aren't you going to tell me?"

"We're not responsible for what we dream, you know. Dreams are a work of the subconscious."

"Margo, then."

"Pretty close." And it was a close call, too. What if she'd *been* there? It was frightening. Where did a vision so perverted come from, anyway? I decided to bury it where it belonged, in some secret closet of the mind. That closet already bulged with hidden imagery.

Five-thirty. Blue light began to edge around the shutter blades.

"What day is it, anyway?" I stroked my groin affectionately at the zone of the residual good feeling.

"It's Sunday, Saint Valentine's. Happy Valentine's Day, sweet Jerry." I saw once again the subtle flushing of her heart-shaped face.

"Then *be* my Valentine."

"I will. Just as soon as I have the baby."

Always the baby! A wet dream rightly timed would have prevented that.

I got up, sighing, and went to take a shower. In the shower as I played with myself I replayed the dream on the black velvet screen of my all-night porno movie. It was even better, awake now, than asleep. I added extra footage—closeups of those footballers' wide eyes as I ejaculated. Maybe they had erections, too. The dirty flick became a full-blown feature film complete with shower room orgy, soap and all. The venturesome young James Corey, his rusty-ringed dork and my own had starring roles. I took care to edit out the offensive last words—*fucking faggot.* This motion picture was a work of art.

I watched the tell-tale pearly strands swirl down the drain. I dried off, put on jeans and jacket, and went to the kitchen to brew coffee. In the bedroom Linda and my rival, the baby, were once more asleep. I took the mug of coffee to the terrace and settled into one of the campaign chairs. The shredded canvas still supported my shower-fresh behind.

The sun climbed above the sawtooth ridges, striking deep into the notches of ravines. The edge of the sea grew luminous. Then the rays lit the faceted waves like the scales of monstrous fishes. Some Japanese fishermen held casting lines with patient dignity. In their shore boots, visored caps and short jackets they were by-passed veterans of a forgotten war. I hoped the kelp-cutter would float by to cut a new path through the seaweed, but the day was a holiday for all.

Surfers got out of a car, stashed their clothes, and stomped bare feet on the cold ground. With strong rhythmic strokes they slipped out throught the surf. Surfing built good bodies. They sat the boards like water bugs, waiting for the waves to mount. It was a stand-off between fishermen and surfers. No one liked to tangle in the hooks and lines. In a while the fishermen reeled in the lines and waded down the shore toward some rocks. White supremacy again—*Surfers Rule.* In Japan things would be just the opposite. The surfers caught their waves.

It was going to be that kind of day. I undressed and got back into bed. I tried to sleep, awaiting dreams. But those that came were abstract, without passion, lacking bodies of any kind. When I awoke at ten o'clock the distaff portion of the bed was vacant.

They were all in the living room, pets included. The children gobbled chocolates from a giant heart-shaped box, a gift of our good friend there, the Colonel. I knew what he had in mind. Presently he would take Linda to the study or the terrace to tell her endless boring stories of the war, or to seek a little sympathy because of his deserting family. Linda would listen patiently, as she did to almost any tale.

Thoughtful Brenda had remembered to pick up some valentines at the Country Store. I opened mine and read aloud:

> *Red are the roses,*
> *Violets blue,*
> *I have a Sweetheart,*
> *I wish you did, too.*

"That's very nice, Brenda. How did you mean it?"

"Oh. That's the wrong one, Jerry. That was supposed to go to Everett. Here's yours." I opened the valentine. It was one of the flowered sort, with a dignified inscription:

> *To one who, being silent, says it best.*

"What can I say, kid? Many thanks."

"You can watch TV with us tonight. If you want to, Jerry," Starkey offered, when Linda and her narrator had gone.

"Yeah, Jerry," Brenda seconded, "it's a special. *The Saint Valentine's Day Massacre,* by the Capone gang."

With grim satisfaction I watched the walls of the garage in South Chicago grow bright with vivid reds. The kids had tinkered with the tint controls again. I rooted for the killers and their tommy guns, not one active homosexual among them. After the easy victory, 7–0, the winning team piled into a fleet of cars and drove away. On the floor of the garage the losers kept on bleeding.

What to do now? To sleep, perchance to dream, *that* was the answer. In that blameless state, all rules suspended, I could explore forbidden limbos.

But the night was not well-slept after all. Like every other being over whom I sought control, my subconscious self refused to go where guided. Instead of clandestinely dreaming, it rummaged through the attic of the past.

What had *my* mom been like? She was always called Mother, for one thing. She liked to keep everything straight: her bobbed hair, her steel-rimmed glasses, her ironed blouse, her pleated flannel skirts. In her study—or *office*, it was called—she kept neat stacks of magazines and papers. Even had I felt free to read them, the periodicals were not of the sort that would nourish the imagination of a growing boy.

Once, when I was twelve, this Mother had given me a special book. The book had no pictures in it, but diagrams of an alarming nature, similar in geometry to those of sixth-grade math. *LOVE FOR YOUNGSTERS* was the title of that book. "Read it," she had said. "And don't let me see those hands loose in your pockets again." If only she could know how far those hands had strayed! Rather than a ruler she might have used a *knife*.

Mother had endured my years of high school at Eagle Rock, insisting on good grades, and suffered through the weekends from boarding college. My room had been pre-empted by her literature. I slept on the studio couch with its scent of lineament and talcum powder.

No sooner was I safely in the service than she had gone away to England on some kind of missionary work. There she had died of combined chill and fever. I saw her now, six feet down, the headstone prominent within the village graveyard...in everlasting pleated skirts, flat soles pointed skyward, on her features a permanent frown. If the words *REST IN PEACE* were engraved upon that tablet they would be not a plea but an injunction.

And my father, Wellington Carr? Mother called him Willy. He dressed in high style and smelled of strong cologne. He wore a small mustache and a large pocket watch. The dial had a sprightly second hand that Daddy often glanced at, as though hoping it might go the other way. I remembered him best in an essay, composed in his honor for Father's Day.

* * * * MY DAD * * * *

MY DADDY, WHEN HE COMES HOME, ALWAYS PUTS THE THING HE HAS BRUNG IN OUR CIGGAR BOX. SOMETIMES CANDY. SOMETIMES MONEY. SOME TIMES A STIK OF GUM. OR SOMETIMES A BALOON OR TWO.

HE ALWAYS SHUT THE LIDD OF THE CIGGAR BOX. "GUESS" HE WOULD SAY. THEN WE WOULD HAVE TO RESSELL FOR IT. BUT I WOULD YOUSUALLY WIN.

ONE TIME I FOUND AN EAGLE DOLLAR. ANOTHER TIME A WISSELL. ANOTHER TIME TWO PAKS OF GUM. ANOTHER TIME HE WOULD NOT LET ME OPEN IT. HE GAVE IT TO MOTHER INSTEAD.

"WHAT IS THIS?" MOTHER SAID.

"IT IS FOR YOU." SAID DAD.

SHE LIKED THE PRESENT, WHATEVER IT WAS. I THINK A PEACE OF PAPER. BUT HE DID NOT SHOW ME THE CIGGAR BOX ANY MORE. ALL THOUGH WE RESSLED AFTER THAT.

"THE END"

JEREMY CARR (AGE 7)

That was my last tribute to my father. Early that summer My Dad had set out upon a journey that had no return ticket. Mother had discarded the cigar box, along with many other things. I hoped I could be a better Dad to these offspring. Though come to think of it, I had yet to receive a gift of any kind on Father's Day. That day would be coming soon enough, and in the truest sense of those words.

12.

"I think it's ready, Jerry." Finally. The odors of the standing rib roast had penetrated every corner of our home. I was famished from a day of heavy housework and weary of concessions to the kids.

"You'd better call the hospital, Jerry. And the doctor." The Baby.

No sit-down dinner after all. I drove to Santa Monica with special care.

"We'll send her to Delivery," the nurse said. Strapped to a wheeled table, Linda was pale beneath white sheets. Her abdomen had swollen alarmingly. I kissed her cheek and gripped her wrist—suddenly small and childlike. When she was gone I felt truly alone. I sat under the lamp of the private room with a handful of comic books from Starkey.

"I think it might be quite a while," said the nurse, popping in. "It's going to be a rather large baby." Nine o'clock. I began to feel conventional first-night fidgets. It was all right for Linda—she'd done it three times before. The woman was practically a veteran—no need to worry about her. I started worrying. What did the nurse mean by *large?* Ten pounds? Thirteen? Twenty? I followed the career of Captain Marvel.

A FAREWELL TO ARMS. That's the book I should have brought. *It was like saying goodbye to a statue,* Hemingway had written of the officer's farewell to his love as she lay dead in childbirth, raindrops beating on the windowpanes. A shiver shook my spine. It was raining on the roof of this hospital, too. An unaccustomed tear graced my eyelash.

I got up and went down the corridor. Only my own footfalls echoed in that septic hall, fluorescent-lit. Where was everyone, in bed? I peeked through the steel door of the delivery room. There lay Linda in the tomblike gloom, arms crossed in silence.

"Please don't disturb her, Mr. Carr," said a nurse at the duty station, "she's sleeping now." Sleeping? At a time like this? There wasn't going to *be* any problem.

"It's going to be another hour or two, at least. Why don't you go out and have a drink?" Just what the doctor ordered! The lady in starchy whites had a real head and heart like all the rest of us.

The neon cocktail glass with a red cherry in it cast an emptied reflection on the sidewalk. An establishment selling alcoholic drinks could not call itself a bar in California, said the law. HUNT 'N HOUNDS, said the curly green letters of the cocktail lounge that wished to be an English tavern, a little bit of *Olde Hollywoode* right there by the shores of the Pacific. I sank into a bar chair and ordered Black Label—a double-on-the-rocks.

"You must be thirsty," said the drinker to my left, a male about my age or younger, in a good-looking Harris Tweed jacket.

"Hungry too," I answered. "I've been waiting three hours, for a baby."

"Then let me buy you a drink. Is it your first time?"

"My wife has three more at home, I believe."

"*My.* You seem very young to be a father all the time. She must keep you sort of busy." And he smiled. Those words brought a painful reminder—I had not been laid in more than three weeks.

"Just how young would you say, exactly?"

"*Certainly* not more than twenty-five." Only recently I'd turned a youthful thirty-three! The younger man and I had both worked at Fox, it developed, and in set design too. He named famous pictures and assorted movie stars, their sayings, doings, their intimate preferences.

"I suppose you *know* about Drake Randall?" he continued, confidentially. I supposed I did. I'd heard tales about every name in pictures. I was getting slightly nervous, and more than a little drunk.

"I ought to get back to the hospital now." Scotch double-potion number three had left its ice cubes high and dry.

"*Lis-sen?* Jerry? You can call there from *my* place. It's on your way. I'll even fix you a sandwich. You don't want to starve all *night,* do you?"

Another studio fruit—as I'd suspected all along. What the hell, though? How far was he prepared to go with it?

The top floor apartment had an ocean view, and white walls hung with flashy watercolors — scenes from expensive musicals. Flung about the white string rug were satin pillows, orange and pink and purple—the decorator *Fever Colors.* "Why don't you take your shoes off, Jerry? Here's the phone." A *Princess* phone, naturally. "I'll make us both a little something to drink." He passed through a beaded curtain.

"No, we're not quite ready to deliver, Mr. Carr," the nurse informed me. "She's been laboring very evenly. She has strong abdominal walls." Didn't I know it? "Doctor's waiting. If you like, I'll check again. Hold on." I laid the receiver by my ear, the illuminated handset on my stomach.

"*Well!*" said my new acquaintance, in a calypso blouse and cut-offs. "You certainly look relaxed for a new daddy." He placed the drinks on the rug and a palm on each knee. "I'll bet you're more than *hungry*, aren't you, Jerry?" The receiver crackled at my ear. I let my lids fall shut. A touch on the thigh made my pulse jump.

There it went, the belt buckle—*clink*. And the descending whine of the zipper—z-zz-zzzzzzt, pulled with authority and dispatch. And then *dit, dat, dut*—the snaps of my boxer shorts. My pants were on the floor.

"*My...*" said the genial homo, before his lips closed on the glans, sweeping swiftly to the root. His hot breath stirred pubic hairs and cooled my perspiration. The experience had never been like this— muscles limp as rope, no distraction, all feeling focused on that slippery, greedy shaft. Below the cleft his tongue touched nerves whose sense I'd hardly known. My slackened spinal cord had slipped into the core of the urethra that tingling all its length let loose a gush of generative fluids. *Father of millions!* I gloried to myself, testes hard as gems, penis spurting wildly. I gasped into the Princess phone's mouthpiece.

"I think we're ready, Mr. Carr," rasped a voice in my ear. "Perhaps you'd better come back now."

"This little fellow just won't *quit*," remarked my host, still kneeling. It was *he* who was having the sandwich! As my empty stomach growled and churned he once more performed the operation.

"Here's your boy," said Dr. Wangler, holding up a howling bundle of wrinkled purple flesh. He *was* a big boy, too. The nurse wheeled in Linda, her blonde hair in strands on wet cheeks.

"Hello, Jerry," she whispered. "Was it hard for you, hon?"

"Easier said than done, little mother."

She began to nurse the baby, who took immediate possession of her breasts. Thirty minutes old, and he knew what he wanted. At the age of thirty-three I wasn't sure.

13.

"Oh, *Mommy!*" began Brenda's complaint as she threw her extra weight upon the unresisting couch. "I think boys are just *awful*." It was clear that she wanted to speak to her mother alone. But Linda was busy nursing Casey and I was petting Randy on the hearth.

Furthermore, we were both taking marginal pleasure in a yet un-scratched recording of *Eine Kleine Nachtmusik*. We were a slow-motion picture of domestic ease.

Brenda's open mouth and widened eyes refused to surrender their expressions of acute personal shock and chagrin.

"Do you know what those two boys were doing?" she challenged Linda. As I made no sign of leaving she launched her sordid tale. In the shower Steve had been demonstrating a familiar boys' trick to Starkey, a willing and interested student. Neither had been prepared for the lesson's climax: an unexpected flow of Stevie's first pubescent juices. Though Steve was pleased, his younger brother was scared witless. "You broke a white vein!" he'd yelled, alerting Brenda. She had sent them straight to bed, half in shame and half in sorrow.

"Oh, Mommy," she went on, "why do boys have to be so *dirty*? Can't we do anything about it?" Linda had no instant answer.

"Boys are like that," I began, in quick defense of my gender. "It's different than with girls, you know. Our private parts are always at hand, so to speak. A permanent temptation. Guys are always primed and ready, I suppose. It's our nature."

It sounded like a goddamn *weapon* I described, instead of the timeless instrument of racial preservation. This was surely more and less than I had meant to say. Linda looked tolerant, even sympathetic. But I had won from Brenda only an expression of restrained disgust. Yet *they* had no such problem, with everything tucked comfortably away inside, as though designed for travel instead of holding down the nest.

Linda put away her nursing breast as the baby still groped for it. She was having such a problem at the moment.

"It's the design of our anatomy," I maintained, passing the buck to the Creator. "We're meant to *throw* the ball. Not *catch* it." What kind of idiot metaphor was that? I should have kept my chauvinistic mouth shut. There was a hopeless, gross absurdity in even attempting to tell these ladies about the time spent by the human male in merely having erections—a lifelong torch-bearing marathon, from the diaper to the shroud.

"Well, I'm glad I don't have to play in *your* ballgame, Jerry," scored Brenda through her sniffles.

"You go talk to them, dear," Linda said. "I'll try to explain it all to Brenda." Apparently she had not yet explained it to her sons.

Steven and Starkey pretended to be sleeping in their sacks.

"It's all right, guys," I said to their blanket-wrapped figures. "Every boy does it now and then. It's only natural. Until you have a girl or get married there's nothing else to do." It was a lie and they knew it. Their stiffened forms made no response. I went on with some textbook mechanics I was sure they'd heard about before.

"Just don't feel bad about it, that's all," I concluded as I tried to exorcise their guilt, in concert with misgivings of my own. "And next time lock the door." Now why had I said that? Then I remembered. I was caught red-handed in the bathroom at the age of ten by a furious and unforgiving Mother. "Don't ever let me catch you doing that again!" she had warned before warming my buns with a hairbrush. The warning had not been a cure.

"Thanks," Starkey whispered. "Are you sure he's going to be all right?" I lifted the blanket from Steve's face.

"Sure, kid. Right as rain," I promised. Steve had missed the last cliché by falling fast asleep.

Part Two

14.

A heaviness hung in the air that day that was more than the weight of the atmosphere. The glaze of milky sky glared deep inside the market, down the waxed aisles, behind the walls of canned goods, back where the compressors hummed and the Muzak played seductively.

The three-page shopping list filled me with impatience, the little things that had no directory or address: *chestnuts, ham glaze, shallots, currants.* The big things, too: the turkey freezing fast to my hand, the twelve-pound ham, the stuffing. And I had to push and carry all this stuff just for an Easter weekend—the price of playing the Big Bunny. I saved the best things for last. Here I had freedom of choice—a rainbow of jelly beans, chocolate rabbits, gaudy baskets, cellophane grass. And the pure-food-color egg dyes. On the way out I bought something for myself—French vermouth and a quart of English gin to complement the stuffed Spanish olives.

At the house no one leaped from the doorway to help unload the groceries. Those kids were taking their vacations seriously! I hauled sack after sack until Linda appeared to say she and the baby had been napping. I expressed my true feelings.

"Well, Everett took the children to some Disney films. They won't be back until later." While I'm tending store, Lieutenant Colonel Vandenberg, retired, succeeds in outflanking me again!

"What's he to them? Their fairy godfather?"

"Right now he's a man without a family. Did you want to see *Snow White,* dear? You still can, you know."

"Right now I'm a man without a wife." I started scuttling around the brick floor tugging at Linda's skirts. "Please, Miss Snow Whitey, don't you remember me? I'm Dopey, number seven. *Please,* pretty Princess, may I have a piece of ass?"

Linda heaved an exasperated sign, as though I were indeed that diminutive creature, and began to stack cans and boxes on the shelves.

"Jerry, you know what the doctor said. The vaginal stitches can't come out yet." I resumed my full stature.

"Well, what's he building in there anyway, the Lincoln Tunnel?"

"It's no use explaining it all over again. It's an episiotomy, not a construction job. I'll be well soon, I promise."

"And in the meantime?"

"Look, Jerry, I know how you feel. There's not much I can do about it now."

"You could help. You used to."

"Honey, I'm just too tired after the baby and the kids and you are all in bed. It's no fun anyhow, it's so one-sided. Why can't you wait a little longer? Think how long I waited before you came along."

"Men aren't very good at keeping savings accounts. We like to keep on spending, recklessly. You ought to know that by now."

"Then go see Margo, or anyone else you want to do it with. I don't care. Really."

"I did. They thought it was funny, just what I deserved. They all have lovers of their own. They're single, with no children."

"Jerry, it's Good Friday," Linda went on wearily, playing her last hole card. "Why can't you take it easy and relax?"

"Why the hell not? I've had a hard day, too. I think I'll take a shower, and jack off. That's what the boys do." And leave the door *wide open* while I'm doing it.

"Anything you want to do, Jerry. Just stop nagging me for a minute."

I broke out the ice, made a pitcher of bone-dry martinis, and took a frosted glass for my solitary vigil in the bathroom. While the shower spray pounded on my scalp I balked at standing there to masturbate like some mindless degenerate now that Linda, the institution nurse, had given her approval. *Yes indeed, we're very progressive here. We used to tie the inmates' hands, you know.* Just to prove it I let the shower beat on *its* impatient swollen head, then turned the shower off. I went back to the kitchen in a bath towel and poured Linda a frozen martini. I kissed her ears and hugged her very close.

"Please, Jerry. Not right *now*. I've got to put the ham in."

"Why not something different in the way of a main course to-

night?" I whipped off the towel. The eager dinner candidate shriveled under her gaze like a wiener on a grill of picnic charcoal.

"Why can't you think of something different for a change? Besides
your everyday Shoppers' Special. And yourself."

"Who just dragged the groceries up from Safeway? It wasn't good
old Ev. He's sitting in an air-conditioned movie with our kitchen
help."

"Jerry, you're really hopeless."

"That's right. There *isn't* much to hope for, is there?" I refilled my
thirsty glass.

"And you're drinking. You know, psychologists say that men who
have to drink all the time are just like bottle babies. They've never
been properly weaned."

"I'm flexible, Linda. Let me suck your tit."

"Just *go* somewhere. Do *something*. Watch television. Read a
book. Don't *bother* me."

Obediently I slunk off to the study and turned on the set. Randy
wagged over to the chair, rolled his eyes and put his paw up. I shook
it.

"You *are* man's best friend," I told him. A quiz show came on. A
battery of colored lights flashed and a woman won a washer, a power
mower and a set of carving knives. She jumped up and down ecstati-
cally in a shower of dollar bills. Maybe *that* would please her, I
thought spitefully. The commercials ran—two for the same prize
products—and then the evening news. Some people in Washington
had found some money, too. But in the wrong pockets as usual—
never in their own. The blacks were rioting in some auto city ghetto.
The cameras showed them getting household appliances for nothing. No waiting around for made-up quiz shows or chintzy government handouts. Those people knew where it was at—drink dance
screw scream and *RIOT*. What else was there to do in life?

And then the *good* news. A man near San Berdoo had shot his wife
and three kids in the brand-new backyard swimming pool—with his
favorite hunting rifle. Just like shooting ducks! And he had the
perfect alibi—God had *told* him to do it. Out of season, too.

I switched off the set to see if we were getting that kind of
reception in our neighborhood. But no exotic voices, demonic or
divine, suggested I do anything at all. I poured another drink. A big
car stopped outside, the Colonel's Coupe de Ville, and all three kids
rushed in.

"Guess what, Mom," said Starkey. "We saw two monster movies. We didn't have to see *Snow White*."

"They were *scary*," cried Brenda deliciously. "One guy got cut in two. His castle fell on him."

"Yeah! He was torturing the maids in the basement."

"He was doing more than *that* to them, dummy."

"How would you know?" said Steve.

"...and another was about an awful *hand* that kept coming after people."

"Don't even talk about that one! When's dinner ready, Mom?"

"Whenever the ham gets done. Jerry brought another kind this time. It wasn't precooked."

So *that* was my fault, too. I'd brought the wrong kind of ham! Why didn't she let Evey do the shopping? Two monster movies would have suited me just fine. It wouldn't hurt to see a little torture. I could have taught that *hand* a trick or two!

"We're going to watch 'The Untouchables,' Mom."

"Don't forget to change the baby, Brenda."

"Who can forget about that?"

Already seven-thirty by the coupon wall-clock—time for my next chilled drink. While we're waiting, I told Linda, I could go ahead and precook the eggs. Maybe that would get me off her back.

"For Easter? Don't bother. Everett's taking care of that."

"What do you mean? He's taking care of *that?*"

"He promised to boil the eggs and color them. That's probably what he's doing right now." And he probably was—spraying squads of virgin eggs Khaki and Olive Drab on the workbench by his Caddie in their big garage.

"What about *me?* What about these special *dyes* here? And six dozen Double-A ranch eggs! What am I supposed to do, make a seventy-two egg omelet? I'm an artist, too. Remember?"

"Who can ever forget! You're being silly, Jerry. You can dye those too. Any way you like. I don't care."

"Well, who the hell's in charge here? Is he still pulling rank? We're both out of the service now, you know. We're civilians!"

"Now you are being childish. Can't you afford to be generous?"

"Generous! Do you think I want to *keep* six dozen fucking eggs? I was looking forward to Easter the way a kid waits for Christmas."

"That's it exactly, Jerry. You *are* a kid sometimes. You only think of holidays. Never the times between, the way the rest of us have to. You've had a good Christmas. What does he have?"

"You ought to know. *He's* got a great house, a Coupe de Ville, and a colonel's retirement pay. Plus compensation and benefits. That's a whole lot more than *I* have."

"He's a lot older than you are, dear," said Linda in her infinite wisdom. "You've got a long way to go."

I sensed a weakening in her gin-fueled defenses.

"I suppose he's bought an Easter rabbit, too," I said, pushing it with calculated malice.

"As a matter of fact, yes, a little brown one. For Casey."

"Well, Jesus Christ! My four-week-old kid wouldn't know an Easter rabbit from a Playboy bunny. Besides, we already have our live-in hutch queen. You!"

"That's really unkind, Jerry. That's hitting below the belt. I had only three before you came. I don't think we ought to talk about our sexual mores now." How like her—to come up with a dictionary word like *mo-res*. It made me feel like some raunchy shit-kicking stud—as she intended.

"Why not, Linda Lee? Hasn't Evey fucked you in the game room yet?" Tit-for-tat. You cunt.

"Jerry!"

"Isn't that where you like to do it best? Because you don't like to do it in the bedroom anymore."

"I've already *told* you a hundred dozen times."

"Prove it."

"God-*damn* you. You half-assed overgrown *child!*"

"You couldn't say that six months ago." I finished another martini, hers or mine—it didn't matter. Why couldn't she just cook the dinner? And shut up!

"I'm saying it now and it's true! You're just like one of the children, and a lot more trouble to bring up. Maybe it's not even possible. There's a limit, you know."

I was seized by a terrible need to slap her. I slapped my wife Linda in the face, exactly as her former husband Harry had. A silence like a vacuum gripped the house. The kids had turned down the crime show to listen. We were getting top ratings for once. Even Casey was quiet in his crib.

I heard the sly guilty sizzling of the twelve-pound underdone ham. *That's* where the blame belonged—right there in the hot smoking oven with that tough pig wrapped in foil. Were it not already dead I could have *killed* it. Sorry beyond ready words, I drained the pitcher into a glass and filled the glass with olives for a meal. The pitcher was no longer frosty. The weather had turned into rain.

"Get out," said Linda very tightly. "Get out now. We don't *need* you anymore."

I picked up a pressed-pulp paper carton of a dozen large Grade-A's, pulled the flap, and raised the carton overhead. I dropped the eggs on Linda Lee's blonde hair. The yellow yolks and clear albumen fell in protoplasmic streamers down the front of her apron and dress. Linda left the room. I took the other cartons one-by-one and dumped another sixty eggs on the waxed brick floor. They made a generous pool of omelet mixed with shells.

"BOMBS AWAY!" I yelled when I was done. I went to the bedroom—formerly ours—and picked up the flight bag—exclusively mine—and went to the bathroom to throw in vitamins and pills and razor and blades. And prophylactics—should the need arise, and grabbed my Levi jacket and a sweater. Then I tugged on my field boots to walk head-bowed through the pelting rain after slamming the front door profoundly, so it could never be opened again. The house shook. I was grateful for that. I heard the baby bawl and the sound of the TV come on again.

The irony of the collective "we" had finally done it. I wasn't wanted by *anyone*. My gratuitous tears mixed with raindrops before I reached the door of the car. I slammed that door, too, rattling the ashtrays. I had at hand the perfect car for a getaway—a two-door two-tone Reconditioned Warranteed Plymouth Fury hardtop, with 250 eager thirsty horses stabled beneath the spacious and extravagant hood, and two-toned twin exhausts. I gunned the engine three times for takeoff, hit the LOW push-button gearshift that engaged the Turbo-Flite drive, and ground on up the driveway—the spinning treads of the whitewalls spitting gravel at the rain-streaked glass of Linda's room. Her egg-smeared face still stinging from its recent slap was probably pressed against it, my oversize tailfin-mounted fast-retreating red-eye taillights distorted in her tear-and-regret-filled eyes. I choked back tears of my own, switched on the wipers, and swerved without pause into the far northbound lane of the Pacific Coast Highway, Route 1. I hoped she had appreciated that gesture, too.

If she hadn't others had. In the two-tone colors—black and white

—of a nocturnal woods-pussy, a cruise car had pulled up on my tail. I slowed the Fury to legal highway speed. An arrest or a night in jail would ruin everything. *She* would win the argument, hands and checkbook down. And I would be driven home in silence, like any everyday rule-breaking curfew-flaunting messed-up juvenile delin-quent, and put on long probation without privileges, including those already lost. The sheriff's car followed in the rain to the L.A. County line and U-turned up a side road to wait for abused and drunken drivers from other broken California homes.

It was Good Friday, I recalled, depressed by further irony. And then more optimistically—the *start* of a holiday weekend!

15.

Where the hell was I headed, anyway? The smart thing, the sensible, reasoned and *mature* thing to do, would be to stop long enough to check the map. That would show not only foresight, it would prove I wasn't drunk. I pulled off Route One at the very next town, Oxnard, and parked on a popular sidestreet among beat up ranch-based pickups. The first door at hand opened to a set from a movie west-ern, a corral of private booths against irrelevant painted vistas of an ultraviolet Day-Glo sea.

At the center was a horseshoe bar. Stalwart long-jawed heavy-handed rustics and their lovelies were set for a spell of drinking on concrete-anchored stools. Those heavies, fixed for the evening with hats shoved back from untanned brows, would have to pass out or be knocked off their perches, like the movies, before an outsider like me would find a decent seat. It was no place to plot a future, or set a steady course.

I went down to the corner—underage Chicanos were taunting their elders into hauling six-packs from the liquor store—and sat at a cafe table under the realistic glare of Day-Brite tubes. I ordered black coffee and spread the MAP OF WESTERN STATES furnished by the auto club.

There it all was, the great western highroad bulldozed from the wilderness. A double-edged red ribbon stretched through thirteen hundred miles and sixteen degrees of latitude, from the fogbound wave-slapped isles of Puget Sound to the riotous Mexican border, where whores were raped by mindless donkeys and cleancut crew-cut marines ate pussy on public stage. But what had that to do with anything? My brain still drifted on its tide of home-poured gin.

The map told me something else. If the long road were a river, a concrete Mississippi, one could see how the commerce flowed. From tributaries of the Great Northwest, trucks and trailers full of boards and hops and apples rumbled downstream to the port of San Francisco and its hookers and hustlers by the Bay, and on to the desert isolation of the sun-crazed counties of Southern California. There, life-giving arteries of northern waters fed a billion hissing rain-birds, their twitterings ignored by scores of narcissistic movie stars, pill-popping perverts, doom-crying Bible freaks in the freeway-strangled Gordian-knotted snakepit of the greater L.A. area.

Why was I taking it out on these unknown and unoffending people in places far from me? Everyone had to live somewhere, doing something. It was only Linda I was mad at, wasn't it? And Everett. I saw beneath the criss-crossed web of roads and streams and boundaries, as a hunter from a netted blind, that the invisible elusive target of my anger was myself.

One black dot of town or city on that map looked exactly like another. I toyed with the names. *Santa Cruz*. Did Santa cruise there? *Eureka! Redwood City*, made of thousand-year-old trees. My head pounded—Linda's wounding phrases ricocheted inside my skull. *If you can't fight 'em join 'em* was a slogan to act on next. I returned to the western bar to buy a drink. A vacancy had come up among the sturdy barstools. The occupant had thrown up and folded in the STUDS room in a nest of newspapers and butts. I sat down among steadfast drinkers and sipped a highball in leisurely sips. Maybe the others had problems. It wasn't an easy life.

On the Oxnard street the rain had stopped. My head felt clearer, too. Like a ray from a distant sun an idea had come into it. I would drive to Big Sur along the coastal route to surprise my old friend Jennifer at her cottage in the woods. A gentle generous understanding girl, *an artist*. And as we warmed ourselves with loving thoughts and mugs of mulled wine, free of interfering children, we would gradually divest ourselves of increasingly superfluous clothing, trading long-lasting soul and body kisses on a bearskin by the slow-burning hearth. That would please Jennifer, too. I piloted the Fury along the rain wet concrete roadbed and at Ventura joined the heavy upstream traffic of U.S. Route 101.

I squirmed in the seat without a seat belt. The cruel words stung like bee-stings, buckshot, bullets, as I recalled them one by one. *Immature. Half-assed. A child.* These from an aging girly who played with living dolls and read herself to sleep with fairy tales. As for a bottle-sucking booze-guzzling weakness, she couldn't hold her liquor at all.

She would have gone on firing rounds of verbal ammo—I was falling in love with the metaphor—like some berserk assassin or maddened psycho housewife if I hadn't stopped her with a SLAP. That was better than a GUN, wasn't it? Easy there, Jerr. I felt the Fury decelerate. The *right* and *only* thing to do was to *take off* as I had, before domestic violence reared its bloody head. I would save my trusty backup weapon, the hand slap, for occasions yet to come. That notion soothed me. I heard the radio again, a chortling baby. It had been there all the time. At the thought of our co-produced infant my red eyes bled fresh streams of tears.

16.

The parkway-divided road at Santa Barbara had carless riders waiting either side of it at all the major lights: youths in big hats and sandals and castoff army gear—some with girls, one couple with a baby, a pair of honchos who looked as though they'd want the car keys around the next bend of the road. For company I picked the last of the line-up, a forlorn-looking kid—his body like a board with clothes hung on it—in sneakers, jeans and a thin red jacket labeled BEARS. His curtain of brown hair had a pink stub of nose sticking through it.

"Hi," I said through the rolled-down window, "where you headed?"

"Same way you are, sir." *Sir?* Sir what? Nobody had called me that since the last good restaurant dinner. The fight must have aged me ten years, at the least.

"Okay. Get in." Courtesy pays, this kid should realize. He seemed a few years ahead of Stevie's age. The boy slumped in his seat.

"What is it?"

"What's what?"

"The short here. What's in it?"

"A two-fifty engine. Twin carbs. Dual pipes. And your obliging chauffeur."

"No headers? A Mexican Cadillac, for sure. Mind if I change the station?" He pulled a skinny hand from a pocket, spun the dial to a top-forty station and turned the volume up, thumping one knee against the glove compartment.

"How come you're out tonight?" I asked, for conversation.

"The old man started whaling on my mom. It happens every time he gets paid. He drinks. He's only my stepdad, really." We had more in common than I'd thought. "I just take off," the boy continued, humming, "and come back when it's over. I got a friend in Pismo Beach. I guess I'll head for Pismo." He folded his arms and crossed his legs forward, letting his head fall down against the armrest. I leaned across to press the safety latch.

"Ten bucks before you touch me," the boy said, moving nothing but his upturned lips.

"I don't want you flying out the door, kid."

"That's awright. I ain't got wings. How about you, mister?"

"I don't go that way myself."

At least I never had. I *did* remember riding in the same shotgun seat, another snotty adolescent waiting for predictable advances. But *ten dollars?* Just to entertain that half-grown little number there between his legs, that hardly made a dent in his blue jeans? And while speeding down a state-patroled six-lane public highway at seventy miles an hour, in a reconditioned semi-customized Plymouth Fury hardtop—*not* a Mexican Cadillac—with not more than 36,000 actual miles on it? The kid must be *nuts.* Not that I was even interested.

"Lemme out at Buellton then. Maybe I can score there."

The teenage free-enterpriser fell into a light doze, hands folded over his portable place of business. The night held other interests. The car burrowed between deep-cut hills, through tunnels—millions of tax-paid dollars lay buried there—and through a blind and boring wilderness. I knew what lay the sunset side of it: the blacked-out fenced-in barracks of the Correctional Facility at Lompoc—that's where this smart-ass kid belonged—and the guarded government estates of Vandenberg Air Force Base and Missile Testing Center, where billions in lethal rockets minded the earth in cunning understanding with its namesake, no doubt—our loving friend and neighbor Colonel Everett. The ironies of Easter week were beginning to multiply like rabbits.

In Buellton I stopped at the Pea Soup Palace, because it made the night air smell so good, and had a bowl of pea soup and a beer to sober up. The boy had a Coke and a burger and went across the freeway to an on-ramp that led the other way. When I left he was standing in a fresh fall of rain, the hair-curtain pasted to his forehead.

I was going to have to think about the Colonel, after all. Perhaps he wasn't such a bad guy, really. What had he ever done to me? Why couldn't I think of him as Everett, a friend? The poor man, retired, sat alone in his new-furnished study or tooled aimlessly around in his Cad. And all he had ever tried to do, to the very best of my knowledge, was to help my overburdened lady with her household chores. And paint some store-bought eggs for other people's kids. It was very touching, really. It turned my head around. I ought to turn the *car* around, I thought in frenzied charity, and go right back home and apologize on bended *knee*.

That would be the best Easter gift of all. It would be *too* good, was the bitter truth of it. I saw myself in the dim curve of backward sloping glass, a five-foot eight-inch bunny, a pacified holiday pet, wrinkling its nose at a carrot, dropping raisins in its chicken-wire pen.

Another and contrary inspiration kept the Plymouth to its course, a reckoning spirit of adventure. *School's out*—you hopeless adolescent drunk! I would do as I pleased. While I did the driving let *them* do the worrying. They would think me *dead* for all I cared, crushed beneath my caved-in Fury in a rain-filled ditch. Or better yet in*ciner-ated*—in a blazing head-on spectacular as I screamed their perishing names.

That was food for thought on Easter morning as they stuffed themselves with jelly beans and Everett's colored eggs. I was spending moods like there was no tomorrow.

17.

I cut off the highway at the halfway point, the town of San Luis Obispo, where the road forks north through Morro Bay to become the narrow twisting blacktop of the coastal route. The rain-varnished streets were bleakly bare under lamps that swayed on cables in the wind. Through distant intersections, headlights darted furtively. I pulled into the hard blue fluorescence of a Standard station and filled the tank, the attendant and myself auditing the chimes of the gas pump.

The only still-lit cafe was in the bus depot, also nearly vacant at that hour, except for a yawning waitress and two teenagers, a boy and a girl, coiled like domestic animals on curved plastic seats. While the waitress rinsed dishes, I had two cups of coffee and a doughnut and went to the men's restroom. It was empty—an enormous private john. I made a leisured tour of the vandal-proof partitions. They bore the usual log of fabulous adventure experienced by highway travelers: their philosophies and poems, hometowns and names and numbers, along with traditional invitations to the perverse.

I AM 14" LONG AND 4" ROUND. MAKE DATE! read one, and beneath it in small print: *I'm interested. How big is your cock?* Another told about the conquest of a gifted and willing partner three times within the hour, each in a different way. FUCK YOU! was the response of one scornful reader. A third writer had observed: QUEERS SUCK.

A hole six inches in diameter had been cut through one partition, a professional-looking job. An amateur artist had drawn hairs around it. They reminded me of Margo's. A pair of balloon-size testicles was attached to a monstrous penis that ran around two sides of this selfsame stall, shooting semen bullets at the door. A target vagina graced the door in outline only. Behind the flush-valve toilet lay a drained half-pint of whiskey in a brown wrinkled sack, the only paper in the house save for a wad of religious tracts stuffed into the holder by the glory hole. *PREPARE FOR THE END IS COMING!* warned a slim pastel pamphlet. I tidied up and left.

I had fooled around long enough. It was time to get moving again. The waitress was bumping plates together in the steaming sink.

"Anything I can get you?" she asked pleasantly.

"A ham sandwich. Two Mister Goodbars. And some Life Savers, please."

"What kind?"

"Assorted Fruit." What was I thinking? "No, Spearmint."

"Going somewhere?"

I sought the meaning behind the words.

"To hell and back," I said dramatically, not smiling.

"Drive carefully," she smiled. I remembered to check her boobs, actually quite ordinary breasts partly hidden in the wet apron front. The waitress went back to her hand-warming sinkful of dishes.

The two young sleepers had shifted postures in their seats, the tousled heads turned away from my departure. I got into the car and pumped the gas pedal, prepared for instant takeoff on my mission to the north.

Contact! I commanded as I turned the key and the engine fired, the twin pipes rumbling on the barren asphalt street. I ran through the check list: *radio, heater, D for DRIVE.* And oh yes, *the brakes.* My boot pressed heavy on the floor as I shot past the towering bulk of Morro Rock. The Fury bored through a shaft of darkness along an isolated wave-washed coast to start the long switchback climb toward Big Sur, where sheer plunging ramparts put an end to Western expansion. *Thus far and no further,* a still greater Power had decreed.

The radio played early rock, a San Francisco station. Getting into that I dimmed the dials and put my talent into driving, taking intricate double turns through black crouching hills, a solitary racer in the night. *Check that, Colonel Vandenberg!* was my challenge on each screeching curve. *Let's see you slide through this one in your corroding Coupe de Ville.*

The storm clouds were shredding themselves on stiff mountain breezes; darts of blue moonlight slanted through. The white patch in the field of boundless dark was San Simeon, no doubt, gleaming like a pile of clean-picked bones. I fled by on the lower road as if it were the castle of Dracula, not Hearst, that I was passing. The car gained altitude with each succeeding canyon draw. No other pair of headlights flicked its friendly high-low beam. What was it like, flying the Atlantic the first time? I ate the ham sandwich. Over the Pacific a ball of green fire moved in parallel direction. A flying saucer, in all probability, prying into California *mo-res.* Why couldn't it pick *me* up instead of hanging out there flirtatiously? I'd go along just for the ride. The fiery disc described a sudden arc and dove into the sea. So much for that—one more rejection. Would that night never end? I thought of gentle Jennifer cradled in her woodland bower. The thought slowed the car to rational speed.

Before daybreak I found the mailbox with her name entwined in painted hearts and flowers. The wheels wobbled down the narrow ruts on weary tires, and stopped beside her jeep. The shingled bungalow was dark, as I might have expected; the door securely barred. I climbed into the back of the Fury and doubled myself on the seat.

18.

"What on earth is out there?" The girl's voice seemed familiar in the not-so-early bright.

"A big chunk of Disneyland iron," said a male's. "Some guy's passed out on the seat."

"Why did he have to do it here?" said hers again, much closer. "Why, I believe that's Jeremy Carr, what I can see of him. A person I used to know in Malibu."

"How can you tell, sweetheart, just looking at his ass? You must have known him pretty well."

"I recognize the ring."

"Are you going to claim the body?"

I propped my aching bones erect. There was Jennifer, all right, as beautiful as always without make-up, in long strands of nun-like hair. The other voice belonged to a burly young man in a beard and a thick plaid jacket with rope loops. I disliked him intensely at once.

"Hello, Jerry. Were you trying to surprise me?"

"I thought I might, Jenny. I just drove north for the weekend."

"You had a quarrel with your wife, didn't you? And at Easter—what a pity! Come in and warm yourself, we're having breakfast. Oh, this is Greg, Jerry. He's my good friend now."

"*Arrivederci,* Jerry," said Greg, exactly as I knew he would. "How's the boy?"

Was it me or the baby he was asking about? His greeting had just crushed my hand.

"Little Casey is fine. He'll be five weeks old next week." It was true! "You ought to see him. He has baby blue eyes."

"I'm glad for you, Jerry. We may have one of our own. Isn't that so, Greg?"

"Sure. A little nature freak, like us."

We strolled downhill to the house that I had always thought of as a country cottage, nestled among rocks and trees in a way that could only be called picturesque. It had a genuine mud-scraper on the door stoop and a rancher's triangle for calling meals. Greg struck the triangle for the three of us. He did it very well. He would be good at all the small things: building fires, sharpening knives, tooling leather belts.

Like a cottage, too, the house was dim inside. It smelled of damp wool and wood smoke. Did fire or water reign here? Jennifer got back among the pots and pans hanging from the rafters and stirred a pot of porridge on the stove. With the porridge she served wine in turquoise goblets and Greg brought out a wheat-paper joint. I knew he would do that, too. Jennifer sat by the hearth against a window, gazing down a channel lined by leaves of live oaks. At its end, like quicksilver, the sea surged metallically. Jennifer still had a lovely neckline, I observed. She smoothed her straight hair back. The light made an aura of her hair.

In the house Greg shed his outdoor aggression. Our smoke, mingling with that of last night's fire, was exactly the right thing at the time. The chilled wine warmed my blood. It didn't seem to matter what we talked about that Saturday. As we chatted, a girl and a boy of three or four ran naked through the room and out into the woods. "It's *my* turn, it's *my* turn," yelled the boy as the little girl giggled and screamed. I watched them frolic in the underbrush.

"They're Greg's children," said Jenny. "Sarah drops them sometimes. She's busy enough with her others."

Just as I was trying to discover how to be a father, Jennifer was learning the art of motherhood. She was obviously very good at it— they had a nice thing going there. Why had she and I never got together? An idle question really, I thought heavy-lidded, in close communication with the view.

"Jerry, old love," she seemed to be saying, "Greg and I are going now. You stay here and do what you want. We'll be back this afternoon."

I climbed up to the loft and fell into downy comforters. "Dave and

Tina!" I heard Greg shout from far away, "Time to wear your clothes," then I was wrapped entirely in a black quilt of sleep.

Like the lid of a great silent box, or a coffin, the sheathing of the roof is what I saw on waking up. I studied the rough-sawn fibers. I didn't want to start thinking right away, or feeling anything, either. After a while I went down the ladder and filled a blue-stemmed glass with Mountain Chablis, squinting through the potion at the altered view. The oak leaves quivered in spangles of lemon and lime in a breeze stirring uphill from the sea. That inconstant surface had changed to navy blue.

A bath was what I truly wanted—to steep half-suspended in a deep vat of amniotic fluid. The bathroom of Jennifer's house, and Greg's too, I had to bear in mind, was a sea chest of personal treasures too intimate to bathe in now—wet towels and underthings, tub toys and muddy boots. I knew the very place. I left a note of thanks.

19.

The Hot Springs Baths, huts of wood and concrete sheltered by the weeds, were reached by a path behind a building that always looked closed for repairs. They hung on the lip of a coved abyss, their fronts open wide to the Pacific, like the scenic spas of Japan. The baths had sides for two sexes, divisions that were often ignored. Hot mineral waters flowed from underneath the mountains that shrugged their tops toward the east, indifferent to Western fashions in mixed bathing. On that afternoon I had the **MALES** side to myself like the transients' plumbing at the bus station. I leaned on the railing, a two-by-four, and looked into the froth-edged pool below.

Seals, sea lions and otters had their lives there, in homes of floating kelp. The sleek dark heads and enormous eyes rose and fell with the tides, uttering exultant barks and cries like hounds at feeding time. Why couldn't our lives be more like that, I pondered idiotically, as I fantasized the family slopping back and forth in troughs of waves. And who would furnish *our* food in our Safeway style of living? *That* was the question, thought the seaside philosopher as he hung his clothes on rusty nails.

I settled by slow degrees into the stinging steamy waters of a hollow concrete square, deep enough to float the body nicely. Buoyant hands, knees, and toes stuck out like little islands. My nerves began to slacken into limp elastic cords.

"—then you shouldn't have let her say that, Rex. It turned the whole thing around. It was imperceptive, ob-*tuse* of you to let her get away with it."

Two white males also in their thirties undressed and got into streaked enamel tubs behind me. One had a mustache and a helmet of curly hairs; the other had hair around the middle but was going bald on top. Neither looked undernourished nor conspicuously fit.

"If that goes for my wife, what about yours?"

"She has her own way of seeing things. And saying things, too." It was the balding one who spoke. "Actually, it doesn't matter. They're all surface substitutes and signals for what she really thinks and feels."

"How do you find out what those things are?"

"I take her to bed and screw her, that's all. We have a language of the flesh."

"I suppose Marge and I are dummies then."

"I think you sometimes fail to articulate in that particular area, Rex. It shows in little ways, her moods and irritations. The way she sits, the way she stands. I've even seen her *scratch* herself."

"And what do you suggest, boudoir leader?"

"*More* communication, not less, of course. But on a deeper, more meaningful level, if you understand what I mean."

"Are you trying to reform my goddamn sex life? Or do you want to eat her out yourself."

"Take it easy, Rex. We came here to relax, remember? You can think about it later on, tonight. We'll all have a terrific dinner, then find a first class motel, near Carmel. We'll talk about it in the morning. In the meantime, enjoy."

"Yeah? Okay then. I wonder what they're saying about us."

"Never mind. It doesn't matter. They still *love* us, don't they? Isn't that enough?"

"I wish they had a handball court here. I could do some working out right now."

Their subject changed to sports and baseball scores, concerns of no personal interest to me. *A language of the flesh*, though, that was good. It seemed a language that Linda and I had once understood. I preferred its speech to all the other useless verbalizing. An instance was last night's slap—a *love* tap, really.

In about half an hour the two splashed from their tubs, slapped themselves, dressed again and left. I heard them joined outside by

A younger man came in, methodically folded his clothing, and leapt to a bench by the rail, almost appearing to go over it. He put his body through a set of startling exercises—yoga I supposed—standing now with one leg crooked to knee—*the Crane?*— and now with chest expanded so the navel touched the spine, and then did astonishing feats of stretching and bending that the muscles and the bones had to yield to—such as I had never seen before and scarcely believed.

The sun, in hurrying descent through cloud banks, glazed his body in a ruddy light as though the tissues shone from within. The movements became perfect ballet. Finally the youth bent over backwards, fingers clasping ankles, genitals directed toward the zenith, remaining in that posture longer than I cared to count.

When the sun-worshipping, sun-worshipped practitioner of yoga had vanished, I was once more alone in my bath. The water's chemistry had turned my silver ring a glistening gun-metal blue, the color of the humping swells and shallow swales that rolled to the rim of the horizon. On that far meridian moved the gray and jagged outline of a fleet in line of war, ships of the United States Navy steaming north to secret rendezvous, sea-links in a globe-encircling chain of armor steel.

Their commanders gazed from lofty platforms as I from mine, but on decks of working sailors, not on pools of playful seals. While they took themselves about the solemn business of the world I lolled in my tank of concrete, a pink and wrinkled baby-like adult. Even as I entertained this idle notion a kind of submarine tub toy surfaced from the depths and took its place among the other floating islands. Its familiar top bobbed brazenly, an anchored dinghy begging to be used. But I had come there to be cleansed, not to pollute the waters.

I walked to the rail for the cold air to dry me, dressed, and went back to the car.

20.

Even in its weekend haste to be in other places, the sun had done a creditable job of sinking in the west. I kept track of its showy behavior along the zigzag stretch of road, until the last sunset kiss of crimson sky to violet ocean was occluded by the headland at Nepenthe. I locked the car and climbed log steps to the hall of that lofty haven, saw the view, and bought an Old Fashioned. The bitters-blended, maraschino-lemon-scented whiskey met the blood of my purified veins.

I had one to watch the dusk turn black, and another to enhance the field of tapers on red tablecloths—already replicated in the strips of windowglass—and a third to toast the lighting of the logs on the grate of the open fire. By then I was nearly as drunk on my foodless stomach as I had been the night before, but in a completely different way. I was ready to say anything to any stranger passing by.

"Is this seat taken?" Here was a girl of superlative attraction in a simple, elegant wool sheath that to me spelled *San Francisco,* even out there in the sticks. I pretended to look under the bar stool, the typical Hollywood fool.

"I don't think so. Please sit down. What would you like?"

"A Margarita, please," she told the bartender, "with very little salt." Seated, she arranged the inside of her purse. "That was kind of you. My name's Sharon."

"I'm Jerry. I'm vacationing. I don't know anyone here, really, at least not anymore. But I love the place, the ocean wilderness."

"I'm here for the same reason. A city confines you to all the same people, the same places after a while. Here you're between two horizons, the mountains and the sea."

I couldn't have put it better. I began to smell a rapport. I could not believe that I actually sat in mutually agreeable conversation with this exquisite-looking girl who gazed at me from the rim of her saltless Margarita. It was simply too good to be true.

"So," I asked, "you've made no particular plans?"

"No. I find planning too far in advance can be limiting."

"I suppose I'm without limits tonight," I said with some decision. "I can do whatever I please." I put down my drink.

"I can, too. Almost, but not quite," said Sharon, turning. "Oh, here's Rob. I'd like you to meet Jerry, dear. Rob's my husband."

"Hi, Rob. I'm a husband on vacation. I just ran away from home."

"Home is where the heart is."

"Or used to be. Where's yours? Your home?"

"Los Gatos. We're staying in Carmel. It's a back-to-nature trip."

Robby could be called attractive, too, in a darkly handsome continental suit and dark styled hair, a boyish well-bred executive. In advertising, I guessed. No, estate management, he corrected. They would be staying at one of the properties that week.

So it wasn't precisely a nature trip after all, even though the great stone house as they described it sat within a wooded park. He probably shed his flared Italian jacket and opened French doors, I thought meanly, returning Sharon's smile. She would look at ease anywhere, indoors or out. Or without that tailored dress at all, in her choker of simple gold links. The Old Fashioneds were doing a job on me.

"Look," said Rob. "We're about to order dinner. Would you join us? We'd be pleased."

Why not make the most of it? They had reserved a table at the apex of the angled room where reflected candle flames made the woods a sacred glade. For dinner we had a robust Zinfandel in company with rare peppercorn steaks, a salad rich in mountain herbs, the aromatic table breads from the kitchen, then black Irish Coffee with fluffs of hand-whipped cream.

During the meal I hogged the conversation in recital of my flight from Linda, beginning with the treacherous ham, the scrambled eggs, and ending right there at the table. Rob and Sharon urged me on with nods and smiles, saying little to each other. The excellent food, the perfect setting in the alpine air, the unexpected flattering attentions were spinning my head like the whiskey, my pleasure tempered only by the swift and radical revisions I was forced to make in my opinion of myself, a shift so drastic it became an irritation.

Here was all the difference between being hauled aboard a lifeboat and being flattened by yet another oar. These were surely the best of companions leaning toward me in the glow of candles, relaxed on their expensive-fabricked elbows. I felt the light vibrant touch of Sharon's stockinged kneecap, and a distinct rub against the other leg from Robby's continental pant.

"That's a marvelous story," gleamed Sharon when I'd finished. "Is any of it true?"

"You don't think I'd make it up for strangers, do you?"

"We're not strange. Are we, Rob? You're the wild one, Jerry."

"How do you spell the word *wild?*" Rob smiled.

"The way we all do, Oscar," said his wife.

After small talk and brandy I said I thought I should move on.

"We ought to move on, too, I think," said Rob. "I'll be back in a few minutes." And he went to pay the check.

"You're a truly attractive couple," I told Sharon, "I wish I had a marriage more like yours."

"Yes, we are attractive, aren't we?" she agreed, attractively smiling. "Everything works for us, you know. We're young, we have money. We have good times together." She had a way of tilting the head as she spoke that did nice things for the lips and lashes.

"It's truly enviable."

"Everything. Except for one tiny insignificant little detail." Pausing, Sharon touched the napkin to her mouth. She was beginning to sound like someone in a goddamn book.

"Which is...I hope you don't mind my asking?" I could talk that way, too.

"Why no, Jerry. I wanted you to ask." She glanced around to see where Rob was. In the Gentlemen's Lounge, I could assume without inspection.

"It's like this, Jeremy," said Sharon smiling broadly, showing even, Northern California teeth. "We have so much, Rob and I, that it's easy to be generous. My husband now is generous in everything. Especially himself." I awaited the particular but didn't hold my breath.

"Don't get the wrong idea," continued Sharon, but now in the manner of a TV drama. "He's not a woman–chaser, a philanderer. Rob, you see, is *gay.*" I looked totally astonished, as though ready to be bowled over by a feather boa. But then I might have known all along. I'd been too busy thinking of myself. The news coincided with the rest of the trip, unnatural as it was turning out to be.

"I don't know what to say, Sharon."

"Well, I thought perhaps you would know, Jerry. I thought you might have known all along. You see, my husband Rob is going to ask you down to the estate house. As soon as he comes back from whatever he's doing now. It's a wonderful house, really, with lots and lots of rooms. A room for every purpose. You're a designer, Jerry. You'd love it."

As I said nothing, she ran on with her verbal script. "That's what Robby usually likes to do on weekends, whenever he's attracted to strangers. Who are also attracted to myself." Sharon took a breather and drained her brandy glass, completely happy.

"That's a bitchy thing to say to me, Sharon."

"Well, I didn't think so, or I wouldn't have said it, would I? You see, I thought you might be that way, too."

I threw down my scarlet napkin and turned on my heel and left. I had no use for her husband—in or out of his classy imported wardrobe. I didn't want her now, either. Or anyone else in the world that I could think of. A world like this was hardly worth saving. Was it still worth driving and drinking in?

From outside the glass door I looked back at the star corner table. In the flattering light of the candles, Rob was once more sitting next to Sharon. Though their heads were close together, I could see that in their own attractive fashion they were laughing.

21.

The car crept into Monterey. The late movie-shows were over, their audience in the streets. Couples, local girls, gangs of boys, and servicemen crowded up against the steamed glass of cafes like watchers at the walls of tall aquariums. The main street was the midway of a county fair, midnight on a Saturday in springtime—two hours before the bars closed, two hours that decided who would wake with sex-eased glands, who with aching heads or hearts or hards-on.

I was lucky to get a hotel room. Parties were going on behind locked doors. I knew what those guests would wake up to. I left my flight bag, a bag of ice, a pint of Ten High bourbon and went out to check the bars. The first two were a din of screams and shouts and amped-up country music, jammed with live bodies to the doorsteps.

A third was dimly quiet—the booths like gilded cages between brocaded walls. Sitters at the bar spun around and swiveled back, showing well-fed fannies in thigh-clutching slacks. Well screw it, I thought—live as you want to live. *"Hurry back,"* trilled a voice on exit. "And next time bring your *purse.*" The night was even colder. A salt wind was blowing from the sea.

Down the street was an old-time saloon behind cut-glass doors and windows. A big stove blazed inside—just what the drinker order-ed. I took a captain's chair at a small corner table and began to shell peanuts as I drank.

"Hey. What become of *my* drink?" asked a tall boy before me, a marine. "Some bastard drunk it while I was on the *phone.*"

"It wasn't me, Corporal, believe me. Sit down, I'll buy you one." He sat down at attention or nearly so. The crew cut made him look about sixteen.

"I called her twenty times. At least. There's got to be some other dude. I *know* it. She's my fiancée, you know. The one in Boston. The one I'm going to marry. The bitch!" He ran his broad hands across the short hairs, his black eyes closing to a focus, and went on in a Texas accent.

"No, I guess you *don't* know. Do you. Because you don't know *me,* Buck Willock. Good old Corporal Buck. Or buck corporal. Who may have his *balls* shot off before he sees his girl again. Oh. Ex*cuse* me, ma'am. I'm sorry."

"Three dollars, please," said the waitress. I pulled out a ball of loose bills. Buck downed his Seven-Seven like a soda and held up the glass for a refill.

"Ohhh, Claudia! I need that girl tonight. Before I fucking ship out. She was gorgeous. *Is* gorgeous. And in bed she was...I don't know. In bed she was gorgeous, too." He lapsed into a wavering revery about the lost and faithless Claudia. I wondered what Linda was doing now.

"If she was here right now I'd *eat her!*" Buck the Corporal said.

"Another round, gentlemen?" The waitress was back again. She looked patiently tired as did other nearby customers, who with tired patience edged their captain's chairs away from ours.

"Sure," said Buck. "Keep 'em coming. We're all friends here. *Aren't* we, ole buddy?" I said we sure were, if friendship meant anything at all.

Beneath the tiny table Buck's knees were rammed against my own. There wasn't room enough for breaking contact. Besides, they gave a radiator warmth. On the other hand I didn't think I ought to push back, even if my tablemate felt nothing from the neck on down. He was over four feet sitting, and a lot more erect, and except for right now in top combat condition. Corporal Willock struggled to his feet.

"Gotta make a *head*-call," he mumbled, weaving off around the other tables. In a while I heard quarters bonging in a wall phone and clanging on the floor and then the slam against a wall of the receiver.

"Last call!" the waitress was announcing, confirmed by the fast-running clock. "Last call for alcohol. Drink up, everybody. Motel time." I stared at others present, seeing them as mismatched motel mates.

"Fuck her. She don't answer," said Buck almost in tears. "She run off with some other dude, the cocksucker. I *know* it. I wish he was here *right now!*" His big fist banged the table and a glass jumped to the floor. It was time to move my legs. And drink my drink.

"Hey, Corporal. Hey, *Buck*. They're closing. They really are." I stuck out my watch to prove it. Buck had fallen into meditation behind interlocking fingers. He widened two slots around his eye-holes.

"Well, let's go then, old buddy. What're we waiting for? You got any women up there? You got something to drink?"

O-*kay*, I thought, be charitable. I helped him up as the chair fell. As if by wires he pulled himself together and walked out the door and down the street, one foot on the curb, the other in the gutter.

We stomped up the slick linoleum staircase. The other rooms were silent; the key made a clatter in the lock. *"Claudia,"* Buck moaned again. The hall refused an answer.

When I brought drinks in heavy tumblers from the bathroom, the shape of Corporal Willock lay stretched across the bed. He was on his back snoring, hands behind the close-cropped skull, thumbs behind the ears.

Jacket, shirt and tie he had managed—they lay tangled on the floor. The grey-green pants gripped his ankles, arrested by the obstinate shoes. I eased them off. In long black socks, white skivvy shorts and T-shirt, he looked at peace, as though laid out for a special service, his dog tags the sole badge of ceremony. The front of the shorts rose tent-like in what was unmistakably one hell of an erection. Then I remembered. It was Easter morn.

I stood by the window with my heavy drink, the sea air whistling through the sill. Bar signs and cafe fronts had long ago blinked out. Here and there a car door slammed, a starter ground. Night walkers prowled the sidewalks.

"Hurry up, Kurowski. We gotta get back," said a voice directly beneath me.

"Just a *minute*, Jackson. Ahhhh. It feels just as good goin' out, you know that? Maybe better. Wow."

"You pissed all over my shoes, you prick. Get back in the doorway, asshole. Here comes the patrol."

"I can't get it back in my pants. Some *fag'll* come along and grab it. Won't you kindly help me, friend? *Please?*"

"Shut up. They're slowin' down. It's the cops."

A squad car pulled up opposite. Its station calls rasped through the window, none of them for me. The policemen called out to some town girls and the girls leaned on the car door, laughing. In the cracks of the pavement below a dark stream had spread toward the gutter, but its maker had since fallen mute.

Far from a time of consecration the entire Easter weekend, it now seemed, was coming to be dominated, no—*utterly profaned*—by the ubiquitous male organ and its magnitude of functions and ugly guises. At least my family would be free of it, and of me. Too late now to hunt those multicolored hard-boiled eggs in Malibu. The good Colonel Vandenberg, inspired, had probably done a perfect job of camouflage, baffling our miniature task force in its mission of search-and-destroy. Well, I hoped it made them happy. Linda too, God rest her gracious soul and careworn body.

22.

Thinking of my wife's physique I turned to look at Buck's. He was well built, all right, for a normal American male—one of those tight-sinewed tough-boned bodies grown in wide open spaces like the range, the face and hands permanently suntanned, the features more those of country boy than soldier. Why did he have to fight some foreign war?

I longed to be in bed also, but his limbs spread like roots on the mattress. And how about that thing in the middle there—his what's-its-name, standing like a stake on his claim? What would Corporal Willock feel, if he *did* feel, about some civilian stranger sliding up alongside anything like that? But then I myself, a veteran, wasn't going to spend the night on the flat cold floor of my very own rented hotel room. I shed my clothes and pulled the light-cord. Shyly, shivering in my jockey shorts, I slid in bed beside him.

Abruptly the snoring ceased. Fumes of oxidizing booze hung in the air above us. I studied the papered ceiling, where some prodigal bedtime orgy had left is awful stain. Then, like the long arm of the law, the hand of Corporal Willock seized my wrist, swung it over, and clamped my palm firmly to his crotch. His range-bred member lunged from its cotton tent. Buck caught it in my fingers, shaped a fist, and taught it how to move to his cadence.

"Umm. That's better," he grunted, kicking off the skivvies, skinning up the T-shirt. One hand cradled his crew cut; the other fell heavy on my shorts. My waist shrank tight as Buck's as he sucked air. His ribs rose, his hips sank—then shot up like a mortar. Whatever male feeling he had felt, I was feeling too—a spasm that came with a shudder on the shock wave of Buck's quick release.

His empty trunk came down again and rested on the sheets.

"Hey, that was okay, man. Do you think you can find us a towel?" I went to the bath, rinsed out my shorts, and took a warm wet towel to the bedside. My bedmate hadn't moved.

By the light of the municipally-funded street lamp it was evident that Lance Corporal Willock, U.S.M.C. active duty, had scored an impressive strike. From just below the hollow of the throat and following the line of body axis, a slim translucent ribbon extended to the source of its supply, infiltrating, and at some points saturating, a parallel trail of downy hairs that flowered to a thicket at the groin.

From a horizontal vantage point, the view across the plane of the abodomen resembled that of wind-smoothed terrain: here a patch of hardy mountain growth at the timberline, and just beyond a mighty storm-stripped pine rooted among rounded boulders— Buck's firm and symmetrical balls. I wiped his chest and crawled into bed beneath the thin cover. Buck rolled aside, my arm around his middle, his warm cheeks heating my belly. It was a different kind of warmth than I had ever felt with Linda—more like that of a hibernating bear without its coat of winter fur. Buck resumed his snoring.

The self-winding watch read four o'clock. It *ought* to run after its workout. Though my flesh ached for sleep, my brain was not ready. Its visual extenders, those windows of the mind or mirrors of the soul, my drink-crazed sex-glazed eyeballs, were turned toward the ominously clouded ceiling and its blots like the come-stains of a giant. Even as I scrutinized the lewd Rorschach shapes, the hidden profiles, their outlines grew subtly enlarged. Just another mouldering *Picture*—a fresco—*of Dorian Gray*, old buddy. Would I look as young that morning as I had the night before? The odds were dead against it.

To aim so high and sink so low. Did Oscar Wilde say that? The quote said it all, didn't it? My nagging brain was merciless. I would rather have listened to Linda were she there. What was all the guilt for, anyway? A couple of guys whacking off on a night that happened to be a special time for Christians, a minority among world faiths. That's all. It couldn't be the kind of sin that Jesus died for. That was Onan's problem.

I tried, but ultimately failed to imagine the buckets, barrels, *vats* of mankind's seed being spilt that very instant. And in useless futile ways of endless variation. Maybe one sperm cell in a sextillion ever reached its natural goal. Spendthrift Mother Nature. Stingy Father Time. What a neat pair *they* were.

And what kind of pair were we? Me and the soldier at my side there, snoozing like a babe in its innocence, my corrupting fingers dangling in his private parts? We had only done what Steve and Starkey nearly had in their sibling-interrupted shower. And what had I told them? That it was *all right*, hadn't I? But they were *boys*, still growing up. Like Buck. Like me and Jimmy Corey. But I was now for all intents and purposes a MAN, by virtue of age, wisdom and experience—trial by war and peace, in love and marriage. And once-successful suitor to any number of reciprocating girls and willing ladies.

Maybe Linda was right. Maybe I hadn't grown up, *matured* yet. And just possibly never would. Perhaps, if tonight were any indication, I was headed back down the time-track toward permanent regressive boyhood, while the kids sped by in rapid transformation to complete adults, like by-passing trains in a science text illustration of the Doppler effect. *En passant, mons cheries*—a line for the people at the birdcage bar. Well, how about it, Linda Lee?

As light through muddy waters, the dawn began to seep through brownish drapes. I got up to take vitamins and aspirin. In the flight bag were the unused condoms. I got back into bed beside Buck, who snored the good snore of a warrior. Finally, my exhausted brain conked out.

It was the tolling of the bells that awoke me, a full and fervent ringing through the founding mission town of Monterey. Good folk out there in the real world of sun and April flowers would be putting on new clothes and going to church, there to raise their heads in hymn to clear and lofty ceilings.

My vision focused on a red translucent sail, Buck's outstanding ear on the rim of his crew cut equator. I examined its web of veins. Then peering around a muscled shoulder I found his trusty sentry still alert. *The morning watch*—blasphemous thought. Buck rolled over grinning with his eyes shut, and saying nothing, caught my head in the spread of his fingers, deftly as an air-filled ball. Like a player shooting baskets he centered his aim by instinct and found the instant target—his own crotch.

That was the name of the game, alright, that mad forbidden act that stopped the wind and made the blood rush. I had been its easy subject more than once. Here, roles were reversed. My neck went stiff in resistance, then yielded to Buck's Marine strength. His downy hairs tickled my nostrils; they inhaled his personal odor of the great outdoors.

Going down on the *Day*, perhaps the memorial *Hour*, when our Lord had arisen from the dead. A one-way ticket to Hell! Well, I'd make it a trip to remember. Sliding down Buck's thighs I set to work in earnest. It was a hard-acquired skill, I learned through gasps and aching jawbones. It was not called *unnatural* for nothing! Biting my lips I pressed on, though my eyes filled with teardrops.

"Yeah-uh. That's getting there," my partner in carnal crime declared agreeably. "A little more pressure at the *end* there, friend."

Seeming to have the hang of it, I cinched the bald scrotum.

"All *right*," Buck called out as his hips heaved and swerved, a colt bolting home to the stable. I gripped the rearing flanks, palms on his rump, as he struck out at a gallop.

"Go, Jerry, go!" He was plunging through the big barn door—"It's *ready*, man. Wow. *EA'CHUR HEART OUT, BABY!*"

The taste of earth's fertility suffused my palate, the age-old flavor of the founding sea. On the flood tide of Buck's fulfilment I was borne away once again—this time between the hard-locked joints of his combat-ready kneecaps.

"I guess I'll take a shower," Buck yawned with his knees up, giving me an upslope view of the scrotum. At my touch the skin crinkled, shrinking tight to its profligate twins. The pouch had a life of its own, distilling in perpetuity the salts of its ocean origin.

"You keep on doing that you'll make me horny," said its owner, getting up. On the wreckage of the bed, a survivor on a raft, I spread my own arms and legs while he showered. Overhead the threatening stains had lost their menace, as after a passing storm.

Well, well, I thought in casual resignation—a cocksucker confirmed at last. And today of all days, the Resurrection. I should have listened to Mother. I might have known. I *should* have known it the very first time, when the boy down the street had shown me a ready-to-go erection. Only playing Tarzan, he had told me—an unknowingly potential Jane. And the times after school or in the bathroom, with Billy and Bob and *Jimmy* and...wasn't that enough?

Or thumbing on the highway, getting done by queens or salesmen for an ego boost. How about all *those* times, old buddy? How about the time at the hospital? Yes, but that was an emergency...*Lis-sen!* You're thirty-fucking-three, a husband and a father, my heedless head ran on.

Those times were different, another inside voice was quick to comfort me—you only laid back and *enjoyed.* But the kindly spirit of true understanding did not in the end prevail, even though this was *the very first and only time* that I had taken between the same two lips that had kissed my wife in holy wedlock (but in other places too!) and had brought to complete and actual oral-sexual discharge, the fundamental procreative organ of another human male—however horny—and swallowed his COME.

Don't forget or overlook that important little detail, chum. And *relished it*—just like your dreams. You faggot.

A fucking half-cannibal was more like it. Or a *vampire*—even worse—tapping the vital juices of a Texas boy-marine sworn to the service of his country. Cells absorbed by the bloodstream stay in the system *seven years,* I'd heard—the period of cyclic rebirth. How's that for cosmic realization, Jerkoff Jerry?

I was getting a heavier sermon than I could find in any church, my throat as parched as though I had delivered it. I went to the steam-clouded bathroom and poured a little whiskey in a water glass. Buck whistled as he whipped the moisture from his back with a damp rolled towel. If he were still half a boy, he was more than half a man, I acknowledged, in review of his tapered back, his washboard ribs and trunk, his tender loins.

"Here, let me do it," said his friendly host in fond demonstration of the toweler's art. Buck's hide rippled with the grooming.

"Are you ready?" I asked.

"Sure! Let's have a great big breakfast. I could eat a horse."

"Me too."

"You look like you just did, man. You look pale."

"Well, it is a big one, Buck." He blushed as though no one else had ever told him. "And still growing."

"My war club. I'm part Indian, you know. My daddy's one-eighth Cherokee. That makes me one-sixteenth, right? I don't know what it does for me. Extra stamina, I guess."

At that point in time who could say? It was nearly twelve noon. Buck found the parts of his uniform and pulled apart the bedclothes for his missing shorts. The waistband bore his name and service number.

"What's the W.W. stand for, Buck?"

"William Wilson Willock, Junior," he said with a little pride. Straight in the seams of his tailored dress-greens he was a different person clothed than before. He led the way downstairs and through the wainscot lobby, heel-cleats clicking on the floor tiles.

"Checking out, boys?" the day clerk inquired from his cage.

"We'll be back soon," I said, "to pick up our things."

"Well, please don't muss the bed. Will you, fellows?"

23.

It was a cool day but windless, the sun barely shining through a springtime haze. We walked up the street to the luxury hotel and ordered two Club Breakfasts, with Screwdrivers instead of orange juice. When our waitress wanted proof of Cpl. Willock's age he flashed a false I.D. card. He'd be eighteen next month, Buck told me, then went on about his home near Texarkana on the Texas side.

He'd left school to help his father, a foreman on a ranch. But his father had developed an affliction of the lungs, and was smoking three packs a day at the pool hall, drinking, without a job. His mother worked in town at a grocery. His brothers were married and gone, and Buck had joined the Corps.

As for hometown girls, they were all right for ordinary screwing, he said, but everyone knew what they did in bed or auto. So there was not much available in the way of a private affair. Claudia, though, was different, a girl with a lot of class he had met on an Eastern weekend. He loved her. So much in fact that he had never even tried to make out. That would have spoiled it. They planned to get married as soon as he got back from a duty tour in Asia, Buck said without conviction. His dark eyes took on the hooded far-off look of the previous night's drinking, the look of the permanently landless, used to moving on.

Over sausage and eggs I asked if he'd eaten prairie oysters. Sure, said Buck, every branding time. He liked them better than real ones—slippery in odd-smelling shells. Ranching was a hard lonely life. The hands didn't go to town to raise hell every weekend, I found out. They didn't earn that much. They were silent and shy with each other. The Big Sky does that.

Sometimes, he said, they rode for days and days along the fences and got themselves off in their jeans, just rocking forward on the saddle horn. It was a different picture than the films showed. He knew about a cowhand, he said as he continued through another Screwdriver, who had buggered a horse so severely that the animal had panicked, locked its sphincter, and run off with the cowboy's cock. It was a risky business anyway, he laughed—you were likely to get a lap full of horseshit. I considered the tale apocryphal, but I didn't use the word to his face.

While I waited for the check Buck took some coins to the phone booth. He was gone a long time. I had a smoke and more coffee and watched the other hotel diners, well-dressed families having decent Easter meals of turkey, ham and ice cream—just like down home in Malibu.

"Hey, she's home!" cried Buck, returning with a wide prairie grin. "They're just eating chow in Boston. They call it supper back there. It's already five o'clock, their time."

"Does she still love you?"

"Sure. I said I still loved her, too. She had to show a visitor around last night, some dude from out of town. She'll write me right away. Her cat had some kittens, Siamese. And she scratched her new car.

"We're going to get engaged. See this ring here?" Buck turned the big brass ring with the red garnet eye and the *Semper Fidelis* graven on it, a knuckle-enhancing accessory so handy on rougher occasions. "I'm sending it special delivery. I sure hope it fits."

In our room I mixed some Ten High and water but we only tasted it, a toast. We took off our clothes and did some things together that we both appreciated, mussing the freshly made-up bed after all. I was not the same person, either, as at 1130 hours. I had the curious sense of recyling through another's being, a mingling of dissimilar selves.

I couldn't tell how Buck felt. For a while he didn't speak at all. We went down to the fishing pier and had a beer there and walked to the end to look west toward the horizon through a mist. The sea was calm without reflection. Flights of gulls were scavenging the scraps of seafood dinners.

"Hey, Jerry, old buddy. I'm not drunk now. I'm glad I met you, though. Because you may be the last friend I see here. We're probably shipping out this week." The seagulls screeched and wheeled above a pail of cut bait. A Japanese fisherman ran out and shook his fist at them. *"Banzai! Banzai!"* his friends were shouting from a cafe.

"Well, it meant a lot to see you too, Buck."

"I don't know how it's going to work out over there. Sixteen fucking months. It's so fucking far away, you know? It's like a man getting shot into space."

"I know what you mean."

"In a funny way I'm scared. Not of dying. Yeah, dying, I suppose. In a place I don't even know the name of. And nobody there knows mine. Except the Corps," he said grimly.

"I worry too, Buck. Almost every day about something. But they're things that aren't likely to kill me anymore."

"I'll send my F.P.O. number. And you write back, okay? Here's my girl's address. You write her if you don't hear from me."

"You'll be all right. You're Buck Willock, built like a horse, with the blood of the Cherokee behind you."

"Yeah. I wish I believed all that. I gotta get back for chow, and get my gear together."

I drove out of the town and up the bay to the gate of the base where he was temporarily, terminally stationed. He swung the car door and we shook hands in the time-honored customary way of Americans shaking hands in America, and he straightened his khaki tie again and then the creases of the uniform with the red-flannel chevrons of his grade, inspecting also the polish of the shoes, and then walked severely erect with headgear secured, visor squared to the horizon of his vision, to the M.P. guarded sentry gate both vehicular and pedestrian, but only the first of the infinitely multiplying gates and doors and ports and holes and hooches and hatchways and jump-ways that were the still invisible but presently viable constructs of his pathway to the future, concealed in the time-warp lattice space-frame of the currently conjectured universe according to God's plan and the best minds in science. His identity challenged and his person qualified to pass, Lance Corporal "Buck" W.W. Willock walked even more erect though smaller in stature, following the rule of diminishing perspective, down the two long blocks of sanitary military street-grid, having for companion traffic only the few slow-moving cars of visitors, and executed a smart right turn before vanishing in measured strides on clicking heels behind a grey mass of building posted B–315 ORDNANCE.

I started up the car and drove away.

24.

I had no feeling for the Sunday road bobbing with bright-painted vehicles like a parade of metal eggs. I had no interest in my two-tone Plymouth—French Vanilla and Aztec Bronze—and just allowed the car to pick its way along the crowded lanes, starting and stopping on demand. I was grateful for the Torque-Flite pushbutton gearshift that didn't need any help from me. Their assignments completed, the divisions of my being were all on weekend leave.

My heart, or its stand-in, was back there in the un-made-up bed of the hotel room. And my conscience, its well-meaning guidance neglected and ignored, had finally decided to shut up. I felt it sulking back there in the bare rear seat like the wives of willful Sunday drivers. All right, you'll see, it probably muttered to itself against the rolled-up rain-streaked window. My head was light as April air between the flat white sheets of general overcast. For a driver the Fury had a dummy at its wheel.

Even Carmel's famed Seventeen Mile Drive was not an acceptable diversion. Tourists from all over the world were out there, rejoicing in the twisted cypresses and barking seals. Instead I fell into an end-of-the-weekend melancholy. What would I say to Linda? She to me? Did I really want to go home? And had I ever *really* been missed?

I ascended into the soaring elevations of Big Sur, the car once more in my control. I drove through woods, past Nepenthe and its holiday tipplers, down a long descending transit of the strictured road. The road darted snake-like along the canyon ridges, now as though to launch the driver off a cliff, then across high-spanned roaring gorges. From underneath bridges, armies of fir and redwood marched in ranks of forest greens, from the near but not visible sea to distant summits. At those heights, holes had opened in the clouds, pierced in passing, and rays of strong western sunlight struck theatrically through. *That's more like it,* I thought smugly.

I drove maturely, not in the Grand Prix fashion of Good Friday. I took time to park the car along an inside curve beneath a canopy of fir boughs, an authentically posted *REST STOP*. Springwater spouted from a pipe stuck rustically in mortared stone. *DO NOT DEPOSIT TRASH. THINK SCENIC!* a nearby sign demanded. I took a long drink, pure refreshment after all that had gone down before.

To the west the guest of the Forestry Service gazed into a widening chasm. A stream churned and tumbled far below, sawing a course through bedrock to unite with the conquering sea. It had all the time in the world. Toward the inland mountains the twin slopes closed to a ravine. A little footpath led irresistibly among the evergreens on a thick brown carpet of needles, twigs and seedling cones. I took a camera from the trunk and followed it.

Away from the road the whoosh and squeal of motorcars was lost to hearing, as in a hush of fallen snow. My boots sank deep into the turf of centuries. Moisture oozed and ran in rivulets—the mountain's capillaries. The trail narrowed with its depth of penetration, at length marked only by broken branches. Colorful deposits of matchbooks, crushed packs of menthols, and spent condoms gave way to untouched toadstools and sculptured fungal growth. I trod lightly, an

Indian scout. Up ahead in a brightening light the space between the tree-trunks broadened.

I stepped into a vast spatial vortex, a cone of air that opened to the sky. Walls of rock spread right and left around a promontory at the core, a water-rounded island between parent streams. From a cover of holly and juniper rose the solitary trunk of a splended time-bleached fir. High above its tip a blue eye blinked open in the cloud-bank, a contact with outer space, should the cylinder of polished wood elect to launch itself.

But secure for the ages on its granite throne, the trunk already transcended its own kingdom. A burst of setting sunlight—God's amber gels—lit the clearing and turned the trunk pure gold. High in the subject audience of trees sang choruses of birds, forest murmurs. *Siegfried's Rhineland Journey!* And why not? The rocky rise became his funeral pyre.

Easy, boy. *Down,* Jerry. But my fancy had already slipped its leash, was off and running, romping through the woodland with wild excited yelps. I sat down on damp moss to wait for it. Gnats and small mosquitoes buzzed around my ears.

Well, what else does it remind you of, I asked patiently—a waiter at commercials for the scheduled show to start, a doper ready for the next hallucination. *A Cathedral in the Pines.* Well natch, stupid. Even the meanest lung-choked, fornicating, defecating, forest-vandalizing *tourist* would have noticed that. That should have come *first,* you asshole. Especially today, before the big pagan Wagner set and its bad associations with a certain late regime.

A chance to make amends then! Truly contrite I knelt in wordless prayer, the rock a natural altar faced by gloomy redwood aisles. I tried to genuflect as seen in church or movie but could not remember rightly the sequence of the gestures. Suppose, like some garbled trans-Pacific cable, the message were to transmit wrong? Ants crawled in the boots and up the legs of that failed forest penitent.

What other thing I wondered, still waiting, crushing ants. The prow of gray rock might be that of a ship, a heavy cruiser, its cavities the scuppers, the tree its radar mast. But the image did not convince. A warship underway through virgin timber was a vision to rebuke the most abused and over-taxed imagination. It was foreign and surreal.

Whatever the scene put me in mind of, I ought to take its photograph before the light failed. And get out of the woods before dark. Why hadn't I thought to take Buck's picture in uniform? Or better still—buck-naked? I framed the setting in the reflex mirror. The focusing ring froze on what I saw, but couldn't believe. The scene was too outrageous. For the view revealed through the wide-angle lens was that of the very morning, there reduced in image but before me exploded to heroic scale—the nether aspect of Buck's Texas-size genital center—the massive rocks supporting through their crown of brush a skyward-leaping phallus...

I AM TEN FEET ROUND AND
TWO HUNDRED FEET LONG. MAKE DATE!!!

I'm interested, I confessed to myself. How big is the rest of you? I decided to take a closer look.

Up the right-hand fork of the clearing a fallen log made a bridge. Scrambling across on hands and knees reminded me of King Kong crashing from his jungle turf to toss invading sailors to a reptile-filled abyss. But on this dusky crossing nothing moved but the waters, in rippling musical rills. I struggled up the cliff toward the tree.

Standing at the foot of the colossus I stroked the silvery silken slickness of the trunk. The inscrutable graffiti of their lives beneath the vanished bark had been left there by long-perished termites. Even after Buck had gone this glory would remain, his woodsy memorial, until the sins of California pushed the land into the sea.

A lump of leavening passion had risen in my jeans. What remained to be done was best done quickly. Glancing up, down, and sideways I shucked them to my boot tops. And standing straight as Buck had in my memory of him, I shot my last reserves of seed into the void, to float to sea among the gurgling waters.

For you, Buck Willock, whatever your fate may be. My head swam in a vertigo of ecstasy. In mind I saw the tabloid banner: *HE FUCKED A FOREST AS MOSQUITOES STUNG HIS ASS!* And the remembered headline of a hanging: *JERKED TO JESUS.* At that instant the sole of my boot slid from the slippery stone; the enclosing cone of woods flew swiftly upward.

Bound tight in lowered jeans my feet struck shallow bottom in an icy rock-bound pool. I climbed out and shivered on a boulder. My camera dripped water. I had ruined the picture, too. My balls are like two walnuts, I thought incongruously. And my *thing* has shrunk up too, the little monster—just what it deserved. There was something wrong in the legs, though. The left knee was swelling, growing painful as it warmed. It did not support my weight. What I had then, I reasoned, was a probable fracture of the knee-joint, the biggest in man's body, I recalled. Though crippled I felt strangely lightened. With the aid of the shattered kneecap I had lost my burden of guilt.

It took an hour to crawl from the bottom of the funnel to the edge of the no-longer virgin woods. By then it was dark indeed.

25.

Again I let the car do the driving. I stuck the stiffening leg in the carpeted well, punched button D and let the wheels take the course of the road like a skateboard with an engine, all the way downhill to the level of the sea. Too tired for the project of new imagery I re-ran old movies in my head: *King's Row* for its double amputee (where's the *rest* of me?), John Ford's *Long Voyage Home, CITIZEN KANE,* as the shell of San Simeon reeled back into oblivion. Then the road from bush country was channeled into U.S. 101. As I by-passed the bus station at Obispo I wondered what new features played upon the restroom walls.

After that came a featureless passage between undulant black hills humping up and down like waves of earth. Now and then gigantic trucks and trailers hurtled by on hissing tires, the running lights like those of jeweled creatures from the sightless ocean depths. While aspirin dulled my senses I tuned the radio, my mind drifting with the airwaves.

Then Vandenberg again and its fields of siloed missiles, the neighboring fresh-air farm for trapped malefactors, and at last the roadside business strip at Buellton. I turned off the freeway to stretch my good leg and get some gas. I half-expected to find the kid in the red BEARS jacket still propped like a scarecrow at his corner stand, a holdout for the righteous ten-spot, his hair-drape whipped to shreds by wind and rain. When I saw that he was gone I missed him. Now I knew a little how he felt. I hoped a charitable driver had paid the standard fee.

As the tank filled, the aroma of the Pea Soup Palace came across the highway on a teasing breeze, stronger than the smells of fossil fuels. I couldn't leave the car to follow it—the leg was already like a cast. I drank a Coke and saved the can for future reference. *I'm a non-ambulatory cripple*, I thought with pride as I signed the service tab.

When I glided down our drive and cut the engine, my home was as dark as any haunted house, as dead as any doornail in that well-slammed door. Was the door then permanently fastened; would it be opened by any living thing? Or had they all deserted to a place of no address with their protective proxy father, Colonel Vandenberg, returned to active duty?

Such were my anxious musings as I sat silent in my disconnected four-wheel space module, its metals crackling in the night. It might as well have been another planet I had landed on. Where was the the homely welcome for the sole survivor of Big Sur Crotch? Of Wounded Knee revisited?

Maybe I should lean on the horn.

A lamp lit in the bedroom. Out came Linda in her light blue robe to stand ghostlike beside the Fury's window.

"Are you going to come in," she said at length, "or aren't you?"

"I can't."

"Then I'm going back to bed."

"My leg's broke, Linda."

"That's not funny, Jerry. And I don't want to hear it's your middle one. It's been a long Easter weekend."

"See for yourself." And I showed her.

Linda viewed the swollen limb with alarm and then relief. The knee solved all our problems! No futile arguments, no rebukes, no recriminations. It was a different Jerry she could deal with now, a Jerry she could be kind to. Linda went to the kitchen and brought me back a drink. Presently Everett came over to inspect the casualty, then drove me to the local all-night clinic. As I waited to be examined, an orderly shot me full of morphine. A guard on duty at the Nike base, he told me, had just put a bullet through his foot. Now what, I wondered as I faded, would ever make a soldier do a thing like that?

That Monday a surgeon set the kneecap and put it in a cast. I lay in bed awhile before attempting crutches, and by the end of the week I was lounging on the terrace soaking up rays of sunshine, sucking drafts of springtime air. The troublesome burdens of home and work had been swept away as if by magic broom.

A half-assed overgrown child. The very words she'd hurled at me Good Friday. And there I was, a half-legged, half-dependent adult. Linda Lee couldn't have done better had she waved a fairy wand and got her wish! What she had *really* meant was a half-assed overgrown un-*manage*-able child. Now I could be managed, along with her four other charges. She could treat us all alike—Big Mother. Actually, I was getting the best of her favors. She rocked Casey to sleep in his hammock and spent her time with me.

In contrast to my outdoor fall, Linda's insides had healed rapidly. She resumed our intimate relations, once more taking the lead. Flat on lounge or mattress I had only to flash my Red Alert and she was there to handle the emergency, a twenty-four hour private nurse. Best of all I had no competition from the Colonel. He had to take a back seat to my injury. A freshly-broken leg was hard to beat.

I compared my new weapon, the handicap, to the one I had so heartily endorsed only the previous week, the old-fashioned commonplace ever-ready hand slap. Alongside the sophistication of the fractured knee the slapping hand was nothing, a crude elementary expedient, the side-arm of domesticity. Once employed, the hand slap had to be used repeatedly, with grave risk of escalation from the other side.

Whereas the handicap, in my present experience of it, need be deployed but once. Then it kept on paying off, hour after carefree hour, day after leisured day, without further thought or effort. I felt like a small dependent state threatening its Big Sister nation. Always, one held the implied intent of not getting well, of breaking another leg, of limping off to a still more lenient sponsor. It was a power to be kept in reserve, not spent in feckless spontaneity.

But as the kneecap knitted and I hopped about with greater ease, Linda sought my help with the baby, with the laundry and other chores. The handicap was compromised. It was not the perfect weapon after all. For long-range dependability it would be necessary to stay in the cast, or to suffer a major bone-crunching disability. The ultimate weapon was a device I could ill afford.

Then as I drove out to find new jobs and renew old friendships, the familiar frictions came back in proportion to my range of freedom. I was not always found where I was meant to be. But Linda was happy with the baby, humming and cooing, offering her breast. There were no complications in Casey's feelings. As for our own, we had a guarded truce.

The truce had come about through a major tactical error. After a time of making love to my handicapped person, Linda had shared a private confidence—Everett had a handicap, too. The unspecified war wound within the last few years had made the Colonel impotent. That was his military secret! The thoughtless woman had betrayed it. She had thrown away her trump card, a king of hearts, forfeiting both my envy and respect.

26.

The week the cast came off I had word from a late confederate in the war between the sexes. The envelope arrived without a stamp. In its place was the printed word *FREE*. Sure enough, there was Buck's name and number and a San Francisco military post address. The ink was streaked and blotched, as though the letter had flown unaided through the rain. The notepaper had for its emblem the picture of a huge helicopter.

> *Hi there, Jerry. I guess you wonder what happened to your old friend Buck. Well he is right here in good old N.A.M. I cant tell you what part because they dont want the enemy to know where I am at.*
>
> *We see a lot of things here I cant write to you about. At least not for right now. I can tell you though that we have movies and all the coke and cold beer we can drink. I am having one right now. We have some women down the road too. So everything is A.O.K. If you dont walk too far or fly too high. If you know what I mean.*
>
> *We are supposed to be sent out to another unit. I would like to finish my duty tour right here. You cant kill a man for hoping. Can you? I guess I shouldnt use the word KILL. I mean it dont sound right for these surroundings.*

A buddy from San Antone just popped a beer for me. So I am going to drink it while its cold. It gets hot here in more ways than one. If you understand what I mean by that remark.

Take it easy for right now and write to Claudia for me. I didnt get her last letter.

A Marine, BUCK (full corporal now) WILLOCK

P.S. When you get to Monterey again please have a tall one for me!

I wrote back to tell him what I was doing and a little bit about my injury in line of duty in the woods. I tried to make it sound funny for him. I hoped he would stay together for those fifteen or sixteen months he had to go yet and visit me when he got back. I would write to his girl as he requested.

This letter brought no reply, and after a while I did write to Miss Claudia Bronson at her Boston address. In a few weeks she answered. She had not heard from Willy either and wondered if anything were wrong. Actually she hadn't known him very well. He was so different from the boys she knew at home, the son of a Texas rancher. The life sounded so romantic. He was a friendly boy with a winning smile. She would feel bad if anything had happened. Now he had two friends to depend on, even though she personally disliked that war.

Claudia herself was engaged but would not marry until her fiancé had his degree in law. She wished my marriage and my children well. I wrote, but never heard from either one again.

Part Three

27.

For mid-Gemini the month had cryptic aspects. The stars flashed messages on moonless nights from countless constellations. The sun burned the haze of the morning beach, where claws of gulls had spelled out hieroglyphics. We all had early suntans.

Again I was involved with the ocean. Should all else fail there were always more waves. Both the sea and I were promiscuous.

Good weather brought more jobs, one of them in photography. I was hired to shoot backgrounds for a swim-wear line, an excuse to hang around the playground of my bachelor days—the bay, the harbor and the pier. I would do my work, catch a wave and linger at the pier until sunset. Like the dazzling seascapes of Turner the scene burned in a gilding light "that never was on land nor sea." That light appeared upon my film.

The harbor waves, combed by pilings, diffused a luminous vapor. Like the castles of Linda's fairy legends, the aging pleasure buildings would soar upon this tinctured mist, ablaze with sunset fire. There rose the turrets of the Merry-Go-Round, the silvered canopy, the mirrored sun-flamed glass—the very sense and substance of romantic vision. The prancing steeds, fabled beasts, and flying pennants were those of a storied tournament from far away and long ago. These reflections, overlapping on the shore, flowed like a golden syrup.

One evening as I shot the last transparency the head of Leonard Faircycle popped from a tower window and made a ridiculous face. I pretended to take its picture.

"Oh, I *hate* this endless publicity," Leonard shouted through the carousel's din. "If only they'd leave me *alone*. I'm not just another pretty *face!*"

"That's not exactly an ivory tower you're living in!" I shouted back.

"How *true*, alas. Why don't you come up, Jerry dear?" I packed the camera bag and climbed the stair, in spite of the dubious endearment.

In Leonard's white apartment, shot through with brassy light, the carousel boomed through the old plank floor like the heavy beat of doom.

"It'll stop soon," said Leonard. "At six o'clock. We have Anchors Aweigh, the Marine Corps Hymn, the Air Corps Song. *Anything* for the service."

"Nothing for us grunts, though," said a boy in khaki shirttails, his bare feet propped on a wicker chair, in his hand a scarlet drink.

"Oh, this is *Rocky*. Don't you love that name? Rocky Romano from South Chicago. Little Sicily! Show Jerry the mark of the Mafia, Rock. And *oh*, let me fix you a drink. We're having Campari-soda, with a *twist*. A Negrito! That's what they sip on the Rialto, you know, in *Venice*. Venice, *Italy*, of course. It's very Venetian here tonight, don't you agree?"

The clatter from below had ceased, and these last words of Leonard, nearly shouted, hung emphatically in gold-specked air.

"I noticed that myself. Except for the music, we could be at Saint Mark's, on the Canal."

"You *do* understand! You see, Rocky? I don't exaggerate *everything*. Rocky thinks I simply make things up!" Leonard went into his kitchen; the freezer door slammed. An ominous rumble followed— the slam of doors that locked the painted horses in their roundhouse for the night. It was good to hear the tinkling of the drinks.

Rocky reached out to shake hands, pointing to a blue spot by the thumb. "I'm only in the Army, not the Mafia. That's where a pen stabbed me in junior high. And I'm Tommy, Tommy Romanchak. From Rockford, Illinois." We shook hands. He did look Italian, I thought. He had that kind of olive grace.

"I'm Jeremy Carr. From Eagle Rock. No one ever called me Rocky, though." Or was ever likely to, now.

"Here you are, boys, fresh and *frosty*." Leonard was the perfect host again. "And here's to your next assignment, Rocky, my pet."

"Wichita Falls, Texas," said Rocky, rolling his Roman eyes. "There's nothing down there but the dust. At least it ain't Asia. Yet."

"Rocky's going to do a little soldiering, and then he'll be out in a year. You can stay here anytime you want then, Rocky. *I'm* the one who's going to do the *traveling*, a fabulous trip around the world! and *paid for* by Columbia Pictures."

As the sunset faded into purple, Leonard began to leap around the room, fluffing pillows, lighting lamps. It *was* like the salon of a river steamer, drifting from a darkening shore.

"And where are they sending you, Lenny?"

"Well, first to Pinewood Studios, in England. Oh, I'll meet all the famous names, I suppose. *Gielgud, Olivier,* the others. It's so *civiliz-ed* there, you know? They call us *poufs.* Can you imagine? There's *such* tradition in the British. And then I'll go about the country and collect some *real* antiques. You won't *know* this place when I get back!"

"Will you send me something, Lenny?" Rocky asked.

"'Of *course* I will, pet. But you won't know what it is until you get it. Otherwise, it won't be a *surprise.*"

"I don't care, as long as it's something I can spend."

"Now don't be greedy. I've never let you down yet, have I?"

"Just the opposite, Len." Rocky winked across the room.

"And then we're going deep into *Arabia,* to do *Conquest of the Dunes!* The budget's twelve million. *Eighteen* before we're finished. Oh, I'll have them stitching there for *months.* All that gold braid, those garments like silk skirts, the *burnoose,* you know. And those heavy, heavy cloaks spun from goats' and camels' hair. The *boys* sew, too, I understand. They *all* have those monkey-like fingers that just make the needles *fly.*

"We'll see all the *really* ancient places. Cairo, Alexandria, Tang*iers.* Where they've been sinning successfully for thousands of years. And Petra! *The rose-red city old as time.* Ali Baba had his caves there, hollowed out of marble for his treasure trove."

"Is any of it left?" asked Rocky. "I think my drink's gone."

"Well, I doubt if they've let any *jewels.* Here, I'll get you another. I can see that *you're* ready, Jerry." I handed him the glass.

"I don't think there's anyone living there right now, Leonard."

"Oh, well," he said from the kitchen. "We'll only be there for a day. And anyway, we'll have our Arab *guides.* They're marvelously handsome, you know. And they *always* leave their women at home, poor things. They have to scurry around in black *veils.*

"And then we'll float down the Nile, on some Peter Lorre kind of riverboat, with servants in red fezzes fanning the whole time, and visit all the *tombs.* You know the pharoahs were buried with *erec-tions? Embalmed* with a gold-plated *hard-on!* If you'll excuse the French."

Leonard brought three Camparis-with-lemon and put one in my hand. The drink was half vodka. "How would *you* like to have a four-thousand year old man?" He playfully patted my knee.

I flinched, even though the knee was not the injured one. Despite the lost weekend in Monterey, I considered myself to be at least half virgin, where other adult males were concerned. Leonard withdrew his hand.

"When the picture's done we'll see the old *romantic* countries. Spain, for those festivals of lace and leather. The A*lhambra,* of course. And *Rome,* Athens, all the rest."

Leonard had begun to show signs of travel fatigue and took a big slug of his drink. Rocky, quite drunk, had gone into a fit of giggles. Leonard, fortyish, sleek and portly, had hair of a dark abundance that belied a true color and age; and the hairpiece had tilted starboard by a list of several degrees.

"He's just a child at times. But I love him just the same," sighed Leonard, squeezing his bulk into the same rattan armchair. "He'll get over it." We had a moment's silence while the bodies met.

"What are you going to do about this place, Len?"

The thought was sobering. "Oh, *I* don't know. I was going to leave it with a friend. But he's *so* unreliable. You don't know *who'd* be here, or *what* I'd find missing. If the place was here at *all!* And then I thought of Sheila, but she'd had it full of *lady* friends. And now I just can't decide. Who *can* you trust?"

"How about me, Leonard? I need a place to work away from home."

"Well, it's not exactly ideal for *working*. But you *are* a married man. Someone to rely on."

"What would be the terms?"

"Well, you would pay the rent, only a hundred a month. And the *uti*lities, of course. And keep things neat and clean, and take care of the *ferns.* They need more than water and air, you know. You have to dust the leaves so they can *breathe.* I think they *listen,* too. So don't tell any secrets!" Leonard squeezed out of the armchair, the wig still askew, and moved energetically about the room again, dusting ferns and palm leaves with a feather duster. Rocky laughed again and wiped his eyes with his shirttail. I felt he didn't want to see Leonard leave.

"Is it a deal?"

"I'll have to *sleep* on it," said Leonard as he paused. "Don't you want to take a nap now, Rocky? You have to get up at *four*, don't you?"

"Yeah, I guess I do," he said, throwing off the khaki shirt, sucking in his gut. He freed the brass buckle and started up the stair.

"So long, Jerry. Maybe I'll pay you a visit."

"See you, Rocky. Take care."

"He's a sweetheart," said Leonard at the door. "But he *does* need someone to look after him."

"Don't we all. Thanks for the refreshments, Lenny. I really like your place."

"I'll let you know about it, Jerry. *Buona notte.*"

The following week I took a call from a studio secretary who connected me to Mr. Faircycle's office.

"It's all right," said Leonard in business tones. "We're going to leave this weekend. You can move in Monday. I'll send you pretty postcards from the *haute monde*. And in case there's any problem, call Miss Schlegel here at the studio. She'll be handling all my accounts. Please take any personal messages. And don't forget about the *ferns*."

"Don't worry, Leonard. You be careful of those mummies."

"You be careful of those swabbies! *Ciao.*"

At the time I wasn't certain what he meant.

28.

The promise I saw in the arrangement was not instantly clear to my wife. She hadn't been consulted, for one thing. "How will you pay for it?" was her first question.

"It's not that much, Linda, and down there I can earn more. It's closer to the center of things."

"And spend more, too, if I know what things you mean."

"It's only going to be for six months, while this movie executive's in Europe. It's just a trial run."

"And what will become of us?"

"You said you didn't need me. That I was just another mouth to feed, or words to that effect."

"That was another occasion. Before you broke your leg."

"It'll be the same as before, Linda. I'll be home every night, unless I have to work—if I should ever get that busy. You have the kids to talk to, and Everett if you want."

"I've gotten used to seeing you around, hon." Here she pressed my arm.

"Look. It will be like going to the office every day, the way other husbands do. You can't object to that."

"I don't suppose I can."

"Then we're agreed." I kissed her forehead, finding new grey hairs.

That Monday I rented a trailer to haul my board, books and files down to the pier. I had depended on Steve for some muscle but the surf had come up. Starkey came along instead. As I drove I directed his attention to spots of special interest: a house I had built, the site of a great party, the scene of a recent auto wreck involving people I'd known, the place where I had lived by the harbor before the fire changed my life.

"Wow," he piped, as I jack-knifed the trailer at the Merry-Go-Round. "You mean you're going to *work* here?" Even to a boy of Starkey's age the idea verged upon improbability—our environment was that of a seething summer's carnival.

Cars baked like biscuits in the midday sun; the breeze smelled of popcorn and fish. Down on Muscle Beach the body-builders toiled, lofting bodies, hoisting weights for an audience of indigents and retirees. The shore was a carpet of flesh. From pinball arcades came mechanical whines, bells and machine-gun fire. And the carousel played its marches. In Leonard's rooms each note was bugle clear.

"I can always wear earplugs," I rationalized, panting from a load. "Or do my drawing nights. This is only a sort of headquarters, Starkey, a place to stash my gear."

"A place to steer your gash," the boy said saucily.

"Just help me put these things away. Okay?"

I swept the shelving clear of fancy lamps and Grecian statues, of blown glass and racy novels, and put there books on building crafts. We stored away the splashy oils, campy movie posters, piles of velvet pillows, fashion magazines, decor.

"What kind of person lives here, anyway?" asked Starkey, thumbing copies of *American Nudist* and *Muscle Galore*.

"Put those in the closet there. Oh, he's a man I used to work with at the studios. They're all a little weird, you know. They have a very different life from me and you."

"Yeah, I know. Is he a good friend of yours?"

"Not really. It's a simple business deal. He's gone away to make a picture; I'm here to do my work. Here, help me lift this. My knee hurts."

Though plants and wicker furniture remained, the stripped apartment no longer seemed the setting for a Tennessee Williams tragicomic drama of the South. It was shipshape, more like the quarters a mariner might keep. I went to the kitchen, or galley, opened one of Leonard's beers, a Heineken, and hauled it aloft to the bedroom. That room, an octagon half-glass—what did it resemble? The *Captain's cabin*, of course, without question. My own command at last. The crowds that swarmed below were a motley crew at dockside begging passage on my ship.

And the *bed*. The four-square platform was an island floating in a sea of shag. The painting at its head, though, an aggressively male nude, would have to go. I unhung it. I lay back on the spread of green velvet; the mobs down below disappeared. I had window-pictures of water and sky, each with a different view. Starkey's feet pounded on the gangway—the cabin boy with hot dogs.

"Here's yours." *Sir!* "Onions and relish. You don't mean you're going to sleep here? It's more like a playhouse," the child said. I might have described the grownup Miss Landau at her performing best, but didn't. "Is this why you rented the place?"

"It's what you'd call unique, Starkey. It's one of a kind."

"No wonder. I'll bet they had some boss times here."

"They used to have movie stars. Sports stars. Writers and designers. People like that. Some pretty crazy parties, I suppose."

"Who are you going to entertain here, Jerry?"

"Oh, I don't know. Friends. Customers. Some V.I.P.'s perhaps."

"Mae West, Joe Blow and Captain Marvel. Who else?"

"Let's go for a swim."

The boy had become a good swimmer. He was getting ready to surf. In the late afternoon of the harbor, small waves nudged the hulls of fishing boats, their owners painting trim or cutting bait. We swam around the buoys and anchor lines as gulls cawed overhead in spirals of flight and glide. The carousel was a distant tinkling music box in air that held a golden melancholy, the distilled essence of that place and time. How could I describe it to the stepson stroking at my side? His colors were those of early morning.

Popping wide-eyed from a wave crest, a glossy head stared at us and vanished. We were startled, too. Then I laughed. The seal's charmed look had been that of Leonard—without his bathing cap of nylon hair.

We closed the apartment and drove toward the house I still called home. I stopped at the Country Store for groceries, at the Malibu Pokey for a beer. I asked Starkey to come in for a Coke.

"Naw, I'll stay in the car."

"What's the matter. Are you tired?"

He twisted his head toward the yellow pickup, its bleached body heaped with poison sprays.

"Don't you want to see your father?"

"He wouldn't even know me. You're my father now."

Where I had thought to break a link, this boy had forged one.

29.

"Do you think we should do it? Or shouldn't we?"

"You already know what I think, Jerry. You don't have to ask me again." Linda was rocking the baby, who had just then fallen asleep, and pulling wisps of hair from her eyes. It was time for a trip to the hairdresser. She looked tired, I had to admit.

"Then I won't ask anyone over."

"That's perfectly fine with me."

"We can watch the Fourth on television."

"I'm not going to argue with you, just so you can run off in the car. I know that trick by this time. You can leave any time you want."

"What about the kids, though?"

"Well, what *about* the kids! They'll be out there on the beach beating bongos, drinking beer, or worse. That's enough excitement for me, my dear. For Casey, too."

"How about the fireworks? We don't want to be without those, do we? I can still drive down and get some. It's Independence Day, Linda."

"Jerry, you don't *have* to take every holiday literally. It's one more excuse for goofing off, getting drunk and spending money. July Fourth is only one more endless weekend. I'll be glad when it's over."

"Just try telling *that* to our forefathers. They'd hang you for being a witch."

"My God, you can be ridiculous! *Be* independent. *Do* what you want. Jerry, I *just—don't—care!*"

"All right then. I'll go down and watch the rockets on the pier."

Exactly what I planned to do, anyway. It was one of those often sultry Fourths, the clouds hanging overhead charged with latent energy. As good a time as any to get out—before the weather reached critical mass.

Like the landing of a fantasy invasion fleet, fireworks blazed along the shore—pinwheels, sparklers, roman candles—without the customary sounds of battle fire; firecrackers had been outlawed. Instead we had their safe-and-sane substitute, a civic celebration on the pier. $10,000 UP IN SMOKE! the evening paper promised. I got to the apartment, lit the cabin lamps and leaned out a window, captain of the view.

A Navy carrier had heaved its mighty anchors in the bay. All day long the ship's boats had hauled devoted patriots to the great steel cathedral of the hangar deck, where flights of avenging angels sat with folded wings. Now they ferried white-ducked sailors to the pier. Flocks of them passed below my window, some with a seaman's gait, but most with the walk of farmboys. In his warning of the swabbies it was surely not this tide of fresh-scrubbed youth that Leonard had in mind.

The carousel was idle, the horses poised in space. Could that be the sound of a human, then, at the apartment door? Lately some of Leonard's closer friends had come around. I guessed what they wanted and had just let them talk, cooling their lust in the hallway.

But that night the door swung open to a sailor in tailored whites, wearing on his face a shore-leave grin beneath a lick of red-brown hair. He held his hat in his hands at his middle, like a boy on a formal call.

"Howdy, stranger," said Ship's Fireman McCoy. "May I come in?"

I looked hard and swallowed. "I didn't know you were coming. How did you know I was here?"

"It's Leonard's apartment, right? I saw the light."

"Welcome aboard then, sailor. You've come to the right place."

"I know you, the man from Malibu. Where's Len?"

"Leonard's doing the continent. Can I get you a drink?"

"That figures. L.A. wasn't big enough. I'll have a beer."

While I fetched our drinks I could collect my thoughts. What was he doing *here*—this dream-time sailor—in the same room, at the same time, more at ease than I? His beer, my scotch—we clinked our cold glasses. As before, he lit two Lucky Strikes and handed one to me. I smoked, though it wasn't my brand. Pegging his hat on an African mask, Mickey sank into a peacock chair, thighs spread as wide as an earlier redhead's on the rocks of a California stream. This ruddy sailor dressed *left,* his white pants told me, as he looked around the room.

"The place looks changed."

"Not really, Mickey. I'm only looking after it till Christmas. That's when Len gets back. Tonight I'm down here to relax."

"You picked the right time for it. What else do you do?"

"Oh, take pictures. Draw houses. Design things. Stuff like that."

"You must be some kind of artist, like Lenny says he is. He makes a bunch of bucks designing dresses. He sure knows how to entertain."

"I know. So do I. I have a wife and four kids, though."

"I wouldn't let that stop you." Mickey grinned. A great thump followed the remark—the first salvo of rockets, then a rain of whistling sirens. "Let's go topside." He stood up with his beer. "We might miss something.

A door in the tower bedroom opened on the roof, a flared skirt painted aluminum. Mickey fingered out another pair of cigarettes—hand-rolled—and lit one. "Panama Red," he said, squinting. The night smelled of burning weed and gunpowder.

The rockets soared...exploding parasols, umbrellas, chandeliers of rainbow jewels...red, blue, then gold again, a dazzle in our eyes. Each burst brought a chorus of sighs from below, and a crunch of mock thunder, delayed in the low-lying skies. A galaxy of falling stars finished the display, their colors soon ghosts in the darkness.

"Ten thousand dollars up in smoke," I said to Mickey, as he sparked another joint.

"Good show. What'll we do now?" Answering the question, he

stepped inside the tower, loosed the Navy kerchief, and pulled the jumper over his head. He spread himself out on the giant bed, the joint between pinched fingers. "It's hot," he said. "Here. Take it."

"I think I'm stoned already." High on the Fourth of July on more than marijuana, I fell to the floor on my knees.

Even if compared to the incomparable Miss Landau, the sailor half out of summer whites was something more than usual to behold. His green eyes—the very color of the bedspread—flickered under copper-color lashes. His navel was a blind third eye. He shone from brow to belly in a breathing sweat, in the beams of the pink and amber spotlights. The bed was a private stage, Mick my leading actor. As if at my direction, he placed his hands behind his head. In the armpits bloomed tender orange tendrils—a patented COREY design.

The impudent nose, the ears, the eyes; the crinkles, dimples, freckles—all were those of Jimmy Corey, a Jimmy Corey grown but still a boy, his latter incarnation there before me. I held my stony breath. Then, rising on my knees, as an acolyte tends toward an altar, I made the solemn vow: *"I want to go all the way with you, McCoy."*

"Go right ahead."

First I removed the polished shoes, slick as patent leather, and placed them side by side. I drew off the sleeves of the long black socks and placed them in the shoes, and paused a long moment before the next momentous step. Reaching forward, I unfastened the fly.

I laid back the stiff laundered flaps, first the left, then the right, and stood to grasp each pantleg by its bell-bottomed cuff. In one smooth motion, like the cloth of a magician, I whisked the white trousers from his legs. Ten thousand red-gold hairs stood up, from his ankles to the hem of his skivvies. There, in the expanded left fork of that frail and accessible garment, lay the part-revealed object of my quest. Would it be anything like Jimmy's—or *more* so? It was more than I dared hope. Perhaps I prayed.

The magnitude of the next imagined act delayed its action. Like the captive of his fragile shorts my heart beat on its rib cage. The minutes passed like hours...that was heavy dope!

"What's keeping you?" asked the sailor.

I spread the vee of the skivvies and skinned them off entirely. I might have gasped. The spotlights converged at the root of the trunk, and *there*—like the needle of a sundial at high noon, like a magnetized bearing to the planet's core—stood a noble member perfectly erect. Neither short nor tall, thin nor stout, but arrow-straight, it was a median of all dimensions, a carnal standard, *a golden mean.* It was uniformly round, delicately veined, and had a polished dome-like cap.

And the testes, twin cherubs worked in living stone, were its firm and enduring foundation. At the monument's base was a frieze of fiery curls, as at a martyr's stake in immolation.

"Why, it's like a little *statue!*" I cried out.

"Yeah, that's what they tell me," Mickey grunted. "Lenny calls it the Saint." He *would* be the one to name it. But his faith would not permit him to perform baptismal rites. That was *my* duty, now.

"Saint *Mick* then! I bless you." I knelt to perform the deed.

A drop of sparkling liquid, clear as dew, had issued from the spotted dome and formed there a magnifying lens. The drop ran down the shaft—a tear of benediction! I bent to kiss the Saint. Presently a warm, life-giving liquor refreshed the earnest convert.

I sank back on my haunches to regard the saint within the context of his parent body, bathed in mystic light. The skin wore an alien flush, a fine supernal radiance; and while Mickey himself had passed into a meditative state, the Saint yet stood steadfast on his rocks of faith.

"Why don't you get into bed?" said Mickey in a whisper. I turned off the lights, turned back the sheets, and lay down close beside him, face-to-face. "I like to sleep with someone," he said, his hand beginning to explore me, my own sweeping up and down his back.

That was my first shared night in that bed of amazing encounters. But the bedroom—was it really a ship's cabin, even with a live sailor there? The Saint, the act of worship and its consequent reward, our platform in its ring of pointed windows, made the room a kind of...chapel. A Seafarers Chapel by the sea! A space benignly shaped to our special kind of service...what could be more perfect than that?

At the end of the pier the ship's bell tolled, and from a long ago reading of *The Tempest,* in the days of Eagle Rock High, the lines came drifting back to me:

Full fathom five thy father lies
Of his bones are coral made
Those are pearls that were his eyes
Nothing of them that doth fade,

But doth suffer a sea-change
Into something rich and strange
Sea nymphs hourly ring his knell:
  "Ding-dong!"
Hark! Now I hear them—ding-dong bell.

What would little Starkey make of that?

As though at that bell's summons, sailors from the carrier began to stream down the ramp, some in taxis, a few in private cars, others with the shuffling stride of drunkenness. A body thudded hard against a carousel wall; window-glass tinkled on the sidewalk.

"Knock it off, Jackson!" a sailor shouted.

"Get this sucker *off* me, man," the voice was rich bass Negro. "Or I fix his ass for *good.*"

"Leave him alone, Price."

"He started it, the pig-fucker."

"Wipe the blood off your nose. Not on your *sleeve*, goddamnit."

"Lemme yours."

"Bleed then. Let's boogie."

Leonard knew whereof he spoke.

30.

The morning air was clear, free of cloud, smelling only of the salt Pacific. A hole in the view at mid-distance showed where the carrier had been. My sailor was still with me. He awoke and rubbed his fingers through his hair, alive with natural oils and rusty highlights.

"What's to eat?" he asked, boy-like.

"What *else?* Well, there's Leonard's downstairs deli. Kippers, lox, bagels, beer. Olives, cheese, pastrami. And frozen rye bread. We've also got some eggs."

"I remember now. When I was here last. Do you think he's got strange tastes?"

"Meaning you?" I watched him jump up naked and scamper down the stair. I made the bed and gathered clothes, putting things in drawers, the way a person will when he wants a friend to stay. On the rug I found the skivvies with their black service stencil: MC CRORY, M.J. He was not the real McCoy after all! Not that it mattered now. The important things were genuine enough. He called me down to breakfast.

Mickey had laid plates of scrambled eggs on the plank table, milk and catsup, too. He sat bare-skinned with his feet on the bench, the centerpiece of the buffet. He didn't dress for meals? That was all right with me. I couldn't take my eyes from his mobile Irish face and busy hands, his energetic body. There was joy in Mickey's every move for both of us.

It was a breakfast not soon forgotten—so near, so far from home.

At ten the music started. It could interrupt my work but not my pleasure. It was time to get away. I knew exactly where—to a little mountain stream up a canyon, a place not unlike Big Tujunga, a place hardly anyone knew; one that Mick could appreciate, too. He took some old clothes—his own I realized—from a closet, and began the act of getting dressed. He addressed the full-length mirror while I, the second witness, sat with a beer at the table.

First the drying—no, the *patting* of the skin after his shower, and the thorough examination this entailed. Then the vigorous stroking of the muscles, scouring of the hollows, and the rubbing of the scalp till the hairs stood out in tendrils, hanging in his eyes. He showed the whites of his teeth as he combed the red hair forward to the eyelash line, cut it with a comb—a little to the left, and flung it back both sides. The longer side he worked into place, all but the hairs of the cowlick.

"Leonard's pretty funny," he was saying at the time. "Once his wig came off in bed while he was doing it. After that he made a turban to wear around the house." He artfully displaced a few strands.

"He got a Turkish dressing gown and pointed slippers. From the Wardrobe Department, naturally." Mickey rolled a pair of Navy socks, unrolled them up his ankles, rolled a T-shirt to the sleeve-holes, and sheathed his trunk in the same fashion, with a final tug at the buttocks. Like putting on a *condom*, I couldn't help but think.

"He bought a hookah from Morocco. Lenny really goes all the way." Mick stepped inside his blue jeans, pulled them up and smoothed the legs. He gently tucked his scrotum—just so—inside the soft denim flaps, and snapped the halves together. Hanging out like a rubber-necking tourist, the Saint, I suspected, would be last.

"Do you smoke hash, Mick?" He did a total re-check in the mirror.

"Whatever I can get. Like anything else, you know? I don't much like to drink, though." That was bad news—we had conflicting habits. Alcohol and hashish didn't mix. Mickey sucked in his waist, flexed his narrow hips, and flipped his pride-and-joy into the pantleg, easily as an angler nets a fish. I bagged the uniform for him to put on later.

Once afoot in the wilderness, I found the dirt road and then the secret trail that led us to the tree-shrouded pool.

"Where are you taking me, buddy?"

"Away from the city. Back to nature."

"Do you think I'll be safe? There's a wasp."

"They only sting when they're hurt."

The pool was shallow, stagnant in the summer heat. On the black mud bottom floated clouds of green algae aswarm with darting tadpoles—giant sperm. Dragonflies flew about like aimless helicopters.

"It's sure dry here," said Mick, "like just before a fire."

"We'd jump in the water then."

"I don't feel like swimming. It's dirty, and it stinks."

Perhaps it could never be the same as the first time, in any human experience. But the sandy boulders, *they* were okay, smooth and dappled under branches, a little too warm to the touch. We took off our clothes, as I had *then*. Mickey folded his and sprawled out on a rock, in alternate sunshine and shadow, and let the Saint enjoy the view. Despite the visual distraction I could still hear the story that Mick was laying out.

Now *his* dad, it seemed, had not been around long, either. His father had been flattened by a tractor when the boy was only four. And his mother—she'd run off with a farm machinery salesman to upper New York State. The people at Welfare had placed him first in an orphanage, then as a ward of the court in a series of foster homes.

In the first he'd been liked too much by the mother, causing friction in the home. In the second he was treated too fondly by the man of the house; then by the teenage daughter of a third. At sixteen he'd joined the Navy. The last set of foster parents had faked the papers for him. Though he had problems in the service, it was still a better home than all the rest. It was cleaner, for one thing, and he had his own space.

"I think I'll get wet," said Mickey, rising, "and cool myself off." His heat-expanded, drooping member hung inches from my thirsty eyes.

"Would you like to do anything else first?" I said, throat hoarse and dry. He picked me up and pitched me in the pond. I stood thigh deep, dredged a gob of muck, and slung it where he lived. "Hey, *sailor*. You're out of uniform!" I yelled. He jumped in. We rolled in the bubbling ooze like crocodiles.

"You boys enjoying yourselves?" inquired an authoritative voice. The voice of authority wore a Smokey Bear outfit and whistle. The man also carried a gun.

"We were looking for something I lost," I said, rinsing mud.

"You won't find it here." He was lighting a pipe. "This here is a *protected* area. You'd better clear out, before I write you up for trespassing. Or poaching out of season." He smiled a knowing smile.

"We can't leave soon enough," said Mick as he pissed a yellow rainbow in the torpid pool.

In uniform again, he got out at County Line, and stuck his head back in the window, the hat cocked on his brow. "See you Friday," Mickey said, "at eighteen hundred." He walked ten feet and jerked out his thumb. I left him. In the rear-view mirror I saw a Jaguar slow and stop. Already I was jealous of its driver.

31.

"And how was your Independence Day, Jerry?" said Linda at the range, apron and hair astray—her Cinderella act. In one arm she held the baby and his bottle. "Here, you can take him for a while. He wouldn't go to sleep all night." He was heavy, too, and gaining every minute.

"Oh, the fireworks were okay, I guess. Nothing new, really. A ship came in, a carrier, with a whole lot of sailors on board. Civilians, too. I spent the night down there because of heavy traffic. Then this morning I had to look at property, a place with a pool. I met the agent." White lies *perhaps*—but think of feelings spared! "He hasn't set a price on it, yet."

"You should have seen it here. It was wild! The neighbors had some fireworks from Mexico. Randy and Casey went crazy. And Brenda drank too much beer, of course, and got sick." Linda brought out some paper plates. "She said they were smoking marijuana down there. I hope the children won't get into anything like that."

"Lord forbid!"

"She's a fink," said Starkey. "They tore each other's clothes off. We saw a lot of ass."

"Some boobies, too," said Steve. "Big ones!"

"What a way to talk," said their mother, frying wieners. "You should learn to respect the human body."

"Yeah, wait until you're married, boys. *All* of it's sacred then."

"I guess I won't get married for a while," said Starkey. "I think I'll get myself an apartment and play the field."

"You got plenty of time to look around," Stevie said.

Linda dished out potato salad.

"You look relaxed for a change," said Linda, when we once more found ourselves in the same bed. "You can get up tonight and feed the baby. I've had it, thank you very much."

"All right," I agreed. "Which story are you reading?"

"Rumpelstiltskin."

"About the girl with golden hair who lures a prince into her tower?"

She nodded. Was it *my* tower she was thinking of?

"A likely story. You'll have to get your hair done first." She'd have to dye it red. For one thing.

"I certainly would, if I had the time to run around that you do."

I didn't really mind the night shift. It was probably a father's duty. Lying awake until Casey began to scream would give me time to think, something I hadn't done too much of lately. It was time, yes, more than time for a good hard look at life's daily ledger, before too many pages flipped by. Or somebody tampered with the books. A little introspection was what I needed. A deep, soul-searching look at my inner reality. What *did* it all mean, anyway—the whole gigantic ball of sticky wax? Recalling tests I'd passed at Eagle Rock, and after, I undertook a speculative self-examination:

PART A. Existential evaluation. Score 5 for each section:

   1. Compare the nocturnal emissions in the tower

*chamber experienced by the following participating
partners:*
   a. Melody Landau and Buster Mirador
   b. Mickey McCrory and Jeremy Carr
   c. Mickey McCrory and Leonard Faircycle

That was simple. There *was* no comparison.

2. True or False. Circle one letter only of each pair:

T F *In the above-mentioned encounter of McCrory
and Carr, greater pleasure was experienced than in
that of Carr and Corey.*

T F *Greater than with Buck Willock*

T F *More fun than Linda Lee Fedderman*

The first two I could decide in the affirmative. On the last I would
suspend judgment. Its subject snoozed at my elbow.

*PART B. Word comprehension and vocabulary quiz.
Score 10 points for each section:*

*1. Compare the described nature of the character,
Mickey McCrory, to any three of the following in
consecutive order of choice:*

   a. a field of daffodils
   b. a summer's day
   c. a living firework
   d. a blaze of glory
   e. a joy forever

c. was good, *d.* better, *e.* the best *(e, d, c)*

*2. Relate the description of the personage, St. Mick,
to any of the listed phenomena. Select two:*

   a. a lightning rod
   b. a tower of power
   c. a Holy Entity
   d. a tool of the Devil
   e. a feast for the gods

There was hardly time to choose, c or e, as I flew on to the next test
question:

3. Sentence completion. 20 points. Select the word that best satisfies the meaning of the passage:

The subjective feeling both foreseen, experienced, and physically demonstrated in respect to the above referenced Saint was one of _____ .

horror, fear, loathing, hatred, revulsion, pity, aversion, annoyance, acceptance, accommodation, affection, respect, admiration, adoration, adulation, exaltation, ecstacy, love, loss

Love. To say the least.

PART C. Verbal analogies. Score 15 for each item:

1. Oral orientation. Choose from below the phrase that best parallels the concept, pink and pulsing:
   a. rare and juicy
   b. rough and ready
   c. willing and able
   d. firm and vibrant
   e. symmetrical and pure
   f. upright and devoted
   g. red, rowdy and delectable

My hasty mental pencil encircled every one.

2. Describe in a hundred thousand words or less: What is a penis?

I had no time for the essay-type question. I threw down the pencil and raced to the shower to furiously masturbate. I came once, then again. I had not even turned on the water—hot or cold—in that dry, reverberating shower stall. Nor had I paused to reckon the score of the examined self. Whatever the sum, it had a value beyond ready calculation.

When I came back to the bedroom, the baby had started to cry. I searched for the bottle without finding it while Casey kept on sobbing.

"Can't you be patient for a *little* while?" asked my wife's voice from the darkened bed. I knew from its inflection it was me that she addressed. I groped in the dark for an answer.

"Patience is a two-way street, you know."

"Jerry, you'd try the patience of a *saint*."

32.

That same week the Colonel again returned from Florida. As before, his estranged wife Martha was not with him, but the two children were. Philip was a frail suspicious youth in glasses and not, it was apparent at once, in line with his father's concept of the name—that of the Macedonian conqueror. Philip had a disquieting head of bright red curls, an inheritance, I was told, from the mother.

Valery, a year younger, was pretty in a slim athletic way, extremely animated, and what the father liked to call "a real live wire." Everett was looking better, too. It was clear that he drew support from his children. Now he had his own troops in the field.

As the two families picnicked on the beach, Everett told Linda the history of Fort Myers, Dry Tortugas, the Caribbean. Steve would teach Philip how to surf—so he said. The girls were of the same age and interests. Only Starkey felt a little out of it. He would be a mascot when the others chose—like Randy. Like me, he was a misfit at the party. As they talked I catalogued excuses for the forthcoming Friday night.

"I have to see a client," I told Linda. "I hate to have to do it on a weekend night, but a collection's due."

"Collect it while you can," she advised, in a small advance from her bank of wifely wisdom. "You may not always have the opportunity."

"A client isn't always in the mood, you understand. They don't always have the funds ready, either."

"A good client's rare. I know that, Jerry. You don't find one every day." What the hell! Was she kidding too? And just how much *did* she know?

"There aren't many around like Everett." There. That settled it.

"There's hardly any need to be jealous, you know."

"I guess you're right again, Linda Lee."

Jumpy with anticipation I scoured my teeth and gargled, showered twice, and shaved, nicking my chin with the razor. Would Mickey be there? Or wouldn't he? And how about the Saint? Suppose they *both* caught the duty at Mugu? I didn't even drink before getting in the car. It was no ordinary cock I was about to suck.

I was at the pier an hour early, while the carousel still clanged its boring tunes. I adjusted all the windows and smoothed the green bedspread. What a contrast to Mickey's pink and orange! Then I dusted all the plants, whispering sweet nothings to the palm fronds. The ferns were a healthy yellow-green. I flicked dust from the masks along the staircase, and gave the one that had worn Mickey's hat a love tap. At last I took a stance at the window, chin cupped in hands, legs spread behind like the props of a surveyor's transit.

A white sailor suit was raised upon the ramp crest, a hat, the tie, jumper, pants. A big hulking swabby—what a downer! He shouldn't even *be* in such an outfit. He tromped down the ramp in a peculiarly insinuating manner, as though he had seized to himself the proper moment for a white-dressed sailor to appear. He cut around the bottom of the ramp and took a passage underneath to the men's public restroom.

A lot of hanky-panky went on there, Leonard had once told me, in vivid and arresting detail. The vice squad was reported to lurk behind holes in hollow walls, prepared to shackle any non-respecter of California's penal code. If this intruding sailor were caught in some misdeed, real or purported, it would only be what he had asked for. In a few moments he came out again, adjusting his fly, and vanished beneath the slab of ramp to reappear along the farther promenade. He was probably getting ready for a date. No one wants to take a piss the minute he gets inside his girl's house.

As though my ears had ceased their function, a sudden void of silence drained the air. The carousel had stopped—*six o'clock*. There was nothing to see or hear. I turned away and tuned the stereo. Then *Mickey* was in sight, halfway down the ramp, covering the intervening sidewalk in clean jaunty strides, as though upon the open decks of a seagoing vessel, his hair a red flag in the sunset.

I leaned out to yell as he passed below the window, but Mickey strode on beyond the stair, and turned at the corner. What did that mean? He wasn't *lost*. I looked out one side, then the other. I ran downstairs around the building, peering into every nook like a player in a game of hide-and-seek. But there was no Mick McCrory to be seen. Maybe it was all an illusion, a wishful waking dream. Things *had* gotten a little out of hand lately. I hauled myself upstairs again, dejected. There sat Mickey at the table, cleaning a lid of grass.

"I thought you'd never come," I panted.

"I had to make a call around the corner." I had heard about that nearby apartment—Glenn and Glenda's—the brother-sister team of local druggists. "Here's a little gift for me and you." I had another rival now—his dope. Mickey licked a white Tops paper, stuck it in my lips and lit it, then took it back again for long hard draws, sucking in his stomach as his lungs stretched. He rolled two more. "Let's go upstairs," he said, holding smoke, exhaling.

This time he stripped off all his clothes, as though in quarters, and stacked them in a neat square by the bed. I took off all of mine, Linda's watch included, and we stood in dusky light as the joint passed back and forth. When the tip burned our fingers, Mickey dropped the roach on his tongue and gulped, like a frog that has just caught a bug.

About the standing human male in full erection there is something of the comically grotesque: he can neither stand still nor run away. Tumescent males together are more peculiar still, some atavistic purpose reasons for us, as in the often-heard expression—*fuck or fight*. Arms and legs entangling, we flung each other on the bed. I couldn't grip Mickey's body close enough. And the *Saint!* Red, ready, and delectable, he was a harbinger of pure devotion and delight.

"Let's try it this way," said Mickey, husky-voiced. He turned a full one-eighty, locked on me as me to him, and made our circle of the flesh complete. I never knew which of us came first—it seemed to go on happening for a long, long time. "I thought you'd never come," said Mickey finally, as we lay close as brothers in the faded light.

That was another big step, for me at least, on the steep ladder down from the topside world of normal sexuality.

Once a person is known in a carnal way, all else seems to follow without effort. Along with the cover of protective clothing, fears and reservations have been cast aside; speech becomes as effortless as breathing. Our communication didn't need many words. We were learning our own body language.

We lounged about naked, had some beers and a dinner; smoked some more, played some records, and then like friends of long acquaintance, went up the stairs to bed.

Mickey stayed on through the weekend.

33.

Upon my eventual return to it, the house was dull and silent. I heard only the crash of waves on the shore below—the promise of our marriage being dashed upon the sands of time. I went about the task of unloading bags of groceries—half-hearted offerings to neglected kids and wife. It would take more than tasty proteins and extra carbohydrates to shore up that shaky estate.

Two of the cats woke up as I came in, yawned, stretched, and sidled to the kitchen for their din-din. They rubbed against my pants cuff, mewing and fawning; but behind their cynical affections I saw their true feelings—those of scorn and disillusion, like the rest. I threw them each a chop.

I made a man-size drink and watched the evening TV. In a plush-couched contemporary-looking living room, a set, famous actors were entertaining one another. They enjoyed each other's jokes, oblivious to fifty million house guests, one of them myself. Starkey came in and sat down on the coffee table, joining us. In the light of the flickering tube he appeared to be gnawing on a bone.

"What did you kill, kid?"

"A spare rib. We had a barbeque next door. Everett cooked it. And Valery played her records. They're groovy. You should have been there."

"I'm not so sure about that."

"Where were you, anyway?"

"Oh, I had to get together with a friend out on the pier, a kind of reunion. I had the fresh seafood. Delicious!"

"Who was your friend?"

"A clergyman. Someone you wouldn't know."

"I don't much care for seafood myself. Except tuna, in tuna sandwiches."

"This wasn't tuna. But we did have a sandwich." Jesus Christ! *This* kid was no dummy. Lay off, Jerry. You dopehead.

"You sound a little weird. Maybe you spend too much time there."

"Who's to say?" And who's to *know?*

"You'll see. I think I'll go to bed now." Starkey left. The gnawed bone lay congealed on the table—like Adam's rib.

On the assumption that its status had not been radically changed, I went to the bedroom and rummaged in the closet, and found there remnants of our Halloween. I got into one of Linda's nightgowns and the frilled lace cap for her curlers, and perched her pair of granny glasses on the wolf mask that I'd found. I crawled under the alpaca by the reading lamp and held—in two rubber paws—a large picture book, the page turned to a portrait of Red Riding Hood at a critical moment of her house-call. As I waited I replayed my new memory tapes, those of the lost weekend I had found above the carousel. I had a new swelling of the groin, and put my knees up.

Oddly enough, Linda was carrying a basket when she came in, the one that carried her knitting. Linda put it down and shook her head.

"I imagine that's meant to be amusing," she said.

"Be glad I'm not a real one."

"I wish you were a real one! What the hell *are* you, Jerry?"

"A sheep in wolf's clothing."

"You can say that again."

"And who the hell are you?"

"I thought I was your wife."

"Think again, precious, before I eat you up alive."

"I don't think you're man enough to do it."

I leaped from the bed and seized her in my hairy rubber paws. But she simply stood there rigid, entirely undelectable. Not rigid—*frigid* was the word that came to mind. My wife was frigid. That explained everything, including my behavior of the past few weeks. I had been driven to it—by her frigidity. I returned the icy stare.

"It's only a matter of time now, isn't it?" said Linda, as a tear formed in the corner of her eye. I visualized it dripping down her nose, suddenly sharp and pointed and turning to an icicle, like a sad picture in her book. But my comic vision failed me. This woman was really hurt!

"I'm sorry, Linda. I really, really am. I just had to get away for a while, to really think things out. You see, I wasn't sure how much I was actually needed here, now that Everett's back. You get on so well together."

The tear had stopped mid-track. "And whom do *you* get on with?" The ice was turning to fire! She had easily finessed my contrition card, a deuce in our little game of Hearts.

"Right now, I can't even get along with myself." There. The basic Mother Instinct Test. Would she pass it?

"That makes it unanimous then." She hadn't even tried!

"Well *fuck* it! What's the use of even *being* here? I might as well not be around."

"Go wherever you want to, Jerry. I'm going to go to bed."

"Where's the little baby we used to see around here?"

"I put him in with Brenda. He's asleep."

Linda went to the bathroom. I heard the shower run. It was no use even putting on a scene now. I got out of the absurd costume—that would lead to more trouble, driving, if I were stopped by the patrol —and put together all of my preferred belongings, as though in preparation for a six-month trip abroad. I had everything but my passport. I took that, too. There was no making sure when I would see the warmly-textured walls of those mellow rooms again.

I cried a little, leaving. The pier, when I arrived, looked utterly deserted. It dripped with heavy dew. Through a thickening mist the foghorn bellowed, and the bell tolled seven times.

34.

At ten the music started. It permeated the tower as it dominated the pier. The day was overcast, cool but humid—the mountains, sea and sky steeped in grey. Gulls wheeled beyond the windows and sat upon the sills. Their cries, harsh and raucous, were those of scavengers at best.

And the apartment. Stuffed with tacky furniture, it looked hokey and contrived, the make-believe playpen of one more Hollywood queen. Even the plants had wilted. I watered them but didn't speak. They could think their own green thoughts that Monday morning, or listen to the music smite the walls.

But the noisome center of distraction where I chose to dwell had two restoring elements about it: my photo file and drawing board. I could save myself through work. Until Friday came.

Mick appeared on Friday in his usual carefree mood, had a joint to make it freer, and felt more liberated still when told that I had taken a fixed residency, that I could never go home again if I had any pride at all.

After that he came down often, whenever he got away. He had other offers on the highway; but the tower, as it had for me, became his refuge too. We would climb the stair to watch the night fall, a kind of vesper hour when the carousel was dumb; or do our special thing together, sometimes on the floor.

Or sometimes we dressed to see a movie, drive to Hollywood, or cruise the Sunset Strip. Nightclubs once crowded by the movie set carried new acts on their banners: The Byrds, The Animals, The Doors. At shops full of black lights and posters, Mick could buy any kind of pipe or paper he might wish. Their illicit use, the risks of getting busted, were what really turned him on. He said he felt like a gambler rolling for high stakes.

The clubs and gay bars refused to serve him liquor. Even though he might be more than welcome, he would never pass for a legal twenty-one if the vice squad came around. So he might as well use dope. It was hard to argue with such reasoning. I wished I were that age myself.

When Mick drove us home into thick coastal fog, I had time to look at others hitching rides. No matter how appealing, he never picked them up, and I would stare instead at miles of blank-front buildings that had the look of backlot scenery, as though nothing lived beyond the gleaming street. Then ahead would be the lights of the tower, a beacon in the fog, the foghorn booming; and I would think of the house to the north, that now-vanished lantern in the dusk.

On nights when the cloud closed around us, extinguishing the world ashore, the old wood structure creaked and sighed to the strain of unseen tides. On those nights we slept very close.

One hot August day Mickey got off early, stripped on arrival, and went up above for a smoke. I was finishing a drawing when a modest sort of tapping came low upon the door.

"Can I come in?" asked Starkey with two ice cream cones. "One's for you."

We took wicker chairs and began to cool our tongues by the window. The fan turned idly, stirring flies, and the palm fronds waved in tropic heat.

"You know what it reminds me of?" the boy began. "An old-fashioned drugstore in the movies, with those funny tables and chairs. All you need is Coca-Cola signs and candy jars. Did you know Coca-Cola was a drug?"

"A long time ago, yes. That's why they called them drugstores, and Coca-Cola, coke. A marble soda fountain would be nice."

"And a soda jerk. Whose clothes are those?" He nodded.

"Oh, that's a painting outfit, for a job."

"A sailor suit?"

"It's only navy surplus. Here, I'll stash it in the closet. How's the family?"

"Mom? She's fine, and the baby. The rest of us went down to Ocean Park. Phil and Valery had to go on all the rides. They're down below on the Merry-Go-Round.

I imagined I heard Mickey's bare feet on the staircase. *That* would be a stunning introduction—Mickey bounding bare-ass to the floor, the irrepressible St. Mick ahead of him. We'd have to get up, I supposed....

"Starkey? I'd like to have you meet my clergyman friend, Saint Nicholas." They would be at almost equal eye level. But no, in deference to the other's higher station, it ought to go the other way around:

"Saint Mick, allow me to present my stepson here, young Starkey." Correct protocol, although bizarre. What then? They couldn't very well *shake hands,* could they?

"Pleased to meet you," the boy might say. But Starkey was no hypocrite. I could be busted on a felony charge right there—corrupting the morals of a minor—by wrong-righting agents of the vice squad bursting Dick Tracy style through the splintered door. *The Crime-Stoppers!* Maybe Leonard would have known how to handle it.

Those were footsteps in the hall. The doorknob rattled.

"Hello, everybody!" shouted Brenda. "I caught the brass ring. Everybody got free rides!" The other three filed in behind her, nice-looking kids in clean shirts and blue jeans, tennis shoes and suntans. Philips's nose had peeled.

"What an extraordinary place!" exclaimed Valery. "You do have a way with things, Mr. Carr. It reminds me of Fort Myers, the Officers Club. They flew the cast-iron furniture from New Orleans, and the walls were pecky cypress. It really *does* have charm!" Her auburn hair fluttered in the fan's slow breeze.

"Oh, where does this go?" cried Brenda, following the parade of painted masks up the staircase. "These are really ugly. Barf!"

"That's my private *retreat,* Brenda!" But she was already in it, the others close behind. I heard only the beat of the Merry-Go-Round, but I saw in mind, upon the green slab of bed, my laid-out, live-in naked sailor boy, the resourceful St. Mick in charge of things, the tour group at a respectful distance. I crept on up the stair.

"It's a *marvelous* view, Mr. Carr. How did you ever manage it?" That was Valery again. Except for these young strangers, the bed, in fact the chamber, was unoccupied.

"You might call it an act of fate."

"It's so romantic here I don't know how I'd *stand* it."

"It's so romantic here I don't know how I'd live," said Brenda.

"Do you always want to live on a pier, Mr. Carr? Was it your idea or Linda's?" How could Philip ask such a thing—the snit!

"My idea entirely, son. I thought I'd stay down here and face the music." That was a Message from Garcia—a dispatch from Carousel Control he could carry to his own C.O.!

"We ought to run along now," Brenda said. "Everett's going to pick us up downtown."

"Thanks for showing us around," said Steve. "We'll tell Mom all about it."

"Yeah," Starkey added, "she can't wait to hear. Take it easy, Jerry."

"Anyway I can, kid," was the tired, trustless reply.

No sooner had the door shut than I raced back up the staircase, three steps at a bound. There lay Mickey like a skinned opossum, a pillow between his legs, squirming on the bed in silent laughter.

"Where the hell have you been?"

"Did you miss me, Jerry? I wasn't dressed for company. I was getting some air on the roof." Stuck like a squatting gargoyle on a tower of Notre Dame! I sat beside him to watch the children climb the ramp, Starkey in the gutter far behind.

"The blonde girl's cute. Is she your daughter?"

"My wife's, first. Why?"

I caught the musk of Mickey's armpit as he laid a sweaty arm on my neck. "I'd kind of like to take her out sometime," he mused, squeezing the pillow in his thighs.

"Then you'll have to ask her father."

"I go for blonde chicks. I think I'm just naturally horny."

"You know what you can do about that."

35.

PISCES (Feb. 20–Mar. 20) A fortunate time to visit with friends and to make new plans for the future. Repay any social obligations you may have—you will be repaid in kind. Opportunity for sea voyage may present itself, but avoid all motion at the time of full moon.

A sea voyage for Pisces! What else was new? I had already scanned the evening paper, its horoscopes and business forecasts, when Mickey brought to the apartment an acquaintance of his own. He and the friend, another sailor, had been drinking or smoking dope or both, judging from their diffident ambiguous remarks, symptoms of a middle-level high.

"Jerry? I want you to meet me good buddy here. My *ass*-hole buddy. This is Yeoman Spencer. Terence. Henderson. Originally of Terrytown, in Tennessee or thereabouts. You can call him by any of those names. Can't he, Henderson?"

"You can call me Terry," said the friendly-looking sailor with a cherub's smile. He had Navy-issue glasses and white uniform, and a reverse-curve kind of figure like a question mark, with a cherub's round stick-out behind. The Navy had not yet turned that figure to an exclamation mark, as it had with most enlisted personnel.

"Terry's got a little surprise for us, Jerry. Something he's been saving, just for tonight. Why keep us all in suspense here? Why not go ahead and whip it out?"

Reaching deep inside his fly to the very rock bottom of his briefs, Spencer fished out a ball of aluminum foil. "From Casablanca. Grade A Numero Uno kief. Or at least good hash." Mick took the ball, unfolded from its wrinkles a lump brown as beeswax, and smelled it with a delicate look. He rubbed it in his palms, broke it into pieces, and laid them in the petals of the foil beside a lighted taper.

From Leonard's closet he brought a tasseled hookah and filled the bowl with wine. That was mellower, he told us. On the living room floor he a made circle of light—votive candles in cups of scarlet glass. Then he took off all his clothes, stacked them as usual, and sat cross-legged at the head of the circle to prepare the water pipe of hashish.

"You can be at ease there, too," he said to Spencer. The good-natured buddy removed all that he wore but his jockey shorts and the thin gold chain of his St. Christopher medal. He sat beside Mick and flexed an arm, stripped but by no means bare.

On a chubby right bicep perched an angry blue eagle, in its talons a snake-like banner. *MOTHER*—the pink ribbon read. The opposite forearm had a marcelled lady with bee-stung ruby lips, the name *ANN* linked within a bleeding heart to the initials *S.T.H.* On that bicep was a standard skull-and-bones above the legend: *U.S. NAVY–DO OR DIE!* The death's-head had a rose in its teeth. On the crest of each shoulder sat a butterfly, and his nipples were labeled HOT and COLD.

"It's not exactly what I wanted," Terry apologized. "I asked for Atlantic and Pacific, but I didn't have the dough."

"He got drunked up in Dago," said Mick, molding hashish in the sieve. "They threw him in the brig."

"Yeah, my *tits* were still bleeding."

I still wore my jeans, but with only a few moles and a pimple to show, I felt naked. "What's next?" I asked the tattooed sailor.

"I dunno. Maybe a sub across the chest here. Or maybe just some waves with the periscope up, or a Chinese dragon down the back. The Navy don't like to have you do it anymore. It spoils their image, they say."

We sat within the circle jungle fashion, knee-to-knee, as Mick sucked on the hose with hollow cheeks.

"I read about a sailor, an admiral," I began, "who had a whole fox-hunt on his skin. The hunters and their horses went around his chest three times, and the hounds around his waist." As a fleck of ash grew on the lump, Mickey took a drag and held it. "All you saw of the fox was his brush. The rest was up the admiral's rear end."

"A Rear Admiral!"

Exhaling slowly, Mickey passed the ivory tip. Terry puffed and started coughing. "You want to see the rest of it?" he gasped.

"I've already seen it about a thousand times, every time we shower up in quarters. Show Jerry."

Terry stood up and pulled down his shorts and stretched out the sheath of his penis. *NORTH POLE* was printed on the top side and *SOUTH POLE* underneath it. On the tender sac of each testicle was a staring blue eyeball without lashes. The penile tip had a portrait, that of a horsefly at rest.

"I never saw anything like it," I said.

"And you probably won't again." Terry pulled up his shorts. "I had to be passed out when they did it. I couldn't screw for a month."

"In Japan all the gangsters used to get tattooed, the *yakuza*," I recited from a book on the art. "The tattoos were like suits all over their bodies, except for the hands and feet. They used to show them off at public baths."

"*Hey*, that's what I'll do next hitch!" cried Terry. "I'll go to all the baths in Yokohama."

"And get yourself massaged all over, Spencer. *Gee*-sha girls."

"They can fly their flag from *my* pole anytime."

"...After the gangsters died, or got killed, the others peeled their skins off. They cured them and kept them around the house. Like works of art, you know?"

"Christ!" Spencer said, nearly choking, as Mickey slapped him hard on the back. His hornrim glasses bounced across the floor.

"Pull yourself together there, Henderson. Here. Take another toke."

I reached out for the glasses, but Mick said not to bother—he only wore them to look smart. We smoked up the rest of the hashish...

...In a Bombay station—a tunnel of curly steel—swarmed twenty thousand white-robed Hindus. Some rode away in shuttered carriages. Others turned into white-trousered sailors running the length of a hangar deck—longer, mightier, *steelier*, than any football field. The sailors became wheeling gulls. I saw squadrons of paper gliders, flights of Ping-Pong balls... Were my eyes shut or open? In either case, should they be kept that way? Stealthily I raised an eyelid...

Two ruby lights still flickered, the candles guttering out. Terry's head nodded on the HOT and COLD taps. Where was Mick?

A hot breath spun my head around. There it was—eye to polished eyeball—a black face straight from Hell! Teeth set in a vicious grin, brass ring through the nostrils, rivets through the forehead, on top of that a red rope wig—just what I might have expected! Mickey dropped the witch-doctor's mask. Like a broken kewpie doll, Terry had keeled over sideways.

"Let's haul him up the stairs," said our leader. "He wouldn't want to wake up like that."

How did any of us want to wake up? Between sheets, I was trapped between two swabbies, neither in the rightest state of mind. Pressed against Terry's cheeks on one side, by Mickey against mine on the other, I was snug as a bug in a rug, warm as a wiener in a bun...but wait. What dull probing presence blundered there? Certainly not the Saint!

"I don't think I can do that, Mick. It's gonna *hurt*."

"Go ahead," he hissed. "Let it in."

"*OUCH!*"

"Relax, goddamnit, you're stoned enough. Stop thinking."

His hand began to rub me with a pungent oil; the motion soothed me forward as his pressure pained me aft. A thrust drove me deep into his mate's cherubic rump; I thought of peaches, melons, breasts.

"Go on," Mick said harshly. "He likes it." And drove me home— through a ring of unbelievable snugness. "Grab his crank. Thaa-at's it. Now we're wired."

Whose grunts? Whose groans? Whose sighs of pleasure, whose sweaty juices intermingled there? I felt three different spasms—then the bed lay still. It was a dirty joke come true, a pain and pleasure sandwich, a triple trial and error—but I'd *liked* it.

Suppose—by wild mischance—Buster Mirador had been watching from the stairwell? Our slippery skins would be worthless as wet rat pelts! What did Terry feel? He didn't stir. And how would Mick look now—if I faced him? Would I catch a carefree Irish grin? Or the baleful eye of evil—like the mask of jungle terror down below? That would be *the real McCoy* of a radically different order! I did not look around. I fell into a narcotized sleep as filigrees fled across my eyelids.

I woke at Terry's back—a wall of buff waiting for its mural. Here and there were traces of Mickey's color—orange, stains of Leonard's Mantan Lotion. Terry's backside already wore designs — on each round cheek the three-bladed screw of an oceangoing capital vessel. The North-South polar axis bent to no particular direction; the horsefly at its tip appeared to doze.

A morning smog obscured the tower windows. Our ship lay becalmed in the doldrums, belayed in the horse latitudes. Three bells.

36.

The summer and its pleasures were drawing to a close. The holiday I had least needed to celebrate, Labor Day, came soon. The beaches would be beautiful but vacant. Then Halloween again, Christmas, another year. I couldn't believe it. How long had I known Mickey—intimately, that is? Two short months. And how many times had we done it? I counted the calendar's red circles: just twenty-nine. The circles were less frequent there of late.

In return for these encircled squares, I had loaned Mickey money from time to needful time, and sometimes the keys to the car. I knew where most of the dollars went—to the sibling pharmacists and their unfranchised drugstore. But where did he go in the Fury? He'd be back in an hour, he would promise, but that hour would always be the darkest, just before a sleepless dawn. He might arrive then, red-eyed, out of cash and cigarettes, with barely time to hitch a ride to Point Mugu.

Had Mick another interest? Probably so. How could any human heart, however dulled and satiated, fail to beat in strong affection for this paragon of red-haired sailor boys?

Who could the monster be—a young executive? A movie star, a starlet? Or a pampered homosexual at the top of Beverly Hills with an Olympic-size pool full of frolicking male nudists, Greek statues all around it, a garageful of imported sports cars. How could I, a struggling artist in a bedlam of crazy sounds, compete with anything so grandiose as that?

But the idea wasn't realistic. Why would he come to the pier then, to share good times with me? My worry was abstract, a fear that someone else would take him. My jealousy as yet had no object. What form would that object take?

Now, when a sailor suit skimmed the crest of the ramp at sunset, it would not always be that of Fireman E-4 McCrory, or that of a uniformed stranger, but one that belonged to that jolly jack tar, Yeoman Spencer Terence Henderson, a Petty Officer Third Class. Terry eased the anxious hours of waiting there for Mick.

He made few demands of any kind. He was content to lie back with a beer and a smoke and simply be allowed to talk. His speech took on the lilting native rhythm of Appalachian hill folk, a manner descending from Elizabethan times. *Dith-y-ram-bic* might be a dictionary term for it, but his words had their own way about them and made a soothing music to my ears. Listening to Terry in narration was as pleasant a pastime as watching Mick in action.

"Now my mom, she was *nice*," a Terry story would begin, perhaps in the Seafarers Chapel. "She always took my side in everything, and stood up strong against my dad. My daddy though, he was *tall*, and one mean bastard at that. Poor, too. We never had much money in the hills. There ain't no gold there, only coal. Somebody else's, too."

"Our clothes we wore one of us after the other. The meals was worse than in the Navy, and all we had to sleep in was this one tiny *room*. Me, my mom and daddy and my brothers. Wet nights the chickens come inside, too."

"Now my older brother Tom, he was just about four*teen* then, he had to bunk with little Tim and me. And you know what, Jerry? He'd try to poke me in our bed *every night*. Usually while Mom and Dad were doing it, so they couldn't hear the noise. *Stop that*, I would say to Tom, but not too *loud*, naturally. I didn't want Daddy to get down on me, too. I didn't want Timmy to hear, either. I think he just pre*tended* to sleep. Playing possum, don't you know? Like he's afraid he might be next. I sure *will*, my brother Tom would say, just as soon as I get quit of school. And that was three more years, if he could even graduate!

"Then Dad, he used to beat me in the daytime, not 'cause I was *bad*. Just for something to do when he was feeling down, like. It was getting kind of tiresome, Dad belting me by day and Tom poking me at night, *nice* as my mother used to treat me. One way or another, my behind was hurting all the *time*.

"So I thought, I was *twelve* then, I thought I'd just run away from home. I done it twice before. So I took Tommy's books, history, geography, math and the rest, and sold them to a man for two bucks. I was going to take off as a carnival hand. The carny was hauling out of there that weekend.

"But my daddy, he found out. He took away my money and went and bought some mule, white lightning, you know? And he come hauling in that night drunk down to his shoes, which was missing, and missed his bed, too. He whips the blanket right off me and Tom and Tim, just as Tommy's doing it.

"*Boy!* he yells, I'm gonna have to whip your *ass* off, like it never been whupped before! And he yanks off his big leather belt. It had brass studs all over it, like he rode a motorcycle, but we didn't even have a car. He wasn't going to beat my brother *Tom*, you know, only little Terry. It wasn't fair. So I skinned right out of bed before he grabbed me. Tom was mad now, too. I reached up on the mantle for the squirrel gun. That was one long rifle. You could punch a squirrel's eye out at a hundred yards.

"I stuck it straight in Daddy's belly and I said, *Dad,* I want my money! He snapped his big belt, like to *hit* me, you know? So I fired off the rifle in his gut. Now *Mom* was angry, too. And my baby brother Tim, he begun to cry hard. Believe me, Jerry, I was *miserable.*

"My mom, she lit the lamp, it was *kero*sene, and before you know it there's the neighbors, Hennesseys and Ables and the Smiths—he's the Sheriff, and my daddy there bleeding up a storm! Me, I'm just standing there buck naked, with the squirrel gun dragging on the floor. It was what they called circumstantial evidence."

Terry had taken off the needless glasses, as though to review the State's exhibit in his head.

"So they took me off and stuck me on the chain-gang. *Me,* just a little bitty twelve-year-old, though I looked older. With all them big buck niggers and the *MAN,* with all his whips. He used to put me in the sweat-box, just for stealing eggs. But the niggers, they were *real* nice. The wouldn't hurt me atall. It was nicer than at home, that part."

While I tried to picture these events, foreign to my experience, Spencer went to get himself another beer.

"So one day," he continued, wetting his larynx, "we're way out in the boonies, patching up some potholes in the road with hot tar. And this one black stud, *Jack,* I think his name was, says *Terry,* you chase on up to that house there and fetch us a bucket of cold water. 'Cause he could see they got a well. He was a kind of foreman to that crew.

"I took the empty bucket, I was thirsty myself, and run up to the house. It was white all over. And this real nice lady, she has a new store dress on, comes up to the front door.

"You just come right on in, child. *Child!* Out there on the fucking chain-ball road gang? She opens up the screen door for me and hustles off to fill the bucket from the inside pump. It was so cool and dark and *nice* in there I didn't want to leave, thirsty as my friends might be. I could spot them through the screen door in the dust, their tongues hanging out like carpets.

"This lady says, why don't you set yourself down, child, and have some of these here biscuits? A whole *pie* tin, with butter running off! I just fixed these for Claude and Wilbur, she says, but I think you need them more. And she brung out some jam and some jelly, *honey*, too, and a glass of ice tea. Wilbur and Claude was her prize beagles, she told me, while I was putting down the tea and biscuits. Their family name was Wright.

"Well, it was hard setting down to that clean table, it had a cloth on it too, while my black buddies was out there sweating in the sun. They were *shining*. But where else would they be, is the way I had it figured.

"Would they like something too? this lady asks. It was too much! They were *criminals*. So I says...Are you still listening, Jerry?...I says, Ma'am, I don't want to go out there *again*. The lady, she don't say nothing, just tears out of the room and runs back with a dress and a bonnet. Here, she says, you go ahead and slip into *these*, child. I hope they fit. They was hers when she was little. So I run out the back door, sort of skipping, while my friends was coming up the front.

"I hopped a freight out to California, not in *those* clothes, naturally. I would of got raped. But they gave me a hard time on the cars all the same. I rode on up to Fresno and learned how to pick peaches. Then a man took me in, he had a ranch, and I got to finish school, almost."

I was thinking less of Terry than of Mickey. It was almost nine, but the Henderson chronicles ran on:

"Then Uncle Sam, he called me to my duty, and I got into my first Navy hitch. This one's the second. I couldn't believe my luck. They put me right into *pig*-boats, diesel subs, and the Captain—he made me his mess boy. To make up his bunk and fetch his chow, you know? *He* used to bugger me, too. Morning, noon, or night, it didn't matter. Sometimes I thought I'd be better off back home. Tom, he'd quit school, and my daddy probably wouldn't beat me anymore. But the skipper, he was nice, and gave me things. Look at this crocodile wallet. It's *real*."

I leafed through the folds of worn leather and the sleeves of warped glassine. They held his I.D., a driver's license, some addresses, and a soiled calling card: I AM PLEASED TO HAVE MADE YOUR ACQUAINTANCE AND

YOUR STORY HAS TOUCHED MY HEART. FUCK YOU VERY MUCH. In other sleeves were wrinkled photographs, a few clipped from magazines, one, the picture of a pig. I flipped to a color snapshot.

"Who's the girl? She's really pretty."

"Oh, that's Ann, the skipper's wife. He gave that to me, too."

Terry hung the wallet on the rear hem of his pants. Mickey wasn't going to show up at all, I guessed, resigning myself to his absence as I brought up four cold beers.

"How was it on submarines, Terry?"

"Not *too* bad. Even with my duties I had it better than the rest. It's cramped, you know? You get sick of smelling sweat and diesel oil when you're weeks out to sea. Then the crew, some of *them* were doing it. There ain't too many places to do it in, Jerry. Nights, they'd go up on deck.

"So one day, we're out in the Pacific, one day this kid who hasn't been aboard too long, and wasn't too smart either, *this* kid comes up to Larry, he's the skipper, and he says, *Captain, sir!* I think we got a little problem here. And he tells how the Electrician's Mate tries to poke him in one of the torpedo holds. I was standing right there to get the skipper's bunk squared away.

"The crew is pretty square in general, sir. But some is pretty *queer.* I think we ought to report it the minute we get back to Pearl! So Larry hangs an arm around the kid and says, you're *right,* son. That's exactly what I think we're gonna do. I'm glad you told me *now.* And he just sets back and cracks his knuckles. That Larry, he was pretty cool.

"About sundown he sends the kid up on deck, we were charging our batteries then, and pretty soon the First Mate pops out of the conning tower, and he's got a pint of rum. So he walks the kid aft and hoists the bottle.

"He says, *Roger,* the kid's name, he says, *Roger,* have a drink. He pulls a long one himself, half the pint, and hands it to the kid. It may not be your *first* drink, he says, but it's going to be your *last.* He comes forward, slams the hatch, and goes below. Then the skipper, he blew the tanks, and the submarine submerged."

I held a beer, speechless.

"After a while we squinted out the 'scope. We couldn't see nothing of Roger, but we *did* see what looked like a bottle. If Roger had a piece of paper he could've left a note."

"Like U.S. Navy, Do or Die?"

"An S.O.S. *Sink or Swim.*"

"What happened to the Captain?"

"Oh, he went back to his wife. They *had* four kids, you know."

"And what happened to you then, Terry?"

"They sent me up to Tripler for surgery. I had a new plastic asshole put in."

Conned again! Couldn't anyone be serious? Except my *wife?* Apart from its lurid ending, the yeoman's bedtime story had lulled me nearly to sleep. I pulled back the covers for Terry and got into bed behind him, sinking once more between the twin tattooed propellers. Plastic or not, the tight clasp of pleasure brought an almost immediate release.

37.

There had been a summer season up in Malibu, too. I confirmed it by the simple act of driving there between adventures on the pier. As though granting visitation rights not yet formalized by law, Linda had been cool but cordial, and brought me up to date on family happenings as she rocked and spoke to the baby. I wasn't asked to hold bottles or change diapers—that she could do for herself. Instead of Heineken beer or mixed drinks, Linda served tea or soda.

Brenda took a liking to Philip, I learned, about the time his glasses broke. When that wore off he had followed her, but not much had come of this late interest. Linda called it puppy love. Valery and Steve took walks to distant coves, but no one was sure what they did there. When asked, Steve would only say, "We talked." And Starkey—his companions had been Randy and the surf. He was too grown up for Superman.

An honorable mention of Everett was always saved for last. He was still negotiating with his wife. A dysfunctional impotence was often curable—did I know that? So the back door to an affair might still be open. The front door, too—should *I* ever care to use it. Like the spider on the wall, she was weaving a new web of intrigue. In the meantime, the good news—Uncle Stanley had sent her some money. That was a comfort to us both.

"And what about yourself?" she would ask, in the final minutes of our mini-conference.

"Oh, I do the same old things, you know. Work, sleep, and body-surf. Sometimes I go to a movie." That numb conclusion would, usually be sufficient. But on this particular Sunday she had tacked on an addendum in the form of a questionnaire.

"What else have you been doing, Jerry?" She'd also poured some real drinks—frosted juleps from a Southern recipe.

"Nothing, that I can *think* of. Well, I had to get the car fixed. The water pump. It needs tires, too." I sampled the mint of the drink.

"Nothing you can *speak* of, is what you mean." Like crushed ice, Linda's eyes sparkled fleetingly. She blushed, but in a non-attractive manner—another sort of Pink Alert. Linda bit her lip, then spoke quite softly.

"Jerry? What's really happened to the two of us? Since I was your golden princess, and you were my shining prince?"

"When was that, Linda?"

"It seems ages ago, now."

"I don't know. Maybe I've been transformed. Isn't that what often happens to princes?" I gave a loud croak like a frog.

"What's happened to our *marriage*? That's what I'm really asking. Can't you understand?" The ice thawed to a tear, still a gleam in her eye, but trembling.

"Maybe the magic's gone out of it," I said, and drained my frosted julep cup like the Captain of a Mississippi sidewheeler.

"And into that boy on the pier?" *Steady as she goes there, Jerry.*

"Which boy is that?" Which *pier*—I should have asked. I bit down on my tongue and felt my sphincter tighten. *Shoals ahead, sir!*

"The one you chase around at night—*naked.*" The damned ship had just run aground!

"Who the hell's been spying on me, anyway?"

"No one's been *spying* on you, Jerry. You're not that important to us anymore."

"Who's my sworn eyewitness then, to this purportedly disgraceful carnal act? Name my accuser, if you please. It's my citizen's right to know, and your duty to tell me, as long as we're man and *wife.*" As I reached for her hand she folded it in the other.

"Only Brenda and Philip," she explained with perfect logic. "They were going to visit you the other night after a movie. They saw *Our Man in Havana*, a story about spies, I believe." The full-grown tear had started down her cheek—first drop out of the pipeline.

"Exactly what are they supposed to have seen at my place? Did Philip get new glasses?"

"The two of you together, playing in the tower bedroom. He looked young, Brenda said, and was covered with tattoos—*or bruises.*"

Abandon ship!!! The water flowed freely, some of it falling on Casey, who clenched his fists and started crying, too. I reached out to take him in my arms.

"Don't you *dare!*" screamed Linda, suddenly rising, eyes aglare through teardrops like searchlights in the rain. "Don't you dare touch him, you drunk—you drunken *fairy!*" Linda and the baby fled inside.

As I slunk out to the car, a shipless captain, I nearly collided with Starkey and the dog. Randy skipped to one side on the unmowed grass; Starkey slipped eyes-front through the bed of yellow daisies. So Brenda had told *them,* too—becoming one of the great mischief-making finks of female history—and all out of simple penile envy! Sly Philip had probably told his dad, the Colonel, but for completely different diplomatic reasons.

Somewhere in the trackless depths of space, such spiteful deeds as these would trace their record, if only in the form of thought-waves leaving Earth to reach at last the all-recalling memory banks of the supreme Cosmological Computer, light years or centuries hence.

When Terry, full of fun and beer, ambled down to the pier that night, neither he nor his tales nor his ornaments amused me. I was a sorry host. I had failed the cross-examination. And *she* knew all the answers.

38.

My phone calls, if they were relayed at all, were directed to the studio-apartment. My mail was delivered there, too—stuffed into a tin box at the foot of the stairs where any literate citizen could read it. A weekly **LIFE** and **TIME**, daily billings, and the so-called literature of my trade were the usual haul. Sometimes I received personal letters. They were addressed to Leonard Faircycle, billets-doux of the many affairs neglected during his journeys. One day a letter came for me. It was from Leonard.

The long envelope of delicate paper was gorgeously decorated with a collector's sample of bright Spanish stamps, as though its message had won some sort of prize. Some of the stamps were of Franco. How could he have licked those? I was prejudiced before opening the letter: Leonard was always a facile opportunist, unhampered by any restraint. That was a principled reaction; sleeping in his borrowed bed with one of his borrowed boyfriends had absolutely nothing to do with it. I slit the envelope. The pages, of course, had been scribed in purple ink:

16 Agosto

Saludas, Don Jaire!

A wee bit surprised to hear from Old Castile? Well, I'm surprised to be here! We were all down in Syria, or some such place, where the picture began just beautifully! Gorgeous sunrises, sunsets too. Turning wild desert sands to waves of bronze and violet, and sparking jet-black eyes in sun-bronzed faces like lamps in bedouin tents. So romantic!

A lot of these fascinating people are paid as extras in "Conquest of the Dunes." If I must say so the pieces I designed look better than their own homemade clothing, mostly rags. Fit better, too! Except for Master Dexter X, the so-called star of the film, who had to bring along his own couturier—from Paris! So things were in a bit of a stew.

Then the winds began to blow, the sirocco or monsoon, or whatever they call it. The devil wind! We got sand in our eyes and in the cameras. In the food and liquor too. It was wretched. Even then it was better than the flies. The natives go potty anywhere. And then some people got shot! Just before the big studio reception at the palace of a handsome young sheik. You'd think they'd be a little civilized after several thousand years!

So I decided to forget the whole fucking thing, at least until the wind stopped blowing. Or until Mr. X comes down off his high horse and gets back on his camel. If she can ever decide what to wear! Myself and three dear friends—you'd just love them, Jerry—hopped a jet to Gibralter and hired a Mercedes limousine.

David and Felix, and Melissa from the prop department, made a cozy group of four and toured the Costa del Sol (The Sunny Coast) from marvelous Marbella through Malaga, Almeria and Granada. We dined at three-star restaurants all the way. Everything is built of red tile and stucco—none of that tacky California style!

Then Cordoba, Madrid, the Prado. And bullfights, bullfights, bullfights. Beauty and the Beast! No wonder Mister Ernest loved it here. Speaking of beauty, the Alhambra's not what it's cracked up to be. Or rather it is! The alabaster's crumbling and the fountains don't work, and there were crowds & crowds of foreign tourists.

Otherwise the country's fine. Lovely, lovely views of Spanish leather. Even the police. They are magnifico! I think I may be in love again. There's more than one gay caballero in this town! Then on to France. Felix wants to see the Cote D'Or, wherever that is. Reminds me of a chummy little N.Y. Club, the Coq d'Or—which everyone confused with Glory Hole! But that's another story.

Have to hurry now, to a fabulous dinner at a villa, flamenco afterward. And then—who knows??? The damnable manager is here again. You'd think they'd never heard of deluxe suites for four (or more!) charming people.

Hope to have the flick wrapped up by November, then back to Tinseltown in season. Oh, if a darling redhead from the Navy should show up, just say I love and miss him. And can't wait to see him on return. Too bad you don't swing that way! But one man's meat, etc. Kiss the ferns for me. And do be careful.

    Aficion,

      Leonardo

c/o American Express, Barcelona (with a lithp!) Espana

I read the letter twice and stuck it in a drawer among other decadent objects: cigarette makings, certain magazines, a tube of K-Y, starchy towels. I washed my hands of it. I ought to do some work.

A sharp wind, clear of smog, blew from the mountains. A few figures strayed along the beach, hunched against the stinging sands. *Searchers of the Dunes.* The carousel was silent; the wind made a mournful tune.

That afternoon, as though summoned through the U.S. mails, Mickey came down to the pier. As usual we went up to the tower. It was warm there and still, as within a winter greenhouse. Mick settled in the sunniest corner and began to free himself of clothing. I gave him the Spanish letter. As he read, he shed his uniform in an absent-minded way, an article for each paragraph ending. At the letter's conclusion he was nude. Rolling on the rug, Mickey laughed.

"He's really far out! There's no one like Leonard. He's a ball!"

"Don't you wish you were with him?"

"Len? Are you kidding? I wouldn't be in Spain for anything. I feel at home right here." He lay back smiling on the faded shag. The coppery lashes fluttered, and a sunbeam at his middle made his fork a burning bush. Mick's fingertips began to groom the pubic hairs—those forever-flaming faggots!

"He loves and misses you and wants you. It says so right here in the letter."

"I hate that kind of sentimental crap. He's just a father figure."

"What about when he comes back? Won't you want to stay here?"

"It'd be like joining a sideshow. Len's a freak."

"What am I then?"

"My best friend and buddy, like I told you. Not an A-hole buddy, either." He cocked his head in a solemn look, confirming it, as my hand slid up a leg toward the light.

Was it really *Saint Mick* that I touched there? Maybe *that* idea was only sentimental crap! Leonard had been the first to think of it. Maybe I should think of something else; it was better facing facts when I was able.

Let's see now. What we have here, Jerry, is a truly remarkable piece of natural engineering—hydraulics linked to solar energy. See how the sensors lift toward the sun, how the skin slides easily on the sun-warmed shaft, a blood-filled lifeline under pressure. How did it feel *inside*?

There was also something dangerous, like a blade that slips too loosely in its sheath.

"What are you thinking of, Jerry?"

"I'm thinking what a nice dong you have. What are you thinking, Mickey?" The green eyes closed.

"Nothing."

It was pretty goddamned ingenious. The generative cells, those tiny tadpoles, were grown right there in the gonads—*two* of them, a safety factor of one-hundred percent. The sac's wrinkled folds were like radiator vanes: they kept the little buggers cool. The manufactured products were conducted to an inside holding tank, well-protected by muscle and bone, where they awaited further orders from higher HQ.

When the signals came through, loud and clear, lubricating fluids were injected to assist in systems delivery. All other channels were pre-empted. The rest was automatic. It was a work of diabolic simplicity!

The device had another safety factor—it would function by itself when overloaded. It squirted all over my hand. The substance gleamed in the sunbeam, liquescent.

"That felt good. I let it run out like a faucet."

"Do you think I could feel that way, too?"

"Let's find out, Jerry. Drop your drawers."

That night I treated Mickey to a seafood dinner at Sinbad's on the pier, and while we dined I repeated Terry's stories, though not in the way they'd been told.

"He's a good storyteller, that's for sure," said Mick. "That's all those hillbillies know how to do, is tell tall tales."

"It wasn't so? About the sub?"

"Not for him, anyway."

"How about the chain gang?"

"He probably made that one up, too."

"Well, what part *is* true?"

"It's true that he likes to be screwed." The phrase had not escaped the couple in the next fish-netted booth. They were finishing their coffees in silence. "But it wasn't his brother who taught him. His daddy taught him that."

"So he shot him in the stomach?"

"He shot him in the ass." The couple got up and left.

We walked to the end of the pier. The wind had died at sunset; the night was ideally calm. We heard the buzz and click of casting reels where anglers stood along the lower decks under floodlights. The lights kept at bay the darker elements that roamed the pier by night. The waters below glowed bright green. Beyond lay the black strip of breakwater.

Once, I thought I saw an underwater light. You have to glance a little to the side, Mick said, for the rods of the eye to register, as on night watch. He saw a light there, too. Divers were hunting lobsters in the rocks. Sometimes, a groping arm would find a moray eel instead. The ship's bell clanged. Eight bells.

"You like Henderson, don't you, Jerry?"

"Only when you're not around." Mickey goosed me. "Where the hell have you been?" I asked.

"Busy. I may be getting out soon. Sooner than I thought."

"What are you going to do then?"

"Move in with you, bud, down here on the pier."

Our elbows touched together on the jointed pipe rail. I struck it with my silver ring—three times for good luck, once for bad.

39.

Before the portentous move could come about, Yeoman Henderson showed up again. Hardly pausing to think, I hauled a cold six-pack to the tower.

"I got something to show you," said Terry, beginning to pull off his blouse. This time I pulled the blinds before switching on the lights.

"Something I haven't seen before?"

"I *think* so." Terry exhibited an arm with a fresh band of color on its bicep—a wavy green snake that ate its tail. "Do you like it?"

"It looks cute. And kind of harmless. Where'd you get it?"

"I saw it in a tattoo parlor window down on Main Street, payday. I couldn't turn it down. It still hurts a little." The snake gave a lively wiggle as he sat on the bed with a beer.

"I used to go down there a *lot*, you know, me and my buddy Skeeter, just before I joined. We had this beat-up old fifty-five *Chivvy* that burned oil like gasoline. No horn or trim or anything like that. It *did* have a radio. The seats was all ripped out in back, the spare gone, too. So we laid a mattress through the trunk to sleep on. We could screw our girls there when we wanted. Sometimes we tricked with each other.

"We'd work a week or two, here or there, and take off again as soon as we got money. That was my *good* summer, Jerry."

"What happened then?" I lit one of the numbers I had learned to roll with the grass I had learned to buy from Glen and Glenda. We were all neighbors now, and knew about sharing the essentials.

"The car blew up, a *fuel*-line maybe. It was lucky we wasn't in it. Then we went down to Main Street and hung around the bars. They close two to six, you know, so we used to go to sleep in that Mexican church—the cathedral. You could lean your head against a back pew, like you was saying a long prayer. Skeeter, he hit the collection box and we got ourselves a room at this cruddy hotel, the *Chase*.

"We had a jug of Ripple and some weed. I was bombed when I begun to smell smoke. I thought it was the *ash*tray, you know. But it was coming through the transom and under the door. *FIRE! FIRE!* they was yelling in the hallway. I didn't wait for any second motions, just ran down the hall without my clothes—I couldn't find them— and right out into the middle of Main Street. It was full of firemen and hoses."

I took a toke. *Far fucking out!* The twin propellers speeding down the corridor pursued by roaring flames, the bold tattoos on public exhibition—the butterflies and double taps, the pole-star fly, the seeing-eye balls.

"Somebody threw a blanket on me. I sure wasn't *cold*, but I was shivering. Flames was shooting out the upstairs windows like a blow-torch. And the *screams,* they were awful! Guys were falling out the windows, too. It was a hotel full of winos. The fire burned clear down to the lobby bar before they got it out. Four*teen,* they lost in that fire, the paper said. But a lot more wasn't registered. I never *did* get my clothes back."

"How about your buddy?"

"Skeeter? Oh, he never made it out, either. He was up on the fifth floor with a twenty-dollar trick, a lumberjack from Seattle. He was as good a buddy as I *ever* had." For the first time in our relationship Terry looked grieved; a wave of sympathy went out to him.

"How about Mickey? Isn't he a good friend, too?"

"The *best*. But he'll be out soon. Then I'll have to find another buddy, I suppose."

"How come he's getting out?"

"Oh, he kind of screwed up, I guess. He had a fight with some colored dude. So the guy turned him in for tricking with a friend. He's getting a U.D. The U's for *Undesirable.*" Even with the beer and smokes his expression stayed serious.

"How is it, Terry, that when you're here he's not? And when Mickey comes around you don't?"

"Oh, that? It's like trading duty at the base, you know. Sometimes we come here, sometimes we see Trudy down in South Gate."

"Trudy?"

"Trudy Johnson. She's a blonde. Lives by herself in a trailer. Her and her parakeets, her *love*birds."

"Is that why he's not here tonight?"

"Hell, no. He's on restriction. He's up for captain's mast. He wouldn't be there anyway, since she gave us both the clap. Didn't Mickey tell you?"

"*Hell,* no! What about right now? You mean we could *all* have it?"

"Don't worry," Terry laughed. "I guess you never caught it yet. They cure it in a day with peni*cillin.*" The drug's name seemed appropriately derived from the popular word-stem and organ: the ever-present *penis* and its bag of dirty tricks. What a mad invention that was! I hastened to the bathroom for a spot-check. I found no sign of discharge, but a sullen burning lingered there. *Where there's smoke there's fire.* It was the other exit I was worried about; time and place were indiscriminate among fate's victims.

Terry finished off the beer and dressed. "Take it easy, old buddy," he said, dixie cup hat across an eyebrow. He hoisted up his torso fore and aft, the well-seasoned saltwater sailor.

"Easy, or not at all. See you later."

But that was not the last call of the evening. The knock was clear but unfamiliar—it was Linda's first visit to the pier. She stood by the doorway and drank it all in. The ferns, the palms, the white wicker chairs, the ceiling fan, the empty bottles on the windowsill.

"Are you coming in? Or aren't you?"

"Why, yes, Jerry. If I may. It's quite a place. It's a wonder you can work here. It's a little," here she smiled, "it's a little like...a whore-house."

"Are you interested in some kind of position then?"

"Not really, Jerry dearest. I came by to see how you were. I thought perhaps we could still be friends."

"Would you like a drink? Whatever brought that thought to mind?'

"I thought that everyone needs a little freedom." So maybe she and Everett *were* doing it. Could the Colonel show it hard? Or couldn't he? "And after all," she continued, "the children didn't really see you doing anything. At least there's not another woman to be jealous of." Parabolic reasoning supreme!

"Actually, he's only a sailor friend, in the Navy. He was showing me his tattoos. They're quite artistic."

"Are you thinking of getting one, Jerry?"

"A tattoo? Yes. A bleeding heart, big as a prince's, with an arrow labeled *Linda* stuck straight through it."

"That's very touching." She sat down with a brandy to a mature conversation, very different from the one I'd had with Terry. Later, I walked her to the van she'd bought, a red VW camper, bright as one of Casey's toys.

"Drive carefully."

"I've only had two drinks."

"That's my line, remember?" She leaned down for a token kiss.

When the red car had gone I was alone in a suddenly huge and very empty parking lot. The shell that housed the Merry-Go-Round was somehow gravely altered. Traceries of cracks were on the walls, as though vines had lately fallen from their moorings. The skeleton of wood showed through.

I was glad to see the lights of the tower. I had not asked my wife to view its bed.

At eight o'clock I called the doctor.

"Doctor's very busy," said the receptionist, "but you may come in. You've been a good patient in the past, Mr. Carr. What seems to be the trouble now?"

"I won't know till Doctor tells me."

"Very well. We'll try to work you in."

Even in a modern office building, the suite had a period look. Chintz-covered chairs, maple shelves and tables, frilly table lamps were the furnishings. The doctor's wife had been the decorator for his home-away-from-home. The six or seven patients were exactly the sort of guests to be invited there—solid citizens with community ties, Elks or fellow Rotarians. Not one of them comfortably seated there would have anything resembling a venereal disease. I picked up respectable magazines—*National Geographic, Sports Illustrated,*

BOYS LIFE—and sat in a corner by the grandfather's clock for the long morning wait.

"Well, Jerry, how's the youngster doing? And what can we do for you?" Doctor Wangler wore the standard stethoscope and starched white jacket. His fingernails were polished, the skin of the hands wax-clear.

"Oh, Casey's fine. So is Linda, and the rest. I have a little problem I've never had before."

"A non-domestic problem, I presume?"

"An error in social judgment, I'm afraid." I described the common symptoms; the doctor looked. I recalled short-arm inspections in the Air Force. For some reason, they were always held in chapels, the medics at the altar rail. The men, dressed in raincoats, went down the aisle, flashing for the checkers one-by-one. How was it, sitting there at zero range? The medics always looked bored.

"A little surface irritation, is all I can see. The nurse will give you a urine bottle. You can pull your pants up, Jerry."

"There's another place, Doctor."

"What other place is that?" I gave him the clinical name for it. Doctor Wangler began to look severe; he went about the room clinking shut the venetian blinds. Although the suite was on an unobstructed floor, his was still a family practice. He slipped sleek hands into slick rubber gloves.

"We'll have to take a smear for the lab. How did you ever get into such a fix, Jeremy?"

"I'd had a disagreement with Linda. Then I met this couple at a cocktail lounge. They *seemed* nice enough, until they took me to this weird sort of place and got me drunk, or gave me drugs, I guess. Anyway, the man got me in bed with his partner, and before I knew it, *he* was doing something too. It's the first time a thing like that has ever happened to me. I can't even remember their names."

"It's the last time I'll have to treat it, I assume. It's considered a heinous crime. An act against nature, says the law." It *would* be the last time, for certain. The next time I'd find another quack! "We all make mistakes, but that's a very grave one. You have to think of your wife, you know. Although *there*, it probably won't affect her. I'll start you on penicillin. Two-hundred-thousand units should do it."

I left without a hat to shield my guilty face. Somehow the others seemed to know.

Only two nights later Mickey took his turn at the apartment. The lab tests had proved negative. We did our three-way thing without compunction.

"Was it this much fun with Trudy?" I asked when we were done.

"Spencer told you? I don't care. She needed somebody to lay her."

"How about now?"

"That's all over. She can do it with her lovebirds if she wants. I don't even want to see her, the whore."

"Truly?"

"You're more fun to be with than anybody. I really dig on *you,* man."

"Okay."

"I'll have to bring my stuff down from the base soon. Will it be all right to borrow the Fury?"

"Sure, Mick, sure. I guess that'll be okay, too."

40.

Against the wild, aroused clamor of the carousel, I didn't hear the telephone's ring. Drawing a plan with plugs in my ears, I felt its vibrations in the drafting board.

"Hey *JERRY!*" Mickey had to yell. "The car's got a *flat.*" I unplugged an ear. "Anchors Aweigh" was the tune of the hour. "Yeah. Up here in Malibu. The spare's flat, too... Where am I calling from? Your place."

"*My* place?"

"Sure. The car's about a mile from here, with all my stuff in it... How are they? They're *real* nice. Your wife's gonna drive me to the Chevron Station. *What!* Yeah, yeah... I can't *hear* you."

"I loaned you the car because you're going to do a *job* for me. And you're moving into town, not down *here,* for God's sake."

"Sure, I understand, Mr. Carr... *Gotcha.* Yessir, we'll probably have it fixed in an hour... I certainly *won't,* sir!" He hung up.

I put down the pencil and went above to meditate. Damn! What a fix that put *me* in. An hour? She'd have the whole story in a minute— if I knew anything at all about my wife. The time was nearly four.

It was seven when Mickey's new key rattled in the lock. He wore Levis, his civvies on hangers on his back. I'd miss the uniforms, their ties and fitted flaps, their well-known easy access. He wasn't Fireman E-4 McCrory anymore. Who would he be now?

"Hey, they're terrific," said the disaffiliated sailor. "You've got a first-class family, Jerry. Brenda was there; she's real sweet. Her bro's are neat kids, too. The dog jumped all over me. Because he smelled you, maybe.

"Linda poured me a beer. A Heineken's. Then we had a few more at the Malibu Inn. That's were all the movie stars hang out, you know. They have their pictures on the wall, autographed. I saw one at the bar. He used to be in westerns. He kept staring at me."

I opened two Heinekens of our own.

"And you know what? When we got to the station Linda bought another spare, a used one. You've sure got a generous wife."

"What all did you and my generous wife talk about?"

"Oh, she asked how long I knew you. I said almost a year, since the night I drove you home. The night you were zonked, remember? You said I saved your life. She was glad to hear that, believe me."

"Thanks, Mick. What else was the gist of your discussion?"

"She asked how well I knew you. I said well enough to know you're one of the grooviest dudes around."

"You're killing me with kindness. I won't know how to pay you back. The Bank of America's not big enough.'

"Forget it. Then I bought her a drink. She didn't have to pay for everything, you know."

"Not my Linda."

"Then the actor, Grady, he sent a free round over. I thought I'd never get that flat fixed."

"You did, though."

"Yeah, a car nearly creamed me, a Corvette. I pulled my shirt off to jack up the rear and my fly popped open. Linda asked if I'd ever been tattooed. But guess what!"

"I'm afraid to."

"She asked me up to dinner. Can you believe that? Friday night. You're invited too, Jerry."

"She's all heart."

"And good-looking! She's got a tight little bod."

"I don't know how to count my blessings anymore."

"Some dudes have all the luck."

"I don't know why I ever left home."

"You sound like there's something the matter."

"Only a slight stomach-ache, nothing serious. Everything's fine. Go ahead and eat. I bought some steaks."

"You talk kind of strange sometimes. I'm starved! We only had Fritos with our drinks."

"I wouldn't do too much of that, Mick."

"This one's the last." He took another deep toke from the alligator clip and handed it to me. Wearing a tight-waisted western shirt, he buckled himself into jeans. As always his prong hung out till last, like angler's bait. He arranged it in a long even roll.

"Just try to keep your head straight tonight."

"Which one?" Mickey grinned.

"*This* one," I said, and squeezed it. We played a fast game of Touch in the tower. Mick scored a jab to the crotch. I folded on the bed like a jackknife.

"Hey, I'm *sorry*, man." Buddy style, he put a friendly arm around me. I punched him in the gut, but he still sat there. *Our first quarrel.*

"Where'd you learn to hit like that?" I groaned in nausea.

"Reform school, I guess. The niggers."

"They ever catch you?"

"Sometimes. They raped me twice. That's why I still hit back. That and my quick Irish temper."

"I'm the only one who's after you now, right?"

"Right. You can catch me anytime. I won't bite."

A Specialty of the House, that's what Linda had prepared for us. Her parsley potatoes, a crown roast of lamb, mushroom salad, melon balls—served alfresco on the terrace among hurricane lamps. A rosé followed the daiquiris. Then we had brandy, too. As the roast had been the object of our hunger, so Mick became the subject of our talk.

"Did you join the Navy to see the world? Or learn a trade, or what?" asked Brenda, as though collecting news for her school paper.

"I joined to please my dad, really. My foster-father, that is. But I haven't seen much of the world yet. Have you?"

"I've seen California. Aren't you pretty young to be getting out already?"

"Young enough to start a new career."

"Do you know what it's going to be?"

"Well, he's an *Aries*," I interposed. "They're pioneers. Their sign's the Ram, their metal's copper, and their planet is the red planet Mars."

Brenda looked nonplussed, no longer taking copy.

"They're leaders," I said, "like Thomas Jefferson or Hitler."

"Really?" said Mick, grinning. "I don't have to worry, with Jerry around. Now I know why he's got such a groovy family."

"Now we know why he's got such a groovy friend." Brenda got up to stack dishes. "I guess your hair's in Aries, too. It's certainly redder than the boy's next door, whatever sign he is."

"I've been the boy next door, a lot of times. Would you care to take a walk on the beach?"

Our daughter allowed that she would.

"Jerry?" Starkey stayed to blow out the lamps. "Could I ask you a personal question?"

"No need to hesitate now."

"Well is Mickey really your *boy* friend?"

"That's personal? He's a personal friend, sure. And still a boy, I guess, in some ways. I'm a kind of older brother when he needs one. Why?"

"Something Mom said, that's all. About a father figure."

"She doesn't always mean what she says. Or say what she means, either. You shouldn't take those words too literally."

"I hope you mean what you say, J.C."

"Some things never change."

"Another brandy, Jerry?"

We were two adults on the terrace, facing seaward, sunk in the sag of our campaign chairs. A half moon hung listless on a misty sea.

"I'll have one if you do."

Linda tilted the decanter. "He seems a nice enough boy, rather cute and fairly bright. An uneducated orphan, like Raspberry Finn."

"Huckleberry. *Huck.* Does that make me a runaway slave, like Jim?"

"No more than I'm the rich widow in those boys' adventure stories you're so fond of. Do you think he'll stay long?"

"Where, at my place? Only until he gets started. I'm merely trying to give the kid a hand, you know. Sometimes he helps me out, too."

"I suppose it does get lonely. I don't imagine he's the one that Brenda saw naked in the tower, is he?"

"You must be confused. Mickey doesn't have a single tattoo on any part of his body. Though he *does* have one distinguishing feature." In the dim half-moonlight I sipped another brandy, and watched with satisfaction as Linda pursed her lips before she spoke.

"I know you're teasing, Jerry, but I am a little jealous. He's a kind of lost boy, I think, that many a mother could be fond of." And many a father, too, Linda Lee! "I hope he'll find his way."

Then Mick was back with Brenda, and we stood to say goodnight. I'd forgotten I was going to leave, too.

"Come visit us this weekend," said my wife.

"We'd like to but we can't, unfortunately," were the words that came unexpectedly out of my mouth. "We're taking a little trip to Mexico."

"First time I knew about it," said my trip-mate.

"It was meant as kind of a surprise."

"Thanks for the terrific dinner, Mrs. Carr," said Mickey, in a timely show of class. "When we're home again you'll have to visit our place."

For this remark I loved him—that night more than ever.

41.

"One to get ready." From the trusty jaws of the alligator clip, Mickey drew a jet-stream of vapor.

"That's your second jay already."

"Two for the road then. You said I could drive."

He stood on the bench to free the T-shirt of all wrinkles; it made a surgical white sheath from neck to hip line. He shaped the pliable jeans to his thighs, then his butt, folding the flaps of the fly like theater curtains. At the very last moment, out popped the head of the Saint, red-faced and bowing, as though to make a late announcement. But the head was as quickly withdrawn. The zipper sang the key of C before the matinee was over. He put on white athletic socks, white-laced navy blue sneakers, and combed his hair. The ensemble was complete: blues and whites set off by red hairs and freckles, a tone poem fair enough for any foreign audience. Tucked into a shoulder sleeve, a pack of Luckies made an off-balance chip like a coda. Mick patted his empty back pockets and grinned. He was ready.

The flight bag carried cameras and film, travelers' checks and swim trunks. The Fury had a tankful of gas. Mickey locked into a slot on the freeway, another set of wheels in a thousand-mile-long train. The air smelled of salt, petroleum, ozone. I slumped back, jiggling my knee to the radio, glad to be leaving the miasma of L.A. and its adulterous, contaminating influence. The music made me feel good, too. "Puff, the Magic Dragon," "Do You Believe in Magic?" "Eight Miles High" played between Saturday morning commercials.

"They're ads for drugs," Mickey claimed. I couldn't believe it. He explained the puzzling lyrics word-for-word.

"High, I understand. But *eight miles?"*

"They're on a jet." "Hey, Joe" came right after. That I could comprehend—a man taking off for Mexico after shooting his woman dead. "It's the new music," Mick added, beating his palm on the vinyl top. Other drivers looked serious and mean. They were tuned to other stations.

The route was boringly familiar, at the same time new: the cloverleafs, the cutoffs, the over/under passes—a stretched-out roller coaster I had ridden a hundred other times. Now, the farms of oil tanks near Long Beach, the bloated globes like spaceships—one painted orange each Halloween. Then the racks of defused mines from one war or another, the dirty-bird derricks by Huntington Beach sucking Mother Earth dry of her black juices. And miles and miles of tin cans, bottles, papers. I didn't care. I could watch Mickey's one-hand driving, admire his figure at the wheel.

I asked him to pull off at Newport. I wanted to ride the Wedge; it was my turn to show off for a change. My heart sank when I saw it—the glass-green twelve-foot crests, dangled bodies crunching on the shore. *High Noon* at Newport Beach, as lethal swells swept along the sea wall.

"Aren't you coming in, Mick?"

"Hell no. I'll watch." He lit a smoke and leaned back on his elbows.

"It separates the men from the boys."

"I don't see any men out there. It separates your bones from your body." I went in, was taken by a wave on a pile-driving break, and struggled out against the grasping undertow. I was glad to catch my breath.

"Did you see it, Mick?"

"Yeah! A chick's tit fell out while she was running. She just let it hang there awhile, like she didn't notice one was loose."

"I mean me."

"Out there? You all look alike, men or boys."

So much for macho performances! I stacked my swim fins and squatted in the sand beside him.

"You really like girls, don't you, Mick?"

"Sure, they're kind of neat. They can do things we can't."

"I like them, too."

"Not really, Jerry boy. You need women. There's a difference."

"I know what I like best. Let's go!"

Oceanside. Marines at any crosswalk, creases sharp, jaws set all alike, eyes blanked by visors; guts in, chests out as though cloned from their leader, Chesty Puller. One was different: he wore a bulge near his pocket. Roadside Courtesy Shelters had been provided where drivers could pick up a marine already gift-wrapped. The shelters were vacant. The marines took their chances in the sun.

And San Diego. Scores of sailors white as seagulls scrambled up-town, collars flying, to swallow drinks and spill their rusty loads. Like an overworked switchboard, my brain cells buzzed with all of those subliminal mating calls.

Then on through the six-lane pearly gates of Tijuana. Servicemen in civvies jammed the Mexican sidewalks.

"Let it *all* hang out," sang a black to his troop. "Let's get it *on*, mother-fuckers!" Exactly how I felt. But not Mick. His grin turned suddenly grim.

"What's bugging you?"

"I still don't like 'em."

"That was in reform school, years ago. There's ten million others."

"Those are the ones I remember. You never been gang-raped, Jerry."

"Yeah. I guess you and Terry don't count." He grinned again and groped me. We'd agreed to share whatever came along.

We began at the Long Bar, drinking, at a wet slab long as a bowling lane, with brass rail and gutter to match. Mugs of foaming beer scudded down its length. It was funny: the minute you crossed the border you were thirsty, just as everyone was horny later on. We had shots of tequila with lemon and salt, trailed by Mexicali chasers.

As at the tower apartment, lazy ceiling fans blew away the smoke and flies and kept it coolly pleasant in the dry desert air. I watched the sweat stains fade from Mickey's armpits. In the slackened tube of T-shirt his trunk had grown longer—the beltless jeans were halfway down his hips. The Saint would have plenty of elbow room, and his *balls* would keep their *cool*, even though I might be losing mine. It was hard to keep my focus topside, away from his distinguished features.

"Another round here, *por favor.*" Precisely what Leonard might have said, at some posh Barcelona bistro. Not only had I his pad and his lover, but I was also doing a duplicate number on his Latin trip!

"*Gracias, Americanos.*" The barkeep had a winning smile.

"Here's to you, Mick. And the Saint, of course."

"Who? Oh, him. I think he's topped off already. I gotta hit the head." He was gone a long time in that *latrina*. I might as well have been there myself. I found him at the triple-curve distorting mirror, a three-foot midget with a head like a red tile roof. "Take these," he said, yellow pills in palm. "Bennies."

The cool space at the bar had been usurped by two strangers.

"Oh, I'm sorry," said the first, spying Mickey. "Please let us buy you both a drink." He and his tourist friend were...thirty? Thirty-two? They wore aloha shirts and dacron slacks and gold-plated watches of the sort that had seventeen jewels. On their feet, I saw disdainfully, were buckled suede loafers. I knew what Mick was into. He would let them buy us all the drinks they wanted, while we had our own private high.

"We're here for local color," said the heavier one, moving the four of us to a round table. "We're *aficionados*. Fans, you know, of anything south of the border. Aren't we, Ronald?"

"Yes, Lester," said the dark one. "We all know which border you're referring to." Regarding Mickey's legs, sprawled in both directions, I wondered when that border would be crossed, with what resistance.

A mariachi band roamed the Long Bar, serenading tables, picking up wet dollar bills. The rattling gourds, the sad violins, the plaintive brass set my backbone tingling like a xylophone—a *simpatico* buzz of alcohol, benzedrine, and mentholated smoke. The others could swap jokes and rub legs all they wanted, in the manner of inquisitive dogs. I felt free to appreciate the beauty of the festive Mexican night.

"We came here to see the hidden sights," Lester had been saying, sniffing the night air. "Things you don't usually see."

"We came here to get my uncle laid. Didn't we, Jerry?"

"That's what you led me to expect, nephew."

"He *mis*-laid his wallet like a fucked-up recruit. I used to come here after boot camp in Dago. We're just cruising around for some action."

"I can *see* it. A carrot-top in navy blues. With a carrot between his legs." Lester's hands laid more money on the table and dropped below the top. "*Where* did you used to come, sailor?"

"Anywhere I could."

"And any *way*?"

"Anytime." With a sailor's mock grin, Mick let his hips slide forward.

"It's *hot* in here," frowned Ronald. "Let's all go somewhere else."

Lester bought us margaritas at the Foreign Club, Mai Tai's at the Tiki Torch, and thin drinks in a basement where waitresses sat on our laps. My feet were loose, my head flying. And then, there it was, neon letters hissing in the night: THE BLUE FOX—*Supper Club & Dancing*. For the party of four Ronald paid the door fees.

Balconies three sides, a raised stage in the middle—the club was like a small art theater. When the band played a tango the lights turned blue. A señorita glided down a staircase—catcalls, whistles, cheers—and in a few turns dropped the mantilla, a chair-back comb, a pleated skirt. "Take it ALL off!" She tossed them the rose in her teeth, the silk bra, the lace panties. Applause. One, then more marines shuffled on their knees across the stage to the black triangle target. Before an audience of hundreds they performed, in turn, an act of cunnilingus. *"CHOW time!" "Sit on his FACE!"* the crowd cheered. A fight began up there among servicemen. Bottles hit the floor. The lights turned bright as artillery flares, scattering marines like giant roaches.

"That's not really sexy," said Lester outside. "It was kind of *disgusting*, don't you think?"

"It's a hard act to follow." Mickey lit another Lucky Strike.

"Jesus," muttered Ron. "I still can't believe it. Those were *our* marines, too."

"You never did that in the Navy, did you?" asked his friend.

"Don't you like eating pussy?" said Mickey, losing his grin. We paused in an arcade to watch him drain himself. The Saint gave a show of power.

"Certainly not in *that* kind of place."

"Let's all go to our hotel. At Rosarito Beach." Lester touched us both. "We've got plenty to drink. And the beds are simply e-*nor*-mous."

"Me and Uncle Jerry have gotta go get laid."

"By Mexican *whores?* I thought you lost your money."

"We're gonna eat each other. We're devoted sixty-niners. He has six and I have nine. Right, Uncle?"

"I think you're a real pair of *pricks.* You both deserve each other." They turned on their loafers and left us. "I hope you're arrested for *incest!*" Ron called back. Mickey laughed and zipped his fly.

"Where are we going now?"

"To the Hotel Rosarito."

42.

The scratch of the pen was an echo in the tile-walled vastness of the lobby. *M. and J. Carr,* I watched Mick scrawl, *of Malibu, California.* We were shown to a suite on the ocean. *Alone at last,* I thought, throat dry, brain speeding. I wanted to order a drink.

"This is better." Mick took a film container from the flight bag and spilled out another set of pills. "Takes these, with a water chaser."

"What's this we're having now?"

"Bluebirds of Happiness." He shucked the T-shirt, kicked off the sneakers, at last dropped his pants—like the stripper of the *BLUE FOX*—and flopped on a big double bed. I undressed, lay down beside him, and shared his cigarette for a while.

"I don't feel anything special," I said, "except a little cool."

"That's good then." The pitch of his voice had altered, and it lingered in my ear. The night was full of subtle noises—clicks, ticks, and sighings—I had not been aware of before. The waves grew ominously louder, as though a heavy surf were coming up.

And our *room*. The blue walls were bluer, the tiles more sparkling still. I heard them sparkle. The globe of colored glass above the bed spread an undulant undersea pattern. The surf lapped just outside.

"Why, it's like the...*Blue Grotto*," I exclaimed.

"You're always so *impressionable*, Jerry. That's why you're my favorite uncle."

"It's a fucking blue grotto and I'm *cold*. Would you tell me what we happen to be on now?"

"Acid. Pure Sandoz. The world's finest LSD."

"You're certain?"

"For sure. It's the *truth* drug, baby. Now we'll truly get to know each other."

"Now or never, huh?" The voice was not really my own.

I drew closer. *There*—the beat of his heart, like a bell buoy, like the boom of a cavernous hull. Gusts of salty air wailed down his windpipe. *A sea-change?* Absolutely. Were those pearls that were his eyes? They hid behind fluttering veils. But the teeth! They were mother-of-pearl, *pearlescent*. On his arms, in his armpits...there, in the pit of his thighs, the orange hairs swayed like...*seaweed*. Or did they?

Calm, suspended, weightless now, a sly elation seized me. The sea sounds chimed like crystal. We were sea-born brothers of an ocean womb, our home the sea-sucked grotto. I grew faint in the pit of my stomach, awash like a tidal pool. Maybe I was seasick. Diatoms swam inside my eye globes.

Mickey—First Class Fireman McCoy—lit a match, a rainbow flare, bright enough to set the world afire. But the match, a shriveling curl, lit the tip of his cigarette. A cloud swirled up in shapes of snakes and dragons. But of course! His sign—Aries—was in *Fire*. Only Pisces could be a *fish*. That was no sea-kin kindling there, but the son of fiery matter! The hairs, the veins themselves were glowing wires.

"What do you feel?" Echoing through space and time, the voice was rich in menace. Impressions were fleeting by too fast. I grabbed one.

"I feel...I *feel*...I'm in between the deep sea...and the *Devil*."

"Which is it going to be then, buddy?"

"Would I rather sink or swim?"

His trunk turned abruptly, thighs spread like the bat wings of a stingray, a swooping devilfish. His testes pressed my eyeballs, like them, moist and cool...and he was deep deep down my throat, past the palate, down the gullet, on a journey to the center of my being. Then I was deep in his, like him a flowing fluid...fire into water into fire again, forever and ever, *Amen.* The Saint had completed his mission—we were brothers under the skin.

"Do you think you know me any better, Mick?"
   "Sure, Jerry, why? Do you think you know me any worse?"
   "That was really super acid, wasn't it?"
   "The best of all probable worlds."
   "Who said that?"
   "I did, just now. You were listening."

I was at peace then, totally in love with everything. With Mickey's flame-red hair—again; with every constellation of his freckled back...*Gemini*...*Orion*...*Ursa Minor.* With the cosmos still whirling on the ceiling; with the iridescent cockroach dancing on the tiles, lovable antennae quivering as they caught our loving vibes.

The blue chamber turned violet, then rose, as though by chemical infusion. That would be the dawn. The Pacific, as far as I could see, had assumed transparent colors seen only in cathedral glass. Invisible birds sang in choirs, in tongues comprehensible to man. *The best of all plausible worlds,* they harmonized.

On the verge of the divine, I fell asleep.

43.

The world I awoke to at noon had been through a cosmic laundromat and had come out bleached and damp. Instead of rainbows we had rain. The ocean was grey and white, a pale engraving.

Mickey still looked good, though, uncovered on blue sheets. He joined me in the huge tile shower in a hollow mist of steam. That might be Jimmy Corey's slippery spine I'd once soaped at Eagle Rock. This was better. Mickey began to yodel. We spent a magic hour in our bath.

Another hour in the huge tiled dining room, at a table by the sea, speaking low like new conspirators, like spies from an alien realm. The others were the aliens, stolid seated tourists, ordering their usual ham and eggs. If only they had been where *we* had, right there in the same hotel! But the standard American Plan did not include our kind of side trip.

"May we have *huevos rancheros,* please?"

"The special ranch eggs? Indeed," agreed the waitress.

"Dos cervezas, por favor."

"Two Carta Blancas."

"Si, señorita." She jotted down the order and left. Underneath the table I touched my knees to Mick's, lest our magic circuit break.

"She's blonde," he said. "She speaks English just as good as you do."

"Just as *well.*" His knees retracted and were still. "No offense," I added. "It don't matter. I felt like speaking in another tongue today, something different."

"You were speaking something different last night, alright."

"What'd I say?"

"You were swimming upstream through eternity, like a salmon."

"What happened then?"

"I hooked you with a fly."

"No kidding. Did you hallucinate?"

"Sure, I always do. I saw stuff I couldn't believe. I was flying. I had wings like an eagle and scales like a dragon and a long red tail like an arrow."

"That's a griffin, a beast out of mythology."

"Whatever. It was fun."

"So how do you feel now?" The knees were back in place.

"Happy, the way I usually do when I get high enough. What's on the eggs? It looks like blood."

"A Mexican sauce. Aren't you hungry?"

"He must be *famished.*" Our table had two visitors. Lester held their luncheon check.

"We forgot to eat last night," I said.

"I doubt it. Those all-protein diets can ruin you, you know."

"So can booze and starches."

"Aren't they rude?" said Ron. "I'm glad they weren't at *our* party. We're taking a little trip to the bullfights now. A *corrida.*"

"We took our trip already, right here at the Rosarito."

"I think you're a couple of *weirdos*."
"That's not good Spanish."
"It's not anything, as far as we're concerned. Come on, Lester."

"They didn't even ask to pay our bill," said Mick.
"Some people have no manners. They're all like that when they travel." I thought of Leonard and his movie entourage.
"Not me and you."
"We're both completely different. *La cuenta, por favor.*"
"What did you just tell the waitress?"
"To bring the check. Nothing dirty."
"There isn't nothing dirty anymore."

Mickey drove south. We were not in any hurry. Children up ahead on the beds of family trucks would point to us and say things. We pointed back and laughed. The land was brown and barren. The rusty walls of fishing shacks had bright, childlike colors.

At kilometer 38 or 39 we stopped to watch the surfing. The reef breaks were a long way out in shallow waters. Now and then a surfer stood, inched slantingly across a swell, and paddled out again. It was not a spectator sport at that distance.

Campers of the surfers were parked in the ravines. Heads of bleached hair common to their race could be seen there, as California surfers waxed their boards and ate their groceries. A few were smoking dope, Mick observed. They had stereo radios and tape decks.

Farther south lay strands of black stones, round like the eggs of reptiles, that made a grinding rumble in the surf. Brown boys in wet pants collected them in buckets for Japanese-style gardens of L.A.

We drove to Ensenada, to a beach-side hotel smaller than the one in Rosarito. It was tranquil, warm, dream-like. We did not use other drugs or drink much. We slept a lot, together, and took walks in the late afternoon. Beyond the town were only trails through mesquite and dry grasses, between shifting dunes littered with seashells. We lay bare among the dunes and grasses. Sometimes a fisherman would pass and scarcely notice. It was the way of the *gringos*, he may have thought, if he thought of us at all. I shot roll after roll of color film, all of Mick, in all possible poses, like one of Leonard's Arabs in *Conquest of The Dunes*.

We lived in Ensenada three long days and nights before the Koda-chrome and travelers' checks were gone.

44.

Back at the pier some hard news awaited us. Three angry phone calls from a client, two pleas from Terry for a loan, a message of distress from Linda—Starkey's arm was broken—and a mailbox of second-notice bills. The sealed apartment had the dank smell of a jungle. The plants were languishing for want of friendly talk and water; two ferns had given up and died. The refrigerator stank like a morgue.

"I guess the honeymoon is over," Mickey said, dribbling water on a palm.

First of all I called Linda.

"You must have had a good trip. You certainly stayed long enough. I wish I had time to travel, and the means."

"It was a change from living here." "The Wild Blue Yonder" was a grinding clatter in my ear. I took the phone to the tower where the song hummed in the wallboards, sometimes buzzing in the glass.

"I guess you know about Starkey."

"How could he break an arm?"

"Why not a *leg?* Well, he fell off his surfboard. He took too many chances, Stevie said. He broke his forearm in two places. Near the shore as luck would have it."

"What sort of luck is that? Tell him I'll see him tonight."

"He misses you." Missed at last, I thought with resignation. The return of Captain Marvel from Never-Ever Land, just over the rim of the rainbow.

The next call mollified my client; I was badly in need of that check. I'd caught a bug in Mexico *(la cucaracha)* I told him, and would be on the job tomorrow, just as soon as my system allowed. Tucked among the bills was one of Leonard's letters, a featherweight *Aerogramme* from a Kensington address. The cramped words in violet script filled the sky-blue form like embroidery.

Jerry Dear,

This is your addled old Aunt Leonora. And believe me, she's a <u>mess.</u> They're wrapping up the picture out at Pinewood, 9 mil over budget. "Conquest of the Doomed" they call it now. The last two months have been a bloody nightmare! I'll spare you all the gory details.

First of all it <u>rained.</u> In the desert! For what seemed <u>more</u> than forty days and forty nights. I was waiting for the next Noah's Ark to come along. But who would I have taken for a <u>mate</u>? The stars sulked in their trailers and the extras fought over food. Most of our wardrobe was <u>ruined.</u> Everyone got some kind of disease. I was lucky. Mine was just a case of crabs. In the <u>eye-brows!</u> A cameraman noticed at a party where everyone was smoking hashish.

Then dashing Mister Dexter, ripped to the tits, fell off a camel and broke his right leg. It would have been the <u>middle</u> one except for all the padding. So they had to shoot around her with a gorgeous stand-in. They should have done that from the <u>beginning,</u> I could have told them. But His Lordship, the director, won't pay attention to anyone who isn't in front of his lens.

So I took a little sidetrip to Egypt. All of my favorite ruins were underwater. The Russkies are drowning the whole country with a <u>dam.</u> So I only saw a few of the mummies, horrible little shriveled-up things. Who <u>cares</u> if they died with a hard-on! They used to grind them up in England, you know, for drugs and aphrodisiacs. Isn't that <u>gruesome?</u> It sounds like Vincent Price!

I'm here on call right now and can't go out. Unless I leave the horn off the hook to cruise Hyde Park. It's colder than a wizard's dick! Those skinny English boys don't keep you warm nights, even with their darling page boy hair-styles. They all say they want <u>masters.</u> Do you think I'm the masterful type?

It's nearly Halloween. Here it's the Eve of All Saints and they don't even dress up in drag! I like our customs better. I

160

can't wait to fly back to my witch's lair and share it with those
sunny California lads!

Give my love to all the plants and whoever else is waiting
there for me.

Cheers,

Loin

Leonard the Lion Hearted

"What's it say?" asked Mickey at my shoulder.

"It says he's cut you out of his will."

"What would I do with all these plants, anyway?"

"Throw them out and grow some weed. Here. Read it."

"She's a scream," said Mickey having read. "Do you think I'm one
of the 'whoever' ones?"

"Not in my book you're not. You're enshrined in my heart forever."

"It's nice to be noticed," he said.

The mission of compassion sped me to the house alone. The door
was opened by Starkey, his right arm in a cast.

"Hi, Jerry! What'd you bring back from Mexico?"

"Fond memories and lots of photographs. We watched the surfing
at K-39. Outstanding! And caught a T-town floor show. It was fun.
Here's some comics and a hand-carved chess set."

"*Made in Taiwan*. Thanks. Did you and Mick meet any girls?"

"Some red-hot tamales, but they're for tourists. We were travelers."

"You sure know how to skirt the subject, don't you?"

"A time and place for everything, you understand?"

"I get it. Why ask?"

"It's good to be back. Does your arm hurt?"

"Naw, it feels real fine. Could you go for some Indian wrestling?"

We had a Linda Lee dinner and a peaceful sort of evening while the
children played games without argument. Children? Steve's and
Brenda's voices were those of young adults. I played chess with
Starkey. He was good. He was beginning to enjoy his new handicap,
just as I had mine. We were all on our good behavior, it seemed. That
night, for example, I had nothing to drink but wine.

"You look well," said Linda as I started to leave. "How's Mick?"

"He's fine, too. And how's Everett?" I went on, in a kind of farewell duet—or duel.

"In splendid shape," was her *riposte.* "He comes over quite a lot."

"I didn't see him here tonight."

"He's in Florida, with the children."

"Then they're fine, too. In fact we're *all* fine. I guess there's absolutely nothing to worry about. Well, take care of yourself, Linda. And let me know if there's anything at all I can do."

"You know what you could do if you wanted to. We're all alone up here. I hope you're happy though, Jerry. I really, truly do."

"Happiness is where you find it, hon."

"We know where you've been looking—not exactly under the welcome mat."

"How could I be happy without a home? Home is where the heart is, Linda." I gave my wife a quickie hug and kissed her on the mouth. She felt plumper than before. Was she losing her figure, or what?

Mickey's feeling was domestic, too. He cleaned all the rooms and put our things away. He was teaching himself how to cook. I came there from work as he once had from the Navy—to eat, drink, smoke and go to bed. That made the trip to Mexico emphatically worthwhile. Maybe the truth drug—*Bluebirds of Happiness*—had done it.

One night I had fallen contentedly asleep when a knock fell on the door. It was Terry again, full of beer. He drank another, told a tale, and joined us in the bed. It was like sleeping at home with his brothers, he said, back there in hilly Tennessee.

Long after midnight I awoke clearly startled, follicles tingling in my scalp. Yet another presence, squat and sinister, manifestly occupied the room. It hovered by the head of the staircase. Abruptly I was blinded by the pink and amber lights.

"*Wake up,* Cinderella, the ball's *over!*" The bald angry figure in the soiled British trenchcoat was that of our well-traveled landlord.

"Just what do you think you're *doing,* Jeremy Carr?"

"Doing? Why, only looking after things, Lenny."

"*What* things? The apartment's nearly vacant. Except for *my* bed."

"We put all of your things in the closet, Leonard, where they'd be safe and dry." Young Henderson awoke, grinding fists in puffy sockets, rippling his tattoos.

"I can see *you're* not in the closet anymore."

162

Mick sat up as if on duty. The swabbies harkened to their master's voice.

"Three of my former *friends*," the voice went on. "And in my satin sheets! How many sailors do you *need*, Jeremy? Is that what you mean by *safe and dry?*"

"It was all in good faith," explained Mickey. "Nothing's missing."

"Nothing's missing but my mind! I can't understand what you're saying. In four short months my native *tongue's* been turned around!"

"Well, you haven't lost the use of it, Leonard. Six months, you said you'd be gone, remember?"

"Six *months?* I wouldn't know what *country* I'm in, let alone what apartment. It used to be my own *pied a terre.*"

"Cool it, Lenny, it's still your pad. Here, try one of these." Mickey offered him a just-lit joint. "You're probably suffering from jet-lag."

"I feel I'm in a *time-warp*." Leonard sat on the bed and started puffing smoke. Burning seeds ate holes in the legs of his trousers. "There goes my Saville Row suit," he complained, killing sparks.

"What happened to your thing," said Mickey, "that you used to wear on your head?"

"My *perruque?* They *lost* it—in customs! They searched everyone for hidden dope. And *everywhere*. Just because we had been to Algiers. It was so *embarrassing*. I'm considering a lawsuit against the U.S. government."

"I'm glad it's not us you're going to sue."

"Yeah, Len. We were on a little trip, too."

"I can *see* you were. A trip around the *world*." Under the twin spotlights the stains were all too clear. I pulled up the green bed-spread. *"You've* certainly come a long way since I left you, Jeremy."

"I guess we all got a little surprise tonight."

Leonard yawned. "I've simply got to get some sleep now, children, your poor mother's worn to the *bone*. Tomorrow's Halloween, and I don't have a *thing to wear.*"

"Where are you planning to sleep, Len?"

"*Where?* Oh. I hadn't thought. I should have given thirty days' notice, don't you think? I'll just curl up on the *love*-seat, if none of you mind. I'm simply too tired to care." The naked pate bobbed down the staircase.

"He's all heart," said Mickey, dousing lights.

"And you're all hard again."

"Let's do it one more time," suggested Terry. "It might be our very last chance."

45.

Terry had been right, so far as further fun and frolic in the Seafarers Chapel was concerned. By the time we came downstairs Leonard had been up for hours, sitting at the telephone, his hairy legs crossed. He wore silk socks and garters, a Japanese kimono with a purple iris print, and a white silk scarf around his head. The effect was that of a hotel guest who has just survived a Tokyo earthquake. Now he was telling all his friends:

"Oh, it was *horrible,* Milly. You can't *believe* what it is to deal with people like that. I couldn't trust them for a *minute. Yes? Yeah-uss.* No, I'm *not* going back, no matter *what* they paid me. *Diamonds* wouldn't do it...NO! Not *one word* to anybody. They can take the whole bloody picture, camels, sand, and Arabs, and shove it up their corporate bloody *ass!* They want me down at Metro. They've been after me for *years.* Yes! And they'll pay me *thousands* more, with a *credit!*

"Oh, hello. Help yourselves to coffee, boys," said Leonard, interrupting himself, blowing smoke from a cigar. "And there's rolls there if you want them. All right, they're *bagels.* Eat or die."

"Oh, some friends who were here to greet me. They gave me a little surprise. I'll see you then for cocktails. Yes, of course. At *seven.*" He hung up and patted the scarf. "I've got a *million* things to do today, boys. Why don't you help put my furnishings back? Oh, never *mind.* You'd better get your own things together. I'll have someone do it next week.

"And Jerry, don't worry anymore about the *rent.* In fact here's a *hundred.* You'd better start looking for another place." Leonard wrote a check on his knee and dialed another number.

"Here. Don't worry about anything, except each other. *Yes,* Gordon, and I've been longing to hear from *you.*" The monologue took on an intimate tone as Leonard took the phone up the staircase.

Exiled from the Garden, like Adam and Eve and the apple. Three slippery smart-ass serpents. Let the green ferns weep. I *knew* we had done something wrong. Mickey, dressed for once, started pulling clothes out of closets while I shoved drawings into Safeway cartons. The rest would have to wait.

"I guess I'll be heading back," said Terry, in sober blue serge. "I'll catch you later. If I can."

"Yeah, we'll let you know about the house-warming, Spencer," said his ex-Navy mate. "We'll throw a pillow party." The carousel was cranking out some military theme.

What if I'd stayed in the Air Force? I'd be out in six more years, fit-and-forty, another life ahead. If I hadn't cracked up in an airplane, or been found out-of-uniform with a soldier, sailor or marine.

Then I would cruise the world, seducing red-haired youths of every nation—if that's all I wanted to do. A lucky stroke—to have red hair become my first-time sexual fetish. Suppose Jimmy Corey had been a three-toed albino dwarf? I'd be in real trouble then—never satisfied. The whole wide world would not be large enough.

And how about Linda and the rest, the absent family I'd just recalled to mind? How satisfied were they?

"What's running through your head, Lucky Pierre?" said Mickey. "How about loading the car?"

"I'm wondering where to go next. I feel like a fucking outcast."

"You'll get used to it, Jerry. I've felt that way all my life."

"I'm sure as hell glad we're together."

"All right then. Lenny wanted me to stay."

As soon as I'd marked the rental ads, we made an all-day tour of city streets. Too near, too far, too noisy, too *nice*. It had to be something both of us could live with. As we drove through the canyon at sunset Mickey saw the hand-lettered sign on Channel Road: APARTMEANT FOR RENT. "Whatever it is we'll take it. That apartment's meant for us."

How true! The house was a wedge between streets that collided at Pacific Coast Highway—the very intersection where our lives had first crossed. Seen from one side the building was a Swiss chalet, from another a bleached shingle hulk. A single palm stood up in front like some organic flagpole.

The apartment, a second-floor railroad flat, had one long room like a motel lobby—a kitchen and a bath at one end, a glassed-in porch at the other. The porch had an alcove for my table and a corner where two single beds made one. I liked that idea—six feet from work to pleasure. Bands of sliding glass faced the ocean, the glare cut by slats of wooden blinds. Around us were the leavings of a party and a roomful of debris.

"They left in sort of a hurry," the landlady explained, offering me a broom. "I only had time to put the sign out. You're the first. It's eighty a month, furnished, plus utilities." I gave her Leonard's check. "You don't have pets or children do you, Mr. Faircycle?"

"Just ourselves. We're related. He's McCrory, and I'm Carr."

"Carr and McCrory. It sounds like a vaudeville team. But you don't remember those days, I suppose. Here's the keys, Mr. Carr. These are for the front doors, upstairs and down, but that one's usually open. And this is for the service entrance, for deliveries."

Fantastic! Furnished view apartment with private rear entrance—or emergency escape route! Mick sat on the beds and lit the first illegal joint. "Funky but nice," he mused, holding smoke in his lungs.

Kneeling on the mattresses, leaning on the sill, we could watch the canyon action I already knew. I had frequented the block of false fronts opposite, gleaming in the sunset like a row of gold teeth: the Casa Mia, a gay beer bar, the Friendship's prow on the sidewalk, an A&W root beer stand, a gourmet restaurant—*Le Croix de Guerre.* And up the street the TUMBLE INN, an asphalt lot, the bisexual cocktail lounge and steakhouse. That night we checked them all— for Halloween, no I.D.'s asked or given.

In the morning I put on trunks and called Linda from a pay phone to ask if I could borrow her van. She said I could—later. Then I started barefoot through the tunnel to Will Rogers State Beach. Like a Sunday morning Extra, the walls carried spray-paint headlines: **HOOVER SUCKS** on one wall, on the other **VIRGINIA ATE A BANANA WITH HER VAGINA**, and in crayon, **so did anna**. Among broken glass, hot dog wraps, and rubbers lay a silver slipper and a crushed magenta kerchief, sacrifices of the night before.

The machine-swept sand was fresh as a hospital's clean sheets. White gulls policed the beach like tiny nurses. I took smooth cold waves to shore, feeling each time more cleansed of Leonard's worldly decadence, free of the carousel's fever, no longer adrift on the pier. Mick and I had four feet on the ground, a new existence.

Later the same day we had our first visitor. We had just finished putting our clothes away when Linda walked in without a knock.

"Well, Jerry, you seem to be well organized. It didn't take you long."

Like the Adam of Michelangelo, Mick was postured nude on the couch, arm raised on a knee, a leg thrust out as though awaiting contact with its Maker. More comely than the seminal stem of the First Man, the Saint lay across one loin like a lamb chop on display at the market. Mickey, hardly stirring, showed his dimples in a smile.

"Why don't you have a seat, Mrs. Carr? Linda?"

"Yes, why don't you, sweetheart. And how about a nice cold beer?"

"I think I will. Your place looks quite comfortable. You've certainly made yourselves at home." Although her blonde head steered a passage of the room, her eyes kept sliding back to Mickey's groin, just as mine did. It was Linda's first meeting with the Saint. Now we had something new in common.

"It's private," Mickey began telling her. "There's nobody looking in the windows, unless they've got a captain's glass. It's like a ship's bridge up here." It was indeed. Why wasn't I the first to think of it?

"Starkey and the others will be up soon," Linda felt compelled to say, libido yielding to maternal instinct. "They're just across the street. We left the van there."

Reluctantly, as though dressing up for dinner, Mickey wrapped a towel around his middle and took an armchair seat. The blinds laid shifting contours on his back, like the stripes of a restless tiger. They would have to be photographed, for sure, on some less gregarious occasion.

"We brought you guys something." Starkey pushed his way in the door, a tray of capped cokes in his sling.

"Yeah," said Steve, with two big sacks. "Wonder Weenies in a Blanket. They're foot-long hot dogs." Brenda was already into the french fries.

"Just what we were hoping for," I said. "Was that your selection?"

"A canyon specialty, it turns out. You want yours with relish?"

"Anyway it comes." The three sat around the cable-spool table in front of the gas log's fake hearth. On the mantle Mick had tacked a poster of a huge Hawaiian wave, and a photo of a stocky girl in only fins and goggles. The pictures would show visitors where our heads were at. Steve said the diver's titties looked unreal. He didn't believe a wave that big, either.

"What makes *you* an expert?" Brenda asked, chomping. Steve made a feint at her breasts. They had ripened, I suddenly saw, like two of that year's avocados—as Mick had been aware all along. His parted legs and forward slouch allowed a glimpse beneath the bath towel. Brenda looked away at the ocean. If any felt discomfort, they were she and I.

"What'd you do for Halloween, Linda?"

"Oh, we had a little party. I was a witch this year."

"She tried to dress Starkey up like Peter Pan. The boy who never grew up."

"Peter *Pansy*," Steve said. "The little freak had wings."

"That ain't me, you son-of-bitch!"

"Hell, no, Stark," I interjected. "You're Billy the Kid. We'll have some target practice next week. If you think your arm is up to it, Straight Shooter."

"It is, whenever you are." He began to crack ice between his teeth.

"And what did you two do?" Linda said to me.

"Oh, we didn't bother to get dressed up."

"No, you didn't have to."

"I couldn't decide what I wanted to be."

"Have you now?"

"For the present. Come on, I'll show you the sun porch."

Linda and I sat down side-by-side on either mattress. I heard Mickey's deeper voice join the others.

"I can appreciate that you're good friends," said my wife. "But do you really think you ought to be sleeping here together?"

"There's plenty of room. What difference does it make? We're both men, aren't we?"

Linda's heel had touched an object on the floor. She picked it up and laid it on the sill—a half-used tube of K-Y lubricating jelly, half-wrapped in a half-congealed washcloth.

"Not any difference to you, perhaps. You're much older. But Mickey's practically a youngster, still a growing boy."

"No one's a simple *boy* anymore after growing up in foster homes, reform school and the Navy."

"Don't you think it's slightly immoral?"

"Our *mo-res*, you mean? Are you going to go into that?"

"What you do is your choice. I think Mick should have a chance to know some girls."

"He's had plenty of girls. He likes people."

"I like people, too, but I've never had a girl friend to sleep with."

"Well, why don't you try one, Linda, while you're waiting for your prince to come? There aren't many princes left, especially for mothers with four children. Try a princess sometime. She might surprise you."

"I'm only trying to help you, Jerry. You needn't be unkind. I don't want to see you chasing princes, either. As you say, they can be transformed." Our voices had begun to rise against the outside traffic noises.

"Only by fairy godmothers."

"The kiss of a toad can do it." Linda swilled the dregs of beer with gusto and wiped her fingers on the stiffened washrag. I knew then that she would stop at nothing.

"Well, how many toads have you kissed, Linda Lee?"

"How many *men*, I keep asking myself."

"I wonder, too. Keep right on asking."

"I thought you might have an answer. Or have you given up?"

"I haven't given up on anything. I guess I don't know when I've had enough."

"That's where you're different from a woman, Jerry." Linda rose.

"Come on, everybody, let's get going," called Brenda. "Before those two start arguing." The children left to find my Fury. We could trade cars again on the morrow.

"Thank you, Linda, for the use of the van. I'm sorry if it seemed to upset you."

"It's certainly not the *car* I'm concerned about. It's you I'm thinking of, Jerry. At least you're closer to us here than on that crazy Merry-Go-Round."

"Within calling distance. As soon as they put the phone in."

"We'll see you then soon, perhaps for dinner."

"I'd sure like that, Linda," said my roommate. "Your cooking's really super. I wish I could take lessons from you." Standing up, he let the towel slip, and caught it with a grin.

"Why, thank you, Mick. Don't let Jerry starve you."

"No way, Linda, and I won't let him have too much to drink."

"He does need looking after."

"I'll try my best, Linda. Haven't you?"

"Yes, Mick. I'm sure you will, too. I think I trust you." *Jesus*. Were they never going to quit their game of verbal Ping-Pong? Would Superwoman go back to planet Krypton? Would Linda never leave?

"Goodbye then, Linda." Linda left. As she left Mickey flung away the towel and fell on the sofa, laughing.

"That'll teach her to knock first!"

His next move was touchingly boy-like, affectingly human. He finger-combed a lock of hair and fixed me with a look of total innocence. *Where had I gone wrong?*—it seemed to ask.

Leonard didn't wait to be asked. He told us all about his Halloween that night as we went about our packing.

"Oh! It was absolutely *marvelous*. Way up in the hills, you know, by the *Hollywood* sign, where the silent stars built palaces and castles. This one had a moat and a drawbridge. It didn't work, of course, and the whole place is crumbling. Like the *Fall of the House of Usher*, or the one in *Sunset Boulevard*. All the better, for *our* Halloween! It was full of real cobwebs, with *torches* in the walls, and torn velvet draperies. The Great Hall had a table set for twenty-six, a double thirteen, you know, but we had at least *two hundred*.

"You don't have to leave already? Have a going-away *libation* before you go. One for the road! I hope it's not *too rocky*." Leonard wore a velvet robe with fleurs-de-lis all over it and a convincing, well-fitted wig. Blowing smoke from a long ivory holder he brought us two Negritos.

"I can't keep you long, my pets. There's someone upstairs, waiting. A perfect *jewel*. We've planned a trip already.

"We were driven to the castle, in old limousines, and left off at the gates. Everyone wore a mask. It was just like *Phantom of the Opera*, the early one with Lon Chaney. The costumes were absolutely *fabulous*. I was Louis *Seize*, my date was Marie Antoinette. We lost our *heads* for each other! *Judy* was there, with three beauties. *George* and his gang of charmers, and three of the biggest *agents*, with some of their latest finds. It was the party of the *year*, my dears, you should have *been* there. You'll see it in all the papers, probably **LIFE**. *Vincent* was supposed to appear, but *Chaplin* didn't show up, either." The story was somehow familiar.

"Was it any fun, Lenny?"

"Un-*be-liev-able!* Mad, mad dancing, with a Spanish tango orchestra, and buckets and buckets of rose petals, like a great star's funeral. We had *coffins* full of iced champagne, and three catered bars. Two guests fell in the swimming pool. It's been empty for *years.* We could hear *rats* in the bottom, and coyotes howling in the hills.

"Then we all went down to the basement. It was decorated like a *torture* chamber. We had one fan-tas-tic orgy there. After the older ones left, of course. Even the cute little *pages* joined in."

"Did anyone get hurt?"

"Oh, one minor injury, but that's been taken care of. He'll be fine by the end of the week. Those S&M queens never know when to stop. You can't tell *them* it's only a party! They were all on *speed,* or worse."

"Lenn-narrd?"

"*YES*, gorgeous, I'll be right up! *You can start without me,* as Tallulah used to say. Or was it Marion?"

"That was you! Last night in the dungeon," came the cry from above. "You couldn't get your royal *tights* off. We had to do it *for* you!"

"I think she *dreams* of whips and chains. I've really got to say goodnight now. Be good, boys, and don't forget to *shtup* each other."

"Hang on to your schlong," said Mick.

"Mine, or anyone else's. Here's a farewell *kiss*." I spotted in the quick embrace, nearly hidden by the white silk scarf, two angry purple bruises. Had his face been as pale before? I looked back from the top of the ramp. The tower's gothic windows were blacked out, the glazing bars like frail white crosses.

In our joined beds I heard the cafes fill again, the cries grow shrill, then raucous. Presently a prowl car came along. Some of the noises ceased. I heard the solenoid clicking of the signal change, the squeal of tires on asphalt. Would it be like that every night, always?

My hand began its customary journey, over the hills, into the dale, my fingers finally closing at the junction of his belly and his thighs. Mickey rolled over slowly, toes turned out, and rooted himself between mattresses.

"Do it," he muttered in the pillow. "Do it now." He was offering up, in its tenderest form, the ultimate friendly gesture.

I reached for the tube in its discovered cloth and anointed both our persons—and sunk where I had not yet sunk before, as far as it was possible to do so. Hands around his shoulders, chest against the blades, hollows of my trunk against his buttocks, I was fastened like a shadow to my mate—so close that every sound was banned, all inside vision banished. Was the mind then finally mindless? Something soared. It was a long time coming back.

"Do you want to do it too, Mick?" I whispered, lips at the nape of his neck. There the ruffled hair was shingled like the feathers of a red bantam rooster.

"No," he said at length. "It already did its thing. When you did."

At those words I was supremely happy.

46.

Linda didn't knock the next time, either. She telephoned. Her wish, as she described it, was for Mick to come up and mow the grass. Stevie was too lazy, or tired from the surf. She would pick up Mick and pay him for his time. Then I would be working, too. I could drive there later, shoot targets with Starkey and pay some attention to our child. Then the whole family team would have its dinner. That was Linda's Master Plan. Like a welfare worker on an obstinate case of social maladjustment, she had decided where her help was needed most.

The plan was flawless. The fault was in the weather. No sooner had she left with Mick than rain began. The rain became a storm, the storm a cloudburst; the dust of summer turned to mud. In late afternoon a mudslide closed the highway. Linda called to say the plan was canceled, the power off, that they would play games by candlelight around the fire. *Beautiful.* I had played those games myself. Why was Providence on *her* side? Fate, it seemed, was always with the keeper of the house.

What about *me*, alone with a drink by the gas log, a wet stain spreading overhead? Too bad Mick hadn't been Ship's Carpenter. Then we could work together days as well as play at night. But such skills had not been navy-taught or natural—he was bored and impatient with tools. I empathized. What was it to work with dead sticks and dry stones when one could charm the lives of other, less privileged creatures, merely by his radiant existence?

And what, I thought rhetorically, was a structure of posts and beams and plastic in respect to the wonderfully wrought, superbly detailed, autonomously functioning, ruddy, ready, red-roofed, red-blooded entity of the boy called Mick McCrory? *Nothing.* Except as one served as shelter to the other.

No construction in the history of the world, however intricate and noble, could compare in simple everyday and everynight wonder, to that walking, talking, and yes—*fucking* miracle that at each passing breath renewed itself, like *fire.* That was a heart-warming thought to go to sleep on, if I could. What were they doing now?

"We didn't do much of anything," said Mick the next evening. "Except eat and play kids' games. Starkey gets sore when he loses. Your old lady's a great little chef, though. She sure knows what she's doing."

"Don't tell me. I married her. Did you get any sleep?"

"Well, I tried to on the living room couch. I woke up with a tongue in my ear—Randy's. Are you jealous?" I hung out my tongue and panted. "I did think about your daughter. But I don't think she thought about me."

"I did."

"All *right* then. I'll take you to a movie, Jerry. Linda laid a ten on me for yardwork, even though it rained."

It was not ideal, working at close quarters, when I had to spend time at the board. I would awake, drink coffee, and start tracing lines while Mick was still a bundle in the corner of the beds, not stirring till the phone rang. Eventually he threw off the covers, lit a Lucky, and exposed himself to light of day. He would yawn, stretch, and lean on the board, naked and smelling of warmth.

"What's this, Jerr, our dream house?" he might ask. "Where's my wardrobe, and the whirlpool bath? Where's the marble fireplace?"

"I don't even know where the house is going to be yet."

"Why, by the ocean, don't you think? On a cliff like Linda's. We both like the ocean, don't we?"

"Sure, but in different ways, if birth signs mean anything. Mine's a water sign, Pisces. Aries is in fire." Ash was falling on my work sheet.

"And you're scared of getting burned?"

I brushed away the ashes. "I'm more scared of being left out in the cold, I think."

"Sit over here in the sun, man. Let's have a little toke."

A working deadline would thus become as flexible as Mick's young body.

So it might be all right, I concluded, if he went to the house days and earned some spending money, so long as I could supervise at night. That kept it all in the family. At the house I was made to feel a father again, as in the spurious role of uncle I sometimes played for Mick.

Whatever my position, counterfeit or not, his was even better. He was flattering with Linda, provocative with Brenda, serious with Steve. He liked to race along the beach with that other Irish redhead, Randy. The two were alike: frisky, eager for affection, more than ready to please. The setter's name could serve them both.

Mickey's powers to give pleasure soon made him an adoptive member of the clan. I felt pride in the success of my protegé, envy that the star was not myself. Only Starkey kept his reservations, and these to himself. Casey was a non-discriminating baby. And nothing was expected of those uncommitted delegates, the house cats.

Something else had changed between Linda and me: she no longer seemed to care how much I drank. Mick could always drive me home, she would remark as she poured another stiff one. I saw beyond this new liberality a warning more sinister than all the times of sore reproach. It meant that she found me expendable. For Mickey there still remained hope.

"No thanks, I've had enough," were words I learned to repeat on more than one occasion.

"Suit yourself," Linda said one night as we were leaving. "We'll expect to see Mick this coming Thursday."

"Am I invited, too?"

"Well, of course, Jerry. What would any holiday be without you? You can bring the champagne if you don't mind. It's going to be a big sit-down dinner."

47.

So why did I feel thankless, that clear Thanksgiving Day? Mick had got himself up something special in a pink rodeo shirt with pearl snaps, white low-rise corduroys, cordovan boots and belt, a matching gauntlet for his shockproof watch. Why compete with anything like that? To this red robin of our dynamic duo I was only playing batman. I wore my customary go-to-hell ranch wear.

A chain of cars sat end-to-end in front of side-by-side beach homes that blocked a glimpse of the Pacific Ocean from Topanga to Malibu Pier. A party five miles long was under way. At one house or another any stranger could walk in. I *knew* some of those people. Why not stop right there?

"Relax," said Mickey in his tight, bright clothes, passing me a joint between cupped fingers. I glanced in the mirror for a cruise car, already turning slightly paranoid. But that was how I felt about the banquet—Linda's upcoming sit-down dinner.

The day was good for surfers on the long breaks at the pier. The sea was shining indigo, a sea of ink. Like a dry wide river of air the wind flowed from distant mountain passes. The hills were the tawny gold of rustling grain. They were ripe for a harvesting by fire.

Leaning on the gate was Starkey with his rifle, his small face shadowed by a gaucho's hat, the arm-cast like a wing in a bandanna. A century before, a few years older, he'd have held up the stage on El Camino Real. I jammed on the brakes and shot my hands up. "Drop your weapons—it's the One-Arm Bandit!"

"We're in real trouble now," grumbled Mickey, slouching out. "I thought you said this was the *safe* way."

"We took a chance. It was this or the redskins, and you know what *they* do to a man before they're finished."

"Let's not even think about it, pardner." He clutched his scalp and groin in mock horror. Starkey's look stayed grim. Casey had got loose and squatted bare beneath a bush, teeth around a bottle's nipple, white hair stringy in the wind. The West was still a little wild at this outpost. From the kitchen came the scent of prairie sage.

"I guess it's okay for you guys to pass. If you still want to." Starkey waved his gun. "No tricks, though."

"Don't take our lives before our money, friend. He's got a price on his head." I nodded mine at Mickey's. "He thinks he's a fast-draw artist."

"Jackrabbit McCoy. Faster than a bullet."

"I heard aboutcha, Jack. I'm faster."

"Oh, hello," said Linda at the door. "I see you brought a baby, too."

"We found him up the road," I said. "Headed for the Mexican border. A gringo wetback. He didn't have any papers."

"He's a funny little tyke. Do you think he understands us?"

The silent child studied us with cool blue eyes. His mother there, in some kind of cowgirl skirt and blouse, a concho belt and bracelets —who did she think *she* was? She had even let her hair down. Thanksgiving had become a masquerade.

It was beautiful out on the terrace, out of the wind in the winter sun. I was following the silhouettes of surfers. One was Phillip; another Steve. Presently four Vandenbergs would join us, then Brenda and her high school friend. His was the new Triumph in the driveway. As Linda filled our goblets with ice cold chablis I was at peace with the hour and all those living in it. Here was a home that didn't *need* a full-time master.

"Aren't you coming with me?" The whites of Starkey's eyeballs gleamed beneath his bandit's hat. The sling held two boxes of cartridges.

"Sure, kid, why not? Let's go shoot something. Anything to keep our hand in."

A short way south along the beachfront the cliffs gave way to a ravine. Beneath a graded dirt road ran a six-foot corrugated storm drain, a shooting gallery ready made, sunlit targets on the rocks beyond its throat. Bottles whole or broken sparkled like a mound of scattered jewels. Rifle locked in his left arm, Starkey dropped prone and squeezed off a clip of .22's. He shot a tight pattern, clipping bottlenecks without a single miss.

But I had been a Marksman in the Air Force. I picked off random pieces. We set up a tin sign, OPEN HOUSE, and perforated the letters, destroying the name of the realtor. When I hit the metal culvert, bullet heads whined off the walls.

"Hey! You *kids* down there. Don't you know what day it is?" I knew what man it was, a neighbor, Dr. Fritchy. "Why not do it somewhere else? Then we can be thankful, too. Or better yet, Jerry, why not join us for a drink?" I nodded and passed the rifle.

"Christ," muttered Starkey, dusting off the barrel. "Do you have to go drink there now?"

"I'm only making a social call, just so they won't be mad at us."

"Always an alibi," he sighed. "I'll see you at the house. Don't miss the turkey."

"I haven't missed yet, have I?"

"There's a lot of things you miss, Jerry, things you don't even know about."

"The Shadow Knows."

"Yeah, but not the substance." Was this still a ten-year-old child? He might be watching too much television for any mortal's good!

Another purpose in visiting the doctor's house was to check up on my work—the way a good physician follows the progress of his patients' diseases. The new bar, made of driftwood and seashells set in plastic, incorporated blenders full of frozen daiquiris—the answer to a sharpshooter's thirst. From the raised elevation I surveyed the living room, its fifty glass feet of ocean view, its forty or more selected guests—associates or patients of Dr. Harold Fritchy. The doctor ran a clinic in interface therapy in self-aware Beverly Hills. His estate had a supervised guesthouse, twin Swirlpools, and vine-clad security fencing with electrically-operated gates.

That afternoon all eyes turned inward, away from the dazzling sea. Who was he or she, this or that attractive—sometimes rejective—guest? The first lip-numbing daiquiri would help me figure it out. I spoke to a woman in a sari with a cast mark and long red nails, to a jolly couple just returned from Iceland (it was green), to a bearded gentleman with heavy lips (the rent-a-cop), and to a slim, vulnerable-looking youth in his twenties. In a little test of insight I figured him for Gay.

"Your face seems somehow familiar. Have I seen you somewhere before? The Polo Lounge? The Gala? The..."

"I don't go to public bars," said the slender young man in the slim-fitting Brooks Brothers suit. "I'm a second-year intern, preparing for a practice in psychiatry. And you?"

"Oh, I design and build things. I remodeled parts of this house."

"You're successful then."

"Oh, thank you, miss. I think I will." A maid had passed a tray of daiquiris. "Professionally, yes. Right now I have a few domestic problems."

"Her friend or yours?" he asked coolly. He sucked on a plastic party-pick, gazing past me at the wide Pacific view. An oral erotic, I was certain. You could spot them every time.

"At the moment it's difficult to say."

"And no need to say it today, is there?" He had moved to the side of a tasty-looking girl in an organdy skirt and halter, who whispered in his ear before they joined an older couple. I looked about the room for future clients, as the intern had doubtless done, too.

At five o'clock a maid addressed me. She had not brought a tray of fresh drinks. "I think it's your home, Mr. Care. They say your dinner's ready, and to please come back real soon."

"Then I really must be leaving," I replied, sucking dry the delicious rum-saturated ices, green as summer sherbet, cold as Greenland.

"Well, be careful, Jerry boy," said Dr. Fritchy, with a firm professional back pat. "And don't forget that I'm here when you need me. We all have little problems now and then."

"The same goes for you, Doc. And many thanks." I walked wide-stanced as a sailor down the glaring sunset trail, pausing on the way to pluck a garland of fragrant wildflowers.

"What's with the weeds?" said Mickey at the terrace door.

"A nosegay of posies for my bride. I'll mount them in a crystal vase. Smell!"

"You'd better get it on and carve the bird. And try to sober up. We're all starving."

The extended dining board was set for ten. On a field of blinding white glittered Linda's best silverware and china. Everyone was seated, fingering the stems of champagne glasses. Linda and her clever hands had arranged the table thus:

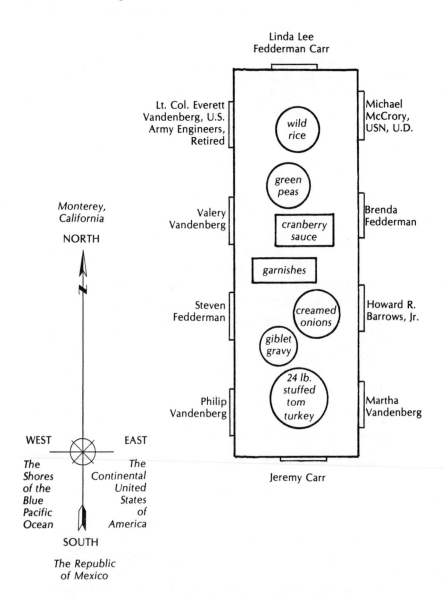

The symmetry of the seating plan did not allow a place for Starkey, who had drawn up a stool to my left. Seated on my right was the newly-reconciled wife of Colonel Everett. I assumed that her Fort Myers major had found a younger love, the usual resolution of such affairs. Martha Vandenberg, in her well-constituted forties, was another redhead in view. The probable gray was a titian shade, like the model on a kit of Clairol products.

Brenda's new friend, Howard Barrows Junior, was a handsome youth in a striped tie and a seersucker jacket. Howard was black. Let's see...with Mickey and the Vandenbergs there were *four* redheads of various persuasions, four natural blonds of the Fedderman strain, one head of ebony hair, one retired greyhead, and one with careless hair described as BRN on my California driver's license. A platinum blond—Casey—was asleep in his crib, doped on eggnog. And then there was a *fifth* redhead—Randy. As I finished counting heads, the redhead to my right raised her glass.

"Here's to the gracious head of the house. Long may he reign!" Martha toasted. She meant *me*—I suddenly realized.

"And here's to its gracious heart, lovely Linda Lee," I responded, downing the champagne. Now let's see what these *hands* can do, I thought, like an aborting surgeon, switching on the battery-powered blade. The knife sliced through the roast like crisp meringue. First, for the guest of honor, I started piling turkey on the plates.

"What would you like, Mrs. Vandenberg? White meat or dark?"

"Oh, I'd prefer the light, I believe. It does look delicious. Thank you, Mr. Carr, that's lovely."

The question might sound odd, put to Howard. *Will you have breasts or thighs,* I might ask. But that was even worse! I shouldn't have been drinking. "I'll have a little bit of each," the boy said helpfully.

"And I'll take a leg," declared Brenda. "With lots of chestnut dressing."

Mickey I didn't have to ask. He was a confirmed breast man, as I supposed I was. The plates bobbed round the table until each was full and I could sit. Why all the ceremony, I pondered. The sit-down dinner was *her* idea. An outdoor buffet would have matched our costumes perfectly. Now we were stuck in straight chairs between fixed partners.

I especially resented Philip on my left. It wasn't right that he should bear upon that spindly neck and fragile skull the same flamboyant banner as my best friend Mick. They had nothing else in common but their years. I was glad that Stark sat between us.

Was Martha Vandenberg of Vicksburg, Mississippi, accustomed to sitting down with dark folk? If not, that was her tough luck! Howard was quite bright, I had been gathering, and would go up to Stanford in the fall. The problem on the starboard side was Mickey, who wasn't talking or even grinning much. Brenda had turned her cold shoulder, leaving Linda to dilute his envy. His attention to her was shared partly with the Colonel. The Colonel's daughter tried to make a conversation come alive, but her mother....

"Of course, in the part of the country where we were brought up, it wasn't in the least unusual to have so many of our chestnut coloring present at the table. Why, when our immediate family and all the aunts and the uncles and the cousins and their kin got together for the holiday festivities, there might be as many as *thirty*, can you imagine? Although some of that red hair was found on the pretty little heads of the youngest ones, and some among the silver locks of the eldest. And some distinguished old heads they were!

"My mother's side of the family was said to be auburn-haired from way back before the Rebellion..." I stared at the fading ocean—out there it was still a nice day..."from County Cork in Ireland, from a pretty little village on the River Lee. Now isn't that a nice coincidence for our first holiday together, Linda Lee?"

Linda agreed that it was.

"Well, all the time that I've been sitting here recollecting our ancestry, Philip and Valery's, and I do think I've perhaps gone on too long, please excuse me, I've been wondering where yours came from, Mr. McCrory. Do you know?"

Mickey looked up from his cold plate. "My what?" Why, your fabulous, illustrious, internationally-renowned, red-knobbed *shillelagh*—you dingy doper! What did you think we were talking about?

"Your attractive red hair, we were discussing down at this end."

"From my mother, I guess. She was Irish. Now she's dead."

"Well, I'm very sorry to hear that. A mother can be important at any time of life, not only when she's helping a boy to grow."

"It depends on how important, and to whom," put in the mini-savant who gnawed a wing beside me. Starkey winked.

"A mother never questions why or when," said Martha sweetly. "Her affection is naturally there all the time. I believe you'll come to recognize that simple truth, young man. Won't he, Linda Lee?"

"When he starts growing up, I think he will."

"When she starts growing old, is what she means."

"That's not a very pleasant thing to say in front of guests," said his mother. "Is it, Jerry? Why don't you talk to him, dear."

"I'm talking to you, Starkey."

"I can hear you."

Midway through the dinner the mood began to mellow. Flushed by drafts of French Colombard, eleven alimentary canals had gone to work. Martha Vandenberg praised the menu. "Why it's almost exactly what we might have had at home. Isn't it, Everett?"

"I don't know, is it? We've had so many homes in the service. She learned how to do things in the South, you see," he said to Linda, and was off on another service story. I heard the names *Pearl Harbor, the Solomons, Saipan, Truk.*

"Oh, I didn't know that, sir," said Mick, blotting gravy from his pink western shirt, where a shift of Brenda's elbow had put it.

"Is Mr. McCrory closely related to your family, Jeremy?" asked Martha.

I poured more wine. "In the strictest sense of blood relationship, no. But he is a very, very close friend. Of the whole family. Mickey's very helpful, you see. Sometimes he helps Linda. Sometimes he helps me. Sometimes he helps us both. I think he helps us *all*, at one time or another."

"But you and Linda have separate living establishments, don't you?"

"In a manner of speaking, yes. She lives here. I have a small but efficient office space in Santa Monica where I sometimes stay the night. It's much much closer to my work."

"It's closer to most everything," echoed Starkey like a parrot from his perch. Linda had been right—the spoiled little cripple was getting out of hand!

"Then Mickey lives with you?" asked the persistent colonel's lady.

"He *is* residing there, yes, until he gets his own two feet on the ground. Or four wheels, whichever comes first."

"I see. I suppose he's your close companion then, a kind of houseboy to look after the little things. How nice that must be for you both!"

"Yes, I suppose it is, Martha. Though not so nice as when you have a *man* around the house. Is it?"

Martha put a napkin to her tightened lips. Mickey was the first to leave the table—before the fruit compote could be served. Brenda and Howard excused themselves; we heard the Triumph start. The other two teenagers split. Starkey and the dog left together. There remained four adults and scores of dirty dishes. After coffee, the Colonel left too.

I mixed a batch of after-dinner Stingers, but the two wives merely held their glasses while they talked about children and food. Some night I'd get that loose-lipped Dixie lady loaded all alone and pop the loaded question: *Could Evy get it up?* And if not, *why not!* But tonight was not the night, I somehow knew. I took the Stingers to the study and flaked out on the couch.

When I opened eyes again they were aimed at the TV screen. Black and white shadows chased across it—a girl, it would seem, in a middy blouse and hair-clip, a boy with a pushed-up hat and nose. The boy, when he grinned, resembled Mickey. He and the girl were in an open car, a studio *process shot.*

"That's a '32 roadster," I heard Stevie's voice say, "a model A."

"Yeah, but it's not powered." Starkey there.

"Who cares?" their sister said. "It's not the car that counts."

"We know, Brenda, it's the singer, not the song." *The Stinger, not the stung,* my head rhymed dreamily. The boy had parked the car and kissed the girl.

"The dinger, not the dong," said Steve.

"You're too smart for your britches, you foul-mouthed surfer boy."

"You're not smart enough for anybody's yet. Did Howard drive you home, or did you hitchhike?"

"Shut up. Let Jerry sleep."

"Where is everybody?" I gaped.

"You mean Mickey? Or Mom. She took a walk."

"Yeah, she's somewhere down the beach."

"Maybe you should take a walk," said Starkey.

"And miss the movie? Just for that I will."

Beneath a low crescent moon the sand was faintly lighter than the wine-dark sea. I saw no moving figure anywhere. I walked up the beach and down again in cold bare feet, following the fringe of wavelets. At the foot of the ravine I sank into its channel, then struggled up the shore to a gaping black hole, the culvert of the day's target practice. Did my own eyes deceive me? I looked askance, like a sailor on night watch. There was a light at the end of the tunnel!

Noises, too. Sounds of furtive scufflings, like those of monster sewer rats, fled along the walls. Sibilant whisperings pursued them. I crouched in the weeds at the abutment. A feeble red dot bounced back and forth.

"S-sssss-tt!" I heard, then an exhale. The echoing pause told me more.

"How does it feel now?"

"Wonderful." A silence, only the trickle of the stream. My clinging wet jeans were colder still.

"Oohhh. Do that again, Mickey."

"Like this, Linda. Ssssssst-ufft-ufft. Take it."

"Mmmmmmn, I think I'm beginning to feel it."

"That's it, you're learning. Just *suck* on it."

"Oouuw. It's hard to catch my...breath!"

"Take it easy, baby."

"But it's getting near the end!"

"Don't lose it."

"OW!"

"You blew it." A sigh... "That's all right, Linda. Better luck next time."

While I shivered in the prickly weeds, my two beloveds shared a stick of marijuana in a storm drain. What should I do now—stomp right in and join them? *Can you spare a smoke there, mates?* Who would spring for it first—if either one? They had probably consumed the last shred. Or should I steal away like an Arab—*The Shadow Knows?* The speaking tube of steel supplied an answer:

"Do you think he knows we're down here, Linda?"

"Who, Jerry? He's watching an old movie, *Andy Hardy Makes a Date,* or something. If he isn't already passed out."

"That's good. He wouldn't miss a Mickey Rooney flick for anything."

"Too bad they never met!" My wife had made a *funny.* The stoned couple giggled in the pipe. I heard muffled words and noises, then harsh metallic rasps of faster breathing. I crouched there numb, listening.

Now that I knew their meaning, my ears caught every nuance,

each faint echo of itself. It wasn't every day or any night that a husband got to hear his boyfriend screw his wife in a storm drain! The sordid subterranean mating ended, in resonating moans and smacking lips.

"*Uhhmmmnn.* That was so *good,* Mick." Kiss-kiss. "You were *so* good to me. I needed that."

"Me too, Linda. It's been a long time. For a *house*-boy."

"It's been a long time for a house-*wife.* Oh! My skirt's all wet."

"We're lying in the middle of a stream. Remember?"

"Well, nothing matters now. Does it, Mick?" More liquid kisses blended with the ripplings of the tiny corrugated cascade.

"Was that better than with Jerry?" Mickey asked.

"Why, that wasn't the same thing at all! It couldn't hold a candle to what we did, lover." More smacks and sighs... "How was it with him and you?"

"Are you *kidding? That was *kid* stuff. Don't make me laugh!" laughed Mick-the-Motherfucker in the vault of our practice rifle range. Now was the time to have a GUN—a Thursday-night *Thanksgiving Special.* God help Saint Mick, the fallen idol. And me, his phallic worshipper.

I picked up a rock and hurled it through the shaft. It bounced and boomed along the metal ribs like the toss of a live grenade. I scrambled up the bank, shredding hands and feet. Let those fornicators do what they wanted—a noble heart had cracked! I trudged along the road past Dr. Fritchy's dark estate. Should I pay him a midnight distress call? I thought of guard dogs, floodlights, shock treatments, injections.

At the hard edge of the Pacific Coast Highway I turned my bleeding feet toward Mexico, another gringo wetback without papers, hope, or home. I slouched along the pavement, grimly aware of the Doppler effect exhibited by swerving trucks and autos as drivers punched their horns. This was no *process shot,* but a *location take.* Let them hit me when they wished. I was beyond such mortal cares. They could wrap my mangled corpse in a tarp and stick it in the icebox down at City Morgue. The minute he came of age, Starkey could collect insurance and set about avenging my untimely end. Meanwhile, *Death before Dishonor!*

A pair of lights slowed down and crept behind me, tires popping gravel on the shoulder of the road. A sheriff's car? A night in the

Malibu cooler might save us one and all. But I knew the brittle tapping of the Fury's piston rings.

"Come on. Get in," said Mickey as he tried to guide the wheels along the narrow strip. He stopped the car some yards ahead and stood against the door. He grabbed my arm as I shrugged by him.

"*Listen,* Jerry. I'm sorry I balled your wife. She was sorry for me because of Brenda. She *asked* me to. I swear it!" I leaned across a fender like a captive of the police and kept my mouth shut. "I'm still your best friend, Jerry," said Mickey, tender now. "Why don't we just go home?" He wrapped a warm arm around my neck. I was sobbing.

I suddenly twisted free and kneed my best friend Mick in the bull's-eye of his crotch. I got into the Fury and fiercely slammed the door. I turned the key and drove away, shuddering with cold and fear, tears and empty laughter.

48.

If that was a black Thursday, Friday was blacker still. Tormented until daybreak by ferocious dreams, I lay all morning in the blind-dark room, a solitary voluntary prisoner of the divided bed, now a size too large for me. I wallowed in the hollows that Mickey's shape had made, on bedsheets scented by his odors, his pillow a sponge for my tears. But for this moist evidence I might have been a ghost. Only Mickey's willing grin, his vitalizing touch, his red flag of randiness, the blessings of the Saint himself, were agents still able to revive me.

The phone rang. Was it the Sheriff? Dr. Fritchy? An attorney for divorce? The Department of Public Works about their storm drain?

"Jeremy Carr...Visuals," I answered.

"I'm John, the electrician on that remodel. There's outlets missing on our plans here." I hauled myself from bed to check the drawings in a hasty count of double-convenience outlets. Sure enough, the plans lacked two—just as I did! "Check," he said. "If there's any more foul-ups I'll call you." *Hang on, John!*—I wanted to shout. Who knew when another voice would call? The phone resumed its dull impersonal dial tone.

Within the Greater Los Angeles area of the time, there existed a perversion of the entire telephone system. By dialing the instrument's own number the caller was delivered to an open network—*the Crosswire*—connecting to every other self-dialer. In a vast electronic limbo, disembodied voices floated night and day.

I dialed and listened in: teeners making dates, hyping drugs, tripping; adult obscenities, grunts and groans, sometimes a skull-piercing scream. I was glad to have this phantom world so near at hand. I dressed my graveless corpse and dragged it down the stairs, across the street to the Friendship for the Happy Hour—5 to 8—and started drinking doubles. It was like sitting in a cell of glass. The others at the bar were couples now, I the friendless loner. Instead of *WE* it's only *me*, I thought in despair, grieving.

I started calling Linda from a phone booth, a busy signal every time. The sly seductress had the phone off the hook while she played House with her new playmate beneath the big alpaca tent—or was she trying to call me? *The HELL with her!* She could call until her ring and index fingers dropped. I tore my name from the phone book, both the white and yellow pages. Just let *anyone* try to find me—let alone those gay deceivers!

I crossed to my prison on the DONT WALK sign. Staring from the mirror a tragic mask confronted me. I poured a glass of scotch and stretched on the floor by the mantle. What were they doing now—still belittling my performance? Two against one, united witnesses. No, *seven* against one—with all the others, and the dog. And soon to be seven to *zero!* Reaching behind my head I opened the valve of the gas log.

Eleven o'clock. How long would it take? Fuel gas was lighter than air. It would fill the ceiling first, an inversion layer. Then the rooms, last of all flooding the floor. Suppose the windows weren't tight enough? Suppose the water heater blew up first, blasting the wrong tenants? I'd run out singed and ridiculous—not even a successful suicide. How would I live that down? I turned the gas log off.

Drowning? I could drop my clothes by the ocean with a note: *I saw, but still forgive you.* What the hell was that—a terminal Valentine? *I'll see you both in Hell!* Vindictive but spirited—with no sure guarantee. *TOO LATE FOR TEARS, TOO SOON FOR LAUGHTER.* Perfect! Those words would endure—unless my clothing were washed away first. What if I didn't roll ashore until next week, waterlogged and bloated, a sight for sorry eyes or any others? Maybe I could fake it all and run away; but that was insincere, a foolish cheat. Who would I be then?

Listen, Jerry, this is better still:

1. Climb into the Fury.
2. Fasten seat belt.
3. Drive to Santa Monica Pier.
4. Charge down the ramp for takeoff at 100 mph.
5. Fly over heads of bug-eyed fishermen.
6. Sink the car off the end of the pier.

What a scene—the Big Splash, as from a killer whale, the waves against the shaken piles, the greenish headlights beaming upward like the ports of Captain Nemo's submarine. Too bad I couldn't film it! Lobster poachers would extract me from the cream and bronze coffin made-in-Detroit at a depth of *full fathom five,* and the bell would ring with reason for a change. Even Leonard, roused from towering excess, would send to know for whom the bell tolled.

I dressed in my customary clothes, the way I'd be best remembered, emptied all the ashtrays, and set the kitchen straight. I made the beds and threw away the K-Y. At last thought I dialed my own number. In a bombardment of verbal graffiti, a background of wailing sirens, the Crosswire had gone berserk: *Eat it. Poppers! I'm commmming. Balls!* At the first station break I hollered, *"Mickey! I want you back."*

"Hang up, you fucking queen," a deep voice bellowed. *"Jack off,"* recommended another. Free advice—why not take it? Because I had promises to keep. Otherwise death would have no sting. I combed my hair and brushed my teeth a final time. On the medicine cabinet's top shelf I spotted one of Mickey's film cans. In one, I knew, were Mexican barbiturates. I poured their number—about twenty—on the pink of my open palm, and studied the poison-green capsules. I gulped them down with scotch. That was a simpler way to go—I was getting too damned tired. I went to bed and shut my eyes for keeps. On their lids—twin radarscopes—I detected a fleeting white image bound for trackless space. *jeremy carr, visuals,* the vanishing card had read.

49.

My eyes instead of staying shut flickered ever more widely open. My pulse pounded faster, too. My every sense, in fact, was tuned to Full Alert. What was wrong with those Mexican barbs? It was *speed* I had dropped—twenty green caps of it. I'd be flying for a week! There was *no way* I'd be able to O.D. myself that weekend. A fickle fate had sold me out again. I played a record, drank a beer, and took the Fury for a run on the highway at the hour when the bars barred their doors for the night.

Twos or threes or singles hung around each clutch of stoplights: sailors for Mugu, marines bound for Pendleton, strays from any state—destinations yet unknown. A living three-dimensional Crosswire, the pulsing widespread crossroads of the West. In place of panting voices without bodies, here were breathing bodies without beds.

"Where you headed, sailor?" I chirped to the first one with his thumb out.

"Most anywhere right now." A Texas accent? Oklahoma? "I lost my wallet. *Ayund* my paycheck. My girl's picture, too." His gay-rull?

"Let's go to my place," said my chemical aggression.

"Long as you get me back to Long Beach, in time to stand up for inspection."

"It's a deal." A ten-*dollar* deal, I had it figured, but right then worth a hundred. I hung a U toward the Canyon. Thirty minutes later the boy lay on the bed.

Wasting not a movement nor a moment, my fingers seized the corner of the thirteen-button fly, each anchor-stamped black wafer representing an original state. Let's see now—what were they? New York, New Jersey, Virginia, Pennsylvania, *Delaware*. And then across the top: Connecticut—Rhode Island—Massachusetts—*Vermont*. My hand was already inside the generous flap, searching the seams of the skivvies. Bypassing other states, I yanked off the pants and drawers to begin an instant service of the serviceman—proof positive that other squid could come from Mick's abundant ocean.

I loaned the Oklahoma boy a five, drove him to Long Beach, and took an early-morning walk along the Pike. The desolate amusement zone, the idle pleasure rides and strange constructions, was a launching apparatus for a race that might never return. I went to an open restroom, the wooden stalls cut with foot-round holes in a line like the rifling of a cannon. What was the action there of a busy Saturday night?

At an uptown bar, dank and cheerful, I sat by a sailor drunk on beer. Within the hour that swabby sat beside me in the Fury, ejaculating in the middle of a bean field. The car swayed in the wind, dust settling on the sperm-flecked serge of his navy blue bellbottom trousers. I returned the spent sailor and drove south.

In a highway culvert I seduced a lone marine as he lazily chainsmoked his Marlboros, and that night took two soldiers to a cheap motel. The good-looking one was willing; the other merely watched. We talked and drank six-packs and slept on separate beds.

On Sunday a marine got *out* of the car. If I were standing up he'd deck me, I was told. But I couldn't have stayed down, my head still speeding. On the road I saw objects that weren't there. I picked up a straggler in a Stetson who looked real enough to drive me home. He stayed the night on Mickey's split of mattress.

It hadn't been a really lost weekend, I considered, totaling the body count: 2 sailors, 1 soldier, 1 marine, a cowboy still at my side. Five (5) hardy dicks for sixty-six bucks, or a little over $13 each, including travel. And I hadn't had time to be lonely, or occasion to remember their names. The amphetamine fever had been cured.

"Well, who's been sleeping in *my* bed?" demanded Mick, suddenly present in the cowhand's hat and hand-tooled boots and one of our old beach towels.

"A fine one you are to be asking, McCrory. What's been happening in mine?"

"Not a goddamn thing, you asshole. We've been calling you the last three days. And I've been sleeping on the couch. I brought you some of Randy's fleas."

"Nothing else?"

"A letter from the missus."

"How come you couldn't lift the phone when I called?"

"We thought we'd let you cool it."

"I damn near cooled it forever. If those uppers had been downers I'd be stretched out here for good." Mickey laughed a fiendish laugh, whipped off the towel and stung me.

"Hey! Careful of my *hat,* man," the waking cowhand said. He was red to wrists and neckline and white for all the rest. A trail of hairs ran down his boney middle. "Name's Mack, McPherson. From Prescott." He held out a long red hand and Mickey shook it. The hand picked up a half-smoked butt; Mick struck a match. The cowhand hawked.

"Well, be careful of the *bed* there, Mack. 'Cause that's my favorite roomie."

"Since when, I'd like to know? And for what reason?" I snickered through my anger at Mick in hat and boots—a holster either naked hip was all he needed. Mack took a drag and hawked again.

"It ain't so different from a bunkhouse here," he muttered. "Except that's a little more private." He covered up his private part, a long one. *They only come out at night*—I thought in secret glee—like *king* snakes or rattlers. Jesus! My whole fucking *world* was centered on those junctions, I saw in sudden panic. And half my time was spent in hot pursuit of them. Mack took his clothes to the bath.

"We worried about you," Mickey said. "Linda says she can't forgive herself. She wants *you* to. Here's her letter." The letter was a folded sheet from one of Starkey's tablets, sealed with a strip of scotch tape.

"*TO A SHINING PRINCE,*" I read aloud.

> Once upon a time there lived a lovely princess, far away by a lonely seashore. Her friends were the morning breezes, the sparkling waves, the seabirds and their night-songs, and the moon that pierced the clouds like a ghostly, beckoning galleon set with silver sails.
>
> But no ship came to bring her true companionship, or to bear her to a happier land. Once a huntsman came and asked for lodging. Though rude and vulgar in his ways he left with the princess three lovely, fair-haired offspring. And though her loneliness was eased, she did not see the man again.
>
> After some time had passed there arrived at her door one day a prince in a shining carriage, ivory and gold in the sun. Though her heart was lost at once the princess dared not then reveal it. By great good fortune the prince was persuaded to stay and again, in time, gave to the grateful princess yet another golden child.
>
> But the prince was not content to be a prince in name only. He had other worlds to conquer, and wonders to perform. So once again the princess learned to console herself in the love of her gifted children, and in the tender care of the animals, green plants, and song-birds which a kindly Mother Nature had entrusted to her.

Like a walk-on movie extra the Arizona cowboy stood in the alcove auditing the letter, the hat held in sinewy hands as though he stood in church. Mickey nodded to go on:

> Now this prince in his travels had befriended yet another, a prince of fiery coloring and reckless, youthful ways. The Red Prince and the Brown Prince, she named them in her mind. When the Red Prince came to visit, it was the princess' eldest daughter who caught his flashing eye. But the daughter loved another, a Black Prince, who had stolen her young heart away.
>
> The princess, when she saw what had come to pass, was sorely troubled by the fierce gleams of jealousy in the emerald eyes of the Red Prince, and by the troubled look that came into the brown eyes of the Brown.
>
> So on the night of a great day of feasting she took aside the Red Prince to a secret cavern and said that he must go. —Only for a price, the Red Prince said. —Name it! If it is within my power to give, you shall have what you desire. But you must promise never to return.
>
> It is you, my fairest princess, the Red Prince said. Though her heart would break in twain the princess then surrendered, so that her daughter and the Brown Prince might be saved.

I folded the letter. "What a pile of horseshit. Where did she find a fairy tale like that? It's crazy."

"She wrote it," said Mick defensively. "It took the whole weekend."

"How do you know?"

"She asked me to help her. Brenda helped too."

"Jesus Jumping Christ! You expect me to *believe* such a story? A child would know better than that."

"It's true, Jerry. She wanted to console you, she said."

"Where's the Blue and Pink and Purple Princes? I suppose she hasn't met them yet. And who ever heard of a *Brown* Prince? What ever happened to White?"

Mickey snatched the letter back. "You don't know when you're well off, man," the Red Prince said.

"I guess I'll be going now, fellows." The cowboy twirled his Stetson. "That's an interesting story you just read there." He cleared his throat. "If you can spare some change for smokes and eats I'll be obliged.

"Here's three and some coins, Mack. It's all I've got left."

"I do thank you all. You be good now."

"Ride on, cowboy," Mickey said.

"Far as I can," Mack replied, walking tall out the doorway. I moved to the window to watch him stalk on stilted heels toward the cafe, the last outsider to rest his head where Mick's had made its mold.

I turned to find Mick studying the weekend's inventory, carelessly left on the drawing board. I grasped at the score-sheet, but he closed it in a fist and grinned maliciously.

"Some expense account here, Mr. Visuals. Are you deducting these five tricks? They can't *all* be dependents."

"I made the whole thing up, like Linda's letter."

"Your cowpoke here looked real enough. Did he poke you?"

"He didn't have nowhere to hang his hat."

"*Anywhere* to hang it. You talk like he does. So that's what you did with our sixty-six bucks. Seventy!"

Ours? Before I knew it I had seized Mick's legs and thrown him. He punched, then pinned me face-down in a hammer lock. I understood that I was going to be raped. *Another first.* Mickey raped me. He released my twisted arms and panted in my ear, "It's been a long time, mate. I missed you."

Turning to his face I did the only other thing I hadn't done before: I kissed him, tongue in cheek.

"I'm glad I didn't lose you, Jerr," he said when the kiss was done.

I was glad I hadn't lost myself. We had all been marginal victims of recent drug abuse.

50.

Though I had both suffered and celebrated the hour of the prodigal's return, I had no following sense of long endurance. I knew our reunion for what it seemed—a hollow phallic victory. Soon or late, by means and methods not yet wholly known to me, *SHE* would have her way and take the spoils.

Not for a sober minute was I deceived by the cute and cunning parable of princes, nor by Linda's air of sacrificed nobility. That was a fiction she could change at any time. The small engagement I had fought, with and for Mickey, was little more than a holding action. With large reserves of patience, will, and home support, she could win the war if she wanted. What did she really want?

More to the point perhaps was what did Mickey want—besides sex and dope and money? More basic still, what did Mickey *need*? A father, mother, brother, lover, girl? A car, a job, a future? Probably all of those in one form or another—a substantial order for any one person to fulfill.

Early in December I swam in heavy surf, the water slate grey and bitter cold, and the next day had a sore throat, chills and fever—the typical winter flu. Mick took a share of the bedding to the other room and set up camp by the gas log.

"I hope I won't get it," he said, taking long drafts of orange juice, wearing clothes. In the form of a morning drizzle, the foul weather season had begun.

"If so, it'll be the one thing you didn't get lately."

"I didn't get Brenda. She's the one I care about. She thinks I'm not quite normal."

"Because your skin's the wrong shade?"

"Because your bod's the wrong shape. For someone I'm supposed to be sleeping with."

"How much does she know?"

"Enough, I guess. It isn't what they know up there. It's what they think, her two brothers. I couldn't handle it without hurting 'em."

"I suppose I'm not normal then, either." Mickey's eyebrows went up. He laughed, then grew serious.

"It doesn't matter about you, J.C. At thirty-three they're not expecting any miracles. And anyway, you're not their real dad. Just the baby's."

"So what does that make you?"

"I can be a husband. And a real father, too. I like balling chicks."

"Linda's no typical chick, Mick. There's more to it than balling, no matter who you do it with." That was a familiar quote—it was one of my wife's.

"Like you proved to me last weekend with five guys on the road?"

"What else would I do on all those speedballs? I was lucky to be alive. Suppose you'd caught *your* wife screwing in a storm drain? For Thanksgiving! What would you do?"

"I'd kill 'em." I was shocked. He seemed to mean it.

194

"How, Mick?" I was seized by violent sneezing. Mickey moved away.

"I'd *fuck* 'em both to death. Him first, that stuck-up nigger dude."

"That's *sick*, Mickey. Howard's never done anything to you."

"Not as sick as you are, Jerry—and I don't mean just your cold." He sat down at the cable reel, rolled up a huge three-paper super-jay, and feverishly began to puff on it. The clouds of smoke from green and uncleaned grass set me to coughing. I took a snort of bourbon and got back into bed.

"You know what?" called Mickey from the other room. "I've been thinking." A trick he'd learned from Linda! I waited. "I think I'll see about getting a job." I counted four more hits. "I'll see about it first thing tomorrow."

"Tomorrow's Saturday."

"First thing next week then. I'll check the Sunday Classified." The portable TV came on with a talkative serial about the lives of sorely troubled adults. As their long complaints became a soothing lull in my ears I prepared to sleep away the flu. When I recovered there was one thing I would want. That was Mick—on any terms, at any time.

Actually and to my great surprise he was up and dressed early, in a pressed pair of pants, suede chukkas, and a green nylon windbreaker. He had combed and sprayed his hair, and was bringing a glass of juice.

"Thanks a million, Mick," I croaked. "Where you off to?"

"Hollywood, man. I'll check the employment agencies, maybe the used car lots."

"Wheeling or dealing?"

"We'll *jutht* have to wait and *thee*."

"You taking the car?"

"Naw, you might need it. Just give me five to eat on. Thanks. *Later.*"

Another kind of Saturday, a day of total rest. Whatever life moved upon the highways would have to move without my help. I picked up a book, THE MASCULINE EGO, Myth or Mister?, then fell back asleep.

When the phone rang that night it was Linda, calling to ask how I was. "*Real* sick." I gave a long hacking cough for effect. "With the flu. I'm in bed. Did you want to speak to Mickey?"

"No, not necessarily. How is he?"

"I couldn't say at the moment. He's out looking for a job."

"I do hope he's successful. He needs something to keep him occupied."

"There's not many things he does he can get paid for," I sniffed.

"Don't be negative about him, Jerry. He needs all the encouragement he can get."

"You've done your share."

"That was a mistake, I admit it. He's your boy now."

"Who told you that?"

"He did, last week. He said he'd rather die than hurt you." My bitter laugh became a cough for Linda. I was happier just the same. She was the other burning end to that same candle.

"Isn't that just like a prince?"

"You can't be very sick to joke like that, Jerry."

"It was a fairly funny letter." The line held a fairly long pause.

"I meant it with all my heart. I really did," said Linda, and hung up. No wins, but no heavy losses, either. It could still be anybody's ball game.

Mick returned at noon the next day. He'd brought the Sunday paper, and sitting by the bed as on a business call, made a show of turning to the want ads.

"Let's seee. Accountant, architect, *artist*. *Auto* mechanic, rear end. Sounds good. Baker, barber, bouncer, boy. *House*-boy. Must live in. Hmmm. Benefits plus wages. Here's the number." He reeled in the phone by its cord.

"Cut the crap, Mick. Where were you?"

"Me? Oh, I met a friend along the Sunset Strip, in a Mercedes. He offered me a job."

"A blow job?"

"Jerry! How can you be so *crude?*" Mick put down the phone and sat erect, legs crossed like a secretary's. "*Well,* Mister Robert, de *Beau*-ville that is, happens to be one of L.A.'s great designers. He told me so himself on the way to his apartment. A twenty-sixth-floor suite above the Strip with a view that just won't quit, with floor to ceiling mirrors, and lamps about six feet high, and a lot of gold chairs. Robert's an interior designer. That's where all the money is. He knows Leonard, too. He's got closets full of English suits and racks of Italian shoes."

"Go on."

"We drank some French cognac and sniffed a little coke. He played his four-thousand-dollar stereo. *Montovani*. When we got out of his monogrammed sheets there was a hot bath ready, a sunken tub with a Jacuzzi. Then his val-lay brought us breakfast, strawberries with crêpes suzettes and iced champagne. *Trays elegant*, he told me."

"So what's the deal?"

"Oh, he's doing expensive remodelings up in Beverly Hills. I can be part of his staff, or just drive him around in his Mercedes sports car. All expenses paid plus one-fifty a week. If I agree to stay at his place."

"Did you agree?" Mickey straightened out his legs and shook his head. He took my hand and faced me.

"What the fuck would you do, Jerry?"

"I don't know. I never had that kind of offer to refuse."

"A kept boy." His head drooped like a puppy's. "It makes me kind of sick."

"It makes me even sicker. I don't make that kind of dough."

"What do you think I ought to do?"

Sitting up I draped an arm around the striped green jacket, of the sort that team players wear. "It's up to you, Mick. I don't know what to tell you."

"If for only once you did."

"I'll do what I can for you, Mickey." With the latest firm bid for his body, the ante had been raised all around.

51.

When my nose stopped running, other fluids yearned to flow. Mickey moved back to our mattresses. "I always look after who's looking after me. Screw it, what the others think," was his simple but eloquent statement of prejudice overcome by principle. That was another item for my tape archives, a future quote for whom it might concern.

Though Christmas was a fortnight away, in the morning I gave Mick the keys and sent him downtown with a hundred dollar check. He was back before dark with his presents.

"For you, Jerry." He drew out a long yellow box. "Your beloved Cutty Sark. And this is for Brenda, 'cause it matches her blue eyes." He unwrapped a turquoise bracelet.

"What's the book?"

"*The Fountainhead,* for Linda. About an over-sexed heiress and a frustrated architect, the clerk said. She whips him while he's laying her marble hearth. Like the cover?"

"It doesn't tell me much. Did you get anything for yourself?"

"Wait a *minute.* He took a large parcel to the bath while I mixed a Cutty-soda. I turned from the counter to find a transformed Mickey, a sleek male model wrapped in tapered suede.

"It looks great. What is it?"

"It's my *car* coat, Jerry. See these pockets? They're for rally gloves and maps and spending-money. Maybe a couple of jays."

"Well, it's beautiful, Mick. You're dressed like a prince."

"Right! Now all I need is the carriage."

"Like a Mercedes SL-300?"

"Forget it. Who needs a job like that?"

"The whole glamor trip with all the trimmings? With breakfast, lunch or dinner in a great big curtained bed?"

"Ro-*bare* is pretty strange, Lenny told me. He likes things I wouldn't do with anybody. Besides, he's always after me. And he wears too much perfume. *Persian Melon.*"

"Every pleasure has its price, every vice its measure," rhymed the tentative devil's advocate.

"There's a price I wouldn't pay." The well-clad puritan admired his reflection right and left, then across each shoulder, to see how the car coat fit the contours of his ass. The skirt hung just below the hip bones. He shook out his hair as in an open sports car.

"All I need now is red leather gloves and aviator shades."

"I'll give you those for Christmas, Mick. They'll have to do until the right car arrives."

"You're too good to me, J.C. You know that?"

The next week Mick had a job. What sort of job was that?

"A chauffeur, to help with Christmas shopping. It's a chance to earn some cash and wear my car coat."

"May I ask who your new employer might happen to be?"

"Sure, Jerr, it's Linda."

I was still for a while. "Her idea? Or yours."

"I just happened to be here when she called. She lost her driver's license."

"In her purse—or in the storm drain? And where's your chauffeur's certificate?"

"Forget it, Jerry," Mickey said. "She needed someone to help with packages and parking, for five an hour. She wants to make up for Thanksgiving. If you want me to I'll tell her *no*."

I brooded on the table. I would rather have listened to the Crosswire. The only job in town! What the hell, I thought, yielding to the spirit of the season, they can't just do it in the parking lot. Let *him* watch the kids and run the wipers. She might even buy me a present —God forbid.

"Save yourself while you can, Mick. I'm only a drowning orphan in a storm, tied across the railroad while the dam breaks."

"You don't really mind?"

"Live as you want to live. Don't forget where your home is."

"I won't forget you, Jerry." He squeezed my nearest cheek.

The shopping expeditions went into their second week. "What do you do downtown all day?" I asked Starkey. He had opted to stay at my place, and I bent to light the log. "I hope nobody's lifting any loot."

"Naw, we've got everything we need already. We go to lots of movies. We saw *The Carpetbaggers, Dr. No* twice, a couple of Disneys."

"All of you?" My matches were damp again.

"No, Mom and Mick go other places. They said they're looking for something special. Here. Why don't you try one of these?" Starkey handed me a gold-and-purple matchbook and offered a significant look. *THE ROYAL COACHMAN, Wayfarers Hostelry & Taverne,* the pretentious letters heralded above a Sepulveda Boulevard address— the same kind of matches I'd found in Mickey's car coat.

That night I found excuse to visit the motel. When I laid a ten beside the register, the desk clerk snatched it like a Kleenex. "Excuse me while I catch the switchboard. It's a very busy night." It was easy finding Mickey's adolescent script, full of curls and flourishes. *M. & L. McCoy* had been guests of The Royal Coachman on Decembers 17, 20, 21.

"Friends of yours?" the clerk inquired.

"Relatives, a nephew and his aunt. They're visiting."

"A very busy couple. We only see them afternoons. It's number thirty-two at the end, sir."

"Well, thank you for your help. I ought to try it here myself once."

"The same private suite? They seem to enjoy it. I shouldn't let them know you've been here?" I laid out a five, the Lincoln portrait up. "Thank you again, sir. Another time."

In the dark curtained window of #32, I caught only the reflection of bewildered plants. I went on to the *Squire's Taverne*, where iron chandeliers like prisoners' cages were chained to false wood beams. From the polished oak bar I might have spied the two, snuggled in a tight corner booth. But what had I expected? Why not reserve the room for Christmas Day and hand them the be-ribboned key, a little sprig of mistletoe?

In the meantime I would maintain cordial relations with the five-buck-an-hour hustler and the fornicating mother of four. My tardy futile anger I swallowed with my drink. I lit a Kool from a *ROYAL COACHMAN* matchbook, ripping out the gold-tipped purple matches one-by-one. *She loves him, he loves her not,* I counted. The latter came out last. What other motels had they visited?

On Christmas Eve, Mickey gave me what I wanted—a generous gift of himself. How could he afford it? Had Linda's image been a third participating partner? I didn't ask. Mick's reward was a pair of red kid-leather driving gloves with knitted inserts, and green-tinted aviator's sunglasses. From his earnings he gave me another handsome gift, a rancher's sheepskin jacket. I might have forgiven him anything. But with *her* my charity ceased. Wrapped in our accessories, we drove up to the house for the ritual opening of presents.

The children tore through theirs in short order, like acquisitive adults. Only one object held interest for me. Linda took her time in opening it, a cluster of boxes within boxes. The last, a plastic watch-case, she opened and snapped shut, and sending me a dire look, retired to the once-shared bedroom. After a while, nutmegged egg-nog cup in hand, I followed her, and let the unlatched door creak slowly open. Linda sat hunched on the wrinkled fur spread in her Snow White pose, weeping.

"Don't *touch* me, goddamn you," she cried, resisting any contact. "I knew you could be heartless. I never once suspected you could be so terribly *cruel.*" Half-sunk in the furry folds of the alpaca, the open case revealed its secret treasure: a gold-and-purple matchbook from the Royal Coachman Inn, and its companion, a gold-and-crimson three-pack of lubricated Trojans. "What if the kids had opened it, you idiotic fool! What sort of Christmas would *they* have?" Amidst Casey's wails and Mickey's mellow laughter I heard their quarreling voices from the other room. The dog was barking, too.

Linda didn't like her present! I offered a suggestion. "Maybe Steve could use them. Even Brenda." Linda glared. "Well, how was I *supposed* to feel with you and Mickey doing it there daily—like Mr. and Mrs. S. Claus without the little elves? I have some feelings left too, you know, even at this season."

"Amazing, Jerry. Yes, I suppose you do, infantile as they might be. Just how the hell do you think I felt when you and Mick were doing it at your place, spilling *sperm* all over one another?"

I made a tentative try with my hand again. The response was much more positive—Linda slugged me in the mouth. I slapped her wet cheek. Fists clenched like armor, she stood up straight with rage.

"You get your ass out of here, Jeremy Carr! I don't want to see that face of yours around again. *NEVER!* Not in *my* house. I want you out of here *RIGHT NOW.*"

I wiped my bleeding lip on the virgin sleeve of sheepskin, returning her tear-bright stare. I pivoted, stalked through the gift-clogged living room, and turned to Mickey in his car coat at the door, his green eyes indistinct behind green lenses.

"Are you coming?" I held onto the doorlatch.

"I think I'll catch you later, Jerr," he said at last. I didn't slam the door or even close it before driving the long lonely miles back to the Canyon. Poor Casey's first Christmas—I hadn't had the chance to run his little train! I licked back a salty teardrop.

The bars across the street were closed or nearly empty behind strings of blinking lights—a row of pinball games without their players. Nearly everyone had a place to go on Christmas Eve. I was going to have to feel sorry for myself—again.

An empathetic rain began to fall. Raindrops would fall on the Pacific, keeping the water level high; and on the rows of royal palms along the palisades, on the palm-frond Nativity displays that looked like early trolley stops. The rain would be falling on the floodlit robes of Wise Men, on the store-window models of Joseph and Mary, on the Babe in his wet straw motel.

Linda and Mick, Mick and Linda. The carol sang its tireless refrain inside my tired brain cells. I had a drink and took some pills and retired to the un-doubled beds. Mickey's solo slab of mattress was barren as a ransacked tomb.

"*Baby, won't you light my fire*," chanted sexy Jim Morrison from the Friendship, on a jukebox record of *THE DOORS*. Now, like the pouring winter rains, a cold and bitter fate had come and *pissed* on it.

52.

"Hey Jerry! What's up?" asked the youthful-sounding voice through the unrelenting magic of the telephone exchange. Not a bad question, considering the nature of the times, the climate of the day, a wet one, the fifth since Christmas past.

Surfeited with every excess of the season I had turned away from drink and its drafts of self-pity, from drugs and their stagnating aftermath, from nourishment itself—save for skimmed milk and orange juice. I was staging a silent fast of protest. It was time for reality to change its ways before the New Year even got started. Resolutions, too little, would always come too late.

Sleep was knitting up the addled sleeve of care. I lay snug abed at noon, my mind a montage of Mickey, Jimmy Corey, and their kind; my fingers tempting yet another slim withdrawal from exhaustible glandular reserves. The indulgence was forestalled by the ring of the prescient black handset. As though touched by a frostbit fairy, the flowering will to abuse myself withered on its stalk.

"Not too much, Starkey. I just try to keep my head up. How about yourself? And the other lads and lassies up Malibu way?"

"We're okay, I guess, except we're starving. The turkey's all gone. We're eating candy canes and fruitcake. Casey drank the eggnog, but there's beer left, and some green stuff at the bottom of the freezer. Artichoke hearts, maybe." There it was—the last report from deep-freeze Little America, just before the ice-caked wireless went dead forevermore.

"How about your mommy and her driver? Can't they make it down to Safeway again?"

"Oh, those two. They took off in the van a couple days ago with

Brenda's air-mat in the back, and the fur blanket. Mick said something about Ensenada. That's in Mexico, isn't it?"

"Did they leave you guys any pesos?"

"Naw, there's no money left. The neighbors aren't around, either. Brenda's signing Uncle Stanley's check. She practiced Mom's signature."

"That's forgery, you know, a *felony* charge. Suppose you just hold on till I get there? I'll bring some food and stuff."

"Chocolate malts and double burgers, with some fries. Maybe you ought to spend the night here."

Great. *Father-for-a-Day*, at least, until those child-deserting cheats finished off their escapade across the border. In Ensenada—*Rosarito Beach*...tripping out on acid on the same Blue Grotto floor tiles. Serenaded at the Long Bar, at ringside at the Blue Fox, holding hands et cetera beneath the sweaty cloths of foreign tables.... It was more than mortal mind was meant to bear! Maybe they'd be beaten up and robbed. *That* would bring the high-flying couple down to earth!

I poured bourbon in the souring milk; the fast was over. What could I do to get even? I felt like the bull in a bullring, pawing dirt, while his killers closed in at the kill for the benefit of Leonard-like *aficionados*. But even poor old Leonard, a pathetic painted clown, would have found the balls—*los cojones*—to turn on his tormentors and, armed with tongue and hairpiece, beat the demons down.

The name for that response was *vengeance*, and its energizing agent, *fury*—an emotion that stood tall on the threshold of the feelings that followed the click of the concluded call.

Despite their token isolation, the horde of abandoned orphans had survived rather well. Not one looked worried or ill. In the absence of mindful adulthood their vacation was complete. Gorged on short-order junk foods, they sank back among the wrappings to enjoy TV, budding Californians at their leisured, privileged best.

"Not *another* old Bing Crosby movie," said Brenda in bitchy good humor. "You'd think he was Mister Santa Claus himself."

"Instead of Mister Minute Maid," continued Steve, "and his billion dollars worth of o-jay."

"Bob Hope's even richer," Starkey claimed.

"*Funnier*, too," his sister thought.

"If you had your druthers would you rather be funny or rich?"

Brenda pondered the quiz-like question through the next six minutes of commercial break. "I'd rather be rich," she declared, as *Going My Way* resumed its story, "with just half-a-million bucks."

"I hope you'll show us how," said Starkey, "if you ever find out yourself." The baby sucked bubbles through a plastic straw.

I popped another Bud from the Frigidaire. Snide little bastards—greed and selfish interest shining through their eyes like Christmas bulbs. They would run wherever price and pleasure took them—exactly like their Mom! Maybe little Casey would be different, if he ever got the chance.

Too bad their real Dad wasn't bopping on the door with his load of toxic sprays, instead of Cokes and ribboned pretzels as of last year. This time he'd be welcome—he could treat them as he wished. I was sick of the whole rotten lot of them, as well as thoroughly tired of myself.

"Time's up," I announced as the black-and-white feature switched to a detergent. "It's beddy-bye for everybody."

"But it isn't even *eleven,*" wailed Brenda. "There isn't any school until next week!"

"Just get your butt in bed, girl, and take the baby with you. Be glad you've got something to eat, until you get your first half mil."

"I wish Mom and *Mick* were here," she cried before her door slammed. "*He* lets us do what we want!"

"What are you going to do now, Jerry?" Starkey and the dog were cleaning plates.

"I don't know, kid. I'm waiting for a sign in the sky."

"Don't stay up all night then. See you in the morning. And thanks."

A chill wind had cleared the night sky; stars stared unflinching through the windows. I stretched out on the rug to watch the fire die, Randy at my side. I stroked his silken coat. The only accessible redhead, I thought poignantly.

And then it struck me—a slender stab of hard white light, the beam of my beginning in that household. It slid slowly up my trunk, up the ribs, pointing *south,* I finally realized. The moon was beaming rays into luxury Mexican hotel suites—assuming that the drapes weren't drawn—or through the dusty breath-fogged windows of her *van,* where the missing alpaca spread might rise and fall spasmodically.

If only that bright ray—like a laser—could penetrate my brittle heart or *freeze* it, hard as an artichoke's—then I might find a way to go on living, or at least be able to exist. Never again would I know the need of that ego-inflating divining rod—an erection. I rubbed my rumbling stomach in the rug.

I must have dozed. A harsher light awoke me—the full moon directly in the eye. I scanned the acned features, my body stiff with cold. Midnight by my chronometer. I pulled on boots and jacket and went out to the car. When the engine turned over smoothly I rammed the Clime-Control knob to FULL HEAT.

53.

Even to a sufferer like myself the night held a certain enchantment. Beyond pain I could still find beauty! The vast sieve of firmament let through a billion points of starlight; the ocean wore a wrap of freezer foil. Where were the frosty white miles of concrete leading me? The tiny fuel window read FULL.

Landmarks ticked by on the odometer: canyon exits, intersections, filling stations, burger stands, the Sheriff's empty parking lot—the cops would be hot after holiday drunks—and the clutter of cars at every festive roadhouse.

Like a rider to a Wild West saloon, I pulled up at the Malibu Pokey beside a new black Ranchero with a white skull-and-crossbones on the doors—Harry's new pickup and logo, with the big block letters: PEST PATROL. *U S of A: Best Place to Stay: KEEP it that Way!* preached a sticker on the chrome-trimmed tailgate behind the poison pumps and hoses. Through the painted wood bars of the Pokey I caught sight of the deadly patriot, at his elbow a good-looking blonde whom I knew as a legal stenographer. What better time to greet the Great Exterminator, the other absent maker of that parentless brood?

"Why, Harry! Here's a friend of yours," said Dorothy as I swung the swinging doors. Harry swerved around on the bar stool. He looked the forty-two that Linda said he was. His hair was thinning, too.

"Hi. I'm Jerry Carr. I guess Linda Fedderman's the friend we have in common."

"Oh, yeah? You *married* her—my little old lady, Linda. Hey,

CLYDE! Drive your ass on over here! Let's have some Tom and Jerries. Or make it double shots of Oly chasers, if that's alright with you, Dad."

"Anything's all right with me right now, Harry."

"Wow. So you live with Linda. She can be fun when she wants to. Do the kids stay out of trouble?"

"Usually. We have another one, a boy."

"*Way*-ull, she always was a fast little breeder. Maybe that's why we're divorced. Too many little people in the way."

"The kids seem pretty smart. For their ages."

"*Too* smart, in my opinion. Especially the youngest one. Starkey! I swear the little bastard read my mind."

"So did Brenda," smiled Dorothy.

"What do you mean by that, Dot?"

"Oh, nothing, Harry, really." She turned to me half-confidentially. "Brenda found him in bed with a maid. A colored one. Maybe that helped along with the divorce." Dorothy finished her beer chaser.

"Well, what the hell! She said she was pregnant *again*, goddamnit. She always had something in the oven."

"I think I know just what you mean."

"Dorothy and me only have each other. Don't we, hon?" Harry gave her a pinch. "Maybe that's enough."

"Maybe sometimes a little too much." Dorothy socked down her double shot of rye.

"Well, that's what love is all about, isn't it?"

"Could we have another round here please, Clyde?" I unfolded dollar bills but Harry stuffed them back in my pocket.

"Save your money, Jerry. Someday you'll be paying alimony, too."

Drinking, I learned other aspects of the marriage that Linda had neglected to detail in her views of the affair. Why hadn't I thought to talk to him before, like the prospective buyer of a used car to the original owner? We'd have been spared lots of heartaches later on.

A burglar alarm went off. It meant the bar would close in ten minutes.

"I hear you have some lively parties up at Linda's," Dorothy said, wrestling into a mackinaw jacket. "You ought to come to our place sometime."

"Righto, Jerry, old boy. We have some *real* good times. There's a redhead next door that just won't quit, since she left her fruity husband."

"You *do* like redheads, don't you, Jerry?"

"I never turned one down yet."

Clyde pulled the plug on the jukebox and turned off strings of lights and beer signs. He locked the cash register and padlocked the bar.

"I never turn *anything* down," said Harry, banging his beer stein on the bar. "Except maybe *faggots.*"

"Faggots?" I sluiced the foam around my glass.

"Yeah, faggots. One tried to make me in the Navy once. An ensign! I had to push his gay *teeth* in. I got no use for queers, the cocksuckers. Excuse me now, folks, I think I gotta piss."

"Harry's had a little too much holiday cheer," said Dorothy as she waited, spreading lipstick by the light of the moon. "He heard she married some set decorator from the movies. You know how *they* are. So he worried about the children, turning homosexual, you know. After all, he pays part of their support."

"He doesn't have to worry about that." I began to scrape my field boots on the curb. I had a full bladder, too. "I'm a designer of buildings. I'm doing jobs up and down the coast."

"We've heard about your jobs," said Dorothy brightly.

"Yeah! Call me next time you build a house," said Harry zipping up. "I'll poison your foundations free of charge. I got no use for termites, either."

"Well, thanks for all the drinks. And Happy New Year."

"Catch you later!" yelled Fedderman Senior as the two got in the car and chunked the Jolly Roger doors. A sheriff's car had parked nearby and the driver waved a greeting. The pickup drove off slowly, finally flicking on the double sealed-beam headlamps. *Best Place to Stay,* the car's rear end reminded me, between multiple flashing red taillights.

Where to go now? North to that cold loveless beach house? South to the empty apartment? Or west into the ocean—like the weakling loser husband of *A Star is Born?* I turned east at the end of Sunset and took its twisted path through lush Bel Air, round Deadman's Curve, past deserted UCLA, and down electrifying Sunset Strip, where life still stirred corruptly. I had coffee at world-famous GOO-GIE'S. The banquettes buzzed with talk of films and drugs.

Hollywood Boulevard was dressed up for the season. Fiberglass candles crowned the lampposts; tinsel bells on glitter ropes rattled in the wind. A honeymooner's lane for Mick and Linda! An entire city street in *drag*, was more like it. For here cruised the seekers and the sought-for, swift or slow—street queens, trade, and *FAGGOTS*— giant termites gnawing in the dark at the core of our rotting society.

What if men like Harry Fedderman were right?

54.

Would I be wrong, just to stop the car for a paper—any little English-printed rag from Mexico, with social notes from Lower California? Would those touring adventurers, Mick and Linda, be mentioned there at all? Or not until their time-stripped, interlocking bones were recovered from the shifting tides or sand dunes? Such were my private speculations as I scanned the import headlines at the International newsstand at Las Palmas, pausing near a reader in grease-stained coveralls. He held a thick Christmas issue of *Playboy*, the centerfold snapping in the wind. The boy would have to buy that magazine or put it back, and soon.

"See anything you like?" I asked.

"Just enough to keep my hands warm."

"How about the rest of you?"

"I'm cold all over, man." He slipped the *Playboy* under its lead brick. The cashier began to look at other customers, some of whom were looking at the boy in grimy twills.

"Let's go then. Here's my car, with whitewalls, radio and heater."

The boy drowsed the whole way to the canyon. I helped him up the stairs to the bathroom. Too tired to think about a bath, he crawled abed in tattered underwear. Instinctively my hand fell flat across his middle. I caught his quickened breath. "*Hey*, man," said the light voice, breaking. "I'm not a *girl*, you know."

"I know you're not." I turned my back, but sleep would not come easily. Beside me in the same bedclothes breathed the fresh form of youth in all its flavor, an infinity of inches distant, as within a camper's tent beneath the stars. Could that yawning gap be bridged? Thoughts became visions, then illusions. I felt...was it true?...the scrape of toenails on my calloused heel, a firm blunt pressure to the rear there.

208

The breathing was once more irregular. I waited, then turned to do the things I thought the boy wanted...until he stiffened, snorted, gave a sigh and slept.

At dawn I saw an unfamiliar innocence—in uncreased brow, sleep-swollen lids, bow lips slightly parted. He had long curling lashes. In teenage boys there was often something girlish, as though nature's tougher choices had not been finalized. Perhaps it was the same with flat-chested girls who rode horseback or played baseball. I lifted the covers for a longer look.

Years Mickey's junior, he was slightly built and bore upon that corresponding part of his bare person bare resemblance to St. Mick. To the Saint's blazing bush, this stripling's pubic growth was no more than a shadow. Those were pimples where freckles ought to be. The cool flesh stirred; a hand reached down to scratch the scrawny butt, then tugged the torn shorts up again. The boy turned on his belly toward the wall, taking most of the covers with him.

At nine Starkey called.

"Don't ask me *what's up*. I can't tell you."

"That's all right, Jerry, I already know."

"You do?"

"They're back."

"Alive and well?"

"Asleep and broke. They brought some eats, though. Fritos and stale enchiladas. And Mexican souvenirs. A stuffed armadillo for my room."

"Enjoy it then, Starkey. You may never get another."

"Brenda got a shawl and Steve got a bullfighter's dagger."

"*De gustibus non est disputandum.* There's no disputing tastes. That's an old Italian saying, from the Mafia."

"I wish you'd tell me something new."

"When the time comes, Starkey. When there's time."

"You're not the mystery you think you are."

"Nor you the master."

"Time will tell." He hung up.

"Who was that?" asked the morning's companion.

"Only a son of mine, one of many. My name's Jerry, by the way. What's yours?"

"Alex. Glad to meet you, Jerry." He shook my hand under the blanket. "You kind of remind me of my dad."

"In what way, Alex?"

"Oh, about the same age, I guess. About the same height, maybe. Except he's still in the service. A quartermaster. In Japan, the last we heard."

"And your mother?"

"She's in Reno with my little brother. We live in a twenty-foot trailer. Maybe I should call and see if they're okay."

"Go right ahead there, Alex. Be my guest."

He got into the stained grease-monkey's suit—a scarlet *SMILEY'S SERVICE* stitched across the back—sat down at the drawing board, business-like, and placed a call to a Miss Myra Jensen. "She don't like Missus," he explained while the line rang. "She don't want everyone to know she's got two sons."

"Hi, *MOM?* Yeah, it's me. Your son *ALEX.* Well, I can hear you good, too...In L.A....*Los Angeles!* No, I'm at a friend's house... What? Naw, he's just a *friend.* You needn't worry.

"Well, I might get a job here...Oh, at any service station. They *need* men. With experience." I checked the clock and lit us each a cigarette as Alex listened, his fingers toying with the drafting tools. They were lean mechanic's fingers, black around the knuckles and beneath the stubs of nails.

"Oh, yeah? He took off for good? He didn't take my *rifle* with him, did he?...Well, maybe. I have to earn the bus fare first...*No,* Mom, I'm not gonna hitchhike. Don't worry! Yes, I *remember* what Daddy used to tell me...No, I won't do nothing dangerous or *strange.*"

"Her boyfriend just left. He's a flake," he said aside, puffing out a chain of smoke rings. "She thinks I'm still a kid."

"We know better, don't we?" said the dirty old man to the boy.

"...It's cold here, too. And I miss *you,* Mom. Tell Eric not to wreck my bike. Sure, I'll write you. Next year...That's *tomorrow,* Mom." My God! The kid was right! "Yeah, I'll send you the address. It's right on the Pacific Ocean. No, I don't think we'll go swimming today... Well, g'bye for now. Say hello to Carla and the dog."

"Carla's my girl." Alex's shoulders slumped, relaxed. "She hasn't decided we're going steady yet. Eric's looking after her. My brother.

He takes her to the flicks if he's got the coins. Hey, Jerry, would it be all right to take a shower now?"

"Sure, I'll get you a clean towel." Another front-row ticket to witness rites of adolescence in the bath! Had this become a kind of fetish with me? I could fret about that later, after he dried off. As he showered I took the clothes and sank them in a sinkful of suds. The boy spent a long time at the mirror, squeezing pimples, stroking fuzz. From time to time I wiped the steaming glass, like any good bathhouse proprietor.

"I'm growing a mustache. Do you like it?"

"It suits your looks so far. It doesn't have to be a thick one."

Alex made a heavy adult frown at himself. "I think I'll shave it off. Carla wouldn't like it. She likes boys more her age."

When the mirror gave Alex its approval he allowed me my turn in the bath. I scrubbed the stubborn stains from Smiley's Service; the improved power cleanser wasn't doing its job. "Hey, Jerry!" he was calling from the kitchen. "It's the telephone. For you!" Like any dutiful son, he brought me a mug of hot coffee.

"Who's that?" demanded Linda, before I had a chance to condemn her completely irresponsible behavior.

"My new helper, that's who. Where the hell do you think *you've* been?"

"With my new helper, too. I felt I deserved a little help for a change. We were all getting ready for a change, to tell the truth."

"It's nice to hear the *truth* for a change. Did your change have to be that drastic? Don't answer that—just listen! The children were worried sick. They could have *starved* to death, if I hadn't been there to feed them."

"Well, dear, we assumed you'd have brains enough to do that."

"For Christ's *sake*, Linda, at least you might have called!"

"They don't have lots of phone booths down in Baja, very few that take American coins. Besides, I had to get away from everything, to break entirely free. To find out how I *really* felt."

"And how did you really *feel*? Or should I ask your helpful friendly feeler, Mickey Finn?"

"How long do you think it is since *I've* had a vacation? Not sixteen minutes, like you. Or sixteen days or weeks. Sixteens years ago! With *Harry!* How would you like that?" I didn't answer. I watched Alex try to dry his coveralls. He wasn't much more than sixteen himself. "The change didn't hurt you, either," she went on, "judging from your new answering service."

"You're in no position to judge anything, Linda, not after what the two of you have done. You don't *deserve* to have those kids, no matter how many vacations you think they've cost you."

A pause came in the meeting of our minds while Linda sipped at some refreshment and I tried to recover my syntax. I drank the black coffee and lit up a Kool. *Say Goodbye to Harsh Taste!* was its slogan.

"Well, the same goes for you, sweetheart," she resumed with new vigor. "At least I haven't made a lot of juveniles delinquent. You might want to dwell on that a little while, before you blow any whistles on me, love." *Juveniles delinquent.* The insidious, semantic witch!

"You don't have to make them, you *take* them," I replied, praying for an instant rephrasing.

"I tried to save Mickey. I hope it's not too late. You have no idea what he's been through. He's become like a son to me now."

"Do you like the man in the boy? Or the boy in the man, Linda?"

"Right now I like having a lover, like Mick. And he likes having a woman, like me."

"That's insane. He can't be a son *and* a lover. It's what they call *incest*, Linda. That's one holy *hell* of a way to start the new year!"

"Well, you go start a new year of your own if you want to. We like our lives just the way they are. *You're* the one who ought to turn some new leaves."

So be it, I thought, stiff and grim, turning to the fresh new leaf that wrapped a green towel around its trunk.

"Mom and Dad used to fight like that," said Alex cheerfully, "back when we all lived together. She's the one that usually won, though."

"Then our families are pretty much alike, right?"

"Maybe. I never stayed in bed with a man before. A man like my own father." Alex's skin turned pink against the towel. "I don't think my mother would've liked it."

"Sometimes I wish I'd never stayed in bed with my wife."

The boy began to look uneasy. I offered him a choice of Mickey's shirts and blue jeans, but he tugged on his sodden clothes instead.

"Let's go have us something to eat, kid."

"Oh-*kay!* Yesterday I don't think I had nothing but two candy bars."

"I'll take you to a great place on the pier. They never stop serving breakfast there."

Indeed, the seasoned diners ordered nothing else.

55.

What was I doing, anyway, dragging this callow youth from inland Reno to the far end of the pier? Maybe he would want to see the harbor, the bay of fishing boats the size of trailers, the gulls sailing high on the wind. Maybe he had never seen a lobster scalded or a fish scaled—though unlikely—or had ever ridden on a full-size brass-ring carousel—not necessarily dangerous or *strange* in the way of new experience. Boys, I had found, were curious by nature, adventurous by gender.

The B'low Decks Cafe had a big iron range like a galley's, sizzling with good food and warmth. In that snug hole between the planks and piles it was always somehow the beginning of the day. *Womb-like*, I supposed I might have called it, to anyone but Alex sitting there, shoveling down a platterful of eggs. *Nostalgic*, for certain—a link to recent history in that timber spine to shore. In grease-dimmed photos on the walls, their split grins in the foregrounds, were faces like this boy's. Half a century later, where had these grins gone? Where would he be decades hence? I was getting off my time track. A picture of the Merry-Go-Round in early paint and glory told me why we were there—to pay a call on dear old Leonard, for reasons I would not disclose at the moment, even to myself.

Before mounting the steps to the traffic deck, a one-time prospect for my suicide run, I gave Alex a look down below—a glimpse between stored hulls, coiled lines and tangled gear into a nether-world of pilings upthrust like drowning fingers that lost themselves in mist. Or again—familiar image—dense files of phallic columns, another carnal temple. Or a tunnel of lust—like the storm drain. I sank my hands deep in my pockets. Alex sank his, too.

"*Man*," he cried above the churning surf, "what a place to bring your girl! Like the woods out back at home. It's kind of *spooky*, though. And *co-old*." He shivered in the damp coveralls.

"I know. I wouldn't recommend it. A lot of other things can happen, too." I'd heard of stab-drained corpses found in corners, under canvas, hours or days too late. "Let's get the hell out of here, Alex. I want to go visit a friend." Compared to that howling chaos, a Niagara's Cave of the Winds, Leonard's live-in music box was a refuge of serenity and ease.

"He makes clothes for movie stars. Like Melody Landau," I said in introduction as we waited at the door. The famed designer's voice was clearly heard behind it. "So go with Rodney, if *that's* all your little heart desires!" it challenged as the door flew wide. "No one ever thinks of *my* needs." A pair of feet stamped up the stairs.

"Oh, hello Jerry. *And* your friend! You're early for the party, if *that's* why you're here. We're not even having one this year. It's im-*poss*-ible. She's a bitch beyond belief! And to think she's practically my own *creation*." He tied a ferocious knot in the sash of his Florentine robe, the silk tassels quivering. "I'm flying down to Palm Springs this weekend. You see, I'm really *wanted* there. Fix yourself a drink while I get ready. And give your friend a *root* beer."

"May I use the bathroom, sir?" asked Alex.

"It's this way, sonny, but you mustn't stay in too *long*." Leonard ran his hands through a new set of hairs that had clever streaks of grey sown among them. "He's a cute little charmer, practically a *child*. Wherever did you find him, in *Popular Mechanics*?"

"He's just around to keep me company, Len, since Mickey left." As Leonard rushed from room to room throwing things together I followed with the story of our complicated lives. "I knew you'd understand what's happened to me, Leonard. You probably know what it is to feel betrayed."

"Betrayed? A *thousand* times, dear Jerry." He crammed his secret creams and jellies in a case. "But Mickey always *did* like pussy, you know. I thought you would have learned that."

"My God. That wasn't *pussy*, Len. That woman is my wife. And Mickey's my best buddy, or he was."

"Sorry for *you*. Lucky you have no enemies then, said the spider to the fly. Here! Help me get this bag shut. These are my *personal* things. I don't want them spilling at the airport, you know. Those tourists won't know which way to *look*." I handled the glove-leather satchel like a bomb threat. It was heavy with clanking weights.

"*Actually*," he went on philosophically, "Mickey's just a great big

Irish puppy-dog. He'll lick any hand that feeds him. But he can also *bite.*" Alex walked in to watch in wonder as gorgeous leisure suits were folded into a suitcase, a magician's deception in reverse. "He put the bite on *me* for several hundred, plus expensive meals and drinks. To say nothing of the *other* things he needs." Leonard bounced his fanny on the case and snapped the latch. "He's less like a house pet than a *monkey*. A monkey, you see, is impossible to *house*-break."

"Is that really true?" asked Alex.

"True as true can be. You ought to try it sometime, my pet."

"This monkey's breaking up my house and home," I interrupted.

"I think you're lucky to be rid of *both* of them. Oh, Lord! It's nearly time to go. I hope their plane is comfortable. I *loved* meeting your friend here, Jerry. You must bring him up again sometime, after I get back. We might even find him a *job*."

"Goodbye now, *precious*," Leonard trilled up the staircase. "Be sure to lock the door when you leave. And only take what *belongs* to you!"

Against the silence of the room above we heard the tireless organ of steel pound underneath us. Then a small hard object bounced off the stairwell walls and lay sparkling on a prayer rug at our feet.

"Take *that*, you frowzy whore," sobbed a baritone voice. "And hand it to your sweetie down in *Palm* Springs. I only hope it fits his fucking *cock!*" Leonard pushed us through the door and banged it, pocketing a chain of keys. Outside he held the ring up to the sky.

"A star sapphire. Set in white gold! She had no *star quality*, you know. She simply didn't *deserve* it. Oh well," he sighed. "It's as good a New Year's gift as any. I hope yours is happy, too, boys."

"Sure, Len. We'll try to make it so."

I walked beside Alex on the wind-stripped beach, our heads bent, eyes to the sand. Winter storms had cast up bits of glass and seashells.

"I heard about people like that," he said between clenched teeth. "My parents used to warn me. I never thought I'd meet them in real life, though."

"It takes all kinds to make a world, kid."

"Not for me it doesn't."

In my heart I was ready to agree.

As the year's first hour raced across the nation we followed celebrations on TV: parties in New York, hysteria in New Orleans, mobs on the streets of tall Chicago, crashes on the freeways of L.A. Then from the bedroom-study window we watched the revelry across the way. Bands of straights, bi's, and gays ran from one bar to another—some in evening clothes, a few in gowns and make-up tilting on high heels.

"I'm glad I won't be that way," mused Alex, "and go around like girls in wigs and dresses. I want a wife and kids when I grow up."

"So did I. Once."

"I hope you don't end up like that, Jerry. You're too nice a guy."

"That's not where my head's at, Alex."

We got into bed and lay there smoking until the noises ceased. Gently I touched the boy's shoulder. The thin blade flinched but his body stayed still and unresisting. "There ain't no use in trying," he said softly. "I guess I'm just not built that way, old man."

"No hard feelings, kid, I'm always your friend when you need one."

I thought of friends and lovers, not merely those of *my* bed, but all around the globe—in unimagined rooms, incalculable spaces; in pleasure, illness, cold despair—as the old year closed its circuit of the planet. Drowsily, dreamily, and then in dreary realization, I remembered Mick McCrory and our meeting on the corner only one year ago—an anniversary. *Going My Way.* What a way to go! He was probably, even now, coiled tight in bed with Linda. Friendship was a word of many meanings.

The phone call in the morning was for Alex himself, said the operator up in Reno. I went to the bathroom to let the call be private.

"That was Mom," said Alex in his coveralls again. "I think she got a little loaded last night. Anyway, she won some money. She sent bus fare care of Western Union. There's a Trailways leaves at noon, so I guess I'll be heading home. She says I'm the man of the house now."

The new year was beginning with a cleaner slate than I'd expected. What words would fate's willful finger write upon those unformed walls, the frail partitioning of the future—*graffiti* of all the days and nights to come? And how would I be further tricked by Mick and Linda? Time yet remained for one quick resolution. No matter who was slated to get screwed that year, I would not be the solitary victim.

56.

Showers of winter rain that drenched the canyon were curtains to
that stage of my career. Our expensive home movie had run its final
reel, ending for me in double jeopardy, for *them* in starring roles. No
need to stick around to watch the credits. I knew who was responsible for whom.

Time to stretch the legs at intermission. Time for the snack bar and
the Men's Lounge—as represented right across the street at the
Friendship, the gay cafe, Bob's beer bar. The names and faces of their
customers, the bodies too, became as known to me as those of
featured players—more familiar than those of the lost family Fedderman whose fate was off the circuit, off the billings of current attractions.

Sometimes I drove up there with a Sunday headache. Mick would
be in mind but out of sight. The hours taut and strained, it would be
Linda with whom I passed the time. We talked about money, school
reports, trouble on the schoolbus. Or about her woman's plight, an
ordeal she wouldn't suffer through again, she said, in this or any
other lifetime. I would think up equivalent complaints.

"Well, I'll see you next week," I would say as I left, "if things look
any better." We might touch in the way that married couples did, but
it felt like embracing a rosebush. I was better off petting the dog or
playing chess with Starkey, though he had learned how to win
without my help. "Keep your nose clean," he would tell me. We
both knew what he really meant.

Or again, I went to the parties of old friends who were used to my
former ways. Some tried to fix me up with girls they knew, but in
these I had only passing interest—an intermission look. In such
society I grew increasingly indifferent to young and old alike. I was
out for the chase, into the race. In pursuit of my feverish ideal, its
sensations and ejaculating juices, these people weren't merely irrelevant—they were actually standing in the way! I would drink my party
drinks and vanish at the stroke of twelve, a vampire thirsting for fresh
victims, an addict in search of a fix.

Such were my thoughts as I made the rounds at midnight, sometimes scoring, often not; sometimes circling city blocks only to see
my intended swept up by the car ahead. Once I nearly crashed in

heavy fog, steering toward the right lane for a sailor. The object I found to be waiting was a blue-and-white U.S. mailbox.

Luck of the road, I could tell myself, like fact-finding captains of free enterprise. If *they* sought the Almighty Dollar, I was out for the Ultimate Dork, the Moby Dick of human sensuality.

I had signed for a long, long journey—a journey that began with a single shift of gear.

Part Four

57.

Irresistibly, from English Lit. II, the scene evoked the lines of some immortal poet. The words flew into mind like vagrant butterflies:

> I wandered lonely as a cloud
>   That floats on high o'er vales and hills
> When all at once I saw a crowd,
>   A host, of golden daffodils;
> Beside the lake, beneath the trees
> Fluttering and dancing in the breeze.

SPRING! The scent of California wildflowers, touched with sweat and tanning oils, swept the roof of that citadel of male-hood, the Young Mens Christian Association, conceived and built in Mission style. Among the rock-hard limbs of golden athletes I spotted a stray pansy here and there. They always had the sleekest skins, the briefest briefs—usually at half-mast for the effect of that overall tan. The Associates, some with transistors at their ears, sunned themselves on wooden pallets. I hung on the stucco parapet taking in the view.

On the greening hills flecked with poppies, sage, and lupine leaned the great tin letters of the town itself: -OLLYWOOD. When would they put back the **H**? Maybe it ought to be an **F** this time, supplying title to my new scenario, trite as the idea might seem at first or second glance. I spent many a foolish hour there with time and glances to spare.

Nearby were office towers. The workers could look down and envy us anytime they wished. Between other buildings, royal palms stuck up like curiously idle mops. Mid-distance in the afternoon haze I spotted sites of recent affairs—if I could call them such— motels and studio apartments. It was flattering to be invited in by others for a change, even were they not my perfect type. Groveling in strangers' loins was not the perfect way to spend an evening, either, but those times gave a lift to my confidence. To hell with Mick and Linda. Who needed them, anyway?

Just up there off Highland I had made it three times in one night while the record changer played the same disc. "Der *Liebestod*," remarked my partner at a smoking break. "It means *The Love Death*. By Richard *Vahg*-ner." He thrust a thick tongue down my throat. "Let's see if we can make it happen at the *climax*," he said when he had pulled it out again. An artificial-looking purple dawn suffused the room as blue jays cawed in eucalyptus trees. The man's breath stank of rum, I discovered, and his flesh was soft—little things I never noticed till after I'd got off. He was, after all, a nine-to-five accountant, in his thirties, like myself. *Ernie*—if I remembered rightly. But I'd probably never see him again.

The one sunbather I had eyes for was still in a stage of sleep, and seemed likely to remain so, even though his back was turning red. Should I wake him? Then what? The young man rolled over, jockey shorts filled out, exhibiting a nasty case of stomach rash. I took my towel and climbed down the hatchway to the gym.

Basketballs thudded on the varnished floor, sneakers squealed, barbells rattled to a cadence. I heard sharp reports from handball courts, the happy speedy chatter of Ping-Pong balls and paddles. Noise was a part of keeping fit. The Y's central court was an open well of sound where every coin machine and phone call was amplified. Yet I knew that in the cell-like rooms above dwelt silent onanists and worse—adepts in secret vices forbidden by rules of Christian fellowship, as well as by California law.

I descended into man's last refuge, the locker room. The slotted metal lockers breathed manliness like so many Iron Lungs. Sitting down or standing in the cramped sweaty aisles, it was hard not to notice how the other guys were hung. What of it? In the ever-streaming showers on perpetual parade was the U.S. male in all its forms and phases.

But the heart—the nascent core—of the YMCA experience was the green subterranean pool, the American swimming hole glorified in classic square white tiles. Webs of light rays quivered on the ceiling, reflections off the water from a sunlit strip of glass bricks. Like a tribe of hairless monkeys at a zoo, naked boys of ten or twelve played tag around the rim, plunging at the shallow end on top of one another. Would that I were one of those—like the freckled lad who could have been a Jimmy Corey brother. He was wrestling a bigger boy, each astride the neck of a companion, and *winning*, I saw with jealous pride. Just think, I thought, legs swinging from the diving board, in a few years their mechanisms would be operational, too. Their troubles hadn't started. A police whistle echoed off the wall tiles.

"All right! Cut the horseplay," yelled the husky lifeguard.

"This is only combat practice. Watch!"

"Time's up. Take off, you little jerks."

"Just two more *minutes?*" pleaded one.

"OUT!" The guard snapped a towel at his apricot bottom.

"Up yours, you big *fruit!*" The towel stung another easy target. The boys scampered yelling to the shower room, Junior Division, and the guard slammed the steel door behind them. Small fists beat against its other side.

"They give you lots of static?" I asked.

"No. They're okay until they're older. Then I can't handle them anymore."

Two serious swimmers appeared, launched themselves in racing dives, and started swimming lengths along the lane stripes with coordinated breaths. I swam ten laps, took a steambath among young businessmen, and dressed. I felt clean, straight, and manly, exactly like everyone else. I bought a ripe apple from the slot machine, and stepped to the warm street, smiling.

58.

At the far end of Hollywood Boulevard the sun was sinking in a pool of hydrocarbons, swelling in mirage to a gigantic bloody eye. That's how it would look ten billion years from now—a preview of our star become a small Red Giant, as predicted by astronomers in LIFE. It was horrendous: the ocean parched, the cities gone, the whole earth scorched like a pot roast. Why not live for the moment? Where would we be then?

The vernal equinox was near. The rays struck straight along the east-west length of thoroughfare, gilding shabby storefronts, lighting up the pink terrazzo sidewalks and their galaxies of movie stars, names set in five-point frames of bronze. Cute Mickey Rooney, the Court Jester. Clark Gable—the King! And sad-eyed Judy Garland, Queen of the Gays. Only Chaplin's, the most famous of all, was known to be missing, owing to an unconventional love life. *My* name would never be among them. Some were stained with spit and bubble gum. On Dean Jagger's star the first name had been altered by a lipstick to read *MICK.*

Against the setting sun the passersby cast long, weirdly animated shadows, like a company of daytime ghosts. I had to squint to see their faces, but few held my eyes for long. In that whole golden throng I was lonely. I ducked into a dim-lit bookstore, a storehouse of secondhand books. The rows of worn volumes were stacked ceiling-high, tighter than the lockers at the Y. Those were for the body, these for the mind. I squeezed past other readers who frowned without looking up.

ACCOUNTING, ANATOMY, THE ARTS...ASTRONOMY, ASTROLOGY, read the tired ragtag labels. *BOTANY*, a bore, like *CHEMISTRY*. Then *HISTORY, THE LAW, THE* NAVY! *PSYCHOLOGY* next. I felt I was getting warmer. I browsed through unique case histories, not one resembling my own. But down there on the plank floor behind me—I had almost missed the tag—were *MAGIC, MYSTERY, THE OCCULT.* I cautiously began to fish in murky waters.

Let's see now: *Everyday Witchcraft; Effective Spells, Binding and Breaking; CRY WEREWOLF!* A work on out-of-body travel. I thought I could get into that; books on trances, levitation, *MAGIC: Black and White.* The black magicians appeared to have the upper hand. They had more tools and larger followings to work with.

What could be done to make Mick and Linda feel as bad as I had? Would I ever possess that kind of knowledge and control? It seemed the practice of a lifetime, like religion. I did not see myself sticking pins in wax figures, laying curses on hanks of stolen hair. Suppose they started doing that to me? *Double jeopardy* was what I would be asking for. I saw squadrons of demons allied to their cause.

My shoe struck an old scarlet binding and I stooped to put it back in its place. *Methods of Torture and Execution.* There was something I could deal with in a practical way. Though the title itself alarmed me, I began to turn the pages—vivid with terrifying prints. In the life that I lived without loving there grew a sullen longing to destroy.

Plenty could be done in the old times to those who had given offense. They might be boiled, grilled or pan-fried, hung in a cage for the blackbirds to peck, locked in an Iron Maiden *(Linda)*, or whipped, racked and flayed. There was no end of ways to make a body suffer. Every age and nation had its own. In sixteenth-century

Ireland for example:

> "The boy-soldier Mahoney was flung into the bog feet first, tied so that his hands could not support him, nor his feet thrash out. Ranged on the bank were his soldier companions shouting encouragement to him as he went down, to call on the saints for forgiveness to his sins. Sure, 'twas a merciful sight when his head at last vanished and his cries were heard no more. The last we saw were his eyes, just peering over the top of the green-brown mud, and his bedraggled hair, all red and fiery, as it sank below the slow-moving mass of slime...."

So much for the boy-sailor McCrory and his adulterous crime in the storm drain! Or better still, even though my bowels cringed:

> "Upon ye tree was hung ye boye...soe thatte he could not move ennyway. Ye butcher—or it maye have been ye physick—then approached ye boye, who screamyd in terror at what was nowe to befall him. Butte onwards came ye butcher with long wycked knyfe—and plunged it well deepye into ye boye's flank—first to draw blodde to ye pleasure of those gathered there. Hence to tendyre parts of bodye with great gush of blodde and attendant crye from boye—who is loth to bear such payne. Nowe goes ye main member, ye stem so to saye, which splitte in twain at one mightye stroke, bleedyng much, ye twine balls of which did fall to ground with much clamour from ye onlookers, who screamt theyre joye at such happenyng.
>
> Atte nyght there will be much burninge—for ye boye will have expyrred of payne and anguish and hyse bodye must be gyven to ye Lord and Master Satan, for hyse pleasure."

The martyrdom of good St. Mick! Though my breath grew shallow and my jaw tensed, I read on. Were others watching while I gleaned those fearsome words? At the time of the Restoration a prisoner was led to the scaffold....

> "...wherat he was made to strip, down to his loin cloth, which he protested to be allowed to keep on. But which the chief executioner, having regard for the number of damsels and wenches present, compelled him to remove, that their pleasure might be the greater in seeing his manhood revealed in full. So with reluctance, as though this were to be the chief indignity, the prisoner removed his cloth and stood there in humiliation. At that a great roar of approval went up from the assembled females, and hoots from the menfolk, no doubt jealous of the man's splendid physique, comely to behold."

This poor fellow was strung on the scaffold till his tongue turned purple and his eyes bulged out, cut down, and the stomach walls laid open. He was forced to look on while his intestines sizzled in a brazier. The passage did not state what the man had been accused of.

> *"This being done to the satisfaction of all...the executioner did then seize upon the man's privies, and chopt them off entire—holding them aloft to the shrill cries of the females and the mock groans of the men. These also were cast into the flames and burned to cinders."*

After that, wrote the witness, the body had been tugged apart by teams of horses, leaving only the limbless trunk. At that time, "then possessed of a little mercy," the presiding executioner...

> *"...deftly criss-crossed the man's chest, bringing forth his pulsing heart which appeared to move a little in his hand, like a fish caught from a stream, and breathing its last."*

I was queasily, curiously moved. For in this last instance I had not pictured the unlucky prisoner to be Mick. The stand-in for that long-ago sufferer had been a person none other than myself. '

Dreams of vengeance—what a thing! I felt shame in merely holding the book. I shut the catalog of horrors and thrust it back in its hole, the title upside down.

Just then, as though conjured up by mystic powers, a shock of red-gold hair flashed by the shop's front window. There strode a youth in late teens and light denims, heading straight for an objective in long springing strides. I followed swiftly after, nearly losing contact at the first red light, and had almost come abreast when the boy stopped, pulled out a bill and bought a ticket to the Wax Museum. I paid an entrance, too.

In the black tomb-like hall of spotlit figures, we appeared to be the only ones alive. The boy paused before the first exhibit: Bette Davis as Elizabeth the Queen. Nearby stood a headsman, axe on high, like a weight lifter in black mask and leotards. A kneeling prisoner stretched out his neck. Queen Bess was getting even with Essex. Next, a castle basement fully furnished with whips, locks and stocks along fake stone walls—the sort of recreation room a home of Leonard's might afford. A poker waited in cellophane flames to be thrust up any orifice of a manacled wretch in pantaloons and fright wig. How would *that* feel, I wondered. Shrieks and terrible groans played on a tape loop. I leaned on a pipe rail.

"I'm glad I wasn't living then," I ventured to the redhead.

"Yeah, you might not live too long." The thin foxy profile showed a glint of braces as he smiled. My glance shifted swiftly to the front of his pants, just to see if anything stirred there. Two hands seized him by the waist.

"I thought you'd never get here," said the boy to a black-haired girl behind him. "You came in the nick of time."

"I told Mother I was going to a show. Then she wanted to know which one, and what time, and with whom."

"Shades of the Inquisition! We've got to stop meeting like this."

The girl giggled, took his hand, and led him out of sight behind a showcase.

What else was there to look at? I wandered along aisles of movie stars in memorable costumes; past leaders of the Axis Powers—Hitler, Hirohito, Mussolini—safe inside glass cages; and down a line of seated presidents, Kennedy the last. The figure wore a new blue suit and a crop of rich red hair. Envy of that hair had probably got him shot, I speculated. Each head-of-state had a recorded speech for viewers who picked up a phone. Kennedy's hot-line had been crossed with Lincoln's—I got the Gettysburg Address. Then around the next corner: Moses on the Mount as played by Charlton Heston. Ten Commandments were writ on gilded plaster.

At the end, the Last Supper. The tablecloth was stained, the hard rolls dusty. Red fluid had congealed inside cheap glasses. The disciples were sallow, quite translucent, like men who had never lived outdoors. They had nice manicures and were glassy-eyed with wine and grief. The place cards had been switched around—someone had stolen that of Jesus. Among the agitated looks of the diners, only He had a calm resigned expression, as though waiting to settle the bill. He had great liquid eyes and seemed prepared to wait forever, even there in that Hollywood tableau. The only sounds came from the distant torture chamber. The boy and his girl friend had never reappeared.

On the street—that's where all the action was. Lanes of cars, lots of bars, singles of all sexes. I cruised the boulevard on foot, then drove out to the 4-Star, the Preview, the Red Shoes, the Savoir Faire (save your fairy!) on the Sunset Strip, but they all seemed silly and shrill. I grew weary of hearing other males called she, my husband, that bitch! I went home with a studio harpist. Before climbing into the canopied bed, he sat behind a harp and strummed a tune.

59.

Afoot and light-hearted I take to the open road
Healthy, free, the world before me,
The long brown path before me leading where
  I choose.

Those sentiments were okay for hitchhikers, stranded on monox-ide-colored shoulders of the Open Road. Other lines penned by the Good Gray Poet were more suited to my style and circumstances:

You road that I enter upon and look around, I believe
  you are not all that is here,
I believe that much unseen is also here.
  . . .
Now if a thousand perfect men were to appear
  it would not amaze me.

Write on, Walt Whitman! I might well recall those verses in the Fury as the radio played on speeding freeways, on highways going every way but west, on networks like the Crosswire incarnate, made concrete and flesh at any intersection—crossroads that reached around the world.

That was better than stalking back streets and alleys staked out by the Vice Squad or squatting half-drunk on bar stools, waiting for young Mr. Right to come along. Besides, fresh air and changing scenery brought adventure to my life, along with a share of new thrills. I compared myself to a combat pilot out to do a job and bring the plane back, or to a Great Plains Indian determined to count coups instead of scalps. Every occupation had its hazards—if risks were sometimes greater than expected so were the rewards. There was always the open possibility that fast friendships made in car seats might last through an entire weekend.

With wider range and increased highway know-how, I chose another destination every week. For the Friday before Palm Sunday the designated target was Palm Springs, a target of opportunity—if popular rumor could be believed. The resort was said to be all but taken over by troops in desert training, by regiments of hard, hungry, horny, uniformed U.S. Marines. A thousand perfect men on week-end passes!

It was true! A marine from Little Rock shared my motel bed the first night, and borrowed a twenty in the morning when he went to see his girl. Another I found thumbing in the wilderness. We took a hike up a canyon draw where I helped him drop his pants; afterwards he killed a small rattler. With a third I drank tequila through Saturday night. That marine had been in need of money too, I found, when I checked out of the Oasis with small change and a headache. I didn't want another drink. The next best thing was free oxygen, an exposure to pure mountain air. I drove to the foot of the tramway that ascends into the San Jacinto Mountains to an elevation over ten thousand feet.

Waiting for the tram I took time to load my cameras. As well as extra dollars for moments like that morning, the bag held extra film. EAT ME, a hand had crayoned on one cassette container, a secret stash of Mickey's LSD. Without hesitation I gulped down the capsule. I could start feeling good in twenty minutes, the duration of the tramway's climb.

From the window of the swaying cab I tracked its flying shadow. Pools glared through the pines like hidden mirrors. Did naked youths swim there too? It was probably too early in the season. I zipped my leather jacket. It was cold and getting colder—first sign of an early turn-on. No trick of Mick's this time, the chemical was doing its work.

When the cab docked at the top I was high and getting higher, my senses sharp as the needles of the pines. A wind droned like an organ through the fir boughs that danced and quivered where I walked. Other travelers marched to a harsh discordant murmur, out of cadence, out of step. "PLEASE FOLLOW ME," and "DON'T WALK IN THE DITCH!" the guide's bull horn bellowed, like the voice of the Creator taking charge. Good acid had a way of bringing the celestial down to earth. There I could meet it halfway.

I would have to watch my step. One broken leg in God's country was enough. Some pretty colors and surprising sights were all I really asked for—an affair of the spirit, not the flesh. Departing from the group I made my way up a slope of thorny brush and boulders, the cameras, like cowbells, dangling musically on straps. Panting, I achieved the top and sat on a granite slab to rest. I could see a long way in all directions.

Though the spring sun warmed my back, strips of blue-white snow hid underneath the ledges, like blankets inviting me to sleep. Closer, I could see their frozen crystals, rainbow prisms in stray beams of light. I tried focusing a lens but my chilled hands shook. I was freshly aware that they bled—in curlicues, red ringlets, like tattoos come to life.

And the *lichen!* I hopped from rock to rock, each glowing patch of yellow, rust, vermilion a flawless wild creation—pubic growths upon the groins of stone. The swollen mushrooms, the succulent moss, the impudent skin-smooth stalks of smiling flowers! I longed to be a part of all of it, to transmute into sensate components—*organs* if you will—of that adored mountain, there to dwell at peace forevermore.

The tourists could find my cameras, and keep them if they wished. They were a burden to me now, as were my car keys, watch and wallet—all but the silver ring and its watchful symbol eye.

But *wait.* That was only a tiny tiny almost *sub-atomic* fragment of the vast vast universe that exploded on all sides, consistent with our concept of an expanding cosmos—or was it cosmology? *No matter.* It was too too much to ever comprehend. Why bother? It was ALL RIGHT THERE. I collapsed against a tree in helpless cosmic laughter. Like the blood of my own being, sap coursed through the trunk to the surge of earth's many chambered heartbeat, slow with the majesty of time.

All right, I told myself the next moment. If you don't get moving, Jerry, you're going to freeze your *ass* off, as well as miss the last trip down the cable. What a place to come down off an acid trip! You might never make it back alive.

But wait a *minute.* Yonder on the following crest the forest had been seared by fire. The tree trunks stood up stiff *stark NAKED* in the stony glare. I ran over rocks to meet them. The burnt-off bark had left the trunks hard as horn, sleek and glossy—like that singular mast of glory in the highlands of Big Sur, here multiplied by thousands. Were they silvery Crusaders? The fire gods of *Vahg*-ner? The mountain's own antennae?

Rhetorical questions all. In the way of lugubrious answers I knew what to expect. What I saw before me—mouth agape in final confrontation—was a forest of *petrified PRICKS*. Jesus. To come so far and climb so high for that!

A sheet of cloud passed over; the vision grew dreary and dull. A cold foreboding seized me for now. Like the last fulfillment of all the years to come, like the end of man's term on the planet, there rose a graveyard of penile memorials...limitless in number, and stretching from there to eternity...further than the eye could wish to see.

The LSD had peaked early; it was time to be making tracks. Beneath an eerie veil of alto-stratus the snow had lost its sparkle, the lichens were dun-colored scabs. My cuts had dried dark purple, like dead meat. The wind's icy passage was in chords of a minor key, as though the whole range of mountain groaned against my trespass of it. It was *frigid*. I shivered deep inside.

Rocks tumbled where my feet slipped, in small but threatening slides. I moved faster. Skirting a blade-like peak I found myself astride a sheer divide, a few feet wide, but a thousand to ground zero. I hung on the rock spread-eagled—*Eagle Rock revisited*—an X-mark on the mountainside, a human fly. A wind whipped the legs of my blue jeans.

From far below, from another world, the emerald eyes of Palm Springs' swimming pools winked up at me. On the far desert floor—a dead sea—cloud shadows floated like kelp clumps. I was homesick for the ocean, for the Malibu terrace, for the kids. For *Linda!* I knew then that I loved her. You can't let me die *now*, God! Are you listening? If You are, I promise not to do it. I promise I won't do it again!

I had one last hallucination. Just around the corner of the cliff, I suspected, was Moses dressed as Charlton Heston, in his clutch the Ten Commandments cast in 14-karat gold—with the addition of a possible Eleventh: *Thou shalt not covet thy neighbor's....* But the last words were lost on the wind.

I breathed deeply, my panic ceased. No need for divine intervention! I calmly raised a camera and took pictures of the view to remind me of my perch on the abyss. I swung my foot across the gap and made it climb, ran back through the darkening woods, caught the tram as the door slid shut, and rode down among ordinary mortals, the cameras still dangling from my neck.

"Did you get what you wanted?" asked a man in a sportsman's cap.

"A few good exposures. In color."

"You can't beat a single-lens reflex. I hope they turn out all right."

"This time I was careful," I assured him.

That night I went to bed early, with no marine to guide me to rest. Most of them had gone back to base, to their war games and guns and dusty weapons carriers, to steel cots and coarse blankets—their cocks warm in dirty green socks.

Now in the crisis on the mount, I had made no *specific* declaration —at least none that I remembered—as to what it was I wouldn't do again. I had a pretty good idea, though, of what that commitment should have been. Since I had actually survived the day unassisted, it might be wise to play it safe that night. Besides, like any national holiday, Palm Sunday came but once a year.

As for my love of Linda, was it truth or fear that spoke? At this dilemma I stretched myself and yawned. There was nothing to do but to sleep on it. In the morning my head would be clear.

60.

"*A nation of strays and orphans,*" wrote the sage of Baltimore. H.L. Mencken knew his country well—better than his country knew him. Now all the strays were here in Southern Cal, where it never got too cold and they never got too hungry—if a healthy young male were not downright repulsive, and knew when and where to say *YES.* Along with some bucks and a bed came a handy massage where it counted or a friendly pat on the rump, though affection sometimes went a little deeper. That's how movie stars were made, they had probably been told back in Pinpoint, Idaho, or by a body scout along the Sunset Strip. I was cruising that strip now, the car paced to hit the red lights. That way there was time to look around, time to check the scene, the early evening turnout.

Hanging out on curbs, flipping butts in gutters, hitting up a stranger for spare change or a smoke, new arrivals were already typecast by an imitated pose or slouch, by the very fit and fading of their jeans. If smartly packaged they were not alone for long, as demonstrated just that moment by a white Ferrari and a bronze-haired surfer type. The car behind squealed its treads in protest.

My eyes turned to other distractions: sidewalk cafes, strings of glitter lights, billboards tall as buildings. At two o'clock high in my sight line loomed a jet-size tube of fluoridated dentifrice. PROMISE! was the name of that brand. Exactly like those orphans, was my rueful notion as the light changed—uncapped, squeezed, discarded—throwaway people for the throwaway city of L.A. As one concerned first-class citizen, what was I doing to help?

The query evaporated on the smoggy air, for there, a block ahead and standing on the right-lane corner, was a redhead uncannily like Mick. Deft as a fighter plane's touchdown the Fury swept alongside and stopped, window-vent to fly-front.

"That's better than the first time you picked me up," said Mickey, sliding in. "At least you've learned to stop."

"Yeah, I've learned a lot since then. Besides, I haven't been drinking." Did it have to be Mick himself? *The real McCrory?* The dude was just too much!

"We might as well do a number then." He lit one. In the flare of the Zippo lighter I saw signs of change. The face was leaner, almost gaunt, with the start of a mustache. No longer boyish-looking, it was a...*man's* face. In my absence, Mickey had gone right ahead and grown up without me, no doubt with Linda's aid and abetment. What wouldn't those two think of doing next!

"Here," he said. "Take a long drag—you won't get busted. If the fuzz comes along you can eat it." The grin had grown harder, almost cruel. His voice was deeper, too. I coughed apprehensively.

"I haven't done much dope lately, Mick. I've been trying to get my head straight. I found your LSD though." As I told the story of the Palm Springs revelation acid trip, Mickey started laughing in his old style, chortling between tokes, the eyebrows arched like copper wires.

"You're a caution, J.C., aren't you? Someday you'll just fly away. If they don't catch you in a net first. Or one of those stiff white jackets." His laughter ceased. "Do you hear voices often?"

"Only when I'm alone, usually. Hey! I took one of those capsules at the Y once. The pool lit up inside, big as the Roman baths. Or like Saint Peter's! The screaming kids turned into choirboys, or fishes."

"You're on the glory road, alright. Try it at the steambaths once, and see what some of those old queens turn into." I wasn't eager to imagine that. "Those caps were only a hundred mikes, you know. Here. Take these." The capsules rolling in my palm were like twin beetles. "*Black Magic*. A thousand micrograms each."

"Sounds impressive. What's it like?"

"A total wipe-out. A *white*-out. You think you're inside the sun." He took on the dazed expression of a star-struck space voyager. I felt I was losing contact.

"Has Linda ever tried it?"

"She won't use drugs. On account of the kids, she says. Some excuse. She helps me have good trips, though." He grew silent again, smoking, as he had the first time in the car. Was it Linda or marijuana that made him so, or something else inside? Maybe he'd changed there, too. Too soon we were dropping down the hill into the Canyon, the salt air a mist in the sycamore leaves.

"Are you coming up for a while, Mick?"

"Not this time. I left the van out in Van Nuys. Dead battery."

"Then I'll drive *you* home."

"*Ben Dover?* That might not be too cool right now. Thanks anyway. I'll hitchhike. I don't usually wait long for a ride."

I dropped into instant depression. Why did I have to be so goddamn nice, when last month I was ready to *torture* him? I must be as crazy as he said! It didn't seem my world would ever straighten out without a strait-jacket—or a ten-thousand-mike super-white-out! In the meantime I would have a few drinks with my friend Bill the barman at the Friendship.

At the first gulp I knew why I had acted as I did. Despite every hardship and heartbreak, for a glimpse of St. Mick I'd do anything.

When it was all too apparent that the Saint would not appear I decided to try something different. I went to the Tivoli Baths, though not on LSD as Mick had recommended. I wasn't ready for another look at the apocalypse.

I was buzzed in, signed the name *Lynn McCrory*, and left my money, keys and real I.D. inside a metal box. My clothes I piled in a locker in exchange for a skinny towel, and started down a labyrinth that led to many rooms. Narrow cubicles had doors locked or ajar, in some a ready host. One room was a small movie theater where threatening genitalia tangled on the screen like monstrous serpents. In another a TV console flickered on a rug-wide orgy. Through them all oozed the soothing sounds of Muzak, as in any busy shopping promenade.

I sweated for a while in the steam room. Two muscular numbers met, fell in love, and departed. Other bodies sat about on shelves like batteries that awaited recharging. Within a foggy alcove crouched a man-size toad beyond the help of any fairy wand. Moisture fell in droplets from the ceiling; steam hissed from under the bench. *A hellish exhalation,* I told myself, and left. Up the stairs by the EXIT was the ANNEX, end of the line.

Its one ruby globe gave the light of a dim planet. In an instant I felt hands all over, tentacles out of the dark. The towel dropped. Someone or something was at me from behind; in front I was engorged to the hilt. Invisible, I was the center of attention.

An arm held my neck, a tube went up each nostril. *Poppers.* The top of my skull lifted off, I felt myself explode in all directions. Had I come? Or had *everybody?* I came down like an empty balloon. *"Wow,"* I called out, but I heard only slurpings and sighs. I found clean soap and took a long scrub in the showers, as after gym class at Eagle Rock High. Did other alumni know the Tivoli Baths?

I left like a prisoner on parole.

61.

One swallow doth not a summer make. Nor a thousand, either. My thirst and appetite had grown apace; they grew with what they fed on. I went further and further afield, deep into friendly—sometimes enemy—territory, from Mexico to Monterey, from pier's end to Death Valley.

Youths out of school, out of work, out of *jail;* off the base, off the reservation, off their rockers—swarmed across the state of California from any of the other forty-nine. Why hunt the Great White Whale when schools of lesser, just as tasty fry were running? *"—to everything its season,"* sang the Byrds.

In pursuit of a quantity catch I used elastic standards. They didn't *have* to look like Mick or Jimmy Corey or any of their red-crested breed. Brown hair, black, bleached or dirty blond were okay, too. Even a hint of gray, if the bearer were below the age of thirty, yet attractive still. An artist had to draw the line somewhere.

At the rate of three to five a week I checked off their numbers on

the calendar squares, the names code-lined in color. Let's see: at
four per week, average, a good year would yield two hundred
nominal partners, discounting weather, illness or hard luck. In five
years: a thousand at the current rate. In twenty-five: five thousand.
I'd be nearly sixty then—a life's work. If nothing happened in the
meantime.

I began to add half points for repeats—those who came back for
seconds, even thirds. A few had wanted to move in, but that would
spoil the record, an investment I needed to protect. I forgot that I'd
once had a family. I was going to be King of the Road.

The quest took time and energy, and all the money I could earn
from Monday mornings until Friday nights. It took its toll in other
ways: lost sleep, lost articles, lost friends; my sports watch, clothes, a
camera. Then restaurant and bar tabs, traffic fines and tickets. It was
costly to be king of such a realm. Was it any cheaper chasing girls?

What was I getting for my efforts when all was had, said, or done—
beyond a chain of fleeting ties, fugitive pleasures, collective images
to masturbate by, distress calls at 3 A.M....?

That's what I would ask in my Monday morning down moods
when the best of them had somehow seemed to get away. But the
richest catch, too, left me hungry for more, like the proverbial
Chinese dinner. An hour later I was primed and ready for the next
full course. Maybe I ought to keep tabs. I lit up a leftover joint.

That's it, man, I rationalized in Mick's inimitable manner—a record
of memories for the years to come, should I ever retire from the
road—or be forced off it, more likely. Thus when technology
became advanced enough the data could be run through a computer. The machine would tell me what I'd won and what I'd lost, how
far I'd fallen short of my ideal. Warming to the task I typed a sample
form, filling in the blanks at random:

CASE STUDY # 234

Date: Sat., June ?   Time: round about Place: P.C.H., mine Weather: full moon!
                      midnight

Name: Randy Hardy   Rank: Lance Cpl.   Service: U.S.M.C.   Answers to: "Rusty"
Age, Apparent: 16   Age, Actual: 18   Race: Cherokee-Irish   Birthplace: Oklahoma
Occupation: A.W.O.L.   Education: +10 gr.   IQ (Est.): +101   Birth Sign: Taurus
Appearance, Clothed: cleancut, crewcut, round face: smooth-cheeked &
dimpled. Western shirt, ranch boots & jeans, no sox, no shorts (no $)
Appearance, Stripped: lean & hard as hickory limb. horny hands, hairless chest,
flat belly, round butt: smooth-cheeked & dimpled. Big grin, bow legs, bull
scrotum. Indian blood in Irish boy's body!

Did that say it all? Those were hardly the bare statistics. I typed on:

Distinguishing Features: *all of the above. long lifeline, heartline. headline? tattoo:
Death before Dishonor. missing front tooth.*

Skin: *tan, freckled*	Eyes: *emerald*	Hair, head: *russet*	Hair, body: *tangerine*
Height: *6'9" erect*	Weight: *+150 lb.*	Phys. Type: *ideal*	Phys. Cond.: *perfect*
Length: *9" erect*	Circum: *4" round*	Shape: *straight arrow*	Endurance: *not estab.*

A PHYSICAL DESCRIPTION, yes. But how about PERFORMANCE?
That's what really counted, wasn't it? I took three more tokes before
hitting the keys:

Sexual Preference:	M X	M-F X	F X	S-M ?	Other: *"any port in a storm"*
Activity:		Manual	Oral	Anal	Other *"between the buns"*

		Manual	Oral	Anal	
Subject:	# Orgasms	2/3	2	1	1/3
	Rating	E	SS	SS	F
	Remarks:	*"No sex in 2 weeks."* fast efficient.			
Self:	# Orgasms	1	1	1	1
	Rating:	S	SS	SS	S
	Remarks:	*"If able, would do it all over again."*			
Joint Conclusion:		*"Only making both ends meet."*			

RATING SCALE:

SS	SENSATIONAL
S	SUPERIOR
E	EXCELLENT
G	GOOD
A	AVERAGE
P	POOR
F	FAILED
NS	NO-SHOW
OD	OVER-DOSED
DOA	DEAD ON ARRIVAL

Well, *finish* it, Jerry. Don't just sit there with a hard-on!

Stimulants Used: *beer, wine, vodka, marijuana, magazines, visual & manual aids, words*
Expenses Incurred: *above, plus 1 pr. sox, 1 pr. shorts, $18.50 "travel pay"*
Case Prognosis: *GOOD! will probably repeat "if not busted, sent to brig, discharged"*

What more could be said? I lay back on the beds and made love to
my phantom lover, synthesizing double simultaneous orgasms that
taxed us both to our respective limits. Thank *you*, Number 234.
"Rusty."

Limp with release I watched the clouded fluids turn to puddles clear
as rain, then trickle down the valleys of my flesh—lost generations. I
fell into a twilight sleep of half-heard voices, overlapping visions that
vanished at a rapping on the door. I pulled on my pants, hid away the
score sheet, and stood for a long moment before turning the knob.
Could the person present there be *HE?*

"Hello? Oh. It's you."

"Were you expecting someone, Jerry?"

"A client, maybe. Other people do show up, you know."

238

"Are you going to ask me in? Or is someone there already."

"*No*, Linda. Be my guest. Long time no see. Or hear from, either."

"You're hard to reach on weekends. The children wonder where you go."

"They do? Oh, sometimes I just drive around and try to get my head together. Here, have a beer. And please be seated."

"Together with what? You look tired, Jerry. Is there anything wrong?"

Still stoned I started laughing. I'd begun to fill the mental blanks on CASE STUDY #1, Linda L. Carr's, and had come to the Physical Description. How would *she* look in a burr cut, a bright rust-red—this 5'-5" housewife, probably AWOL from her children and her nearest dearest friend? The Distinguishing Features were already too familiar. It was the clear blue eyes and college-level I.Q. I would have to deal with.

"Why the sudden risibility? I don't see anything to laugh at."

"I thought for a moment you were Mickey at the door."

She was thoughtful. "That's what I came here to talk to you about."

"What's there to say at this late date?"

Her thoughts became a rapid calculation, concluding in a sigh. "He's changed, Jerry. You'd know it if you saw him. And not for the better, I'm sorry to say."

"I thought you'd undertaken his upbringing. He's not my baby anymore. It's up to you to tell him where it's at."

"How do I tell him *where it's at* when I don't know where he is? There're things I can't control any longer."

"What is it in particular you think you've lost control of? Or is that too intimate a question?"

"It's serious, Jerry, so please don't be sarcastic, tempting as that may be. I'm afraid he's been using stimulants, and drugs."

"Really? Whatever caused you to imagine that? I hope he's not acting funny, or *strange.*"

"A lot stranger than he used to. It's not funny at all. He gets high on something, and it's not grass, either. He gets depressed and violent until he rushes off somewhere. Then we have no car, and sometimes no money."

In the course of this appeal Linda had been rolling up her sweater to expose her bra. What the hell was she up to now? She couldn't be trying to *seduce* me! She lifted the left cup and the breast dropped out, swollen with a blotch of multi-colored psychedelic-looking bruises. *Her Purple Heart.* I'd bet she'd earned it! I made a terrible face. "How did you ever do that—in the blender? Or is Casey growing fangs?"

For an answer she hoisted her skirt to show a similar contusion of the upper right thigh. "Is that all?" I asked.

"It *is* serious, Jerry. An injury like that can start a cancer."

"Well, how did it happen then?"

"*Mickey.* He had a bad trip and started hitting me. I was turning him into the Devil, he said. He certainly acted it." Linda had loosened the valves behind her eyeballs, already glistening with tears.

"That's not too far from a Red Prince, is it?" I wiped my lips, moist with beer foam. "You ought to be careful with that magic wand, Princess."

"*Damn* you, Jerry, you just don't care about anything!" Inspection over, she stood up and straightened her clothing. "Anything except those *boys,* that is. I don't think you're quite right in the head, either."

"*Le tete a ses raisons.* I'm boy-crazy, Linda. I thought you always knew that."

"All *right,* Jeremy Carr." She picked up her big straw purse—probably empty—with daisies sewn on it, and marched to the front door. She swung it wide for a grand slam. "Don't come crawling back to me when you're in trouble—like the time you broke your leg!"

"I thought you were leaving." Where was my love for her now?

"You don't know what it *is* to be a wife, you homosexual alcoholic!" she shouted for the whole apartment house to hear. The words bounced like bullets off the plaster walls. "Whatever happens now is up to you!"

"So long, bitch," I said. Linda slammed the door.

Before the hinges cooled I heard another knock. There stood Mrs. Haymer for the rent. "I hope you're not having any trouble," she said, checking the figures on the bank check. "Your visitors are usually pretty quiet." Those visitors had learned to use the rear door—the Service entrance. They were rarely heard or seen if they could walk straight.

"My wife is having some problems. I'm afraid she's not really very stable. In fact, that's why we're separated—she imagines things. I can't believe anything she tells me anymore."

"I'm sorry, Mr. Carr. Is there anything at all you can do about it? Can't your roommate help you?"

"I feel he's done what he could. There's not a whole lot more that anyone can do now. The doctors call it schizophrenic paranoia, a psychosis with delusions. I hope I won't have to commit her."

"That must be hard on you, Jerry. And the children, too. Don't you miss them?"

"Of course I do. It's not easy to work it out alone, Mrs. Haymer, but life is often hard."

"Well, you've been a good tenant. You always know how to fix things."

"It's the human things you can't control, unfortunately."

The electric Smith-Corona still hummed in expectation. I sat down and began a new survey:

CASE STUDY # 1

Date: *Mon., June 6*   Time: *fleeting*   Place: *Planet Earth*   Weather: *treacherous*
Name: *Mrs. Jeremy Carr*   Rank: *none*   Service: *terminated*   Answers to: *"Bitch"*
Age, Apparent: *61*   Age, Actual: *37*   Race: *lost*   Birthplace: *discredited*
Occupation: *adultress*   Education: *inadequate*   IQ (Est.): *4-Q-2*   Birth Sign: *Ca*

At the dread word *Cancer* my fingers stopped. It was more like a DEATH SIGN. It took all the fun from the preposterous report. Why go on about APPEARANCES: *deceiving*, ORGASMS: *0*, et cetera? For PROGNOSIS I could simply write *POOR*.

What if she should have a real injury, like me? Suppose she lost a breast? That would be like losing a *ball*—if you happened to be male— only a whole lot more up front. Two would be the max. Her love life with Mick the Tit Man would be over. Her *whole* life, maybe.

How would I feel about that—though it would certainly not be *my* fault? And the kids! I'd have four junior orphans to take care of, and not for only one night, either. The future could look pretty bleak.

Then, just before dying, she would probably forgive me everything.

That would be the cruelest blow of all.

62.

In bed Wednesday night as the eaves poured rain I brooded on the subject. The bars on Channel Road were empty, even silent for a change. How much of my public had caught Linda's words, her flak-burst delivered at my doorstep? If they hadn't, my neighbors were (a) stone deaf, (b) permanently out to lunch, (c) absorbed in vices of their own, or (d) already aware—and indifferent. It was one thing to entertain suspicions, another to have the naked truth shouted through the halls.

Someone was banging at the door again—this time the service entrance. Trick, treat, or trade—*something* scraped against the door. I cracked it. Mickey fell flat on the kitchen floor in a flood of bloody water. *"Ripped to the tits,"* I heard him gasp before a total sensory blackout.

I pulled off the boots with blood inside, the torn jeans only too gladly, the bloody shirt, the sticky socks. Mick lay stripped on the vinyl like a stiff that awaited embalming. Down one calf ran a jagged gash; he bled from a cut in the forearm. The bluish dots in the crook of the arm were not related to those injuries. I bound the wounds with dish towels.

I wiped the body dry, beginning at its core, fluffing up a nest of orange curls. Then chest and outer limbs, at length massaging Mickey's scalp until the red hairs shone. The lips kept a waxen smile. Paler than I remembered, frailer by many pounds, the remains still had the makings of a beautiful corpse. I draped it with our quilt and curled up by its side, like Randy.

By dawn's pearly light it was clear that the patient would survive. The breath hissed through his teeth, the ribs went up and down like a bellows. The quilt had slipped aside and there, conspicuous as usual, like the first to fall out for roll call, stood the Saint, haloed by a sunbeam. The orange hairs glistened in a beady sweat—*like early dew.* How would I write *that* in my report, should I wish to keep current my statistics? The world did not have words enough, nor time, to describe in full detail that ruddy, recrudescent miracle.

At once I knew the answer. From its hiding place I took my camera with the portrait lens and photographed St. Mick and Mickey, bandages and all, on thirty-six rolls of color film.

242

"Are you finished?" murmured Mick, palms cushioning his skull as though interpreting the art of relaxation.

"The last exposure."

"Then do what you want to do, Jerry."

I put aside the camera and knelt to kiss His Mickiness. But in some subtle fashion the Saint had changed, too. Was he also leaner, did he stand as firm? I did what I had so long yearned to do in thought, but the doing was not as fantasized. Or recollected either. Where had *our* love gone? And what a time to ask! It was taking him longer than ever.

What was wrong? Was it my denatured feelings? Or Mick's pale passion, oddly pacified? When the prime moment came, it was not one of fulfillment but of an aftertaste, bitter and strange. Had something been lost in the bleeding? Or was it what had been added to the bloodstream. Mick rolled over to let me have my other pleasure, too. Even that was not the same, on the cold kitchen floor. It was like having sex with a mannequin, a doll from the House of Wax. But the leg bled real blood. Mick sat up to see his wounds.

"How did it happen?" I washed the cuts. Without stitches they were going to leave scars.

"Fell through a sliding glass door, I guess. Or some dude pushed me. I was flying! I dropped in a pile of trash and lost my car coat. I could still drive, though. I guess I'll have to clean up the van."

"Yeah, blood never looks good on the driver's seat." I bandaged the arm with the needle marks. "That's an interesting habit you've got there, Mickey."

"Oh, those? We shoot a little crystal sometimes. Or coke. Acid in the mainline is a rush! My habits don't cost any more than yours, J.C."

"No heroin yet?"

"That's a *death* trip, man. I've only done smack twice."

"There, Mick, you're mended. Here's some Levis and a long-sleeved shirt. What else is new?"

"At the house? Oh, your wife Linda. She gets pissed off all the time, like with your drinking. '*Because I smoke a little dope, because I talk to Brenda, because I don't get a regular job*,'" he recited, in a gross falsetto voice. "It's a hassle. I could make a lot of bread. Dealing, you know? It's like she wants to run my fucking life." Mick got up. The Saint looked tired.

"I know how you feel. Did you ever have to hit her?"

"Uh-huh. We had a little argument," he grunted as I helped him dress.

"We had a fight once. I hit her with an egg, for Easter. A raw one, too."

"Ours was different."

"Tell me, Mick." His eyes were pink, the pupils pointed.

"She said I might have made her pregnant—because she couldn't think of anybody else. She was sure it wasn't you, though. So was I."

"And you *believed* her?" There wasn't going to be any *good* news.

"Hell, would you? I thought she was playing with my mind, like I was only someone there to dump on. Her houseboy!" He tugged on the boots and turned his shirt cuffs. "I gotta split now. Take care."

I rinsed the bloodied towels and clothing—another set of Mickey's scarlet souvenirs.

63.

Though troublesome, the visits had been uppers for my ego. Mick and Linda both knew where to come when everything got bent out of shape: to good old Uncle Jerry's *(Whistle While-U-Work)* Head & Body Shop. They obviously weren't helping each other—neither was capable of that—and they couldn't take care of themselves. Suppose the whole affair *did* fall apart, as it had every human right to. Would I want either of them back? How about their baby—should that ludicrous invention come true? Or Mickey's drug habit—true as true could be. It was *their* bed, let them lie in it. As they unquestionably did—to each other.

On Saturday I set out for Mexico. I too had to get away from it all. The day was brilliant, and though hitchhikers, servicemen and surfers lined the road like pickets, I passed them without slowing down. How often could you do it in broad daylight? Even Kings of The Road had to rest. I stopped along the beach at Laguna to lie in warm sand, swim in cool surf, and get kinks out of body and mind. Sun, sea and hydrotherapy—that would do the trick! But the very phrase itself turned my head in old directions. Other hearts and minds were worth winning. Whose would it be tonight?

It was night when I got to Tijuana. Ten minutes later I was in the Long Bar, tequila at the left hand, beer on the right, prepared for whatever came my way. And two rounds later there it was, a few feet down the bar rail, gazing at the action in the back bar mirror. Short, dark and brown-skinned, he was not built to factory specs. But the close-cropped head, the ready stance, the shirttail hung out like a banner told at once his everyday vocation—that of genuine U.S. Marine. Case Study #567, and the name was...

"Barney. What's yours?" I gave it and ordered fresh drinks for the brand new subject and myself. The alcohol raced with my adrenaline. Another challenge! Should I take it? I glanced again in the mirror. Next to his brown face the one I recognized as mine had blushed a white man's red.

Barney—and I took a closer look—had a flat nose, jug-handle ears—a *jarhead*—and deep-set Mongoloid eye sockets. The skullcap of hair gave the small impish face the look of a grownup...*monkey*. And an animated monkey at that.

"So my buddy took my weekend K.P.," he was saying, "for a fifth of Black Velvet. Payday's not till the fifteenth." He squeezed a lemon slice for his tequila. The fingers, swift and agile, were simian too. The eyes were black holes, like targets. "Say, is anything wrong?"

"A sunburn, I guess. I was surfing. I saw spots before my eyes."

"You stared at me, like you was queer or something."

"I'm married, to a mother of five. I was in the service, too, in the Air Force. I get dizzy sometimes. From flying too high, they tell me."

"Let's get some air then. Here, I'll get the last round." And he did. I rinsed my face at the *latrina*, left a tip for the towel, and once more caught my reflection—but in the big rippled mirror that threw back at me the image of a triple-layer fruitcake with pink frosting, a cherry for its mouth.

Barney darted through the sidewalk crowds, his long arms swinging past his kneecaps, a monkey off his chain. Like Mickey—that throughbred retriever who could never be kept on a leash. We toured the same places, I bought the same drinks. Half-listening I let Barney chatter, but I could only compare, compare. In the closeness of the basement *cantina* I was growing bored and drunk. A sharp blow struck my collarbone—"That's a killer karate chop!" And another my back—"That's where you stick a knife between the ribs."

"That's my goddamn *sunburn*."

"The best way is to sneak up with piano wire," the black eyes glittered craftily, "and snap the gook's head off with a noose." I broke into laughter. He looked exactly like a small hostile Asian, an irrelevant foreign threat to the sovereign United States.

"I'm not gonna hurt you. You're my drinking buddy now. I'll pro-tect you. Okay?"

"Why don't I feel safe?"

"You were falling on your butt, bud. Let's down these drinks and get outta here. How would you like to get laid?" My ears snapped to attention. "I know the nearest whorehouse." They slumped back at rest. "We'll screw the same whore, how's that? I'll fuck her like a *big* dog." A Marine Corps slogan, trite but true.

"Lead the way then, Barney."

The way led through dirt streets good for rolling drunks, past yelping curs and through a court, to a long bleak hall where blue doors opened and slammed shut. Another corridor of sex—I was weary. I sat down on a sofa that probably crawled with lice. A barrel-shaped woman grabbed Barney by the arm like a *federale* making an arrest. "You first," I said, scratching. Ten minutes later he was back. "Let's haul ass!" he snapped.

I found the Fury and drove south past the motels, their red neon *VACANCY*'s extinguished. Others were screwing on those busy bed-springs. Barney for once kept his silence.

"The fucking whore," he said finally. "She took my money, then she wouldn't give me time to get it up."

"You should've tried karate. Or a noose."

"You better pull over, pal. You don't even have any lights. I think I'm gonna heave. I parked by a wall and waited, listening to cicadas as he retched, then peed. He zipped and got in. "Let's sleep it off here."

"I got a better idea."

"I knew you would, from the beginning. But go ahead. I don't care anymore." He unlatched his web belt.

"Let's try these first." I produced the two capsules of Black Magic.

Burning through my back and boring through my skull, an intense white heat enveloped me. Of two red curtains that protected my eyes, I parted one the fraction of an inch, and found myself ensnared in heavy wire. *Heavy acid!* The wire became a nest of pubic hair, part-sheltering one public scrotal egg and a shriveled sheath of penis. A patch of hairs was glued to Barney's belly. Shirt wide open and his thighs laid bare, he sagged in his seat asleep. I raised my head into the full glare of daylight.

Up the road and cresting a hill rose a fabulous white castle in a park of trees and grass—the Agua Caliente racetrack. Fifty yards from us two laborers chopped weeds. One stopped and pointed when he saw me, and they joked in their colorful lingo. They had looked in the window, I supposed. Head low, I switched on the ignition and turned the car around toward open desert.

What the hell! Was that a white-out? More like a *blackout,* for sure. Then I knew. We had swallowed fucking downers—double-duty barbiturates. *Black Magic?* Tricky Mickey! This time he had gone a mile too far—and a thousand mikes too short. My brain sprouted new thoughts of vengeance.

I looked down at Barney's open Y. What, after all, was a dick, its duty done? A wrinkled tube of flesh, good for nothing but a drain-pipe. It wasn't even a pretty thing to look at. Barney's was a kind of two-tone job, tan and crimson. At best the penis was a kind of kid's toy, like a fire engine, a hose-and-ladder made to charge around the room until its rundown batteries made it calm again. *An Instrument of Procreation.* That phrase was for fundamentalists—if they could use it. A heedless stem of headlong lust: that was its true nature.

But ah, the secret life of the vagina, that was something else. A foxy hole with a cover of fleece, it opened at its leisure, at its pleasure—like Venus' flytrap. And entertained what it was pleased to welcome there with grace and warmth, exquisite taste, extraordinary hospitali-ty—so that each lucky guest was loathe to leave. *The perfect hostess!* The party over, it pursed its precious lips in a Mona Lisa smile. You never knew what it was thinking. How well had Linda entertained St. Mick?

Barney stirred. The skilled-killer fingers pulled up his pants and clicked the buckle shut. "Where the fuck are we?" he gaped, knuck-ling his eyeholes.

"Lower California. Upper Mexico. Middle of nowhere."

"What happened last night? That pill must've clobbered me."

"You were gobbled by a hungry coyote."

"It sure felt that way." He lit a smoke. "What do you get out of it, anyhow?"

"Sometimes I wonder, Barney." The word *vicarious* had come to mind.

"Let's go somewhere and wash up."

I drove south to the Rodriquez Reservoir. The lake was nearly full, and silvery when a breeze riffed the surface, like wind in fields of grain. Where the rock fell off steeply it was deep but clear. We stripped and dove into cold water. In the water he was less like a monkey, more like an otter, I thought. Regardless of peculiar shape and features, Barney had a sleek tawny build. It looked native to that naked place. I wished that I did.

We hunkered for awhile on the boulders, tossing pebbles in the lake. Now and then a car passed on the dam breast far downstream. It was possible to hear the calls of insects and of birds—desert quail, and other small rustlings in the sagebrush. We were comfortably at ease, like aborigines. If he were monkey-otter, what was I? A sampling of his nature was already in my blood.

64.

"You must be pretty busy. We don't see you much anymore."

It was the junior oracle himself, in person, licking a Chocolate Revel ice cream cone with the patient repetition of a housecat on a lunch break. I wished he would come to the point.

"My business takes me to many ports of call."

"Your monkey business, you mean. In the port of San Diego?" No doubt about it—the little creep had ESP in spades!

"So what's yours?" I pushed away the drafting tools and folded my arms, waiting.

"Just wondered if you knew what's happening, that's all. I suppose I don't need to ask."

"Well, I'm all ears, Starkey. What have I been missing lately?"

"Mom's been kind of upset." He nibbled the fringes of the pastry cone. "Since Steve got busted." He licked each miniature digit.

"Could you possibly describe the bust for me?"

"Sure. Is it all right if I use the bathroom?"

"Be my guest." I watched the minutes pass. "Not my *tenant*." He flushed the bowl and waited for the tank to fill before returning.

"It happened at the lighthouse. The restroom at Castle Rock." That public convenience had a statewide reputation for casual sex, from truckers on down to vagrants. My heart jumped—as Starkey knew it would.

"The vice squad nailed him. Mom's going to get a lawyer." Steve was still four*teen*. That would usually mean Juvenile Hall.

"And the specific charges?"

"They found seeds in his pocket."

"*Seeds?*"

"Yeah, you know, grass. Marijuana. And a roach. I guess Mick gave him some before he took off." Starkey picked up my pocket knife and started cleaning his nails.

"So where is he now?"

"Surf's up, six to ten. He's probably out surfing."

"I meant the other one. Mickey. Did he leave?"

"He and Brenda, yeah. They may be in Mexico, or San Francisco." Jesus. She was *fif*teen now. "Ace is pretty mad about it."

"*Ace?*"

"Her new boyfriend, Ace Decker. He's got a big bike, a Triumph six-fifty. He's six-feet-six, you know."

"I didn't."

"And black. He's in the Army, in a special outfit called the Green Berets. He's going to teach us self-defense, he said."

"Against whom?"

"Mickey. He gets pretty wild sometimes, and runs around with our Scout axe. He acts like he's *king* up there. When he isn't out of his head."

"Did he ever pick on you?"

"A couple of times. He chopped up my armadillo when I found that's where his stash was. That's why I'm here, to borrow some money."

"And the purpose of the loan?" I saw another runaway, eleven years old, about to take his chances on the road, or worse.

"I want a twelve-gauge shotgun. Or a four-ten, at least."

"I'll have to think about it, kid. I don't want you shooting up the neighborhood."

"You better not think about it too long. Mickey might be back."

"I'll bring you some twenty-two longs for target practice. How's that? You won't have to kill anybody."

"Why don't you come up for dinner? Casey's not feeling too good, either. Mom told me to ask."

"Tell her I expect to be there, if business doesn't get in the way."

Christ. Just as everything seemed to be working out. Why couldn't she handle *her* job for once? With Mickey's help she'd made a total mess of both their lives, I gloated. It richly served them right.

I had other obligations to think of. "Hey, Funnyface!" Barney's energetic voice had crackled that morning from a pay phone. "I'm coming up to see you. I gotta get off this fucking base." Neither an appealing nor gung-ho sort of reason. Still, a promise was a promise —I'd agreed. I was almost looking forward to the company of the walking-talking ape-man. He could keep me off the streets and out of trouble, away from those Hollywood cocktail lounges and their legions of mincing queens.

And now this! I prepared for my errand of mercy—of *charity*, really. It could wreck the whole of the forthcoming weekend, the weekend of the Fourth of July.

"Here's your ammo, Starkey, and some extra rations, for when you're holed up during an attack. Where's the lady of the house?"

"*Twinkies*. Thanks, Jerry. She's in bed with a headache." Linda's standby lie-in strategy of passive defense—I knew it well. And there she was, Queen-for-a-Night as of yore. Casey snuggled in the bed beside her, sucking on his thumb as she pretended to explain a fairy tale. I chucked the little fellow's chin.

"I hope it's not another one about princes."

"No, dear, this is all about a great red dragon who guards a priceless treasure in a secret place. He blows smoke and eats fire. He's very jealous, too."

"Mickey and his drugs? Or Mick and Brenda?"

"*Starkey!*" she called out. "Why don't you take the baby for a while? And fix his bottle. Close the door please, hon."

"And don't listen while you argue. I know."

We stared for a while at one another. Her left eye was noticeably swollen, discolored beneath a layer of grease and powder. Linda struck a more dramatic pose, farther from the lamp. I had already brought a drink. I rattled the ice as at the movies, waiting for the feature to begin.

"Well," she said, as though starting a new chapter in the book, "it's been a hectic time around here lately. We could have used a little help."

"Like mine, for instance?"

"Why not? You're his father, aren't you?"

"Not the latest one, sweets. That's where I get off your lullaby express. I'm not responsible for other people screwing in our sheets."

Quiet, deadly restraint was another favorite among my wife's expressions. She used it now to full effect.

"Just for the record, Jerry Carr, there isn't any baby. If that's what you're about to blame me for—as an excuse for everything you do."

"What happened to the little bastard then?"

"There never was another baby, dear. I missed one of my periods, that's all. I only mentioned it to Mick one night in case there was. I wanted him to feel some responsibility in the world, so he'd feel grown up for once. A man!"

"A manly poke in the eye is what you got for it."

"He's still too immature, and too full of drugs to do anything."

"Is that how you caught me? When I was immature and full of drink?"

"Don't flatter yourself, Jerry. That was purely an accident, one I should have avoided. You're lucky to even *have* a child."

I sat stunned as though struck by a poison dart. I stood up and threw the stale drink in Linda's face. It rinsed off the makeup. She looked bad.

"Go fuck yourself then," I told her. "That wasn't the *real* reason. You wanted to get him off Brenda. You were jealous! *Admit it,* you vicious whoring witch!"

For a long minute we glared at one another like two pairs of oncoming headlights, like teeners playing *Chicken-of-the-Road.* I had the handicap advantage—Linda's black eye blinked. She fell forward in uncontrolled sobs, shedding tears all over the story book. I eased myself down beside her and tentatively placed a palm upon her back. My wife might choke right then and there, I felt. She took a deep gasping breath.

"Oh, Jerry,"—and she pressed my free hand—"I don't know what to do anymore. God *knows* what he'll do to Brenda. He's got a box full of plastic syringes—I don't know how many kinds of drugs. Suppose they don't come back?"

"Suppose they do?" I stroked her vertebrae down to the pelvis. It felt good, like a familiar hiking trail. I was not encouraged to go on.

"Jerry, I'm just plain *scared*." Her look of fright was only passably convincing, but sufficient to deserve a response.

"Don't worry, Linda. I'll think of something." Without thinking I knew already what that something ought to be—a handy, reliable handgun. If she ever had to have a MAN around the house, maybe I could be the strong one for a change.

65.

The apartment was not as I had left it. Someone had switched on the lights. Someone had got into the vodka, had ransacked a six-pack of Budweiser. Someone had smoked cigarettes. *Mickey?* I heard gunshots. Grey shadows leaped around the room—phantoms of the black-and-white TV. On the screen, frightened seamen fired rifles from a raft. A monster reared its ugly head, sent the sailors flying, and shook one in its dripping scaly jaws.

"They don't know shit about jungle warfare," said Barney in his skivvies from the bed. "It serves the swabbies right." A seaman was trapped in a treetop, his rifle of little avail. The monster ate that sailor too—shoes and all.

"I figured you wouldn't be here. How did you get in?"

"Climbed the palm tree and swung in the window." Well, naturally. What else would a monkey do? "I stopped on the road for some brews." He dropped a smoking butt in a beercan and crushed it in his fist.

"Is that where you got the fat lip?"

He curled the split flesh on his thumbtip. "Squids! They jumped me down in Long Beach, the cocksuckers. I was on the corner first. They were big mothers, too. Hey, you can pour me one of those, man, a double."

I brought one. The sailors on the screen had panicked, and ran in full retreat. King Kong smashed a path through the trees. "Then a fag picked me up and tried to grope me. I said I'd fix his lip, too."

"I guess it wasn't your day. Did you ever see an old Tarzan movie?"

"I don't need to answer that question. I know how I look. How'd you like to be called Cheetah all through school? A female chimp at that? It can really screw up a man's love life." The handsome First

Mate, Bruce Cabot, had escaped. "At boot camp they used to call me Charley Apeshit. Not no more, though. I kicked a lot of ass."

"So how's your love life now? *Barney.*"

"It sucks, man."

At my hurt look he said, "Want me to show you?" and reached into his pants for a walletful of photos. Most were of a lovely girl with long glossy hair and black, wide-set eyebrows.

"Why, she's beautiful," I said, impressed. "You're lucky."

"That's my big sister Karen. Here's Sherry. She's my chick." Sherry had cone-shaped breasts, square teeth, and wore glasses.

"She's pretty, too. Do you love her?"

"Yeah! She likes to call me Trigger, 'cause I'm so fast, you know? She knows more tricks than a barrel full of monkeys, and she's only a sophomore in high school."

The natives of the film had prepared Fay Wray for her big date. They beat drums and shook spears, dancing on a wall by torchlight.

"May I look at your I.D.?"

"Go ahead. It's not a real good picture."

The head was shaved bald, the ears stood out straight, the face had an anthropoid scowl. The card was sealed in plastic. BARNABY J. TRIMBLE HT: 5-7 WT: 132 BIRTHPLACE: LITTLE FALLS, MINN would be nineteen that fall, a Scorpio, astrologically *"sexual but dangerous"*. Sex, where was thy sting?

"I'm supposed to be English or Swedish. My grandfather's a Chippewa. I don't much like my name, though. It's too much like a kid's." *Trigger Trimble* then. Why not? Everyone had some kind of identity problem.

King Kong had captured the heart of Fay Wray and hand-carried the girl to his hideaway. The huge fingers plucked at her chemise.

"I wonder how big it is?" I speculated.

"See for yourself." I looked at Barney, then unsnapped his shorts. Out popped an everyday American erection, slightly garish in its coloring, but otherwise as near to normal as any average viewer might expect. "Hey, can you lend me some bucks until payday? My wallet's flat."

The big ape fought a pterodactyl. I had a bird in the bush.

"Will a twenty be okay?"

"Sure. Go ahead and take your clothes off."

"I thought you didn't like to mess around with other men."

"I don't care. I'm not queer. I guess everybody likes to get their rocks off. You paid for it. Why not?"

I undressed and we did it on the bedspread, pausing now and then to watch key scenes, catching up again at the commercials. It seemed a sane and rational thing to do, compared to the action running wild on the tube, to the raw feelings rampant in the household.

King Kong was getting zapped by Air Corps biplanes on the top of the Empire State. I remarked on the building's phallic tower, "tallest in the world" when it was built.

"Made of stainless steel," said Barney, squeezing my hand to himself.

"Ready when you are, Trigger." He fired. A bullet would have gone through my brain.

The King of Apes, full of holes, fell right into the middle of Fifth Avenue. The pelt looked dead as a buffalo rug. Not one piece of equipment in the city of New York was designed to move a fifty-foot corpse, now blocking traffic headed uptown to The Plaza, Schwarz' Toys, St. Pat's Cathedral. The agent of the late great ape, still wearing tails from the ill-starred premiere, made a eulogizing statement for the press.

"It was *Beauty* killed the Beast," he declared.

66.

Car horns blasted in my eardrums. Was that dead ape still blocking the street? Where were the bulldozers, the flatbed trailers, an ambulance? The cars were down below, rolling from the city on fat rubber doughnuts filled with air. July the Fourth, alright, hot and humid as a pot of stew. A steamy fog hid the beach. In the tunnel kids were lighting firecrackers.

Drawn up beside me like a captive bare-skinned animal, Barney jumped at my touch as though caught napping in his cage, and blinked open beady chimpanzee eyes that as yet had no expression in them. I offered him a Kool. Already alert, his ever-ready fingers accepted it.

"What would you do, Barney, if you thought someone was threatening your life?" I watched him light up and take a long initial drag.

"Are you kidding? That's what they teach us every minute in the Corps. I sure wouldn't take no shit." Forcing out a gust of mentholated vapor, he punched the wadded pillow and kicked the sheet off his feet.

"I don't mean in the service. I mean in private life. Like somebody messing with your family, or your wife." I told about the scene in the storm drain, the thing with Brenda, about the Boy Scout axe and drugs.

"Then I'd get me a gun and shoot the motherfucker. I could sleep here all day if it wasn't for the noise." Issuing from Barney lying there in Mickey's former slot, the words sounded positively eerie! Yet what else could I expect him to say? He was not in command of all the facts.

"What sort of weapon do you recommend?"

"I don't know. A forty-five. A P-thirty-eight. A magnum. How much do you hate the fucker's guts? Why don't you get one if it makes you feel better? We got any cold beer left?"

Why not indeed? If any local gunshop were open, that would be the perfect project for an overcast, sultry Independence Day.

"I think it's gone. I'll fix you a Bloody Mary. Don't get up."

"I gotta go." Kneeling at the window sill he peed into a box of weak geraniums—a driver blew his horn on Channel Road. Barney gave the honker a stiff middle finger as he got on with his job. What I had heard from Leonard was manifestly true: however hard you tried you could not housebreak a monkey. No matter how amusing, they were not reliable pets.

In the cloudy afternoon we went shopping, stopping first at the plush multi-mirrored Naugahyde bar of the Hotel Carmel for a drink. The passage to the washrooms led in a peculiar way to the rear of Cow City, and its mural of a spectacular coastline bombing in some future hydrogen war. We had drinks there, too, listening to country-western records, until Barney got a slap from a waitress displeased by the feel of his paws.

When I swung the wired door a small bell rang inside the pawn-shop. The proprietor looked up and dropped cigar ash on his sports page. "Take your time, boys," he said easily. "I got all day." A ball game had its inning on one of the many radios abandoned there. I looked at them, the radios. At the cameras, wedding rings, hunting knives—abused and forgotten merchandise that would never be redeemed—before drifting to the nicked glass case of handguns. The guns were scratched and oily, veterans of mean and vicious acts. I felt guilty as a boy about to buy his first drugstore rubber, a used one, at that. "See anything you like?" the man said.

"How about this one here? Marked twenty-fifty." He brought out a blunt blued gun of foreign manufacture. The model might as easily have been carved from soap and dyed with shoeblack for a jailbreak. "Is it reliable?" I asked.

"It'll do the job," said the proprietor, as though he knew Mick as well as I did and already had him tailored for some holes. He blew off more cigar ash and showed me how it worked.

"What do you think, Trigger?" Barney had strayed over to the porno magazine rack and was rifling through its stock.

"You oughtta see this, man! Two chicks balling each other. They both show lots of gash. And here they're with some stud. He's a hairy sonofabitch." He turned another page and looked up at the gun. "That's a piece of shit. It'll blow up in your hand."

"The magazine's five dollars," the proprietor said. I paid it.

"Thanks, man. I can use this back at the base. Why don't you buy the Alta? Made in Spain for the Spanish. They like to shoot it out."

"It's forty-seven dollars."

"So what's your life worth to you? Or your wife's?" He picked up the gun and sighted likely targets: clocks, lamps, the hairy suitor of the photos, the proprietor's chest. The man brought out a ledger.

"Fill out the forms and leave a deposit. It takes three days to check police records."

"But I don't have a record, sir."

"Same for everyone, like getting married. In case you change your mind." The man stood where the phone was, smoking a cigar.

"Well, fuck it then," said Barney. "I'll take care of him myself."

"You don't even know what he looks like." And then I wished he never would! In some crazy way I wished that it were Mickey there beside me when we returned to Cow City and had another drink, this time at the bar.

Smelling of stale beer and Lysol, the establishment had no other customers to play the country-western jukebox. The offended wait-ress had gone home. The barman was seriously setting up for Happy Hour: first the olives, then the cherries, the lemon peel, the quarter-ed limes. It was boring just sitting, listening to the air conditioner hum its monotone summertime tune. Barney flipped the pages of the magazine, its slick salacious cover sticking to the bar.

"I've got an idea," I said to Barney as he clawed his undershorts.

"Let's go shoot the breeze on the Merry-Go-Round. It's only a block away."

"The what? You gotta be kidding, Jack. That's for kids. Hey, check this one! She looks good enough to eat without a spoon." He took a long slurp on a rum-and-Coke. The barman did not show amusement.

"Not upstairs it's not. I've got a friend there, a big man at Metro. He's always got something going." No matter what Leonard might be doing, I meant to be out on the silver roof, under the rockets' red glare, when the night spread its canopy of fire. Exactly as I had a year ago with Mick—a night that would live in ecstasy!

"Some chicks from the flicks?"

"You never can tell."

"What're we waiting for? Let's move, man."

The mighty music mill was grinding notes; the dazzling wheel went round. And there they were again, white as seagulls—*chicken-of-the-sea*, as they were known in certain quarters—one more flock of footloose sailors off yet another of Uncle Sam's lust-driven battle cruisers. I lagged behind to catch the passing parade of laundered cheeks and fly-fronts, wishing I too were free and single, young enough to enlist, even though I might not last the full enlistment.

"What's keeping you?" hailed Barney, heading for the stair. Three big motorcycles blocked it—Harley Davidsons with stretched forks and dropped frames and mufflers like the jackets of machine guns. "Hogs!" cried Barney, jumping on a seat and pumping the controls. "I wish to hell I had one." I had a vision of a braid-suited monkey in a circus ring, guided on a bike by its trainer. But little Trigger Trimble could probably handle it entirely on his own. A beercan struck my shoulder.

"HEY!" came an order from above. "Get your paws off those machines. Them ain't your holiday rentals!" A bearded head was framed in Leonard's window.

"Asshole!" yelled Barney, but the head had withdrawn. We climbed the wooden stair. The door opened on the same unfriendly face, in a fist a frothing can of brew. Whatever did not show as matted hair or muscle was covered by a leather vest, creased boots and greasy jeans, worn with the look of native hide. As our greeter downed his beer I counted the contractions of his larynx. The back of his hand wiped his ginger-colored beard.

"What's your business?"

"We thought we'd see if Leonard's in, to wish him a happy Fourth."

The man gave a thoughtful belch. "He's in but he ain't receiving. Who would I tell him has called?"

"I'm Jerry. This is Barney, a marine. I'm an old friend of Len's."

"Wait here."

"It don't look like a party to me," said the marine.

Through the half-open door I saw that the apartment had undergone yet another recent change in decor. Gone were the fey appointments, the listening ferns, the frivolous chairs. In their stead were sturdy pieces from the Salvation Army or Goodwill. The rug was like a country trail, the white walls painted black. On one hung a Nazi swastika and a brace of bayonets. The fan on the ceiling had sharp metal blades.

At the table two cyclists played cards. The first wore a cap and embroidered vest—his colors—the other a patchwork of tattoos. An event of extreme unlikelihood was the personal appearance of Melody Landau, on that or any future holiday.

"Let's go," muttered Barney. "They're just a buncha pricks."

"*Hi*, sweethearts," cooed Leonard, blocking our view through the door. "I just wanted to say hel-*lo*." Barney had not captured his interest. He was speaking directly to me.

Lenny too had gone through changes. His head was clean-shaven, he had lost lots of weight. He wore a vest and jeans like the others, but on him they were studio clean. On a wrist and an opposing ankle were red-painted casts laced with wild outrageous symbols like the ones bikers wore.

"What happened to you?"

"Oh, I took a midnight run with Satan's Slaves. I slid off the *sissy* seat. It was *slippery*." Leonard limped into the hallway and shut the door behind him. The carousel boomed through an opening that looked into the well below.

"I fell through that *window*, actually." The sill was four feet high. "*Luckily*, the Merry-Go-Round wasn't running. I *could* have been run over by a flying horse, or one of those...*golden chariots*." What a way to go! Violence was busting out all over, like rockets on the Fourth of July.

"Where were your new friends?"

"Oh, them? They're my *bodyguards.* Isn't that a thrill? You never know what your life is worth until you've *had* one. Or several, as the case may be. Like Miss Mae West and her body-*builders.*"

"They don't seem to do a good job of guarding you."

"*Listen,* Jerry. I really can't talk to you now. I've got to get back to my *guests.*" In the shadows of the gallery he was playing still another role, that of the crippled Quasimodo in *The Hunchback of Notre Dame.* He continued in a loud stage whisper. "Don't let your good friend *Mickey* ever show up here again!" I looked puzzled. Leonard's able hand gripped my shoulder as he hissed into my ear. "He *burned* some people in a *bum deal.*" The door flew open behind him—the bearded one with the beer. "I hope you know what I *meann-n.*" As I nodded, Barney frowned.

"Yes! I'm *coming,* Dirty Dick! Can't you boys do *anything* without me?" Leonard locked the door, leaving us to face the louder music.

"I think the party's over," said Barney outside, staring at some girls of many seasons. Like my own, their attention was diverted to the frisky sea-fresh sailors, their expendable dollars and exploitable selves. "Let's go to your place and get loaded," said the not-quite-as-lovable primate. "There's fuck-all else to do."

What we did then is sweat through the swarming traffic to the Canyon, and sweating harder still mix tall iced drinks that perspired in our sweaty hands, then take off our sweat-soaked clothing to lie steaming in front of the TV. Barney leafed fiercely through the journal, heated to a feverish excitement by the photos of the two ravished women and their hirsute friend. We did a kind of imitation, our skins making wet slapping noises. When we were done, the pornographic pages had been welded together for good.

In a while the fireworks went off. The bursts of many colors dulled by smoke seemed far away, a desultory nuisance that refused to stop, like the hit tunes that pounded from the bar fronts.

Barney left early in the morning to report for guard duty.

67.

Saturday then Sunday were hotter still, for the sun had reappeared and made the beach a playground for its ball of bouncing light. The waves were like bleachers for the surfers. Volleyballers were out in numbers, too.

"We thought we might see you," Linda phoned, almost sweetly. "The weekend's been so long. Thank God, the fireworks are nearly over."

"The traffic's been so heavy. I've had some company, too."

Further introductions would be pointless. On my right, for example, lay a HAWKINS J.R., according to the brand on his shorts. We were separated by a stain at the division of the mattresses where J.R. had wet the bed. His sidekick Spider Sklarek had found a dry place in the floor. As befitted the name, Spider was spare, dark and furry. J.R., or Johnny, was a fair-haired sailor-boy. We had drunk a lot of beer together. But why go into all of that? She rarely felt the need to share everything with me.

"Well, everybody will be going back home today, so why don't you come up? I thought we might have a picnic, a kind of family reunion."

"Including whom?"

"Just the boys and the two of us. Brenda's friend Ace is here, but he has to leave early. For parachute training, he says."

"And Princess Brenda and Prince Mick?"

"I'm terribly worried about them. They did send for money, though, from San Francisco. So I guess they're still all right."

"Where there's wealth there's health, I always say."

Linda made a pause then to reflect on the value of the saying.

"I wish you wouldn't talk like that," she countered. "I thought we might meet as friends. I made your favorite shrimp and lobster salad."

"I *love* seafood. You remembered!" I suppressed a snicker for the sailors stirring in their sleep. "I'll bring you some dry white wine."

"You aren't going to bring your friends along, are you?"

"Not this time, thank you. They have other things to do."

"Well, do try not to be late," said my wife in all sincerity.

The two sailors roused and scratched themselves. Like a fifth, vestigial limb, Spider had preserved in his shorts a leftover half-used erection. They began communications in their salty shorthand language—chirps, grunts and syllables such as dolphins might employ. I let them wash up and have coffee. I did not open any more beers. After a while, dressed and restless, they cocked their white hats and took leave.

"I guess we'll go down to Hollywood," said Spider, "and find us some California girls." "Yeah, we'd like to see some movie stars," said his buddy. "Thanks, mate, for the beer." "And the bed," smirked Spider. Unlike marines I had known, a sailor hardly ever lost his class or cool by publicly whizzing out a window.

It was true for once, what Linda told me. Cars were fighting for the town-bound lanes, often streaking down the shoulder strips to swing in front of drivers intimidated by the wife and kids. On my side the traffic moved as though by enema. Now and then the highway cleared for sheriffs' sirens or an ambulance, once for a sweep of Hell's Angels hogging the whole road. They passed in stately V-formation, arms like ramrods, chests like shields, hair and colors flying—*the Apaches*. Our world was pygmified in mirrored goggles. I was glad when they were gone. While I stopped I bought Linda a green flask of Mountain Chablis.

"Well, thank you, dear." She gave me some sort of kiss. "You're more your old self again. The Jerry who used to bring me presents." She meant the days before her reception of the most expensive one—St. Mick, now on temporary loan in San Francisco. Could that pawned treasure ever be redeemed?

"It's the best I could do on short notice."

"Never mind. It's enough to have you here." Randy sniffed and pawed my legs and Casey stood to clutch them. *"Dad-da!"* he cried. When had I last heard that word? I tossed him in the air a few times, as every good father is supposed to do. The child and his mother held their breaths. Starkey at the door held his rifle.

It was *weird*. Here was the same dank tunnel of the storm drain, the stream trickling down its corrugated grooves. At the far end, in a sunlit disc of clearing, stood Starkey's new target, a lifesize cardboard mock-up of the mighty Mick himself. Red heart, red hair, red features had been painted there, the image thoroughly ventilated in the head, heart and groin. My stepson loaded the rifle. "You shoot first," he said. I squeezed off a full clip of cartridges.

"Nice pattern. Why the elbows?"

"Just for kicks, Starkey. A shot in the arm for your enemy."

"You haven't changed. You're as twisted as ever." He shot off an ear and enlarged the eye sockets. Had they been represented there, the last rounds would have dropped St. Mick and both dependents.

"I know when I'm outclassed, kid. Let's take a walk on the beach." I hoped that would be the last shootout down there at the K-O Corral.

"So what do you think you'll be when you grow up, Starkey?" He carried the gun while I threw sticks for Randy.

"I don't know yet. How about you?" Me? Not a bird, not a plane, I sometimes felt like *Stupor*-man. Or Funnyface!

"I might be a secret agent," he went on at my noncommitment. "Or go into computer programming. I'm pretty good at putting two-and-two together, you know."

"Or taking them apart."

"...anything to get away from here. Why?"

"I thought I'd like to help you. That's all."

"Seems like you've got plenty to take care of already." He paused, took aim, and winged a gull gliding low on the ocean. Our retriever plunged in to retrieve it.

"Fantastic! A moving target with a single shot. How did you learn to lead like that?"

"Only practice. You can see what I'd do with a shotgun."

Randy ran up with the bird in his mouth. The wet feathers dripped blood and the half-lidded eyes stared at air. The beak gaped open and drew closed. I took the gull and gently stroked its plumage. Then I snapped its limp neck and buried it, in the sand above the tide line near the trees, a twig to mark its grave.

"You're expert enough already." I dropped a hand on Starkey's shoulderblade. He continued to look straight ahead.

About a dozen surfers competed for the waves, Steve among them. He dipped his board in greeting, caught a long clean ride, and did a perfect spinout as the waves broke into foam. When he stood, his long blond hair touched his shoulders, so manly had he grown. Bearing scant resemblance to a criminal with a record, Steve had developed a style. In fact all of the boys, including Casey, had made strong advances in their mastery of skills. Could the same be said of me?

At sunset, Linda brought a hamper to the beach and we built a driftwood fire. As darkness fell the flames drew us close, as close as we had been in a long time. The closeness was unlike that within the house, with its mixed ambience of goings and comings. Joking, dining, drinking wine and Coke, we might have been the nuclear family anywhere, at almost any time. How did it feel to be Linda, cooker of meals, mother of sons, two-time wife and recent mistress? It was hardly the time to ask. And no longer my place to ask it.

When Casey was in bed and the boys were at TV, Linda and I were faced with one another. To ease the awkward circumstance she once again brought out the brandy. Beyond the transient pleasure of the postprandial liqueurs I sensed a more serious intention. The custom-made seafood salad would bear a heavy tab.

"You know," she began lightly, lighting candles, "I've been think-ing." The very act I feared and dreaded most! Linda picked up a passing cat and seated herself attractively. The petted cat began to purr. "We've been through some trying times together, many trials and errors. But we still have a lot in common. We aren't getting any younger, Jerry."

"Our friends are, though." It was good brandy, an Armagnac.

"And we do have responsibilities toward each other, toward the children, too. Have you ever wondered how they feel about the way we're going?"

"Yes, I have wondered, Linda. How *do* they feel about the way we're going? And how, for that matter, do we?"

"Well, just look at what they're doing. There's your answer! Steve, in trouble with the law. And Brenda, practically *kidnapped* before she's reached sixteen. All Starkey thinks about is guns. Do you think that's a normal family situation?"

"Do they? Do you? Do you think *your* home life is normal?"

"Look who's calling cats black! A lot more normal than yours, my dear, if you want to come right down to it. The trouble is they have no one to look up to, no one to call a father."

"They never called me anything but Jerry, or J.C. I'll bet they never called the other one Harry."

Linda appeared to be thinking, no longer stroking the cat. I was satisfied sipping my cognac.

"Please listen to me for a minute, Jerry, and try not to take offense. Because I do mean well, for all of us. Los Angeles has multitudes of qualified psychiatrists. They can cure the most difficult of cases, if they're given half a chance."

"So I've heard. Do you think you can afford one? Or even half a shrink, Linda? I thought you were pretty broke."

With patience she replenished her brandy glass and swirled the liquor under her nose. Unlike previous times she had not yet shown a single flaring nostril.

"You could try to get yourself straightened out, you know, before it's simply too late. The whole thing of sex and alcohol is what they call a syndrome. It's really all in your head."

"That's one way of putting it. One place, too."

"Frankly, I'm not looking forward to another divorce. They're expensive and hard on everybody. You might want to consider that."

"Ours would be simple. We could both name the same correspondent. We don't even need two attorneys."

"You would bring Mickey into it, wouldn't you?"

"It's hard not to, Linda. Isn't he the biggest syndrome right now?"

"He's a poor, confused orphan who's badly in need of help. There's nothing more I can do about his drugs and violence. I'm only a woman, don't forget."

"You mean you've stopped helping him? Or he's stopped helping you." There it was—a slight distension of the pinkening nostrils, not due to the bouquet of the cognac, but in tune with her quickening heartbeat.

"I've done everything I could do. I'm concerned for the rest of the family."

"How about me?"

"How about you? You're the one who brought him here! I can live without him, thank you. I wish to God I'd never seen his face."

I tilted the snifter and let the trickling fluid heat my gullet.

"How about the rest of him, Linda? How could you live without that?"

Linda didn't speak. Instead she set her nostrils at Full Flare.

"Who wants to see his face?" I continued. "Who needs to, with his prick between your lips or legs, Linda Lee?"

The hypothetical question failed to produce a proper answer.

264

Linda swirled the dregs in her glass, a tiny whirlpool, and flung the good Armagnac in my eyes. They stung, but I could still see candles. Remotely I heard the staccato sounds of violence on TV. My drooping head rolled side-to-side, encouraging the flow of teardrops. I felt Linda lean over beside me. Her cool cat-stroking fingers massaged the stiff nape of my neck. "I'm sorry, Jerry," she soothed. "Did I hurt you?"

Theatrically I threw my head back. *My eyes, my eyes,* I cried. They focused through my tears on the bank of tall windows. Shining through our star-crossed reflections a fearful apparition had appeared. "Speak of the Devil. He's *here.*"

The skin burned a glowing crimson, a red beard pointed hellward. The eyes blazed over sucked-in cheeks, from the neck hung a sorcerer's jewel. The teeth flashed in a demon's grin—they were Mickey's. Legs astride a road-flare, he was naked. His turn to play the lost redskin at the end of the outcast's trail! It was Linda who opened the door.

Nude save for a headband and the gold-chained crystal prism, our Mick dropped his backside to the floor and there laxed-out completely. As though faint from heat and exhaustion, the Saint rolled limp to one side. Fresh needle stabs marked the forearms.

"I hope you didn't drive like that from San Francisco," said Linda, voice of our innermost concern.

Mickey snorted. "You shoulda seen the truckers cruise my window at the stop-lights, man. One threw a doobie in my lap. It was already lit."

"What have you done with my daughter?" Her daughter now. I'd be her *husband* next.

"She's O.D.'d in the van," said Mickey matter-of-factly. Enough to put any mother's mind to rest! He wriggled his toes to see if they still functioned, stretched out the deflated scrotal sac, and spread his fingers fan-shape, on either side of his chest. The ribs stood out sharply, the skin had a scabrous rash. The eyelids drooped, the jaw fell open as of rigor mortis setting in. The dead gull flashed on my mind screen.

"Well, you can't stay there like that," said Linda, like a housewife preparing to vacuum. But the Mick himself was past scolding. Linda plucked the cover from the couch and tossed it over him—one more victim of the four-day Fourth of July. "What are we going to do now, Jerry?"

"I don't know. Another cognac? A game of Hearts? Canasta, anybody?"

"We'd better go look at Brenda," my wife said with decision.

The back of the van was a trashbin—papers, maps, food scraps, clothes, a Tampax box, dead flowers. At the bottom lay the sleeping bag, Brenda's cocoon, her blonde hair spilling out the top of it. The cloth seemed to stir itself slightly. Lifting up the bag at either end we hauled it to her room. Linda found a wrist and took its pulse.

"She's alive, thank God. Do you think we should call a doctor?"

"A doctor for her. For him the Great Exterminator."

"Please, Jerry, it's no joking matter. They could *both* be dead, you know."

"You said we were all getting older. No one lives forever."

"Christ, you can be callous when you want."

"For some of us it's called sophistication. Worldliness. Or maybe I'm desensitized, like those two, by things that have gone on too long."

"I'm not going to argue anymore. What shall we do about Mick?"

"Why not let sleeping dogs lie? That's what I always say." I went back to pour a cognac, perhaps to blow out the tapers. Now that she needed my help I might even spend the night in Linda's bedroom— or bed.

The sleeping dog no longer lay. He was head-on into the icebox, outlined in its frosty glow. He laid out whatever came to hand—eggs, an eggplant, mayonnaise, hotdogs, a rib roast—and set them on the maple chopping block. The Saint hovered at its edge, suggestively. I could put one and one together, too. I picked up the butcher's cleaver.

"Mind if I have a slice of this?"

Instinctively Mick moved aside, one hand held like a fig leaf, in the other a kind of sandwich. "Go ahead, man. I already fed my head. I got to feed my stomach."

I cleaved a rib of blood-rare beef and shook some chili on it.

"So what all did you do in San Francisco?"

"What all didn't we do, man! Meth, dope, coke, purple acid, blue cheer, reds, yellow jackets, upper-downers, insider-outers. Sex. You name it. We done it."

"With whom?" What was I—the jealous father?

"Why the hippies, man. That's *whom*. Cats who just dig staying high. They're like, you know, another race, man. They might be Martians." He ground a mix of food between his teeth and tried to swallow. "I shoulda put this in the blender man," he choked, "and mainlined it."

"High for how long, though?"

"Forever, that's how long." He drank milk. "Foreveranever. Amen."

"You're never coming down then. Are you?"

"To your place? On you? I seen the light, man. Neveranever. Amen."

"So our friendship is practically over." In the snifter I twirled another splash of brandy, a tired, traditional sort of high.

"In a word, yes, Jerry Juicehead. Now why don't you get off my fucking case?"

"Why don't you get the fuck out, you son-of-a-bitch! And leave us all alone. We're not *hippies*, Mick. Or *Martians*, either. And we're not gonna do all your drugs. You think you can do a burn on everybody."

Like twinned diaphragms of a camera lens his pupils dilated fantastically, glaring deep into my watery eyes. My gaze dropped, freezing on the sparkling stone as though I were truly hypnotized.

"Because it's not your house—*Jenny*. It's *Linda's*. I'll split when she's ready to tell me."

He unlimbered the thin needled arms. He looked to me all veins and eyeballs. St. Mick or no saint, I kneed him in the core of the crotch. Mickey bent double. In a second I was flat on my back, lips bleeding freely. His knees clamped my chest, his calves my arms, my feet were locked under the chopping block. Above me swung that tasty, teasing pendulum, that once-so-tantalizing prize—*Saint Prick*—and Mickey's aching testicles, orange hairs curled in fury. His hand reached out for the cleaver. Where was Barney—now that I needed him? Or the forty-seven-dollar Spanish pistol? An explosion blew the groceries off the counter. Mustard, milk and ketchup splattered on the floor.

"The next one's for *you*," promised Starkey at the pass-through, leveling a double-barreled shotgun ten feet from Mick's red head. In the doorway stood Steve with the rifle. The brothers looked solemn and scared. Like the pungent scent of gunpowder, the kitchen reeked of instant paranoia.

"You can't do it. *Can* you, punk!" challenged high-rolling Mick, his face out of sight above the pendant genitals and jewel. His legs and my chest dripped sauces. His knees let my lungs re-expand.

"Just try me."

Starkey's trigger finger drew tight. Steve was ready, too. A police siren wailed on the highway. Mick slumped back against a drawerful of knives, another section of our handy kitchen arsenal.

"Oh my God!" shrieked Linda rushing in. "You've gone ahead and killed him. How *could* you?"

"*I'm* all right." I got up to bathe at the stainless-steel sink. "Starkey here just saved my life."

The boy split the gun, blew out the barrel, and coolly slipped a shell in the chamber. Linda knelt to wipe Mickey's flesh with a handful of *Stars-N-Bars* picnic napkins. Behind the faint mustache and the wispy red beard, the skin was paper-white.

"Be careful," she warned, "of all the broken glass."

"I'll *get* you," snarled Mick at my back, "if it's the last fucking thing I ever do." I would have to buy the book on spell-casting after all. "You'll *pay* for it, Jerry." The textbook on torture, too.

"Don't talk like that," said Linda in her mother's voice. "It's over now. And no one's been seriously hurt yet." She draped the nubbly cover on Mickey's skeletal frame. Where had he got his sudden strength? Not from the midnight buffet. Nor a handful of vitamins, either. It was speed. He was *speeding.*

"He tried to chop off my fucking dick! Do you think I can forget a thing like that? It blew my fucking mind!"

"Try to let bygones be bygones. You must be exhausted from the trip."

"I'll fix Starkey too, the little fart." Mick's head thrust forward in a terrible stare. "He better start sleeping with that *gun* in his hand, not his weenie. You too, Steve." He paused in a touch of fatigue. "The next time they better not miss," he said weakly.

"The next time you won't even remember." Starkey slapped the stock of the shotgun.

"You boys run along to bed now," said their mother. "We've had enough excitement for one night."

Burned out by the Fourth, my natural son Casey had slept through two near-assassinations and one misconstrued amputation.

Again Linda erred in her judgement. Within the hour we had a county sheriff in the house. Someone had reported an illegal use of fireworks. Mick, Linda, and I sat tensely in living room chairs. I held a red napkin to my mouth. An eye was closing too.

"I didn't know the children had them," she explained. The sheriff looked at the room.

"Yeah," said Mickey. "A cherry bomb went off. We didn't know it was loaded." He wore the couch cover, the headband and the jewel.

"That's no excuse, boy. They're not allowed. Who's this one? Have I seen him somewhere before?" The officer jotted in his black leather casebook. Mick had given him the last name of McCarthy.

"He's only a temporary houseguest," said my wife, "from northern California. A family acquaintance."

"He looks like more trouble to me, Mrs. Carr. You already have one boy with a court case. And who, may I ask, are you?"

"I'm Mister Carr, sir, the husband. I'm here for the holiday."

"Well, you'd better look after family business, Mr. Carr. And take care of that eye." He pocketed the notes. "One more complaint and I'll be forced to take you all in." He turned at the door. "We still have law and order, even here in Malibu." *Love it or leave it, copper!*

"The fucking pig," pronounced Mickey as he left. "Fascist prick nark motherfucker." The combination phrases fresh from San Francisco's changing culture scene were new to my Southland hearing. Linda gave Mick some Nembutals and laid him to rest on the couch. He *crashed and burned,* I would later recall.

I lay down beside her—the Golden Sleeplady—on our bed, but with my clothes on and the shotgun close at hand. The weapon, a .410 Savage, had been given in trust as a house present by then-acting Sergeant Decker of the U.S. Army Special Forces, for the sole and express purpose of protecting and defending the honor of the one whose hand he cherished most, that of Brenda Fedderman.

In the morning Mick was gone, with him Linda's van and its cargo of assorted junk. I hoped he'd headed straight for the Merry-Go-Round, where outlaw *pigs on hogs,* Leonard's scurrilous crew of guardians, could even other scores.

68.

Alright. Suppose Mickey *was* back on the Merry-Go-Round. Wasn't it time that I got off? Time to have purposes not always aimed below the belt, time to belong to a community again, time to rejoin the human race. And more than time to trim the branches of the tangled family tree. Its problems were easily greater than the sum total of my own.

In the absence of the Colonel, who else could lead the way? For though Linda probably could afford a psychiatrist, she would not voluntarily go to see one, not even Dr. Fritchy farther down the beach. And neither in fact would I. We had problems enough already.

As reported by the police a few days later, the van was gathering dust and sea-spray on a parking lot in Venice. Foul words and crude symbols had been traced in the grime by the fingers of expressive Venetians. The interior smelled like a garbage can. Of Mick there was no clue. He was doubtless holed up in some crusty tattered crash-pad with a fabulous ocean view, scarfing pizza pies, shooting speed and acid among hip compatriots. I drove the van to a car wash. The car could begin a new life.

All week I stayed off the highway. It would always be there when it was needed, as would the servicemen, orphans and strays. I heard nothing from Barney, the ungrateful chimp. And failed bodyguard. I slept in her bed with Linda. The feel of the alpaca soothed my sleep.

And Brenda, cause of both departure and return? She trailed through the house like a zombie if she walked around at all. Spaced in front of the TV, forgetting to switch channels, neglecting to take food; in weird meditations on the terrace she had no more presence than a plant. In her lusterless hair she wore flowers, sea daisies—our Ophelia; on her wan face a distant smile, as though wired to another galaxy, waiting for a signal light-years hence.

One day we heard the roar of a cycle. The fixed smile came unfrozen, the lights flicked on in their sockets, the detached persona reconnected itself. As if by teleportation that signal had clearly arrived.

All six-feet-six and two hundred pounds of it, in a solid deep ebony finish, and a fitted white nylon jumpsuit—a sight to stagger anyone's eyes. No need to ask Brenda what she saw in him. No one looked anywhere else. As they entered arm-in-arm she was once more the size of a child, our teenage Goldilocks daughter.

"Jerry," she said softly, "I'd like you to meet my friend, Clarence Decker. His friends all call him Ace." The two had locked contrasting fingers in a dovetail joint. His arm muscles bulged like pythons, I thought. As for the rest of him...

"I can see why." I lifted my eyes to meet his. "I'm indebted to you, Ace. Your present saved my life."

"I wished I was here to use it. I expect you might need it some day."

"Some night, as it turned out. Sometimes you don't know what to expect around this house."

"I do," Ace smiled simply, the words a kind of baritone croon. "You're good people." Well said, Clarence! The man's resonant voice, his vitality, his mellow charm, his charisma were qualities not lost on Linda, either. At my side she became the gracious hostess I had rarely seen before, let alone conceived of as my wife. My wife had usually been the alter side to that ego.

"I hope you'll stay for dinner," she said warmly, as though it were the shotgun of a stranger that had almost removed Mickey's brains. But the blast of that weapon had also cleared the air, a pioneer brand of home therapy.

We had martinis, then dined. Ace was very polite. He talked about his hometown Motown—Detroit, but very little of his training in the service. That was confidential, I supposed, like so much that went on in the world. After each turn of phrase his eyes rolled toward Brenda like wet marbles. I assumed that underneath the tablecloth their knees met. Young love. I felt older.

When Ace rose after coffee, the candlelight bounced off his cheekbones and shimmered on the white satin jumpsuit. Yes, I saw surreptitiously, he wore it on the right. A thick one, too. Ace and Brenda excused themselves to take a walk on the beach. Did they know the uses of the storm drain?

The two had not returned when Linda yawned, put down her knitting and said it was time for her bed. In a short while I followed, undressed in the dark, and slipped in close beside her. I copped a feel, cupped a breast, touched a labial lip and was almost as quickly inside it, surprised as she was. What was happening? we must have asked ourselves.

How could I match what Ace had shown at dinner? How far could his go in, I wondered, plumbing depths. And how did those people do it? Those long rhythmic *lunges,* those horizontal jungle *strides.* That's what came of dancing for a million years, barefoot in the dirt of Mother Africa. Black Panthers—for sure! Throaty growls from shining jowls, glistening hide, rippling flanks, plunging pelvis.... They had it *made in spades,* thought the envious honky racist in the course of having marital sex.

"That's *so fine,*" Linda groaned. "Don't stop now, for God's sake!" When they came was it in long whip-like strands the color of milk chocolate? Physical Science told me differently. I ejaculated.

"Oh, Jerry," and she actually sighed. "Perhaps I've been missing something. Was it ever like this with us before?"

I gave her a throat-deep soul-kiss. "Not really, babe. Maybe we've both matured. It's possible. Let's not talk about it now." Enough applause. I wanted an instant encore, to prove I could do it again.

"You're right, dear. Let's only try to love one another."

Then I did want to talk about it anyway, despite the mutual expressions of trust and tender affection. I stroked her warmest parts.

"How did it feel with Mickey?" Her melting flesh congealed.

"Please let's not discuss it *now,* Jerry." Linda humped her bare back toward me. I wished I had a tool, of the sort that an ear doctor uses, to take one quick peek inside that skull of hers. Whom would I find revealed there on her tiny Technicolor screen—or did she dream in black-and-white? Mickey? Myself? Harry? *ACE.* I could take bets—ten to one. She was never that hot with me before, even the very first time, on the unfinished floor of Colonel Everett's game room. She was horny for that big black stud, Brenda's boyfriend! Innocent though she might appear in sleep, feigned or genuine, she had practically committed *mental incest*—for all abnormal purposes —right there in our conjugal sheets. As so, indeed, had I.

If she could sleep, I couldn't. I tried to think instead. A married pair with children, we'd exercised a prerogative sanctioned by custom, law and church. We'd had sex—a loving relationship. Was it good? Yes. More than satisfactory? Excellent, in fact worth repeating. Did you *dig it,* Jerry? Yes, I think I did. Don't you *know?* I thought I knew what I was missing.

What was missing was what I'd grown accustomed to—the hearty heady contest between male and muscled male—like wrestling! The cinched hold, the tensioned grip, the firm resistance finally yielding as quivering sweating limbs reversed themselves—like magnets. The reckless grasps, slippery-sliding, minds abandoned there...until the cumulative spastic gasp, spuming, spouting, sperming.... Moby Dick harpooned! Uncontrolled, uncontrollable.

The dual thrill, the double charge of *two studs* getting off together, *mano a mano*, boy to boy, hard as hard can be. And *wrestling* from that fleet split second of eternity a moment's realization of universal being. Or some such ideal. *Man's humanity to man,* was how I ought to think of it, I thought unto myself. *It doubled my pleasure,* I might have added too.

My heart, my freshened hard-on, throbbed together to the rolling freight-train rhythms of the heavily freighted words, sound track to my reservations-only motion picture show. At that moment even Barney, his eager merely adequate member, his tough-skinned nut-brown monkey's body, could have played an important part, far superior to Cheetah's.

The more ambitiously-conceived starring role assigned to Mickey had been sliced from the production entirely, for flagrant breach of contract, moral turpitude. The costly footage lay discarded, no—dismembered—on the bloodstained cutting room floor.

Thoughtfully I scratched my groin. Then my buttocks. My thighs itched too, I noticed. I ought to feel relaxed. Was it nerves? I began to itch all over. I leaned at the bathroom mirror, blinking in the light. On the loins, chest and stomach tiny welts and scabs like Mickey's had appeared. They bled wherever I picked them. Crabs? Black Magic? Not the *BIG S*, certainly! I spread a pungent crotch-stinging pyrinate lotion, showered and got into bed, two feet apart from Linda. In her sleep she stirred restlessly, too.

"Scabies," said Dr. Warner the next morning. "Have you been sleeping where you shouldn't, Mr. Carr?"

"On the contrary, Doctor. I've been sleeping where I should."

"Been to Mexico lately? Tijuana? Skid Row?" Tactfully the doctor smiled as he went on with the examination.

"Not recently. In fact I've hardly been anywhere at all."

"Well, the medication kills 'em. Microscopic mites. They'll itch for a while, though. The scabs block the sweat glands, so be careful not to sweat or overheat. You'll have to wash or dry clean everything. Someone's brought some dirty linen to your house."

Like the couch cover worn by Mickey? That *would* be his legacy to the devastated household—a skin disease picked up for free in liberal San Francisco! Where would the little buggers strike next? At Linda, Brenda, Ace? Maybe the entire family, plus cats and dog. Then all of Malibu! At the Pokey, the Sheriff would pin a badge on our star exterminator, deputizing Harry to stamp out the raging disease, an epidermal epidemic. If he branded me the carrier I'd be a marked man for life!

So ran my latest paranoid fantasy as I sat with a mirror on the toilet lid in scrutiny of stigmatizing sores. It could be a long hot summer, thanks to Mick. I swore a solemn curse. I swore that he'd be cooled out forever. In the direction he was headed, that fate could overtake him anytime.

"That's disgusting," said Linda when she found out, simply by entering the bathroom. "How could you do a thing like that?"

"I didn't do it, it was done to me—by Mick, when he tried to axe me in the kitchen. When we tangled on the floor."

"Why wasn't he scratching then?" she asked logically.

"He was probably too trashed on drugs. He *drove* here *naked.*"

"Then why doesn't Brenda have it?" she inquired more logically still.

"I don't know. Maybe her skin's still virgin territory."

"That's not amusing, Jeremy. We can all get it now." Linda dropped her nightgown and demanded an instant on-the-spot inspection.

"I don't see anything yet," I said on my knees, applying the prescribed mite-killing salve in the manner of a royal annointment.

"I could joke about that if I wanted to." She began to get into clean clothes. "You'll have to take everything down to the laundry. We can't wash it here. And you probably can't sleep here, either, until you're positively cured."

"Well, Jesus, Linda, the doctor said the little things were dead." If one night of love could put the magic back in marriage, a good case of scabies could as easily take it out.

"I'm sorry, Jerry, but we do have the others to think about. You certainly haven't minded being absent in the past."

"I thought I was here to protect you."

274

"I think we'll be all right now, thank you. You'd better look after yourself."

All right? Well, I could be *all right* too, doing just what I was doing before the whole bloody thing got started, without risking life, limb and skin. As soon as I stopped scratching, that is.

My bruised eye was another reminder in the rear-view mirror. She was driving me—I knew as I drove townward with the wash—back to those same ways and habits she had only so recently deplored. Whatever happened now would be her fault, not mine. Instead of meekly turning cheeks I should have clipped her one—the hypocrite —as Mickey had. That was the kind of honest treatment she had learned to understand and respect.

As for him, he had obviously cast the better curse. It functioned at all times, at any range, in any weather—like psychic radar. Beneath the new-formed scabs I felt my flesh crawl. Was he in possession of— or possessed by—powers beyond those I had known? It was well within range of the possible.

Then the easy charm, the friendly persuasion, the more-than-palatable teachings of the personable St. Mick and his curly-haired cohorts—twin sidekicks—were only a lure for a fish, a victim Pisces. A cynical disguise, a subtly deadly subterfuge, a front in fact, for dark and dangerous forces that ruled his underworld. The artful Saint had been unmasked—like a second circumcision.

In the heat of the July afternoon whining through the Fury's vented windows, the hairs and sinews of the back of my neck grew as stiff as at an air-cooled horror movie. Suppose Mick *were* the Devil— as he claimed? Or a commissioned agent of Old Nick—*Old Scratch*, another nickname for His Infernal Majesty? That was why he hadn't scratched himself, why Brenda's skin stayed pure. It made a lot of sense. The Red Prince could be a Prince of Darkness.

Unseen, unheard, his whereabouts unknown, he was the ominous invisible menace—the *omni-menace*—of my existence now. What if Starkey had pulled the trigger? I scarcely dared ask the silent question. What if the demon in him knew? Suppose the demon were only one of my imagining, in his mind merely a drug? That thought, too bland for reassurance, too pedestrian for belief, I banished with the coins I ground into the parking meter. Without a personal demon how could I be saved?

When I had dropped the dirty linen at the laundromat I walked over to Richie's Sportware and applied for registration of a Colt .357 Magnum. I bought latches for each apartment window and double bolts for both doors and a tiny glass eyeball to stare into the night. I priced an axe for chopping down the coconut palm, providing Mrs. Haymer let me. If any life other than that tree's were in danger, it was my own.

69.

Not simply doctor's orders, not solely Mickey's threats, real or imagined, nor Linda's cold rejection, but every power in the world, it seemed, was trying to tell me the same thing—to cool it. That was the larger message that was coming through to me, like foul-weather heavy-surf warning signs. I didn't have to ask the stars and planets; I could feel it in my bones. Staying cool was not a bad idea that time of year, the summer's zenith.

Maybe there *was* something a little out-of-bounds, in or out of season, in filling up my guts with alcohol the way fuel was pumped into my gas tank, to track down and seduce young strangers on the highways and byways of the state. If consulted, other citizens might have seconded the notion. Caution, self-restraint were not exactly dirty words, especially in dealings with the Devil or any of his West Coast representatives. *Cool* then, would be the password of the month at my place.

"Hey, Fuck-face! Whatcha doin'?" Though it was one of Barney's toll calls, I resented the tone. Could familiarity have bred contempt?

"I'm keeping my cool." There! I'd said it. I felt better for saying it already. At the moment I didn't even itch.

"Well, you might as well blow it. Your cool, that is. I'm coming over. So be ready to party, pal, with plenty of booze and some broads." Before I could cool that suggestion the coin-fed call had clicked off.

A little sex play wouldn't hurt though, even in my current condition. Besides, it was with someone I knew. The opportunity had been dropped into my lap, so to speak. Why fight it? I wasn't bothered by the nonexistent call girls. They were props for his Marine Corps ego. We'd simply have some drinks and do it in the dark.

I had confidence in the gentlemen's agreement we'd made: twenty bucks a trip in take-home pay, plus fringe benefits, house privileges, and all the free liquor he could drink. That way he wouldn't feel guilty, doing it for pay, not pleasure. And I wouldn't waste my time in fruitless cruising. With a born gift for imitation, the wage-earning ape-man might even get better at his job.

But he was more than a paid playmate. With Barney—*Trigger*—there, I felt secure. I would have both companion and champion. On top of all that I kind of liked him.

Came sunset, the Happy Hour, dinner time, then nine or ten o'clock. Still neither hide nor hair of Barney. What could have happened to the little monk? A duty call, a barroom brawl, a crack-up? Mildly worried, I was hungry and horny, too. The watched phone rang. Through the holes of the earpiece as though constricted in its coils came a hard rasp of pressurized breathing.

"Barney?" No answer. "Charley? King Kong?" As on a Crosswire tensioned into silence the breaths grew harsher still. *"Mickey."* The line went dead. I tested doors and locked the windows. Like the bell of an alarm the phone rang. I nudged it off the cradle and stood back.

"Hello? Are you *there?* Is your tongue tied up? You might say *something!* Or are you doing someone else?"

"I was waiting for a long distance call, Lenny. But go ahead. It's always interesting to hear from you." Leonard sounded breathless, too.

"You can tell me that when I'm *finished.* But first I've got to tell you the news. *It's all bad,* bee-lieve me!" he hurried on hysterically. "It's your friend *Mick.* He has *blown his top."* I heard the ice cubes quake in Leonard's glass. "Completely *flipped out.* And dan-ger-ous!" The theatrical reading of the last words caused him to catch his breath and audibly gulp his iced drink.

"Dangerous to whom?"

"Dangerous to *me.* To you! To him*self.* He's like a devil in the flesh, with a *spike* instead of a pitchfork. You don't know *where* he'll strike next." Leonard poured some liquid in his drink. Someone else shared my misgivings about the recent conduct of the drugged-up renegade redhead.

"What did he do to you, Lenny? And where were your leather-bound bodyguards, like Dirty Dick?"

The virtuoso voice became a hushed whisper.

"I think they're all in it together. *I'm* the one who's getting *burned*. Bricks of grass. Grams of coke. *Now* they're using everything! One grand *in one week*. I can't go *on* like this, Jerry."

"Why don't you fly down to Palm Springs?" A cheap remark— *calloused*. Here was a fellow sufferer at Mick's hands. I had hit the wrong target again. "Why not Mexico?"

"I've got to hang up," he said abruptly. "They're *coming up the stairs*." I was left to the thin plaintive whine of the wire in my ear, and the far-off cry of the sirens. What was happening out there in the great wide world? The night was scarier than any film I'd ever seen. I slept fitfully through frightful dreams that seemed more real than waking, scratching all the while.

70.

Were those dark clouds equipped with silver linings? I never knew. In the morning every cloud had vanished, burned to a vapor by a vicious sun—all but a belt of brown smog expanding to a girdle where the sky touched the sea. On such a day, after such a night, how was I supposed to keep my cool?

I was itching to get into the ocean. Choosing two trusty sidekicks, my swim fins, I headed for the beach, leaving everything else to my nine-to-five answering service. Let those operators handle drunk marines, gay hysterics, psychopaths panting in their earphones. That's what PARALERT was getting paid for, as soon as I could send the month's check.

The waves at State Beach were mounting in a soldierly order, as though in review at a military parade. First came a series of frisky dancing waves like drum majorettes for children to excite themselves, for parents to get wet. Then echelons of medium breaks of five or six feet—the recruits—making clean decent rides for the younger set. Every half hour came the big ones, the artillery display, humping tall and breathtaking in walls like plates of steel.

I swam boldly out to meet them, out where the surface heaved to a trembling crest, skipped a beat, and spilled into a white crackling climax as the wave's spine broke. Shapes of body-surfers shot through it like bullets, features in the arrogant cast of skiers on a downhill run, of lovers in triumphant embraces. I had known such moments also. Now I only ducked.

After each great wave came a boom like buried thunder and a wash of swirling foam that swept the beach—waking tourists, wetting towels. That was called the cleanup set. I swam through the foam to the break line, to the wavering rows of surfers that hung there on the brink, waiting for the wave of the day. The tide was high and getting higher. From below I felt the sucking backsurge, from above the tug of gravity toward the noontime sun.

Waiting, I took my bearings. East beyond the beach and the highway, I saw the walls and windows of the place I lived, in the shadow of the Trojan palm. First to show its uses, Trigger Trimble was either in the brig or on maneuvers to the south. On the pier a mile away in that direction soared the silvery spread of the carousel roof, like a satin sheet on a phallus, a cloak for the unsavory acts of Leonard and his band of thieves, perhaps the demoniacal Mickey. The day was far too bright for his dark powers. Besides, he couldn't swim. Cool in my native element I was safe from his phone calls and threats.

To the west was Malibu, a neat triangulation. I had a fourth point of reference an arm's length to my left, for there, suddenly surfaced like a rusty buoy, bobbed a head of wet red hair stuck flat to the brow above a cheek-swelling grin, a grin directed nowhere in particular. A tuft stood up behind like a red signature. I held my breath. I felt as Captain Ahab might have felt on beholding at the port side of the *Pequot* a smiling Moby Dick. The boy was the ultimate redhead, the redhead of all my dreams!

Was I dreaming? For a moment, like a beacon, the boy's grin flashed upon me. "Surf's up. It's coming. I can *feel* it," the grinning boy grinned as to a friend. My body rose a little in the swell. Was there a wave out there? I couldn't see it, nor anything beyond that sparkling, freckled dew-fresh face. He dipped it, shaped the mouth like a fish, and shot a spray of water at the sun. He grinned at me again, eye-to-iris.

Could this red-haired boy be thinking what I *thought* he did? The thought was farther out than any I had ever had, or could imagine. Just imagine.... *Doing it* right there in the undulant ocean, me submerged, he half emerged.... Then *he* spouting sea-spray, shooting sperm, as ignorant thousands idled on the shore—*me* and the ideal redhead—at high noon! The heady vision made my head swim. I took a deep breath and dove below.

Reflected overhead, the headless body wriggled in the current like a speckled rainbow trout. Finned like mine, the legs kept a cycling rhythm, the hands moved like paddles at his sides. Were they webbed it would not have surprised me. No merman he, but a slim sea urchin, true sea-born brother of the briny deep. On his slippery skin, his slender hips, the loose-tied trunks slid downward. They were hanging by a thread!

At their center—like forbidden fruit—grew a lump as large as an apple. Should I reach for that ripe apple *now?* No voice was heard, no face peered down to tell me. The trunks slipped to his kneecaps. The boy was...*glorified!*

As though lifted aloft by a skyhook the body was yanked out of sight. Those were bubbles that had been his balls. Like a rock I was plunged to the bottom. A shock shook the base of my spine, my brain took a jolt of white lightning.

For a while I might have rolled along the bottom as monstrous tons of water passed above. Had the surfer caught a ride? Was he for real? The wave of the day—a total wipe-out! A total white-out, perhaps for good. Without precedent or warning the brown-belted ocean had delivered a karate chop. Mick's fiendish hand had dealt its deadly blow!

My hands clawed a way toward the air but my lungs, oddly numb, seemed not to breathe it. So this is how you drown, I thought coolly, an everyday drowning in the every-summer month of July, the proper season. I hoped my drowning would not have a red-haired witness. I didn't want *him,* so recently acquainted, to remember me like that.

Of his bones are coral made. In the sun's white glare the billows swept toward me, quilted linings of my ocean bier, the cleanup set. Like a battered clump of seaweed I drifted toward the beach, and touching sandy bottom crawled ashore. Something hurt.

"Are you all right there, fellow?" called a man from the shade of his shadow. "Would you like a sip of Coke?" asked a woman who might have been his wife. A circle of dark heads seemed to surround me. A lifeguard knelt at my side. He was blond, in red trunks. His face came near to mine in what appeared to be a goodbye kiss.

Presently, and from a long way off, came the intermittent wail of a siren. The sound ceased nearby at the parking lot. I closed my eyes.

71.

"Well, you've certainly done it this time. Haven't you, Jerry?" The kind of remark my wife might make. Linda had just made it.

"What are you doing here? And why are you all wearing white?"

"It's a linen dress you gave me once, remember?"

"Yes. And the others? What am I doing here, exactly?"

"They haven't told you yet?"

"I've been sort of out of it lately."

"White is your usual hospital shade. It's the color here at the Veterans', where they brought you as an accident case. You know you've had an accident, don't you?"

"Yes, I remember now. Body-surfing. White's not a shade, Linda. It's not even a color. White is the *absence* of color. It's nice of you to come here, though." I took the hand with our ring on it. "How am I?"

"Right now you're full of morphine. You're in a body cast from crotch to clavicle"—*her very words*—"with a crushed vertebra. The first lumbar they tell me. Does it hurt?"

"It's beginning to. How about the rest of me, Linda?"

"You're once more my knight in white armor."

I squeezed her hand in earnest. "Stop *kidding* me, goddamnit. I can't even feel my own *dick*." A nurse frowned in passing—another problem vet.

"Oh, your primary physical function? It's going to be all right, I believe. They haven't had time to test it yet. They have terminal cases here, you know. They're also understaffed and underpaid."

"Don't ever talk to *me* about cruelty, you heartless bitch."

"You're not a paraplegic, if that's what you mean. We won't have to push you in a wheelchair, with a bladder."

"Well, *thanks a lot*. Were you hoping you would?"

"Of course not, hon." She squeezed my hand back, I imagined. "But we're the ones who have to look after you, you know, as soon as you're released." Already she looked weary with dismay. "It's a month at least before the cast comes off, with bedpans and constant attention. You're not an easy patient. You won't be working for a while, either."

"I a-*pol*-ogize. It's lucky I'm a veteran. I should have been killed in a war. Then you'd have a widow's pension."

"I'm sorry, dear. I can't feel sorry for you like the last time. I have Casey and all the other responsibilities to take care of. I do think you might have been careful, and thought about us for once."

"It's not my fault, Linda." She began to look serious indeed.

"Are you going to say it's Mickey's? Like the scabies?"

"Exactly. You were right. Mickey *is* a tool of the Devil." I told the story of the surrogate redhead. Linda sat beside the cast and braced an arm on it, evaluating the report.

"I don't know how to interpret that, Jerry. I don't know who's crazier now. He's done some bad things, certainly, but that strains even my credulity." Even in disaster she could find a word like that!

"Don't believe it then. You'll see what happens." Linda took away her hand and arm. "There are more things in heaven and earth, Linda Lee, than are dreamt of in *your* philosophy."

"I believe you molested a young boy out there. God punished you. That's my philosophy."

"Don't give me that sanctimonious crap. You don't go to any churches, either. And I don't go after children, any more than you do."

"I also believe there's a rough kind of justice in this world. When you play with fire you're going to get burned, as any child can tell you."

"Do me a favor? Please go find a nurse. It hurts like hell, Linda. I can't even scratch where it itches."

"All right, Jerry, I'll leave you now. Take care of yourself."

"Who else would want to?"

"You never know, do you?"

A nurse jabbed a needle in my buttock.

72.

I was an object in suspension—in suspended animation—through the count of nameless days that I lay there in my cast, subject of the clip board at the bottom of the bed. In the ward, a sick man's barracks, the schedule told the hours: a time to wake and wash, a time to eat, a time to excrete, a time to go to sleep again. The time for medication was the time worth waiting for—the moment for the needle to sink below the skin. Then the hours lost their meaning, the clatter of the ward became a dulling lullaby. I dreamt while still awake.

The steel bed and sideframes were indeed a rack of torment—the pains that shot along the nerves like heated wires, the paralyzing plaster cast and the odors from beneath, the scabs that stung like burrowing termites.

They'll put you in a stiff white jacket, Mick had said. And there I was, his curse come true, twisting in my cast like the captive of an Iron Maiden—*an exquisite torture*—until morphine struck a vein. I had one other solace. In that fortress concrete ward behind steel doors and barred windows I was safe from Mick himself. *"I can call spirits from the vasty deep."* But would they come to such a place if he did call them?

I was after all among old soldiers, unfit though they might be, in oversize pajamas on shriveled frames, on amputated stumps in wheelchairs. Maybe these had once been carefree youths on western highways, full of lust or violence, of love and fear in war. Behind cloth screens or ranked before TV they were soldiers turned pacifist by injury, by wasting diseases, by drugs. They had no world outside. Passive in my plaster cast, I was an uninvited visitor who brought nothing of that outside in.

One afternoon after sheet change and injection I had two outside visitors of my own. Steve and Starkey brought my mail and a *Playboy* magazine. They had shaggy hair and peeled skins from long days in the surf. Zinc ointment on their noses gave them comic masks.

"So you finally caught the big one." Steve tapped the cast like a mummy's case. "That's a solid body job. Does it fit?"

"Over the falls! How did it feel?" said Starkey.

"Like getting crushed by an avalanche, or getting hit by a truck. It's not recommended. I wouldn't do it again."

"You learn fast."

"Yeah, what are you going to break next time, Jerry?"

"I'm thinking about it. What else has happened lately?"

"Some of your customers called. We said you were indisposed."

"And a guy named Stinger. From Oceanside."

"Trigger. He's going to Asia. He'll send you a gook's ear."

"He'd better look after his own." I felt a little less protected.

"Did you hear about the man on the pier?" Starkey asked. "The one that loaned you the apartment?"

"Did he finally get his name in the papers?"

"The front page, yesterday. They found him hanging down between the piles." The boys dropped their voices, more in discretion than respect. "He'd been *mutilated,* the paper said."

"He'd been strung up by the balls, naked," Steve added. "He'd been slashed with a knife. Even his hair was cut off."

"They didn't print that part," Starkey said.

"Everybody knows it at school. The paper didn't say he was a fag, either." Steve looked me in the eye to say our interests and injuries had been too closely linked for his comfort.

"Has anyone heard from Mickey?" I was sweating again in my cast. Flies buzzed where I couldn't reach them.

"How come you ask about him? Is he still after you?"

"Maybe he's the slasher," Starkey said.

"Yeah! Who will he slash next?"

"It could be you or me." Stark was always one move ahead of the game. Steve picked up a Magic Marker and began to draw designs on the cast—first some ornamental slashes, then drops of dripping gore.

"I don't think they're going to like that," I said. "Haven't I been hurt bad enough?" Steve drew two enormous circles on my chest and put dotted nipples at their centers.

"Cut it out," said Starkey. He took another pen and started scrawling blue stars on the plaster. His brother filled in the names: *Mae West, Melody Landau, Mickey Rooney, Steve McQueen.* On the stomach, *Jack the Ripper. Mick the Slasher* at the groin.

"I'm Bertha, the head nurse. What do you think you're doing to our trunk dressing?" She wore white from head to heel. "Are these your children, Mr. Carr?"

"They're my wife's, Mrs. Grable. Write *Betty Grable* there, boys."

"Who's ever, they'll have to leave. You're a patient, not a playmate." I slid the *Playboy* under the cast as she pulled the sheet over it. "Their visiting hours are over. Please don't ask them back."

"*Hasta la vista, amigos.* Thanks for all the news."

As the boys left, other veterans looked up from TV events and sports pages. Once they had walked down corridors like that, shoving younger brothers.

"Could I have a hypodermic now, please, Mrs. Grable?"

She consulted the chart, then a tiny gold watch. "In an hour and thirty-five minutes, Mr. Carr. We can't have you leaving here an addict."

Wheeling smartly about, the head nurse advanced down the next rank of patients, pigeon chest thrust out as though be-medaled—starched major domo of the third floor back.

My heart sank like ballast to the bottom of the cast. Barney gone. Then Leonard! A soul so full of lust and life, strangled by the scrotum. Bad company could do it. Had Mickey been the one? Maybe I had no friends left. Maybe I was better off among these fellow derelicts.

"They're bright kids," said the man in the next bed, a bleeding ulcer case. "I wish I still had mine."

"What became of yours, Larry?"

"Oh, their aunt took them away when I was drinking. Jim's in jail. Frank's in college. Jim's the one who writes."

I turned my head, trying not to feel depressed. A stiff drink would have helped. *Here's to you, Len!* Or Trigger. The letters could wait until later. Everything was better after dark. Cooler, too.

After dark was long after dinner, after day-shifts had gone, after beds had been laid before the night's sedations. I glanced through the mail, mostly bills, and dropped them in a basket. I leafed through *Playboy's* list of summer pleasures, admiring the artwork, coveting the stereos and sports cars. I looked at tilted breasts and swollen pubes, at waistlines, belly holes and backsides. At male models, too, but none excited me. Morphine is a general narcotic. I chucked the magazine across to Larry. It would make the rounds of the ward, a paper mistress, creating stealthy agitations of the bedframes audible among the night's distresses.

But the pleasure of the night was in its nurses, lithe young girls from poorer homes, of darker races than those stiff white matrons of the day. To them a pill or a shot was nothing. "Oh, let me *slip it in*, love," black Madeline might murmur, and the whole ward would breathe and sleep the easier.

73.

In ten days I was out. Not only was the Veterans Hospital understaffed, extra beds were demanded. From warring southeast Asia, casualties still in their teens were flown in, with complex, sophisticated wounds that veterans of other wars might never have survived. New techniques, new equipment would be needed. Careless, freeloading seniors like myself would have to be cared for elsewhere.

It was just as well. The orthopedic surgeon had taken me off morphine and substituted Demerol, a less effective, less addictive pain relief. The broken bone and I would have to shift for ourselves. The painted cast looked like a ghetto wall. For the journey through the halls it was covered by an institution blanket.

Linda had a kind of surprise for me—an aluminum chaise-lounge on rubber casters. I'd be pushed around as on a gurney or delivered directly to the bathroom. Beneath a canopy of canvas on the terrace was where I liked it best. There had been the beginning of our romance. The view was romantic still. I was back in the bosom of the family, Randy at my side, the glossy russet coat reminding me once more of the multi-manifested Mickey. Could this watchful, panting dog be yet *another?* I would watch him, too. I didn't choose to share this superstition with my wife. She had troubles enough, as she reminded me each morning more than once.

Every night I was wheeled to the bedroom where I slept with the shotgun close at hand. But the gun, Linda's presence, or that of the others in the house were not in themselves my security. I sensed in my heart, in my bones, in my *tail*bone that Mick had gone a long way away. Having finished his foul deed he had vanished.

Or maybe—just maybe—he did have a hand in Leonard's death. In that case he was only hiding out. And in *that* case would he ever strike again? We would *jutht wait and thee*—if seeing him again were in a form still familiar. In the clear September light, the terror of those days began to fade, like feverish colors exposed to air and sunlight.

It was clear from the start that the recovery from the broken back would not resemble that of the knee injury. A handicap was no news to Linda. As she herself foretold, she had no sympathy to waste—only charity—and that in short supply. As for the admonitory hand-slap, it was not even to be thought of—she had the upper hand complete. Any smart talk or nonsense and I'd be knocked back on my top-heavy tail, or be left out on the terrace overnight like a parked car waiting for the tow-truck.

I'd be lucky to get meals, pills and bedding with a drink as a reward. She was doing a perfect Head Nurse Grable number on me. *Linda=Bertha.* It was a wonder the two hadn't met. I'd better get well in a hurry, was the message expressed by both.

Not only well in body, in mind and spirit too. Each morning I found volumes stacked by the chaise, or sometimes laid open on the cast to a significant, underscored passage: *They have sown the wind, and they shall reap the whirlwind,* in the Bible. Or words of Aristotle, William Blake, Emily Bronte. . . Dante, Darwin, Dickens. . . with a book of Hemingway or D.H. Lawrence thrown in. It was all coming down on me at once—a veritable cloudburst of literature, the wisdom of the ages to be absorbed in one short spell of backache.

Where was she getting such a list? I found the clue inside a dust jacket from the Modern Library, the all-time writers' Hall of Fame. Stuff she hadn't even read herself! I could wager that by the time we reached alphabet's end there'd be no Wilde or Whitman. Gay witty dreamers, men who played around with boys, would definitely be off the reader's menu.

She was trying to reform my goddamn sex life—by example at that! On the pretext of self-improvement I was being brain-washed like a captive G.I. I had her number—and the hell with it. I'd just take extra pills or pretend to be asleep, or relish behind the Modern Library jacket a Mary Renault novel about true love in ancient Greece.

I was glad when Starkey came to win at chess, or Brenda played a game of monopoly, or I was wheeled into the study to watch monotonous TV. I compared myself to other veterans imprisoned by their maladies for life, to Leonard's gruesome end, to Barney dodging booby traps or bullets. I was *lucky.* Lucky to be breathing, lucky to be alive—so lucky I ought to cry if I had any tears left. Both Linda and I were nearly out of teardrops.

Perhaps the bump on the spine, the bolt of white light, had jolted my head back to sanity in the same way a shock treatment would. I was content to be right there, doing ordinary things as far as I was able. I didn't really *need* to be chasing other males, getting into their pants, manipulating private parts, in order to be happy. To be honest with myself, I hardly thought of sex at all. The change—the *sea change*—had little to do with my prescribed course of reading or even with prescription drugs. It seemed normal to simply exist.

"Are you happy?" asked Linda that night preceding dinner, as she offered a glass of sparkling rosé. How perceptive she could be when she wanted!

"Thank you, Linda. Yes, I think I am, oddly enough, happier than I remember being in a long time. *Happiness is a wine of rarest vintage, and seems insipid to a vulgar taste.*"

"I'll drink to that. You *have* been reading. It's a lovely line. Who wrote it?"

"I don't know. There've been so many words and writers in my head lately."

"Have they taught you something?"

"*Now that you are going to marry, do not expect more from life than marriage will afford.* Samuel Johnson."

"I can't agree with him entirely. I think there's more to life than that."

"*It matters not how a man lives, but how he dies.* He said that, too."

"He wrote excellent dictionaries. Have you read all of Boswell's *Life of Johnson?*"

"I've been dipping into the Quotation Dictionary. Here. You can pick some quotes of your own. I'll have a touch of the *vin du jour,* please."

"That's only a paperback, Jerry."

"*Good things come in small packages.* Look at you, Linda."

"Why? Do you think I'm little? You never told me that before. Or do I somehow remind you of a paperback?"

"Neither, dove. I mean that things don't have to be gorgeously circumstanced in order to be appreciated. I've made that mistake in the past, like living on the Merry-Go-Round."

"That's not my idea of *gorgeous.* That was *dreadful,* about that man. You knew him quite well, didn't you?"

"Friends, but nothing more. I'll miss him."

"Jerry?"

"Yes, love? Give us a little kiss."

"There *is* something I've been meaning to talk about while we're together now. While we're really communicating with each other."

"You've been wonderful to me, Linda. I don't know how to say thanks. Without you I could hardly have survived."

"Don't overdo it, Jerry."

"I mean it. You've given me the prospect of a whole new life. I feel practically reborn already."

"Well, I'm glad. Then the experience was worth it. I want you to do a little bit more."

"Are you making personal advances? It's oh-*kay*."

"There's another person I'd like you to talk to. Just briefly, if you don't mind."

"And who would that other person be, pray tell?"

"Dr. Fritchy. He's coming over after dinner to see how you're doing."

"To see how my brain cells are doing. Isn't that what you mean?"

"Well, the object of life is to know yourself. Sigmund Freud said something like that. Can't you go along with that idea?"

"I already know Harold Fritchy. He's my client. He makes a bunch of bucks off people's sex hangups. Whatever it is they do, he gives them something different. His clinic's like a supermarket in psychology."

"Will you do it for me? Please? It's all I'm asking of you, Jerry."

"Are you paying?"

"Who else pays for anything now?"

"Sure. Let's see what the Doc's pushing this year. It might be funny if the fashion happens to be boys."

True to Linda's word the doctor did show up, in a kind of gabardine golfing outfit with lots of pleats, and split-leather tassels on white buck shoes. I kept eyeing the brown tassels as we talked. The shoe-tops rose and swiveled when the doctor grew tense. Our eye-to-toe dialogue took place on the terrace as I lounged on the chaise by moonlight.

"Well, Jerry." He sank into one of the campaign chairs still doing duty in its shreds. Linda brought a flask of brandy and left us. "You've been through some hard times lately. How's the back?"

"It's holding up all right, Doctor, as long as the cast stays on. I've learned to walk around a little in it."

"It must feel like being a lobster."

"Or a hermit crab sometimes, trying to shake off his shell."

"Odd that you should say that. You know, everyone goes through that process. It's a part of growing up. Yours was a pretty lonely childhood, wasn't it?"

I told him about Mother and Dad of Eagle Rock.

"I see. Your father was frequently absent, and you had no brothers or sisters. Your mother, then, was the dominant person in your life. Wasn't she?"

"Very domineering. She kept me in line with a ruler."

"So you became a draftsman, right?"

"Right on, Harold, the straight and narrow all the way."

"And she never let you *deviate*, did she?"

"Not without getting whipped with a hairbrush. A silver one, like this ring, with my father's initials on it." Dr. Fritchy was a fascinating listener. He was tapping his toes on the bricks.

"And his name, Jerry?"

"Wellington Carr. Mother called him Willy, W.C."

"Have those initials any other significance for you?"

"Why yes, Harold. Yes, they do. *Water closet* is what they often stand for."

"And did anything happen there, beside the usual?"

"You bet it did, Doc. How did you know? I used to...urinate in the bathtub, while I took a shower. I don't think Mother ever knew." A shoe tassel quivered.

"Anything else, Jerry? We all know what boys do, if they're normal."

"I suppose I wasn't then. I used to put may hands...down here ..." I showed him on the plaster cast, happily covered, "...and touch my *thing*."

"You mean your *penis*, don't you? Every boy does that."

"And *plays* with it? Up and down...like this?" I pantomimed the motion.

"Yes, Jerry, I'm afraid we all do. I was discovered at the age of four, with two older boys and my brother. We were all doing it together in the playroom. A bit precocious, I might say, except for my brother. He was nine."

"What's *his* name, Harold?"

"Francis Oliver. F.O.F. *Frig or fight*, he used to tell the girls. I haven't thought of that for ages. He was always a big man on campus, even in senior high."

"Did you envy him? When you got to that grade, I mean."

"I didn't enjoy quite the reputation he did. But then he got there first, didn't he?"

"Harold... Here, let me fill your glass. Harold, tell me something frankly. It's only us two guys. Was his any bigger than yours was?"

"It's not really a fair comparison. Proportionately, no. You see, he was nearly six-feet-four, a basketball center, and it was probably, say... Well, you seem to be conducting the interview, Jerry. I think we were talking about yours."

"Oh, mine? It isn't big at all. Maybe six, seven inches, depending where you measure from. It got stuck in a five-inch roll of toilet paper once while I was measuring." Dr. Fritchy smiled a knowing smile. "That's when Mother whipped me. The toilet paper wouldn't roll back on the roll."

"You've seen bigger ones, no doubt?"

"Yes I have, many times. In gym class, after basketball practice, or down at the YMCA. Two hundred feet is the biggest, I think, hard. You should have seen the size of the rocks!"

"That *is* extraordinary, Jerry." Both golf shoes were twitching now. Putting down his glass, Dr. Fritchy began to wipe his glasses on his polka-dotted ascot. "Where were you measuring from?"

"From ground level. There was no other way. So that was a matter of proportion, too."

"Perhaps you felt a little touch of envy, also?"

"Not at all. It was made of solid wood, in a forest. A *national* forest, too." The good doctor had been patient; he deserved a reward. I related the Big Sur allegory, the legend of the wounded knee, omitting Buck Willock's initials, W.W.W. What would he have made of those?

"It's an interesting story. It has a touch of the poetic about it. You do distinguish fact from fantasy. I'm glad of that. I thought you might have been deceiving yourself, or simply pulling my leg."

"No way, Harold. Your time's more precious than mine. Is there anything else you'd like to know?"

"Not tonight, thank you. It's getting late. I have a free afternoon tomorrow. Perhaps we'll get together then, if you're not busy."

I glanced at my calendar watch. "My time is your time. I'll be right here, waiting."

The doctor went inside and spent another quarter-hour in hushed conversation with my wife, who came out and wheeled me to the bathroom. There I closed the door and confirmed the usual measurement. I groped my way along the wall to the bedroom, to the couch in its stall by the bed.

"You're doing very well, dear. Did the doctor help you all that much?"

"No. I did. But it was interesting, he said. What did he tell you?"

"That you're verbal, and have a good choice of words."

"I've been *reading,* for God's sake! You didn't pay to hear him say that?"

"...that you're more preoccupied with the male than with the female organ, and tend toward the bisexual, perhaps."

"Big deal! You know what he told me *his* problem was? Penis envy! He coveted his big brother's *cock.*"

"I don't believe you. He's a certified Ph.D."

"Don't then. He's the doctor. I'm the patient. You're only picking up the tab. What have you two cooked up for tomorrow?"

"He's going to try a little experiment, to see if he can get to the root of the problem."

"He hasn't touched the tip of it yet."

"Goodnight, Jerry. I'm going to read for a while. I'm glad the two of you had your little talk. At least it's a beginning."

I had disturbing bisexual dreams, deviant enough to keep us talking through the morrow. I didn't want to disappoint the doctor now.

74.

After lunch Linda cleaned the bedroom, helped me into a bathrobe and pajama bottoms, and made me comfortable on top of the alpaca spread. She had closed the shuttered blinds as though in preparation for a seance and placed a book about psychology beside the lamp. She was going to be outdoors swinging Casey in his hammock, and I would be alone with the Doc.

Doctor Fritchy came in, made preliminary small talk and then got down to business. He dropped his bag on the bed and opened it to a pretty array of colored vials and shiny instruments. He brought out a glistening hypodermic kit—*his works,* a vial of alcohol, and cotton pads. He was going to play doctor for real. I thrust out my arm cooperatively. The doctor drew up a few c.c.'s and shot suggestive drops of fluid in the air. I made a fist.

"What are we shooting up today, Harold?"

"Oh, I thought we'd try a little Sodium Pentothal. It will help relax your spine. We're not even thinking of a full analysis. There won't be time for that. It's very costly, Jerry. So we're taking a kind of short cut, if that's all right with you."

"The truth serum, right? I can dig it. Shoot." My wife, generous lady, was paying to get me high! And a nice little buzz it was when it came on, smooth and sneaky, like two very dry martinis on the rocks. Soon I was chattering away as though present at the doctor's cocktail party. The filtered light became a twilight glow. Time lost its meaning.

I heard the voice of a child, a boy of six or seven. How did he get into the room? This was supposed to be a private conversation between two consenting adults. But the childish voice was my own, talking to Mother in her bedroom, by her dresser it would seem. She had allowed me a look into a drawer—it was nicely arranged—and wasn't even thinking of the hairbrush nestled there. I was charmed.

And then, there was *Willy*, my Dad, in his bow tie and shirtsleeves. We were wrestling again—I thought I could smell his cologne—and he *ressled* me to the floor and put a knee in my back—it hurt—and tickled me under the ribs. That felt funny. When he left the room I opened the *ciggar* box. That was no *baloon* there. It was a rubber. Mother saw it too. It made her mad!

There I was at twelve running from the playground, its yells and cries and laughter, with a lacerated knee. I washed the blood off the knee in the washroom and went to a cool dark stall, the one at the far end that always had things scribbled there in colored chalks—hearts and obscene sketches, social notes and dirty words. *J.C. loves J.C.*, someone had recently written. Taking the initials as my own I erased them with a wad of tissue and put my hand in its favorite place. Another hand had tested the latch of the door and the head of a teacher had peered over, seeing something it had not been meant to see. I began to thrash about on the bed. Dr. Fritchy was right there beside me.

"Would you like to be somewhere else?" his voice suggested dryly.

"Yes, I believe I would. I'd like to be...in Big Tujunga Canyon."

And there I was, spying on the nudists, the bouncing breasts and flopping genitals of those excited volleyballers. Then we were hopping—just the two of us—over boulders up the stream bed, they were *hot* to our tender feet, until we came to that cool place under spreading live oaks, all dappled and spangled in the shade, and peeled off sweated T-shirts and dropped our dusty jeans, our young bodies suddenly bare and breathing, and touching as we sat on the rock, the water gurgling underneath like some eternal fountain, the blueflies incandescent in the sun.

Then we had done it.

It was better than I had recalled. I counted every freckle, each gold-orange hair, and our fingers had reached underneath our scrotums—they grew tight, unwrinkling—to stroke the rigid seam that joins the body there, and fastened monkey-like around the shaft of one another's penis. I clamped my thumb to the cap of his as he had done to mine—the sensations were making me dizzy—and then the live juices shot from under all at once, like soda pop from shaken bottles, and we were two boys with our skins flushed and glistening. He said, "I like you, Jerry. I wouldn't do it with anyone else." I had forgotten that. I ruffled his red hair and threw my arm around Jimmy Corey's sun-reddened neck. We plunged into the stream and swam underwater between each other's legs and stood knee-deep to rinse ourselves in the cold fresh flood. Beneath the speckled skin slid the blades of his shoulders; the hard little buttocks were polished. He peed into the pool then, as I did, and the sparkling jets crossed like swords of liquid fire in our pledge of allegiance—*Jim and Jerry*. The flies had droned on oblivious in the ambient blue-amber air.

When I woke it was dark. That was Linda by the lamp, not Dr. Fritchy. She was reading in the book of psychology. My back had indeed ceased to hurt and my body felt wonderfully released, though imprisoned in its cage of gauze and plaster. Linda removed her reading glasses and looked up.

"You must have had a good session, Jerry. You've lost those lines of tension. You look so much *younger*. I'm amazed."

"I *feel* that way, too. That was a real nice treat. Can I have some more tomorrow? Can I have a Coke right now?"

"Not tomorrow, dear, maybe next week." *If you're good!* "The doctor said it takes a while to digest the experience. There's quite a lot to think about, you know." Maybe next week? What was there to think about? We'd hardly got started! With each injection of the truth drug I could relive another chapter in the history of my sex life.

It might be months before we got to St. Mick's finest hours. We were simply going to waste a lot of time. Linda brought the soft drink in a glass.

"So what did Dr. Fritchy have to say?" I said sipping it. "Does he think there's any hope?"

Linda replaced her reading glasses and took on a scholarly look.

"He talked about childhood repressions, about obsessions, fixations, and transferences. I'm looking up some of those things now. He's going to give some thought to the problem, to see where the trouble lies."

"It's usually standing up."

"I *know* that, Jerry," Linda sighed. "I think I understand what you've been through. What's important is how you function in the future. We can't always live in the past."

"Who needs to? It's nice to check up on it, though, to see if it's the same way you left it."

"I wouldn't worry about that if I were you. I think you'd be lucky to leave. Speaking of the present, it's time to fix dinner again."

What a break! What a break-*through*. Here I'd been consigned to basic bed rest, resigned to sexual abstinence, only waiting to get well. *Then*, like a sorcerer manipulating space and time, the gifted psychiatrist had restored to me some of life's most precious moments. Instead of blowing out the feeble candle of desire he had fanned it to a fever heat! The vision newly radiant within me, I did it once again with the tireless, the absent, the immortal Jimmy Corey there on the Malibu bed, thus soiling one of Linda's finest guest towels.

75.

"You see," Dr. Fritchy was explaining to Linda and myself, "the memory has an integral, discretionary filter. It seems to recall whatever has been most intense, life's primary signals, though often what has been merely pleasurable. In times of stress, therefore, we flee from present anxieties to recapture the pleasures of the past, by switching to another channel, so to speak." Linda had turned off the television set. The psychiatrist was pleased by the aptness of his words.

"Marcel Proust did that," I said. "He wrote a book about it. Several, in a cork-lined room." *Le Temps perdu Retrouve* would not be a Linda Lee selection, nor was she about to cork four walls for me. The doctor had not brought his silver key to past events. Instead he was giving us an insight.

"So if Jeremy has such a problem, what we used to call a neurosis, it is probably centered in just that sort of event."

"Like the one I described to you last week?"

"Precisely, and a very good description it was. I wish I had thought to record it." If he didn't—next time—I surely would. "You've probably had a similar experience, Linda. I think we all have." He couldn't be thinking of Big Brother again, could he?

"I remember the first boy who kissed me. He didn't want to stop."

"There you are. Perhaps you sometimes dream about him in a sensual way, or daydream about him, too."

"He had dark bushy eyebrows and a mole on his cheek. I wish I could remember his name."

"It wasn't Harry then," I said. "Was it?"

"There were plenty of boys before him. I was popular."

"Not if you only got kissed."

"I think we should get on with the subject. I'm already past due at the clinic." We glanced at our watches: 9:33. "What I'm going to say, briefly, is that Jerry can't recapture that one special moment of his past, meaningful as it may be, as an on-going present reality. None of us can, unfortunately. So he tries to relive it through others, and inevitably fails."

"You mean with red-headed boys, don't you, Harold?"

Arms folded, Linda bit her lip.

"I wasn't going to say that, Jerry, but it's just as well you did. Whatever image one carries can become an emotional burden. The person, time or place will never be the same. It's like living in a haunted house, among spirits. Like a ghost, that fixation can possess you, unless you exorcise it first." Along with his good shoes and his golfing clothes the doctor had his smarts on that morning. I was listening with both ears.

"That's what Linda tried to do, is exercise him."

"You have a very understanding wife. But that's what ghost stories, terror tales and vampire legends are about," he went on, "the possession of the present by the past, the possession of the living by the dead."

We had a thoughtful pause. The doctor rose. "Life is change. I must go now." Dr. Fritchy took a folder from his attaché case. "I want to leave this with you, Jerry. We'll talk again soon." Linda saw him to his car. The monogrammed Lincoln Continental did not leave right away.

In the folder was a grayed reproduction of a news story next to a graphic flash-photo of a freeway crash. The cars were like crumpled wads of tin foil, bent trim and hub caps scattered here and there. The bodies had been covered with blankets. A bent arm hung out of a window as though waving a careless farewell. The black streaks were blood.

My heart stopped. So *that's* what had happened to Mick! I read the article, getting ready to shed tears.

> A high-speed pursuit near San Bernardino ended early this morning in tragedy. Dead at the scene of the two-car collision were Elmer R. Wheeler, 23, of Colton, California, driver of the first vehicle and his companion, Victoria Slade, 32, of Redlands. Passengers of the second car, Mrs. James J. Corey, 26, and her four-year-old son Toby were pronounced dead at the scene of the accident by police. The driver James J. Corey, 29, was taken to St. Bernardine's Hospital, where he succumbed to multiple injuries at 5:25 A.M. A son James Jr., 7, is reported in guarded condition.
>
> The Wheeler car, a late model coupe traveling east at a high rate of speed, had been followed by California Highway Patrolmen before veering across the medial strip into the path of the west-bound Corey automobile, a station wagon. An investigation has been ordered into possible causes of the accident. The Corey family had been residents of Claremont for the past nine years. Mr. Corey was a native of Eagle Rock, California, and is survived by relatives there.

A September date of seasons ago was written in a corner. The news source was not given. I was numb. My eyes welled like springs. *Three years*, and I hadn't even known. Where he lived, where he worked, whom he married. The two children, the surviving boy, now ten. In fact, except for our encounter I had hardly known him at all. How had he looked when it happened? Did he still have his flaming red hair?

Those were all blanks on my memory tapes, questions I had never thought to ask. I never knew his faults, his imperfections, whatever good he had done in the world only eighty miles east, in Claremont.

James J. Corey, 29, deceased. But *Jimmy Corey* still lived in my head, in Big Tujunga. As did Mick McCrory in the canyon, on the pier. One had been the preview of the other.

Linda moved quietly about the house. She already knew of the event, but not what to say about it. I guessed the doctor's staff had done the research.

"I'm going down to Safeway," she said after a while. "Casey's asleep. I'll be back soon." She sat on the rail of the chaise and stroked my hair. "I'll soon have to give you a haircut. Poor baby, I know how it must hurt. He was your first close friend, wasn't he?" I nodded. "Is there anything I can bring you?"

"Not really," I sniffled. "I can't think of anything now. I'll just lie here in the sunshine. I'd like to be alone for a while."

"Don't get sunburned. You'd better stay covered. Oh, a sports shop called about a gun. You didn't order one, did you?"

"Once, a long time ago. It doesn't matter now. They can keep it."

"We don't need more fear around this house, just a little more love and affection." She kissed my wet lids and went away.

It was a beautiful day, fitting for a funeral. I heard sea birds, the crunch of the surf. And then an eerie kind of silence. Someone else was in the house. The hairs rose on my tingling scalp. *There's only air and fear between us,* a sailor had once said to me, waiting. And now there was only...a *ghost?* I waited. 11:13 A.M.

76.

Whatever it was wore...moccasins? *Sandals.* The soles slithered lightly on the dusty bricks. My head twisted round to right and left but I could not see behind the backrest. It scared me to try getting up. What would I do then in my anchoring cast? Where was the goddamn *shotgun?* The twenty-two? The Colt! A sharp metallic click—a Zippo lighter.

"Hello, Mick," I said to the ocean.

He came forward and stood at my side. He was smoking a long Lucky Strike. The hair had grown thick to the shoulders, so the red hair and beard were one. The bones of the cheeks showed through;

the eyes were like chips of green bottles. He looked a little crazed—a hermit come in from the woods, the jeans and the fringed deerskin jacket stiff with grease and candlewax. The frame was gaunt all over, and the hands—they were tissue stretched on tendons, freckles gone. He *looked* like a ghost. He looked *wasted.*

"You don't seem surprised to see me," Mickey said.

"Only the first time, Mick. Nothing surprises me now."

"Something did. Or you wouldn't be wearing that body sock."

"I caught the wrong wave."

The beard parted in a toothy grin. "Maybe the right wave caught you." He drew up a campaign chair—the chair was as tattered as he—and sat alongside the chaise in the manner of a hospital visit.

"Let's see what we've got here." He threw off the couch-cover—all that I was wearing other than the cast. New decorations had been added: a flowery bouquet from Linda, grotesque cartoons by the kids. The original stars shone dimly through.

"My all-star cast," I said modestly.

"I wouldn't be seen *dead* in a thing like that, as Lenny used to say."

"Me neither. Poor Len."

Mick examined the roster of stars.

"Mae West. Isn't she a little old for you, Jerry?"

"I don't think I'm her type, either."

"Steve McQueen. Dig him. Melody Landau. Another friend of Lenny's. Mickey Rooney...I expected that...Jack the Ripper, in the right place, too. *Mick the Slasher.*" He licked his lips. "And what's this underneath? Jerry's Cherry, right?" He pressed the tender pink bulb like a rubber eraser, regarding it with curiosity as though for the first time.

"Does it still work? You're not dead from the waist down, are you, Jerry? I hope you're not *one of those.* Let's see if it can feel." He blew the ash from the cigarette. I couldn't see the look behind the beard.

"It works," I said, though my voice broke. "*Please,* Mick. Don't?"

"Just checking out your reflexes, Jerry." He dragged on the Lucky Strike and blew out a trio of smoke rings. His left hand fondled me idly, as if it had nothing else to do. He slipped his feet out of the sandals. The ankles were white and blue. I sneaked a glance at my watch—11:35. Where in God's name was Linda?

"We have plenty of time for a visit. The van's gone, with your wife. The others are at school. So be cool. There's so much time for everything, all the time in the world. It's nice sitting here in the sun. Like a sun dial."

He tilted back his head and stared into our star directly overhead and stared at me again. "I see sun-spots. Red spots. A *red*-out. It's strange." The hand took a firmer hold. "It does work, doesn't it? You've been keeping something from me, Jerry."

Despairingly I knew it did. My pulse beat with fear and old passion, even for that madman sitting there. His wrist began to move. I forced back the consequent feeling.

"We used to have some good times, didn't we, Jerr? I guess they're gone now, like most everything else. Time changes things a lot."

"It's changed things for you, Mick. Where are you living?"

"Living? Where? Oh, anywhere, I guess. I was up in Big Sur, way up on the Ridge. It's a trip." The wrist fell idle, the feeling seemingly arrested. I hoped it would go away for good. "Way up in the tall trees in a cabin made of rocks. You can look straight down to the ocean, and straight up into space. We see flying saucers at night. And they see us."

"Are you sure?" The sensation was almost gone. I was sure I could handle it then. The hand made a tighter fist.

"Yeah.... They land way back in the mountains, in national forest land. They're starting a whole new order, the Demi-Men. They'll be taking over soon. Some night when you're cruising San Francisco all the lights will go out, even in the gay bars, Jerry. They'll blow out the candles, too."

"And then what?" The goddamned thing was coming *up* again— the little traitor!

"You'll see a thousand lights all over the Bay, like blinking green signals where they've landed in the moonlight. Can you flash on that? Then everything will *stop*." The hand gripped me now like the handle of an axe. "But that's only the beginning." It moved again. "Already they're picking people up."

"Anyone you know?"

"I knew some dudes that disappeared up there. Maybe they only got snuffed, but I think the saucers got them." It kept to a regular rhythm, that hard and horny hand. "We used to have parties, too. The cabin's all black from the fire. That's all he's got, is a fireplace. A Scotsman, the Mad Scot. He's got red hair, like mine. He heats wine in a big black pot and cooks haggis-baggis in a kettle.

"You know what that is, don't you? Blood and oatmeal, in sheep's guts. Then we get high on everything and rip off all our clothes. We start beating pans and drums and bongos." The fist beat faster too. I couldn't help what I was feeling anymore.

"It gets wild. We jump around naked in the full moon, guys and gals, all ages, everyone fucking and sucking. We pour hot wine on each other, and smear haggis-baggis in our crotch and snatch and hair. We claw our bare bodies till the blood comes. We shoot off our loads at the stars."

"That's when the flying saucers come," I quavered, "the Demi-Men." It was going to happen soon—he had me in his clutch. There was nothing I could do if I wanted.

"That's when dudes disappear." The hand that held the Lucky Strike—the right—had reached into a pocket, and drawn out again, produced a heavy click. The click was not the Zippo lighter. The click was a switchblade knife. Mick laid the flashing blade along the root—*the root of all our evils.*

"Ready when you are, Jerry." The swollen pipe was primed. I felt the blade's cold bite, my heart pumped even harder. *Der Liebestod.* The Love Death. It was all coming all too true.

"You only come this way once," Mickey said. I froze my body rigid as the cast. I wanted time to stop.

Had it? Somewhere in the house a buzzer buzzed—the bedside digital alarm. Time for a pain-killing pill. And then a child wailed—Casey. It was time for the little kid's milk. I felt the knife withdrawn. But I knew what had spilled out on the plaster, on Mick the Slasher's star, and even then became transparent in the sun. *Twelve noon.* Saved by the buzz!

Mick snapped the knife-blade and stood up. He slipped his pale feet into the sandals and clicked the Zippo for a light.

"You couldn't do it, could you, Mick?"

"I could. But I didn't. Don't tempt me, I'm the Devil."

"You really believe that, don't you?"

"Don't you? Doesn't Linda? Didn't Leonard?"

"Did you...do that?"

Mickey smoked. "No, the others did. Lenny asked them. He said it was all he could feel anymore. Things got a little out of hand." His lips shaped a tube around the smoke rings. "He started screaming. He shouldn't have screamed."

"And you *watched?*"

"Yeah, I watched. It wasn't pretty. But I don't feel anything now, either. Except drugs. And pain. And time."

"You used to, Mick." I propped my cast upright and swung my legs around, feet to the bricks. How *weird*. A moment from near-emasculation, from the threat of a terminal orgasm, and we talked together in the frank way of lovers, of losers, of old friends. What a crazy mixed-up world!

"I can't talk about it, Jerry, it's too late. You won't see me again. Keep your head straight. For Linda, or your son. For yourself, man."

Like a ghost he was gone. *I want to go all the way with you, McCoy!* But that was as far as I could go. Weak and world-weary I teetered to the bathroom and made myself decent and clean. I threw on a white terry cloth robe and went to the bedroom to see what could be done for my son. I heard the rattle of tires on the gravel, the squeal of the VW's door. *Dear Linda.* I had a tale to tell. Could I, would I, tell it?

77.

But it wasn't the last time I saw him. It may have been the last time he saw me. After the visit—the visitation—I saw where his head was at, *where he was coming from*. I didn't need the truth drug to tell me. Like me he had lost his last family. Unlike me, he hadn't got it back. He'd gone through lots of changes—changes that left him in deep space not his own, lonely as an astronaut. No flying saucer would pick him up, no Demi-Man save him—the way he was looking now. *What a bummer!*

I had another feeling for him then: compassion. Sorry for you, you devil. Luck of the road, old buddy. Glad you're gone!

Then the cast came off with a surgical saw, dividing like the long halves of an eggshell, and smelling of rotten eggs. I was a long time in the shower, the flesh showing color as it came back to life. I've been re-*born*, Linda, I wanted to say. I'm your new model husband, the Reconditioned Jeremy Carr, warrantied for five more years or 1,000 lays, whichever came first. Would she buy it? That night I believed she did.

I was put in a brace, a laced corset, for another six weeks. In the

meantime I could go to work drawing, at least, at my office. That was
how I thought of the apartment in my new remodeled form. In my
office I would follow my profession, not my *trade*. It would be strictly
business. Not monkey-business, either. I hoped everyone would
understand.

Even Barney, were he there. He had sent a little gift from Vietnam,
a bamboo box with gaudy tissue in it. In the tissue was a black
withered object that was not a severed ear. *A frigger from Trigger,*
his note read. That was the kind of thing you got from such associates.
The box was ugly, too.

Brenda had been looking after the apartment and, on weekends,
Ace. Linda had approved the arrangement, the affair of the blonde
sixteen-year-old and the black Green Beret. "After all," she had
explained, "she does care for him, and she's a junior. They might not
have too much time."

Well did anyone, really? I wasn't sure I liked it—others making
love in my bed. *Our bed,* once upon a time not long ago.

Since Steve was back in school the dope charge had been dropped. But the lawyer's fee had been exorbitant, Linda claimed. Even
Steve called it a rip-off. Starkey had put aside his firearms. We were
almost an average family again, as average as we were likely to be.

One night we visited Brenda. Linda drove me in the rain. I was
preparing to get the office ready for work. The two-tone love affair
could go elsewhere, perhaps to the Royal Coachman Inn. We used
the service entrance to bring in groceries.

"Oh, thank God it's only you!" cried Brenda at the door. "I was
hoping it was Ace. Someone's been calling up and *breathing*. It was
scary! Someone's out there now, watching me. Someone in the
tree."

Barney couldn't have been shipped back already—the little rascal
—not fit enough to climb coconut palms. And why would he be
spying on her? I peered between the slats, through streaming windows.

Something *did* hang there among the weeping fronds, something
bigger than a bunch of coconuts, something smaller than King Kong.
A branch peeled away and it fell. Brenda screamed. It pounced to
the ground like a tarantula and skittered out the gate on two long
legs. I followed reluctantly after, marching stiffly down the staircase
and out beneath the palm into the pouring rain. The intruder ran out

on the highway—Route 1—as the signals clicked yellow, then red. The DONT WALK sign was on.

Did I call out? The figure stopped and waved—as though flagging down a car.

An air horn gave a blast like a diesel locomotive, air brakes hissed and snorted, the truck rig shuddered through a downgrade skid in a grind of down-shifting gears. The cab struck a figure that sailed through the air, then a pole as the big trailer jackknifed. A transformer dropped in a shower of sparks. The Canyon went black as the rainstorm.

Wires snapped and crackled between poles; voices shouted warnings. Cars stopped, their headlights pale drowning rays. The driver swung down from the cab, his knees shaking. The signal turned green. It read WALK. I walked the width of the Pacific Coast Highway.

The body had been flung beyond the railing of the bridge. It was down there in the weeds and broken glass at the mouth of the canyon's storm drain. Flashlights weaved about in the raindrops, then pooled at the figure on the bank. The bare feet were floating, tugged seaward on the stream, the fingers entwined in clumps of grasses. The jacket and jeans were as bloody and torn as though stripped from a butcher's parcel. I saw a white hip and a thigh. From the skull near the ear a pink substance oozed out—like haggis-baggis. I was glad that I couldn't see his face.

The hair was wetly matted and the color gone, as though drained into the red that flowed from underneath to join the quickening flood in rivulets. It seemed so frail, that corpse uncovered there. I wished that I could cover it. The flashlights turned my tears to star-like crosses. If only the stars could be seen!

The sirens were wailing in full cry, like hounds at the end of the hunt. Police and emergency at first, no doubt. The officers would crunch down the bank in black leather jackboots and jackets, in shiny white visored helmets, and pronounce the body DSA—dead at the scene of the accident. Then Michael James McCrory, United States Navy, U.D., would be taken away and the radios would rasp out coded messages.

And St. Mick—what of him? Was he also torn and mangled—*maybe severed from his roots?* I stared for a while at the darkness as raindrops spattered the shore. The storm surf was stirring like some undersea beast; the sea-surge sucked at my shoes. The waves rolled and tumbled, and their tall crests...*crumbled,* in sparks of green sea fire. The sparks lit a vision in my brain.

Yes, the tide would come in, it was coming in now, and the blood of the Saint would flow with it...out into the currents, out beyond the reef, out beyond the deep-sunk reaches of the continental shelf...the sailor gone home to the sea. And with each red cell, encoded particle, an essence of that potent, privileged being would infuse the ancient oceans, amniotic waters of the earth, from which all that dwells upon it is eternally reborn. Distilled through tide, through time, the very elements and atoms of the Saint's late incarnation would transform and inspire that into which they were taken ...*a race of Demi-Men...* Until the sun turned the seas into Fire.

An ambulance had come, and a crane-lift from the power company. Rows of flares were set out—a hundred brief candles—for the hasty observance on the highway. From a distance, the low wheeled stretcher seemed a tiny raft—a *death* raft—lightly adrift upon the glistening road. Lights reflected there were trembling columns that sank countless fathoms to the center of the world.

Linda stood beside the body. It looked quite flat beneath the waterproof sheet, as though nothing of much substance were concealed there. Her hunched shoulders quivered with low, moaning sobs. She herself seemed diminished. I held my wife close but she seemed not to know, though her hand squeezed my own, spasmodically.

Across from us, among shifting strangers, stood Brenda. She was crying, too. A few heads away was another face I knew, that of a boy in rain-soaked blue jeans and a jacket. The coat was a Navy pea coat open to his bare wet chest, the collar turned up, and his hands thrust like spades in the pockets, like a seaman's on night duty. The rusty hair dripped as it had in the ocean, and the tuft stood up behind—a red ensign. He recognized me in a half-formed grin.

The ambulance attendants raised up the stretcher and slid it down the grooved metal floor. They latched the rear door and went up front and the ambulance drove away with purring engine, the whitewalls shooting sprays of puddled rain. The boy darted back across the highway and walked up Channel Road past the blacked-out bars, past darkened cafes, past the ghostly white prow of the Friendship.

We went back to the apartment and lit candles. I sat for a while on the bed with a drink that Brenda brought me. Linda had retired to the bath. What did it all mean—I asked myself. It meant, for one thing, that the boy lived nearby, close to or *in* the canyon. It meant that we would doubtless meet again, on a wave or off it. Then I would ask his name and our friendship would get underway.

Doctor Fritchy had been right. Times changed, things could not be the same. They could be *better*.

I drank to that.